Damn, what was going on here? Ray's brain demanded silently.

This *was* Holly, right?

He wasn't sure anymore but even so, he was fairly certain that it really couldn't be. This woman didn't dress like Holly, didn't act like Holly and, most of all, she didn't *taste* the way he'd always assumed that Holly would taste if he ever thought to fleetingly sample her lips.

The Holly Johnson he knew would have smelled of soap and tasted like some kind of minty toothpaste. Holly was practical. Holly was grounded. By no stretch of the imagination was she some femme fatale who got his pulse running like the lead car in the Indianapolis 500 and his imagination all fired up—like this woman did.

TEXAS
★ COUNTRY LEGACY ★

ALL A COWBOY WANTS

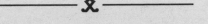

USA TODAY Bestselling Author
Marie Ferrarella

Cathy Gillen Thacker

Previously published as *The Cowboy's Christmas Surprise* and *A Texas Soldier's Christmas*

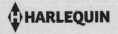

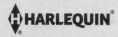

ISBN-13: 978-1-335-20958-0

Texas Country Legacy:
All a Cowboy Wants
Copyright © 2020 by Harlequin Books S.A.

The Cowboy's Christmas Surprise
First published in 2013. This edition published in 2020.
Copyright © 2013 by Marie Rydzynski-Ferrarella

A Texas Soldier's Christmas
First published in 2017. This edition published in 2020.
Copyright © 2017 by Cathy Gillen Thacker

Recycling programs
for this product may
not exist in your area.

This edition published by arrangement with Harlequin Books S.A.

For questions and comments about the quality of this book,
please contact us at CustomerService@Harlequin.com.

Harlequin Enterprises ULC
22 Adelaide St. West, 40th Floor
Toronto, Ontario M5H 4E3, Canada
www.Harlequin.com

Printed in U.S.A.

CONTENTS

USA TODAY bestselling and RITA® Award—winning author **Marie Ferrarella** has written more than two hundred and fifty books for Harlequin, some under the name Marie Nicole. Her romances are beloved by fans worldwide. Visit her website, marieferrarella.com.

Books by Marie Ferrarella

Harlequin Special Edition

Forever, Texas

The Cowboy's Lesson in Love
The Lawman's Romance Lesson
Her Right-Hand Cowboy

Matchmaking Mamas

Coming Home for Christmas
Dr. Forget-Me-Not
Twice a Hero, Always Her Man
Meant to Be Mine
A Second Chance for the Single Dad

The Fortunes of Texas: The Secret Fortunes

Fortune's Second-Chance Cowboy

The Fortunes of Texas: Rambling Rose

Fortune's Greatest Risk

The Montana Mavericks: The Great Family Roundup

The Maverick's Return

Visit the Author Profile page at Harlequin.com for more titles.

THE COWBOY'S CHRISTMAS SURPRISE

Marie Ferrarella

To
Charlie,
Who can still make
My heart
Skip a beat
Just by looking at me.

Prologue

The bouquet of flowers she'd given her mother for her birthday had done more than serve its purpose. The arrangement of yellow mums, pink carnations and white daisies had remained fresh looking and had lasted more than the customary few days, managing to dazzle for a little more than a week and a half.

However, now, as to be expected, the flowers were finally dying, no longer brightening the family room where her mother usually spent a good deal of her day. Their present drooping, dried-up state accomplished just the opposite, so it was now time to retire the cluster of shriveling flowers to the trash can on the side of the house.

But as she began to throw the wilted bouquet away, one white daisy caught Holly's eye. Unlike the others, it had retained some of its former vibrancy.

On an impulse, she plucked the daisy out of the cluster, pulling the stem all the way out and freeing it from its desiccated brethren. After dumping the rest of the bouquet into the garbage, she closed the lid of the trash can, then stared at the single daisy in her hand.

Holly shut her eyes, made a wish—the same one she'd made over and over again for more than a decade and a half—and opened them again.

Then, very slowly, she tugged on one petal at a time, denuding the daisy gradually and allowing each plucked petal to glide away on the light late-fall breeze that had begun to stir.

"He loves me," Holly Johnson whispered, a wistful, hopeful smile curving her lips as she watched the first white petal float away. "He loves me not."

Just to say those words made her chest ache. She knew she was being silly, but it hurt nonetheless. Because in all the world, there was nothing she wanted more than to have the first sentence be true.

The petal floated away like its predecessor.

"He loves me," she recited again, pulling a third petal from the daisy.

Her smile faded with the fourth petal, then bloomed again with the fifth. With two petals left, the game ended on a positive note.

She looked at the last petal a long moment before she plucked it. "He loves me."

This petal, unlike the others, had no breeze to ride, no puff of air to take it away. So instead, when she released it, it floated down right at her feet.

Unable to live?

Or unable to leave?

She sighed and shook her head. What did flowers know anyway? It was just a silly game.

The next moment, she heard her mother calling her name. "Coming!" she responded, raising her voice.

Then, pausing just for a second, she quickly bent down to pick up the petal, curling her fingers around it. She pressed her hand close to her heart.

Turning on her heel, she hurried back into the house, a small, soft smile curving the corners of her mouth. The corners of her soul.

The last sing-song refrain she'd uttered echoed in her head.

He loves me.

Chapter 1

"Hi, Doll, how's it going?"

Holly Johnson's heart instantly skipped a beat and then quickened, the way it always did when she heard his voice or first saw him coming her way.

It had been like that since the very first time she had set eyes on the tall, broad-shouldered and raven-haired Ramon Rodriguez, with his soul-melting brown eyes, all the way back in the first grade.

The beginning of the second day of the first week of first grade, to be exact. That was the day she'd started first grade. Looking to change his luck, her father had moved his family—her mother, older brother Will and her—from a dirt farm in Oklahoma to Forever, Texas.

Back then she'd been a skinny little tomboy and the only reason Ray had noticed her at all was because she was not only determined to play all the games that boys played, she was actually good at them. She could out-run the fastest boy in class, climb trees faster than he could and wasn't afraid of bugs or snakes, no matter which one was dangled in front of her face.

And she didn't care about getting dirty.

All those talents and qualities had been previously acquired in Holly's quest to gain her older brother's favor. She never quite succeeded, because during their childhood Will had never thought of her as anything other than a pest he was glad to ditch. During those years, Will was only interested in girls, and he'd thought of her as just holding him back from his chosen goal.

Ray and Will, although several years apart in age, shared the same interest; but while Will had thought of her as a pest, Ray came to think of her as a pal, a confidante. In short, he saw her as—and treated her like—another guy.

Holly was so crazy about him she took what she could get. So over the years she got close to Ray as only a friend could, and while she would rather have had him think of her as a girlfriend, she consoled herself with the fact that in Ray's life girlfriends came and went very quickly, but she remained the one constant in his life outside of his family.

It was a consolation prize she could put up with until Ray finally came to his senses and realized just what had been waiting for him all along.

It was a decision Holly had come to at the ripe old age of eleven.

That was thirteen years ago.

She was still waiting.

There were times, Holly had to admit, when she felt as if Ray didn't see her at all, that to him she was just part of the scenery, part of the background of what made up the town. These days, because money was short and she had to provide not just for herself but for her mother and for Molly, the four-year-old Will had left in her care when he abruptly took off for places West, she worked as a waitress at Miss Joan's diner.

The highlight of her day was seeing Ray.

He stopped by the diner whenever he came to town—which was frequently, because he was in charge of picking up supplies for Rancho Grande, the ranch that he, his father, his brothers and his sister all owned equally. And every time Ray walked into the diner, she'd see him before he ever said a word.

It was tantamount to an inner radar that she'd developed. It always went off and alerted her whenever Ray was anywhere within the immediate vicinity. She'd always turn to look his way, and her heart would inevitably do its little dance before he called out his customary greeting to her.

Ray had taken to calling her Doll, because it rhymed with her name and she was a foot shorter than he was. She loved it, though she was careful not to show it.

"I'll take the usual, Doll."

The "usual" was comprised of coffee, heavily laced with creamer, and a jelly donut—raspberry. In the rare instance that the latter was unavailable, Ray was willing to settle for an apple-filled donut, but raspberry was his favorite, and ever since Miss Joan had placed her in charge of doing the inventory and placing the weekly orders, she made sure that there were always plenty of raspberry-jelly donuts on hand. It wouldn't do to run out.

She would have made them herself if she'd had to,

but, luckily, the supplier she used for their weekly orders never seemed to run out.

Technically, Holly thought as she concentrated on regulating her breathing and appearing calm, Ray wasn't actually coming her way. He was coming to sit down at the counter, get his morning coffee and donut and shoot the breeze for a few minutes. With any pretty face that might have shown up at the counter that morning.

Or, if he was particularly excited about something, or had something exceptional to share, then he'd deliberately seek out her company the way he always did if he needed advice, sympathy or a sounding board. Over the years, she had become his go-to person whenever something of a more serious nature came up.

This morning, Ray had some news to share with her. Big news, from his point of view.

"You'll never guess what," he said to her as she filled his coffee cup and placed the sweetened creamer next to it. Unlike his brothers whenever they stopped by, Ray hated black coffee. For him to be able to drink it, his coffee had to be a pale shade of chocolate.

Holly raised her eyes to meet his soft brown ones as she set down the half-filled coffeepot, waiting for him to continue talking.

He, apparently, was waiting for something, too. "You're not guessing," he prompted.

"You really want me to guess?" she asked, surprised. But she could see that he was serious. "Okay. But to do a decent job at guessing, I'm going to need a hint." With Ray, there was never any telling what he thought was share worthy at any particular given time.

He nodded, obviously enjoying stretching this out.

"Okay, if you want a hint, how's this?" he said just before he declared, *"The Last of the Mohicans."*

Holly stared at the face that popped up in her dreams at least three nights a week, usually more. What he'd just said didn't make any sense to her, but she took a stab at it. It really didn't matter all that much to her *what* Ray said to her as long as he went on talking. She loved the sound of his voice, loved everything about him, even his devil-may-care attitude, despite the fact that it was responsible for his going from female to female.

"You're reading James Fenimore Cooper?" she asked uncertainly. Why did he think the book title would mean anything to her?

"No, me," he told her, hitting his chest with his fisted right hand. When she continued to stare at him, a puzzled expression on her face, he elaborated a little further for her. *"I'm* the last of the Mohicans."

Holly knew that he had a little bit of Native American blood in him on his father's side, but he'd told her that he had traced it back to an Apache tribe, not some fictional tribe the long-dead author had written about.

"It's too early for brainteasers, boy."

Holly glanced up to see that Miss Joan had joined them, having made her way to this side of the counter. The red-haired older woman who owned and ran the diner narrowed her hazel eyes as she fixed the youngest of the Rodriguez clan with a reproving look.

"Why don't you just come out and tell Holly what you're trying to say while she's still young enough to be able to hear you?" Miss Joan suggested.

But Ray apparently enjoyed being enigmatic and he gave hinting one final try. *"Last Man Standing."*

"Ray," Miss Joan said in a warning tone, "you're

going to be the last man sitting on his butt outside my diner if you don't stop playing games and just say what you're trying to say."

Ray sighed, shaking his head. He'd thought that Holly, whom he'd always regarded as being sharp, would have already figured out what he was trying to tell her.

"All right, all right," he said, surrendering. "You know, you take all the fun out of things, Miss Joan." He couldn't resist complaining.

In response, Miss Joan gave him a wicked little smile. "That's not what my Harry says," she informed him, referring to the husband she'd acquired not long ago after years of being Forever's so-called carefree bachelorette.

Meanwhile, Holly stood waiting to find out what it was that had her best friend so mysteriously excited.

"All right, *why* are you the last man standing?" she asked, prodding him along.

"Because everyone else in my family is dropping like flies," he told her vaguely, playing it out as long as he could. "Except for my dad," he threw in. "But he doesn't really count." Eyes all but sparkling, he looked from Miss Joan to Holly, then said, "We just had another casualty last night."

"Don't see why a casualty would have you grinning from ear to ear like that," Miss Joan observed, then ordered, "C'mon, spit it out, boy. What the devil are you talking about?"

The twinkle in the woman's hazel eyes, Holly noted, seemed to be at odds with the question she'd just asked and the way she'd asked it. Everyone understood that Miss Joan knew it all: was privy to every secret, knew what people were doing even before they did it at times and in general was viewed as a source of information for everything that was taking place in Forever.

"Don't tell me you don't know," Ray suddenly said, looking at the older woman. He was savoring every second of this—especially if it turned out that he knew something before Miss Joan actually did.

"I'm not saying one way or the other, I'm just saying that since you're so all fired up about spilling these particular beans, you should spill them already—before someone decides to string you up."

It wasn't a suggestion, it was a direct order, and if she actually *did* somehow know what he was about to tell Holly, he appreciated Miss Joan allowing him to be the one to make the announcement. After all, it did concern his family.

Forever was a town where very little happened. They had the customary sheriff and he had appointed three deputies—including his sister, Alma—but they spent most of their time taking care of mundane things like getting cats out of trees and occasionally locking up one of several men in Forever who had trouble holding their liquor. Occasionally the men in question had imbibed too much in their singular attempts to drown out the sound of displeased wives.

Moreover, it was a town where everyone knew everyone else's business, so to be the first one to know something or the first one to make an announcement regarding that news was a big deal.

"Well?" Holly coaxed, waiting. "Are you going to tell me or am I going to have to shake it out of you?" It was a threat that dated back to their childhood when they were rather equally matched on the playing field because they were both incredibly skinny.

He grinned at her. "You and what army?" he teased. When she pretended to take a step forward, he held up his hands as if to stop her. Having played out the moment, he was finally ready to tell her what he'd come to say.

"You know the woman who came to our ranch to work on that box of diaries and journals my dad found in our attic?"

Holly nodded. She'd caught a glimpse or three of Samantha Monroe, the person Ray was referring to, when she'd stopped by the diner. The woman had the kind of face that looked beautiful without makeup and Holly truly envied her that. She wore very little makeup herself, but felt that if she went without any at all, she had no visible features.

"Yes," she answered Ray patiently. "I remember. What about her?"

Ray grinned broadly. "Well, guess which brother just popped the question?" Ray's soft brown eyes all but danced as he waited for her to make the logical assumption.

For one horrifying split second, Holly's heart sank to the bottom of her toes as she thought Ray was referring to himself. She'd seen the way he'd initially looked at this Samantha person, and even someone paying marginal attention would have seen that he'd been clearly smitten with the attractive redhead.

And while she knew that Ray's attraction to a woman had the sticking power of adhesive tape that had been left out in the sun for a week, there was always the silent threat hanging over her head—and her heart—that someday, some woman would come along who would knock his socks off, get her hooks into him and Ray would wind up following this woman to the ends of the earth, hopelessly in love and forever at her beck and call.

But then she realized that the smile curving his sensual mouth was more of a smirk than an actual smile. She wasn't exactly a leading authority on the behavior of men, but she was fairly certain that a man didn't smirk when he was talking about finding the love of his life and preparing to marry her.

So he wasn't referring to himself.

That left only—

"Mike?" she asked, stunned as she stared at Ray. "Seriously?"

Miguel Rodriguez Jr., known to everyone but his father as Mike, was the eldest of the brothers. Unlike Ray, Mike smiled approximately as often as a blue moon appeared. If Ray dated way too much, Mike hardly dated at all. From everything she'd seen, the eldest of the Rodriguez siblings had devoted himself to working the ranch and being not just his father's right hand, but his left one, as well.

She'd just assumed that the man would never marry. He was already married to the ranch.

"Mike asked this woman to marry him?" she asked incredulously.

She'd known all the brothers for as long as she'd known Ray, but for the most part, she knew them *through* Ray's eyes and Ray's interpretation of their actions. According to Ray, while Mike wasn't a woman hater, he wasn't exactly a lover of women, either. And he had no time to cultivate a relationship.

Yet, as she recalled, whenever she did see this Samantha they were talking about, she'd been in Mike's company.

Well, what do you know. Miracles do happen.

Ray's news gave her hope.

"Yeah." Ray laughed at the surprised look on Holly's face. "Knocked my boots off, too," he admitted. "So right after Christmas—they want to get married Christmas Eve," he added, realizing he had left that part out, "I'll be the only single Rodriguez male walking around." There was laughter in his eyes as he relished the image that projected.

"Maybe that's because the girls in Forever have the good sense to know that as a husband, you'd wind up being a lot more work for them than most men," Miss Joan quipped.

"No, it's because I've got the good sense never to get married," Ray told Miss Joan, contradicting the diner owner. He leaned his head on his upturned palm as he glanced toward one of the tables where four female customers around his age were seated, eating their breakfasts in between snippets of the conversation they were engaged in. He sighed in deep appreciation as he looked at the women. "There're just too many beautiful flowers out there for me to pick to be confined to just a garden on my own property."

"So now you're a gardener?" Miss Joan asked, rolling her eyes. "Lord help us all."

She glanced over toward Holly for a moment, her look speaking volumes. But she said nothing further out loud before leaving to wait on the sheriff, who had just walked in.

"Morning, Sheriff," Miss Joan said, greeting him

as she automatically applied a towel to the counter and wiped down an already clean area. "Have you heard the news?" She didn't bother waiting for him to respond or even make a guess. "The last of the eligible Rodriguez boys is getting hitched."

Sheriff Rick Santiago's expressive eyebrows drew together in a look of confusion. Alma, in between stifled groans as she lowered her very pregnant body onto her chair, had told him the news about her brother this morning. But this little detail that Miss Joan had just sprung on him hadn't been mentioned.

"The last?" Rick echoed. "I thought Ray was still unattached."

Miss Joan smiled complacently. "I said *eligible,* Sheriff," the woman pointed out. "That implies a good catch. Ray there—" she nodded in Ray's direction "—is the kind you catch and then release after you realize that there's no way he's going to be a good fit for that kind of a position."

Ray turned around on his stool to face the older woman. He looked more amused than annoyed as he asked, "Are you saying I'm not the marrying kind? Or the kind no one wants to marry?"

Miss Joan looked at him for a long moment, her expression completely unreadable, before she finally said, "Well, boy, I guess you're the only one who really knows the answer to that one, aren't you?"

Taking out a number of singles, Ray left them on the counter as he slid off his stool. The wrapped-up, partially consumed jelly donut was in his hand. "Good thing I love you, Miss Joan," he said to the woman as he walked passed her. "Because you sure have a way of knocking down a man's ego."

Miss Joan shook her head, a knowing smile on her lips. "You're not a man yet, Ray. Come back and talk to me when you are," she concluded with a smart, sassy nod of her head.

"And you," she said in a low, throaty whisper as she walked by Holly. "Stop looking at him as if he was the cutest little kitten in the whole world and you were going to just die if you couldn't hold him in your arms and call him your own. You want him, missy? Go out and get him!" Miss Joan ordered the girl who'd been in her employ for the past five years.

Holly's eyes darted around to see if anyone within the immediate area had overheard Miss Joan's succinct, albeit embarrassing romance advice.

To her undying relief, apparently no one had. And the person who actually counted in all this was on his way to the front door—to run whatever errands he had for his father and to shoot the breeze with every pretty girl and woman who crossed his path.

Holly had no idea she was sighing until Miss Joan looked at her from across the diner. While she didn't think she was possibly loud enough to be heard the length of the diner, she did know that Miss Joan had the ability to intuit things and read between the lines, no matter how tightly drawn those lines might be.

She also knew that she owed a huge debt of gratitude to the woman. Miss Joan had offered her a job out of the blue just when she'd needed it the most and would have given her a roof over her head if she'd needed that, as well.

It was Miss Joan who had taken an interest in her and encouraged her to take some courses online, following up on her dream to become a nurse, specifically, an

E.R. nurse, when her dreams of going to college to pursue that career had crumbled. It was Miss Joan who'd had faith in her when she had lost all of it herself. And Miss Joan had come through without a word of criticism or complaint when Holly suddenly found herself a mother—without the excitement of having gone the usual route to get to that state.

She flashed a smile at the woman now, tucked away her starry-eyed look and got back to work. Miss Joan wasn't paying her to daydream.

Chapter 2

"C'mon, Holly, say yes," Laurie Hodges, one of Miss Joan's part-time waitresses, coaxed as she followed Holly around the diner.

The latter was clearing away glasses and dishes bearing the remnants of customers' lunches.

Every so often Laurie would pick up a dish, too, and pile it onto her tray. But the twenty-four-year-old's mind wasn't on her work, it was on convincing her friend to do something else *besides* work.

"You never have any fun," Laurie complained, lowering her voice so that those who were still in the diner wouldn't overhear. Bending slightly so as to get a better look at Holly's face, she continued trying to chip away at Holly's resolve. "You want to look back twenty years from now, sitting alone in your house, watching shadows swallow each other up on the wall and lamenting that you never devoted any time to creating memories to look back on? For pity's sake, Holly, all you ever do is work." Laurie said it in an accusing voice, emphasizing the last part as if it was a curse word.

Well, she certainly couldn't argue with that, Holly thought. But there was a very good reason for that. "That's because that's all there is."

At least, that was all there was in her world.

There was her job as a full-time waitress, and when her shift was over and Miss Joan didn't need her for any extra work, she went home, where an entirely different kind of work was waiting for her. The work that every woman did when she had a family and a home to look after.

In her case, she looked after her mother, whose range of activities was limited by her condition and the wheelchair that had all but kept her prisoner these past few years. She also took care of her niece, Molly, who at four, going all too quickly on five, was a handful and a half to keep up with.

Then, of course, there was the house, which didn't clean itself. And when all that was taken care of, she had the courses she was taking online. Granted, they were strategically arranged around her limited time, but they were still there, waiting for her to dive into and work through them.

All in all, that usually comprised a twenty-three-and-a-half-hour day.

That left a minimum of time to be used for such frivolous things like eating and sleeping, both of which she did on a very limited basis.

And *that,* in turn, left absolutely *no* time for things

such as going out with friends and just doing nothing—
or, as Laurie was proposing, going dancing at Murphy's.

"That is *not* all there is," Laurie argued with her.
"My God, Holly, make some time for yourself before
you're a shriveled up old prune living with nothing but
a bunch of regrets."

Laurie caught Holly's arm to corner her attention
when it seemed as if her words were just bouncing off
Holly's head, unheard, unheeded. Holly was easygoing,
but she didn't like being backed into a corner physically or verbally.

She raised her eyes. The deadly serious look in them
caused Laurie to drop her hand. But she didn't stop
talking.

"They're going to have an actual *band* that's going
to be playing Friday night. One of the Murphy brothers
and a couple of his friends," she elaborated. "Liam, I
think." Laurie took a guess at which brother was playing. "Or maybe it's Finn. I just know it's not Brett."
Brett was the eldest and ran the place. All three lived
above the family-owned saloon. "But anyway, it doesn't
matter which of the Murphy brothers it is, the point is
that there's going to be live people playing music for
the rest of us to dance to."

"Might be interesting if they were having dead people playing music," Miss Joan commented, coming up
behind the two young women.

Rather than looking flustered and rushing away, pretending to look busy, Laurie brazenly appealed to the
diner owner to back her up.

"Tell her, Miss Joan," Laurie entreated. "Tell this
pig-headed woman that she only gets one chance at
being young."

"Unlike the many chances I give you to actually act like a waitress," Miss Joan said, her eyes narrowing as she gave the fast-talking Laurie a scrutinizing look. "Don't you have sugar dispensers to fill?" It was a rhetorical question. One that had Laurie instantly backing away and running off to comply.

Once the other waitress had hurried away, Miss Joan turned her attention back to Holly. "She's right, you know," Miss Joan said, lowering her voice. "I hate to admit it, all things considered, but Laurie is right. You do only have one chance to be young. You can act like a fool kid in your sixties, like some of those pea-brained wranglers who come here to eat, but you and I know that the only right time to behave that way is when you *are* young. Like now," she told Holly pointedly. "Did Laurie have anything specific in mind? Or was she just rambling on the way she usually does? If that girl had a real thought in her head, it would die of loneliness," she declared, shaking her head.

"She had something specific in mind," Holly reluctantly told her.

Holly braced herself. She could already see whose side Miss Joan was on. She loved and respected the redheaded woman and she didn't want to be at odds with her, but she *really* had no time to waste on something as trivial as dancing, which she didn't do very well anyway. She just wished the whole subject would just fade away.

Miss Joan waited a second but Holly didn't say anything more. "Are you going to give me details, or am I supposed to guess what that 'specific' thing is?" Miss Joan asked.

Unable to pile any more dishes onto the tray, Holly

hefted it and started across the diner. With Miss Joan eyeing every step she took, Holly had no choice but to tell her what she wanted to know.

Reluctantly, she recited the details Miss Joan asked for.

"There's a band playing at Murphy's this Friday. Laurie and some of her friends are planning to go there around nine to check it out. And to dance," she added.

Miss Joan nodded, taking it all in. "So why aren't you going?" she asked.

Holly shrugged carelessly. "I've got too much to do."

"Why aren't you going?" Miss Joan repeated, as if the excuse she'd just given the diner owner wasn't nearly good enough to be taken seriously. Before Holly could answer, the woman went on to recite all the reasons why she *should* go. "It's after your shift. I'm sure that your mother is capable enough to babysit Molly, especially since it'll be past your niece's bedtime—and if for some reason your mother can't, then honey, I certainly can."

That surprised Holly. She knew that Miss Joan tended to be less blustery with children, but that still didn't mean that she was a substitute Mary Poppins.

"You'd watch her?" Holly asked incredulously.

"Sure. I've got to get in more practice babysitting, seeing as how my first grandbaby is almost here," Miss Joan answered, referring to the baby that Alma, Ray's sister, and Cash, her stepson, were having. The baby was due at the beginning of January, and as time grew shorter, the woman was becoming increasingly excited.

"I couldn't ask you to do that," Holly protested. "Even on standby."

Miss Joan frowned at her. "Unless my hearing's going, girl—and I'm pretty damn sure that it isn't, you

didn't ask me to babysit this Friday night. I just offered."
With her hands on her small hips Miss Joan fixed her
with a penetrating look. "Okay, you got any other excuses you want shot down?"

Apparently Miss Joan was not about to take no for
an answer. But Holly wasn't ready to capitulate just yet,
either. "I've got classes."

Miss Joan made a dismissive noise. "*Online* classes,"
she emphasized with a small snort. "That means you
can take them the next day. Or on Sunday, if you're busy
making memories Saturday night." The final comment
was punctuated with a lusty chuckle.

Holly blushed to the roots of her long, straight blond
hair. "Miss Joan." The name was more of a plea than
anything else. Though she knew Miss Joan didn't mean
to, the woman was embarrassing her.

"Lots of ways to make memories," Miss Joan informed her, brushing aside the obvious meaning behind
the previous phrase she'd used. She looked at Holly intently. "Okay, like I said, any other excuses?"

"Yes, a big one," Holly answered, unloading the last
of the dishes onto the conveyor belt that would snake
the dishes through the dishwashing machine against
the far wall. "I really don't know how to dance." Because she felt it was a shortcoming, she said the words
to the wall next to the conveyor belt, rather than to
Miss Joan's face.

"Well, that's an easy one to fix," Miss Joan informed
her, brushing the excuse aside as if it was an annoying
gnat. "Dancing's fun. I can teach you. Or my husband,
Harry, can. You want someone younger, I'll ask Cash
to show you the finer points," she said, waiting to hear
who Holly wanted to go with.

Had Miss Joan forgotten that her stepson was in a very unique situation? "Just what he wants to be doing when his wife's on the verge of having their first baby. Teaching me how to dance," Holly quipped.

"Sure, why not?" Miss Joan asked. "I think it's perfect. It'll take his mind off worrying about everything for a little while—and it'll perform a useful service for you."

Holly sighed. The woman was like a Hydra monster. No matter how many heads she lopped off, Miss Joan just grew some more and kept coming right back at her.

"Miss Joan, I appreciate everything you're trying to do here, I really do," Holly said emphatically. "But I don't have time for any dancing lessons, just like I don't have time to go to Murphy's and —"

Out of the blue, Miss Joan gave her a look. The kind of look that made strong men doubt the validity of their cause and rendered frightened young waitresses like Laurie speechless. Holly, however, was made of far sterner stuff than the average person, due to all the responsibility she had shouldered from a very young age.

So she braced herself and listened, hoping she could offer a successful rebuttal.

"You like working here at the diner, girl?" Miss Joan finally asked after a sufficient amount of time had gone by.

Here it comes, Holly thought. "Yes, ma'am, you know that I do."

Miss Joan's expressive eyes narrowed, bringing in her penciled-in eyebrows. "Then if you want to have a job on Monday, you'll go to Murphy's with your friends on Friday *and you will have fun,*" she ordered forcefully.

"Hey, old woman." Eduardo, the longtime cook,

called to her as he stopped puttering around in his kitchen and came forward. "You cannot just order someone to have fun. It does not work that way, but then, perhaps you have never had any fun yourself so you would not know that."

"Maybe *you* can't order someone to have fun, but *I* can," Miss Joan assured the short-order cook in a voice that said she wasn't going to brook any sort of rebellion or challenge, especially from him.

That resolved, Miss Joan turned her attention back to Holly. "So, girl, what'll it be? You going to Murphy's on Friday night and coming to work on Monday, or are you staying home, studying and looking for a new job come Monday morning?" Miss Joan asked.

"You wouldn't fire me over something like that," Holly pointed out with some certainty.

"No," Miss Joan agreed and let her savor that for approximately two seconds before adding, "I'd fire you over your insubordination." When Holly looked at her, confusion in her eyes, Miss Joan elaborated. "I told you to do something and you out-and-out refused. That's pretty sassy if you ask me." Miss Joan smiled at her, and it was one of the few genuine smiles that seemed to register on the woman's lips and in her hazel eyes, as well. "In other words, insubordination. So what'll it be?" she prodded, waiting to hear the answer she *wanted* to hear.

Holly sighed. She'd known in her heart it was going to end this way.

"I'll go," she said.

Miss Joan's eyes met hers and it almost felt as if the woman was delving into her very soul as she asked in a clear voice, "You're sure?"

"Yes, ma'am, I'm sure. I'll go," Holly repeated, still not certain how this had all come about now that she looked back at it. "But I won't dance." That, to her, was as far as she was willing to concede. She absolutely refused to make a complete fool of herself.

At least she would be among friends, she consoled herself.

For the time being, what Miss Joan had heard seemed to be enough, though she shook her head as if despairing over the young woman. "I guess you can lead the filly to the dance floor, but you can't make her dance. Still, something is better than nothing, I always say." She patted Holly's shoulder. "Good girl. Remember to have fun. That's an order," she added with a near growl.

"What did she say?" Laurie asked, venturing forward rather quickly once Miss Joan had made her way to the opposite end of the diner. Laurie looked as if she was dying of curiosity.

Holly began putting down fresh place settings at each table that was no longer occupied. Rather than helping, Laurie just started to follow her around again, oblivious to her obligations as a waitress who was *not* on a break.

"She told me to go out with you, Cyndy and Reta on Friday," Holly told her.

Laurie's eyes all but lit up. They were definitely wider. "Really? How about that? There's hope for the old girl yet." Laurie laughed, glancing over her shoulder to where Miss Joan was behind the counter. And then she turned her attention back to Holly. "So you gonna listen?"

Holly was fairly certain that Miss Joan wouldn't fire her over something as trivial as this, but if she were honest with herself, she wasn't a hundred percent sure. Miss

Joan had been known to do some very strange things in her time, all because she felt she was right. The very last thing Holly wanted was to challenge the woman.

Besides, on the outside chance that Miss Joan had meant what she said, she definitely couldn't afford to lose her job. Granted, there were other jobs in Forever, but she had gotten comfortable in this one. There was the added fact that Miss Joan allowed her to take leftovers home to her mother and Molly.

It might not seem like a lot to someone else, but she was of a mind that every tiny bit helped. Someday, when she finally got her nursing degree and her courage up to ask Dr. Davenport if he'd hire her as his nurse, she intended to pay Miss Joan back for all the times the older woman had looked the other way and allowed her to bend the rules.

Like the time that her mother and Molly were both sick and she had to stay home to take care of them. Miss Joan not only allowed her to take the two days off, but she paid her for them as if she was at work. And, on top of that, she'd sent over one of the waitresses with soup for her mother and niece, and food for her because, "If I know her, that fool girl will be so busy taking care of her family, she'll forget to eat herself."

Miss Joan had been right, Holly recalled. She *had* been so busy caring for the two patients she'd entirely forgotten to eat.

Miss Joan always covered all the bases, Holly thought with no small amount of affection.

Her eyes dancing, it was obvious to Holly that Laurie was making even *more* plans for Friday night. The young waitress looked as if she was ready to go now rather than have to wait until the end of the week.

"If you don't have anything to wear," Laurie suddenly said, turning toward her, "you can borrow something from my closet. We're about the same size," she guesstimated, looking Holly up and down. "I'll be happy to share anything I've got."

Did Laurie think that she was *that* poor? "I've got a dress," Holly protested with a touch of indignation she didn't bother hiding.

"Oh." Holly's response had clearly surprised her. "Okay, then you're all set," she said happily. "I'll come by to pick you up at 7:30 p.m. Friday night."

She didn't want Laurie going out of her way. "Why don't I just meet you there?" Holly suggested.

"Because you won't," Laurie responded. She looked at her friend. "I know you, Holly, so don't even go there. I'll pick you up," she repeated. "And we'll have fun," she promised with feeling. "You'll see."

With all the things she had on her mind, Holly thought, she highly doubted it. But she knew better than to say so.

So instead, she forced a quick flash of a smile to her lips, then murmured something about having "inventory to do" as she walked away from Laurie and headed toward the tiny back office.

Chapter 3

Her time factor down to the wire, Holly stared into the small, narrow closet in her bedroom. She'd been staring into it for a couple of minutes now.

It wasn't as if she was trying to decide what to wear, because there was so much to choose from. There wasn't. She knew every article of clothing that hung there by heart.

She had exactly one all-purpose dress that she'd worn to her high school graduation, to the funeral of a friend of her mother's and to a small number of other, lesser occasions. Money was tight. She saw no reason to spend it on something frivolous when there were so many more worthy items that needed to be bought first—like toys that lit up Molly's eyes and clothes for the girl's ever-growing little body.

The all-purpose, A-line, navy blue dress was certainly still in decent condition, but she had to secretly admit that part of her wished she'd taken Laurie up on her offer when the waitress had suggested lending her a dress for this evening.

The next moment, Holly shrugged the thought away. Murphy's wasn't all that well lit anyway, and besides, she was not looking to impress anyone. She was just giving in and going out tonight so that Laurie and Miss Joan would stop saying she needed to get out more and socialize.

After all, it wasn't as if she was bored. God knew she had more than enough to keep her busy, and she didn't feel a lack of anything in her life. She wasn't looking for a boyfriend or a husband. Her heart definitely wasn't up for grabs.

It was already spoken for.

She'd been in love with Ray for as long as she could remember. That wasn't going to change, and as long as she felt that way, she wasn't about to go looking for a boyfriend. She wouldn't feel right about it. Her heart definitely wouldn't be in it.

She'd never been one of those girls who felt she needed a man at her side to complete her. She knew better than that. She had always been her own person, and that person was as busy as any two or three people had a right to be.

"You know, it doesn't matter how long you stare into it, nothing new is going to pop up in that closet," Martha Johnson said as she wheeled herself into her daughter's small, tidy bedroom.

"I know, Mom," Holly acknowledged wearily, still staring into her closet. "I was just wondering if it wouldn't be better all around if I just stayed home tonight." She certainly didn't need to dig for excuses. She had plenty of those. "I've got that test to study for and Molly's just getting over a cold—"

"At this age, Molly's *always* going to be getting over a cold," Martha pointed out patiently. "And from what I understand, the beauty of taking those courses in the isolating privacy of your own room is that you can take those tests whenever you want—on your own schedule, not the teacher's or whoever it is that's hiding on the other side of that monitor. Anyway, you're going and that's that."

"Mom, what if Molly wakes up—" She got no further. Her mother had raised her hand, calling for silence.

"So she wakes up. I'll handle it. Don't make me feel any more of an invalid than this chair already makes me feel, Holly," she pleaded. "Besides, you wouldn't want this dress to go to waste, would you?"

"What dress?" Holly asked, finally turning around to look at her mother.

That was when she saw it. What her mother was talking about. There on her lap, encased in a plastic, see-through garment bag, was a dress that gave new meaning to the word *beautiful*.

Holly's mouth dropped open in complete awe—and concern. The dress *had* to be expensive. She wasn't about to allow her mother to throw away money on her like that, especially since there wasn't all that much to toss around. They were still paying off the medical bills associated with the car accident that had put her mother into that wheelchair.

"Mom, you didn't—"

"No, Holly, I didn't," Martha quickly assured her daughter.

Her mother didn't usually lie to her, yet there was the dress, on her lap. "Then where did that come from?" Holly asked.

Martha Johnson smiled. "Miss Joan's husband, Harry, brought it over. He said she told him that this was for you and that you weren't allowed to give it back or refuse it, otherwise you're out of a job," her mother said matter-of-factly. She looked down at the dress that was still on her lap. "If you ask me, this'll look extremely pretty on you." And then she looked up to see Holly's reaction.

That was *not* the expression of a woman who was thrilled about getting a new dress.

Holly was frowning.

"Oh, Holly, smile. You look as if you are about to be sent to prison, not to enjoy a rare night out. A *well-deserved* night out, I might add," Martha insisted. She shook her head, her salt-and-pepper hair moving back and forth from the motion. "Honey, I can't remember the last time you went out for fun."

Neither could she, actually, Holly thought. But that still didn't make this any easier for her. Holly bit her lower lip. "Mom, I won't fit in."

"You won't fit in if you wear that old navy blue dress of yours," Martha pointed out, nodding at the dress that was still hanging in the closet. "In this bright, pretty little thing, you'll still stand out," she acknowledged, nodding at the glittery blue-gray dress, "but in a good way. Besides, you're going out with your friends, aren't you? That should make it easier for you."

She really wasn't all that close to the girls she was going out with. Not so much that she could really call them her friends.

Holly raised one shoulder in a helpless gesture. "I'm going out with girls I work with, Mom."

"Close enough," her mother pronounced.

There was no doubt about it, Holly thought. She was going to feel awkward. She had trouble blending in in situations outside of her comfort zone, at work or home. Anything beyond that was no longer in her zone.

Martha took her hand between both of hers, a sympathetic look in her eyes. "Honey, the more you hide, the harder it's going to be on you to come out and mingle with people who aren't sitting at the counter, giving you their lunch orders." If Holly could be outgoing in that situation—which she was—then she had it in her to be outgoing in other kinds of situations. She just had to be drawn out. "My friends occasionally drop by the diner and they all tell me that you're the nicest, most helpful girl there—"

"Yes, but that's work," Holly reminded her. And that was exactly her point. She was fine as long as she could hide behind her job. No one expected any real one-on-one time with her while she was at work.

Martha was not about to accept defeat. In her own way, she was as stubborn as her daughter. "Then pretend you're at work tonight—just don't go behind the bar and start serving drinks," Martha warned with an understanding smile.

"Mom, I—" The doorbell rang, interrupting what she was going to say next. Her head swung in the direction of the front door. "Oh, God, that's Laurie." She glanced toward her mother. "She said she was going to swing by to pick me up because she didn't trust me to come to Murphy's on my own."

Martha looked just the slightest bit impressed, as

well as surprised. "That Laurie is smarter than she looks." Maneuvering her wheelchair so that she was closer to her daughter's double bed, Martha deposited the new dress on it, then announced, "You get ready. I'll let Laurie in and tell her that you'll need a few extra minutes. She'll understand."

Holly's stomach officially tied itself up in a knot. The kind that threatened to cut off her air supply. She pressed her hand against her stomach. "Tell her I'm sick."

"Holly Ann Johnson, you know how I feel about lying," Martha informed her, pretending to look stern.

"But I think I am coming down with something," Holly protested. "I feel feverish."

Martha frowned, wheeling herself over to her daughter. "Bend down," she ordered.

Holly had no idea what her mother was up to. "Mom, I—"

"I said bend down," Martha repeated even as the doorbell pealed again. When Holly did as she was instructed, her mother leaned forward in her chair and employed the classic mother's thermometer: she brushed her lips lightly across her daughter's forehead. "Cool as a cucumber," she pronounced, motioning for her to straighten up again. "No fever present." Her eyes narrowed. "You're going. No argument."

With that, Martha wheeled herself out of the room as the doorbell rang a third time.

Holly sighed. Okay, she silently argued with herself, searching for the pros in this. After all, how humiliating could this be? She was going out with a bunch of girls from the diner, and while they weren't bosom buddies, she did know them, at least to varying degrees.

They'd go to Murphy's, have a couple of beers—or, in her case, a single sangria—eat a few oversalted peanuts and listen to this band that Laurie had gone on about for the past two days.

If guys came by and asked the other girls to dance, leaving her alone at the bar, she knew Brett Murphy—the bartender who was most likely on duty tonight—well enough to have a conversation with him while she waited for her friends to come back.

She didn't consider what she'd do if someone asked her to dance, because she was more than fairly certain that no one would. As far as she was concerned, she didn't think of herself as the type to attract the attention of anybody, except maybe someone who desperately didn't want to leave alone at closing time. And when it came to fending off someone like that, well, she could handle herself in those sorts of situations. Just before he'd left home, Will had gotten interested in martial arts and he'd taught her a few self-defense moves that would come in handy in dicey situations.

Okay, enough thinking, time for dressing, she silently ordered herself.

Hurrying into the blue-gray dress, she had to admit she liked the feel of the material as it glided passed her hips, stopping several inches above her knee—quite a bit shorter than the navy dress.

She wasn't accustomed to wearing anything this short—or this clingy, she thought, looking herself over in the narrow full-length mirror that hung on the back of her door.

The fabric looked almost shimmery, she thought, staring at her image as she turned first in one direction then the other.

Holly didn't realize she was smiling until she caught her reflection.

Running a comb through her hair, she decided to leave it down. After all, she wasn't trying to attract any undue attention, and the dress looked as if it could do more than that on its own.

For a second, she debated taking it off again and slipping on her faithful old navy dress, but she had a strong suspicion that Miss Joan had eyes everywhere, and if she wore her navy dress to Murphy's, Miss Joan would know and get on her case about that.

Besides, this had to have cost the woman a pretty penny, she thought as she lovingly glided her hand along her hip.

Holly took a deep breath. "Okay, ready or not, here I come."

Grabbing her hoop earrings from the top of her bureau—a gift from her mother on her graduation day—she put them on as she walked toward the front of the house. The earrings were the one good piece of jewelry she had besides the small gold cross her father had given her on the first day of school.

She heard voices coming from the living room.

As she drew closer, Holly cocked her head, listening intently.

She could make out her mother's voice, but the voice that was answering her mother didn't sound anything like Laurie—or any other female she knew, except possibly Miss Joan. But even Miss Joan's voice wasn't this deep.

If she didn't know any better, she would have said that the voice she heard belonged to—

Holly's heart began to pound the way it always did

whenever she first heard his voice and realized he was somewhere close by.

"Ray?" she asked as she walked into the small living room.

Ray shifted his brown eyes toward her a beat after he uttered a preoccupied, "Hi." But once he actually focused on her, the greeting was immediately followed by an awestruck, "Wow," and then a joking request for some sort of proof of identity.

"Doll, is that really you?" Ray asked, staring at her and cocking his head as if that could somehow help him clear his vision, or at least allow him to make a better identification of the shimmering fairy princess entering the room. He took a step toward her, staring so hard his eyes all but burned into her. "Wow," he said again. "You clean up really well," he told her, appreciation all but vibrating in his voice.

"Doesn't she, though?" Martha said, pride brimming over in her voice as she, too, turned around to face Holly.

A warm, pleased feeling swept through her, but she told herself that Ray was just being nice. After all, they were friends and they'd known each other since they were children.

"What are you doing here?" she asked him. Holly glanced around, expecting to see Laurie somewhere in the room, but there was no indication that he'd come with anyone.

What was going on here?

"Well, this afternoon I happened to mention to Laurie's brother that I was going to see if Liam could play half as well as he thinks he can, and I guess Laurie overheard me because next thing I know, she's asking me for a favor, saying that she and her friends were going to Murphy's tonight, too. Her problem was that she didn't have enough room in her car for everyone. She thought that since you and I are friends, maybe I wouldn't mind picking you up and taking you with me." He shrugged casually. "I said sure, why not. Why didn't you tell me you were going tonight?" he asked. "You know that I would have taken you—like I am now."

Her shrug matched his, except that hers was tinged with self-consciousness. "It kind of just came up as a spur-of-the-moment, last-minute thing," she told him, deliberately avoiding his gaze.

His eyes swept over her as the corners of his mouth curved in a smile that could only be described as wicked.

"That dress certainly doesn't look like a spur-of-the-moment thing," he told her.

In all the time that he'd known Holly, he'd never seen her looking this good, this, well, sexy for lack of a better word. Did she even know that? That she looked really hot? He had a feeling that, this being Holly, she didn't.

He had a full agenda planned for tonight, but it looked as if he might have to add chaperone to that list. As her friend, he didn't want to see guys hit on her if that made her uncomfortable.

Seeing that Holly was momentarily stuck for a response to Ray's assessment of the dress that adorned her body, Martha came to her daughter's rescue.

"That was a birthday present I gave her last year. You know how Holly is, she saves things until the very last minute—even leaves the tags on until she wears the item for the first time," she added, seeing that there was one telltale tag hanging from the back of the stunning dress. Shifting her wheelchair so that she was behind her daughter, Martha drew close enough to remove the tag with one well-executed yank.

"I knew it would look good on you," she told her daughter, playing her part to the hilt.

"Good?" Ray echoed incredulously. "Doll, you're downright beautiful in that."

"She's downright beautiful without it, too," Martha told him. The way she saw it, Holly enhanced the clothing she wore, not the other way around.

"Mom!" Holly cried, mortified at the implication of the words.

"No, she's right," Ray cut in. "You're a beautiful person, especially on the inside, Doll. I've always said that." He had a feeling it was getting late. "Okay, you ready to go?" he asked, glancing at his watch. He'd expected to be there by now, looking over the crop of women the band had attracted. "The first set is at eight and I want to get there before that, look over the crowd and all that good stuff," he told her.

She felt her heart go back to its regular measured beat. She knew what he meant by "good stuff." How could she forget? If Ray was going to Murphy's, it was because he wanted to see if the promise of a band had drawn any new faces from the neighboring towns and places farther south.

"Well, we wouldn't want you to be late," she told him glibly.

"You two have fun, now," Martha told them as she followed in their wake to the front door. "Don't worry about Molly—or anything else, either," she instructed Holly. "Just for one night, please act your age and not mine."

"Good advice, Mrs. Johnson. I'll see that she follows it," Ray promised the woman with a bright smile. "Okay, milady, your chariot awaits," he told Holly grandly, bowing from the waist and gesturing toward the truck that he always drove.

"I see that your 'chariot's' been freshly washed," she teased as she opened the passenger-side door and got in.

"Can't make a good impression in a dirty chariot, now, can I?" he asked with a laugh, getting in on his side.

Holly made no reply.

She knew that the good impression he was talking about referred to whatever woman he set his sights on tonight, but just for the moment, she pretended that he'd actually done this for her and that he was her date, not just a friend doing another friend a favor.

Chapter 4

"Seriously, Doll," Ray said to her as he pulled away from the single-story house she called home. "You could have given me a call, told me you wanted to go hear Liam play tonight. I would have been more than happy to swing by and pick you up."

He eased his foot off the gas pedal of his Super Duty pickup truck and glanced in Holly's direction.

Damn, but she looked different tonight. He'd been spending too much time looking *through* her that he hadn't realized just how really pretty his best friend was.

Really pretty.

He found it difficult to pull his eyes away.

When she made no answer to his comment, Ray went on talking. "Don't mind saying that I was kind of surprised when I heard that you were actually stepping out for a change."

He flashed Holly a wide grin, the one that the girls he'd been out with referred to as his *killer* grin, except that with Holly, he wasn't trying to prove anything or charm her the way he did when he was out on a date. Since this was Holly, the grin he flashed at her was completely genuine.

"Good for you," he congratulated her heartily, still on the subject of her finally stepping out on Friday night. "I guess you're really not the stick-in-the-mud that you pretend to be."

Holly squared her shoulders, taking offense at the careless assessment he'd just tossed at her. "First, I don't 'pretend' to be anything—I never do. And second, I am *not,* nor have I ever been, a stick-in-the-mud, Ray Rodriguez," she retorted with feeling.

"Okay," Ray allowed expansively. "Exactly what would *you* call doing nothing but working 24/7?" he asked.

Holly sniffed as she lifted her chin defensively. "Being responsible."

"A responsible stick-in-the-mud," he qualified, underscoring the descriptive phrase he'd just used. Then, seeing that his teasing was apparently getting under Holly's skin, he shrugged, dismissing the semantics they were butting heads over. "Hey, it's just good to see you going out, Doll." He inclined his head in her direction, as if that would help him hear her response better as he drove. "Got your sights set on anybody in particular?" he asked curiously.

Yes, the lunkhead sitting next to me. "Nobody," she told him firmly. "I just want to hear the band play, see if they're any good."

Since this was Holly and they told each other everything—even though the dress she had on clearly negated the seemingly innocent reason behind her going out tonight—he took her at her word.

"Well, Liam's brothers seem to think so," Ray told her. "They think he's got real potential. Brett even had a small area cleared off to serve as a dance floor. The way I see it, the music has to be good in order for people to dance."

She smiled, thinking of something Laurie had said to her about the band. "Not really," she interjected. "It just has to be good and loud."

He laughed, remembering what he'd overheard her friend saying as he talked to Laurie's brother. "Laurie just wants to give Neil Parsons an excuse to put his arms around her," Ray said.

"Neil Parsons?" Holly echoed. "Are you sure?"

This was the first she'd heard anything about Laurie wanting to get close to Neil. When Laurie had talked to her about coming tonight, she'd made it sound as if she was trying to talk her into a girls' night out, an occasion where they and a couple of the other girls who worked at Miss Joan's diner would get loud and just have some fun listening to Liam trying to hit all the right notes. Laurie hadn't said a word about wanting to get close to Neil.

Deliberately?

"I'm sure," Ray said casually, completely ignorant of the way what he'd just said had thrown Holly for a loop. "That's what she told her brother. She also said that Cyndy Adams was hoping to catch Ty Smith's eye, as well. Come to think of it, Laurie mentioned Reta Wells, too, but I didn't hear the name of the guy that Reta was looking to corner."

"So they're all looking to get partnered up?" Holly asked.

She was doing her best to hide the distressed feeling that was growing in the pit of her stomach. Why hadn't Laurie leveled with her?

Because she knew you'd never agree to come if she mentioned being interested in catching some guy's eye. You know that.

"It sounded like that to me," Ray told her. And then he shrugged. "But, hey, I could be wrong. And even if I'm right, this just might be a fishing expedition on their parts. I think that if this was a done deal, they would have all gotten paired off before they ever got to Murphy's. So, if this is just in the works, it's all going to be casual," he assured her. Ray slanted a look in her direction. "You *sure* there's nobody you're looking to cut out of the herd?" he asked her.

"I'm sure," she answered firmly. She'd *known* this was a bad idea. Holly glanced over her shoulder at the road they'd just traveled. "Look, maybe you'd better take me back home."

Ray just kept driving the way he'd been going, heading toward Murphy's.

"Sorry, Doll, I told you I don't want to be late for Liam's first number. I'm *really* curious to see how he does. Besides, if I take you back now, that knock-'em-dead dress'll go to waste, since I'd be the only one who's seen it on you," he maintained.

You're the only one who counts.

Why did he have to be so thickheaded when it came to this? Holly wondered in frustration.

Out loud she merely said, "I can always save it for another time."

"C'mon, Doll, where's your sense of adventure? Let your hair down," he prompted.

"Maybe you need an eye exam," she told him with a touch of sarcasm. "My hair *is* down."

"See?" he asked with that same disarming grin. "Halfway there."

Holly sighed and, for the moment, gave up as she slouched back in her seat.

The trip was all but over.

Murphy's looked as if it had been infused with a community of fireflies; it was so lit up that it was visible from a few blocks away.

"I guess word must have gotten around about Liam and his band," she speculated.

Ray laughed. "He'd better be good. If he's not, he's going to fall flat on his face in front of a packed house."

She caught herself having performance jitters for the middle Murphy brother. "I think they're probably more than ready to meet him halfway," she said. At least she hoped so, for the sake of Liam's pride.

Everyone in Forever knew everyone else. That meant that, by and large, they pretty much had each others' backs. While some occasional petty jealousies might surface between the inhabitants of Forever and the people who lived on the surrounding ranches, for the most part, everyone wished everyone else well.

Ray pulled up in front of the saloon. Then, seeing that there was no space to park his truck, he circled around to a larger lot in the back. Usually there were plenty of spaces to be had there. Tonight Ray found that he had to drive up one lane and down another before he finally found a space where he could park his truck.

He pulled it in between two 4x4s of almost identical color—battleship gray.

"Sure hope this means he's selling beer to all these car owners," he commented, looking around the lot.

The offhanded comment caught her attention. She looked at Ray sharply. "Why? Is Brett having trouble staying in the black?"

Brett Murphy wasn't the kind who talked about money problems except in the most casual way, making it sound as if there was no problem at all.

"Mike heard him say something about having a note come due on Murphy's next month," Ray answered.

He and his siblings certainly knew what it was like to have their backs up against a wall and the bank breathing down their necks, Ray thought. They'd almost lost the ranch after their mother had died. Pulling together as a family had been the only thing that had saved them from foreclosure. Even though he was the youngest, the experience had made him hypersensitive to other people's problems when it came to needing money for payments due.

"I think that's the reason behind Brett agreeing to have Liam get his friends together and play tonight. Having a packed house never hurts," Ray told her as he pocketed the keys to his truck.

Holly looked out at all the cars parked outside the saloon. It looked as if everyone in town had shown up, not to mention that there appeared to be vehicles from some of the neighboring towns, as well.

"Well, whatever his reason, I think he's going to be up all night counting the saloon's take from tonight," Holly predicted.

They could hear the noise coming from the saloon

even inside the cab of the truck. She estimated that it would be close to deafening once they were inside the small, rectangular building that was both the place of business for the three Murphy brothers and their home since they lived right above the saloon. "Maybe we should have brought earplugs," she all but shouted to Ray.

She saw him grinning at her. It was the kind of grin that acknowledged he was aware she'd said something to him, but hadn't a clue what that something had been.

It didn't matter to her if Ray had heard her or not; the important thing was being this close to him. She hadn't seen him for the past couple of days and had assumed that work on the ranch was keeping him busy.

Either that, or a new love interest had come into his life. That happened with a fair amount of regularity—like clockwork.

Holly shut down the idea as soon as it occurred to her, preferring not to think about it.

But since Ray hadn't mentioned anyone's name on the way over here—and he would have had there been someone new—she just assumed that tonight he'd be back on the prowl again. One of his brothers—Mike—had made the observation that Ray changed girlfriends the way other men changed undershirts while working out in the hot sun.

What that meant to her was that Ray wasn't getting serious about any of the women he went out with—which was just the way she liked it.

Someday, Holly firmly hoped, Ray Rodriguez would come to his senses and realize that what he had been looking for all this time had been standing right there in front of him all along. The fact that he'd said more than once that he wasn't looking for that special some-one didn't carry any weight with her. It was a rare man who admitted that he wanted a wife in his life, that he wanted something other than to be a carefree, love-'em-and-leave-'em man that all the available women in the area— and some who weren't so available—flocked to.

Just before he opened the front door to Murphy's, Ray bent close to her ear and promised, "Don't worry. I won't leave you until we find Laurie."

The moment he said that, Holly fervently hoped that Laurie and her friends had gotten stuck in some paral-lel universe and had, for all intents and purposes, dis-appeared off the face of the earth for the duration of the evening.

Her wish to that end intensified when, to her sur-prise, Ray took her hand. "So we don't get separated," he explained.

The explanation came with an accompanying puff of warm breath—his—that instantly seemed to sink right into the sensitive skin along her neck and cheek.

For a split second, Holly thought her heart was going to burst through her chest, it was hammering that hard. But she managed to take in, hold and then release two long, even breaths, which in turn steadied her pulse— or got it as steady as was humanly possible, given the circumstances.

She took another long breath before saying, "I'm not worried."

He turned to look at her over his shoulder, guessing she'd said something but the din from the saloon had completely swallowed it up.

"What?" he asked, his voice just a decibel below shouting.

This time, it was her turn to lean forward and bring her lips to his ear. "I said, I'm not worried," she repeated.

Something tightened in his gut as he felt her breath along his ear. It sent a reflexive shiver through a large part of him, which surprised him. Feeling slightly unsettled, his eyes met hers.

And held.

For just an isolated fragment of time, Ray felt something happening, although what that *something* was, he wasn't sure. He just knew it was something. Something unusual.

Something different.

The next moment it was gone.

Whether he'd shaken it off or it had just been absorbed by the noise and the atmosphere, he didn't know. All he knew was that it was gone. And he was relieved.

And maybe just a little saddened, as well.

Turning from her, feeling just the slightest bit unsteady on his feet—as if he'd just gotten up from his sickbed to come here—Ray carefully scanned the crowd directly in front of him.

The band, he could see, was just setting up. Which meant that he and Holly weren't late.

Instead of dwelling on the odd sensation in the pit of his stomach, he focused on being able to hear Liam's best efforts and on finding Holly's friends. He knew he wouldn't feel right about just leaving her alone here. It would be a little like abandoning a newborn on the steps of a church in the middle of the night. There was no telling if she'd be all right or not until her friends found her.

He couldn't very well take Holly with him, though. She was his best friend, but it somehow just didn't seem right to have her standing within earshot as he made his play for whatever female caught his fancy tonight. He could talk to Holly about it later—sans some of the more private details—but he didn't feel right having her actually witnessing him in action.

Not that he could really explain why; it just didn't feel right to him.

"Hey, there she is!" he cried out to Holly, spotting Laurie.

Since he was facing away from her, none of his words found her.

"What?" Holly raised her voice so that he could hear her, although their previous mode of exchange— through close proximity and long, warm glances, had clearly won her favor.

Turning to face her so that she could see his lips when he spoke, Ray repeated, "I found Laurie and the others."

"Great," Holly said, pasting a grateful smile she didn't feel on her lips as she said it.

All good things had to come to an end, she thought. She's always known that, she'd just been hoping that in this case, the end would take a little longer getting there. But then, she reminded herself, she hadn't been planning on coming out in the first place, so that any time she spent with Ray was actually a bonus.

Ray took her hand again and forged a path through the milling bodies of people she knew either by sight or by name. But she really wasn't focused on them—or on Laurie, either. Right now, all that mattered was that Ray was holding her hand.

And then he wasn't.

He'd dropped it, and the next moment she realized why. Laurie, Cyndy and Reta were right in front of her.

"Okay," Ray was saying to her, "Have a good time. That's an order, hear?"

She nodded her head. "I hear," she replied with another fake smile.

The next second, he was plowing his way through the crowd.

And then he was gone.

"Can't believe you actually made it," Laurie was saying enthusiastically, hooking her arm through Holly's. "We've got a table right over there." She pointed toward something in the distance, although she could have been pointing to a kangaroo for all the difference it made to Holly. "You can leave your coat and purse there," Laurie coaxed, drawing her to the table. "So that you can mingle better when the time comes."

She had no intension of mingling, better or otherwise, but to say so at this early stage was just looking for an argument. So instead, she made her way over to the table Laurie had indicated.

Once she reached the table, Holly shrugged off her coat and left it on the back of a chair. Her small purse she took with her. Who knew when she might need what was inside the small purse?

Turning to face Laurie, she saw a look of absolute wonder and appreciation in the other woman's soft brown eyes.

"Wow, no wonder you didn't want me to lend you one of my dresses." Her smile broadened. "You've been holding out on me, Holly."

Holly had no idea what the other woman was talking about. "Holding out?"

Laurie nodded, indicating the dress she had on. "I wouldn't have thought you owned something that special looking. You really do look sensational," she told Holly with the enthusiasm of a true friend. There wasn't so much as a note of jealousy in her voice. "You're definitely not going to have any trouble attracting attention from the testosterone set."

Red flags instantly went up all over the place in Holly's head. This was *not* going to be the uncomplicated evening that she'd hoped it would be.

"I don't want to attract any attention," Holly insisted, all but shouting the words into Laurie's ear. "I just came out tonight to hear the music."

And because you were going to nag me until I said yes, she added silently.

"That's not all you came for. Not in *that* dress," Laurie told her knowingly, saying the words directly into her ear so as to be heard.

There was no warm shiver going through her system the way there had been when Ray had talked to her. Instead, she could feel her stomach twisting for another reason.

She definitely shouldn't have given in and come here tonight. She was just leaving herself open to problems, problems she had neither the time nor the patience for.

The good part was over, Holly thought with a sinking feeling.

Chapter 5

"Look." Holly measured out her words slowly, trying to sound as calm as she could while having to practically shout at Laurie in order to be heard, even at this close proximity, "I don't want to be set up or pushed into anyone's arms. All I wanted when I said yes to you about going out was just a simple girls' night out, nothing else."

Struggling to hang on to her patience—and her bravado—Holly looked at the other waitress to see if she was getting through to her—or if Laurie had even actually heard her.

Laurie had obviously heard because she shouted back with a delighted smile, "We don't always get what we want, Holly."

I already knew that, Holly thought as she attempted not to let her thoughts show on her face even as she zeroed in on Ray. From what she could see, since he was halfway across the crowded floor, Ray looked as if he was talking up Emma Cross. Apparently, if that expression on Emma's face was any indication, he didn't have to do that much talking, either.

A sinking sensation was taking hold of her stomach again. This time it was more personal. She'd seen Ray in action before, when they were in high school together, but it had been a while since she'd been a witness to the moves he could put on a girl when he was drawn to her.

Jealousy began to nibble away at the sedate exterior she was trying to project.

It hurt to watch, so she looked away.

She realized that Laurie was trying to ask her a question. Holly focused on her friend's mouth and finally heard what she was asking.

"What's your pleasure?" Laurie asked.

To go home, Holly thought but out loud she said, "Something simple. Vodka and orange juice, heavy on the orange juice."

"Naturally." The smile on Laurie's lips looked almost *too* accommodating.

Holly had a feeling that if the drink she'd just requested was going to be heavy on anything, it would be the vodka. Which was the *last* thing she needed at a time like this. Inebriated people did stupid things, and she prided herself on being in control. She intended for that to remain the case.

"Tell you what," Holly said, rising from the table, "I'll get my own drink. Be right back," she promised just before she started to make her way up to the bar.

She could feel the music throbbing in her chest, and the ever-increasing din of voices was already beginning to give her a headache. This was *not* promising, she thought darkly as she squeezed into the miniscule space that was available at the bar.

"What'll you have, beautiful?" Brett asked her.

The eldest Murphy brother seemed to materialize out of thin air. She could have sworn that he'd been on the far end of the bar as she'd begun her pilgrimage to the counter.

Beautiful, huh? The saloon owner obviously didn't recognize her, she decided. "Brett, it's me. Holly Johnson."

"I know who you are," he answered, a smile in his dark blue eyes as they met hers. "And you really do look beautiful," he told her, glancing at her dress. A sexy smile curved the corners of his mouth as he gave her a small piece of advice. "You've got to learn how to relax and take a compliment once in a while, Holly. That's the easy stuff. The hard stuff comes later," he said with a wink. "Now, what'll it be?"

What hard stuff? she couldn't help wondering. But out loud she answered his question. "Vodka and orange juice—heavy on the orange juice," she added.

If she'd been expecting an argument—or a joke—neither happened. Instead, Brett replied, "Coming right up," seamlessly capturing two different bottles and preparing the drink that she'd ordered.

Holly opened the small purse she'd brought with her—a purse that had practically no room for her wallet—when Brett placed the drink on the bar directly in front of her.

"How much do I owe you?" Holly asked, taking several bills out.

Brett shook his head. Picking up a dish towel, he

wiped a spot up from the counter. "Beautiful women get the first drink of the evening on the house," he answered with a wink.

It'd been a while since she'd even had a drink. Holly had no idea how much she could safely imbibe, so she'd already made up her mind as to how much she was going to consume.

"I'm only getting the one," she told him.

Brett's smile never faded. "Then this won't be an expensive evening for you," he predicted.

And with that, he went down the bar as someone held up a glass.

Picking up the screwdriver Brett had made for her, Holly wove her way back to the table where she'd left her coat and Laurie.

But when she got there, Laurie was nowhere in sight. However, there was no empty place to mark her absence, and the chair that she had left her coat on before going to fetch her drink had somebody else sitting in it.

There were two guys she vaguely recognized sitting at the table, talking to Cyndy and Reta. Judging the expressions on the women's faces, these were the guys they had been looking to get together with tonight.

Laurie was probably with the guy she was interested in, as well. Dancing most likely. The crescendo of music was growing louder. Liam was obviously showing off his musical abilities.

He wasn't half bad, Holly decided. Since there was no place for her to sit, she inched her way closer to the band. Selecting a small corner of the dance floor, she claimed it, secure in the idea that she was out of the way and could enjoy listening to the band play for a little while.

Without meaning to, as the music seemed to seep deeper and deeper into her, Holly began to sway rhythmically to the beat.

"You know, it's even better if you put down the drink you're holding and move your feet," said a deep male voice behind her.

Surprised, Holly almost dropped the glass. Turning around, she found herself looking at a tall, good-looking male she judged to be somewhere in his late twenties. He had straight blond hair that he wore a little long. The cut succeeded in giving him a rugged, free-range look—and it didn't take an Einstein to realize that he knew it.

His eyes were skimming over her, and Holly felt instantly uncomfortable. "I'll take your word for it," she replied pleasantly and then deliberately turned away from him.

The wrangler didn't—or wouldn't—take the hint and leave. Instead, he poured on a little more of what he had to have assumed was his charm.

"I've always felt that finding things out for yourself is the best way to remember the lesson," he told her. Taking the drink out of her hand, he put it down on the closest flat surface near them.

He'd surprised her. Otherwise, she would have held on harder to her glass. "Maybe I'm not looking to learn any lessons," she countered, reaching around him to pick up her drink.

"Then how about just dancing?" her persistent admirer suggested, removing the drink from her hand for a second time.

"I'm not looking to do that, either," Holly told him firmly, her voice losing its polite edge.

The wrangler moved the drink so that she would have been forced to move into him in order to reach for it again. He blocked her next move, taking a firm hold of her hand.

"That's what your lips say," he told her. "But your hips seem to have other ideas. I'm throwing my vote in with your hips."

Her eyes were icy now, as was her tone. She absolutely hated the idea of causing a scene, but there was no way she was going to allow herself to be plucked up like a piece of candy from a tray, and she could see that this pushy cowboy had more than just dancing on his mind. "You can throw your vote into the Rio Grande, I really don't care."

"C'mon, little lady," he coaxed, grabbing her and pulling her toward him. "Just one dance. You didn't get all dolled up like that just to do an imitation of a wallflower."

"Well, I sure didn't do it to dance with you," she retorted, determined to pull herself free.

"Feisty. I like that," the cowboy declared, laughing as his hold on her tightened, rendering her unable to get away.

For the second time in the space of a few minutes, Holly heard a male voice speak up behind her. "The lady said she's not interested in dancing with you. What part of *no* do you find confusing?"

The way her heart just leaped, even with all the noise, she knew that had to be Ray. How did he get over here so fast? She'd just seen him trying to romance Emma. She sincerely doubted that Emma had said she wasn't interested and had sent Ray away.

"Move on, cowboy," the grabby wrangler ordered between clenched teeth.

With deliberate movements, Ray extricated her from the wrangler's grasp and placed himself between her and the pushy cowboy.

"You first," Ray countered, keeping his voice even and pleasant. Only the look in his eyes, Holly noted, was steely.

For a second, it looked as if a fight would break out. The wrangler was inches away from trading punches with Ray, but then, at the last moment, he bit off a curse and just waved his hands dismissively at the both of them.

"She ain't worth getting my hair messed up for," the wrangler declared. "Looks as frosty as a frozen cone. She's all yours, cowboy." With that, the offensive wrangler stormed away.

Ray immediately turned his attention to her. There was concern in his eyes when he asked, "That jerk didn't hurt you, did he?"

Touched, Holly shook her head. "No, I'm fine," she assured him, and then she couldn't help asking him, "Where did you come from?"

That grin that always made her heart flip rose to his lips. "Well, initially, according to my mother, I started out as a twinkle in my dad's eye—"

Holly suppressed a laugh and rolled her eyes. "I meant just now. I just saw you halfway across the room with Emma."

The second Ray had looked her way and seen what was going on, he'd felt his temper instantly flaring.

But he kept that part to himself, merely telling her, "You looked like you needed saving." He paused, debating whether or not to say something for her own good. "You know, Doll, you have to be careful about the kind of signals you send out in a place like this," he warned.

"I wasn't sending out signals," Holly protested indignantly. "I was swaying to the music."

"Palm trees sway," Ray corrected. "You were moving your hips in a very inviting way. That creep took you up on the invitation." If he hadn't been here, who knew how far this could have gone before someone would have put a stop to it? He didn't even want to think about what might have happened. He knew that Holly liked to think that she could take care of herself, but the fact was, she wasn't as tough as she liked to think she was. "Next time, be more careful."

Blowing out an exasperated breath, Ray turned on his heel, ready to go back to what he'd been doing before he saw the wrangler coming on to Holly.

"Right, no swaying," Holly promised. And then, grabbing his wrist—and his attention for a second— she flashed him a broad, grateful smile. "Thanks for coming to my rescue."

"Don't mention it." Ray shrugged off her gratitude, just happy he'd been in the right place at the right time. And then, because he was feeling pretty good about the whole thing, he decided not to stomp on her ego. "You probably would have decked him if I hadn't been here, but since I was, I figured I might as well tell that wrangler what he could do with his unsavory advances and his big, grabby hands."

This was nice, she thought. Whether Ray realized it or not—and he probably didn't—he'd just been the white knight to her damsel not-so-in-distress. She allowed herself to pretend that it was for the right reasons: because he cared about her, not as a friend but as a girlfriend.

"How do you know they were unsavory?" she asked.

"Easy. A guy like that only has the unsavory kind," he maintained. And then, looking across the floor, he frowned slightly.

Holly turned around, trying to see what had caught his attention. "What's the matter?"

The frown faded as he shrugged, assuming a disinterested air. "Looks like Emma decided she wanted to dance more than she wanted to wait for me."

And then she saw what he was looking at. Emma was in the arms of Dixon Baker, one of the ranchers. She was looking up at him as if he was the smartest, handsomest man in the room—as well as one of the wealthier ones.

Holly looked at the man beside her. "I'm so sorry I messed up your evening," she apologized, trying very hard not to allow a smile negate what she was saying.

Ray merely shrugged, looking completely unaffected. "No big deal," he told her. "If not Emma, then someone else will come along. I wasn't looking for a lifelong partner, just someone to pass the evening with."

The band was beginning to play another song; this one had a slower tempo than the two numbers that had come just before.

Ray surprised her by turning to face her and saying, "Well, since I seem to temporarily be caught between partners, would you like to dance?"

She would have loved nothing more, but the truth was, dancing was something she had never taken the time to learn—and she didn't want to embarrass herself or him in public like this.

"I don't really dance," she told Ray with a vague, dismissive shrug. She thought that would be the end of it.

But it wasn't.

"I don't think your hips read that memo," Ray told her, his eyes dipping down to look at the area under discussion. "Let's see what they've got," he coaxed, taking her hand in his and drawing her over toward the newly built dance floor.

"I don't think this is a good idea," Holly protested again, although she really liked him taking her hand like that.

But he was going to regret this, she couldn't help thinking. Ray was known to be a good dancer and she couldn't remember the last time she'd moved her feet in anything but a determined, forward pattern, going from one destination to another.

"That's the problem here," he told her with a patient, knowing expression on his face. "You're overthinking this. You're not supposed to think at all," he stressed. "What you're supposed to do is *feel* the rhythm in your bones," he told her, once again bending his head and saying the words into her ear to keep from shouting at her to be heard.

Taking her right hand in his left, gently pressing the small of her back, he brought her up closer to him. Just for a heartbeat, his eyes met hers. "Feel it?" he asked.

What she was feeling wasn't anything she could admit to. It felt like someone had lit a match in her core, and it was spreading out like wildfire to all her extremities at the same time.

Her throat was bone dry as she tried to thrust out a single-word response. There was only one thing she could say in hopes that he couldn't read between the lines. "No."

He spread his hand out, his fingers dipping down below her waist as he tried to get her to mimic his own movements, to mimic the way his hips were moving to the beat of the music.

"Now do you feel it?" he asked, then stressed, "Concentrate."

If possible, her mouth had grown even drier than before. There was no way she could say *anything* until she managed to get some saliva back. So instead, she just nodded because she *did* feel his hips swaying and she did try to mimic the movement.

All this while she was desperately trying to tamp down the flames that threatened to consume her.

Holly raised her head to look at him at the exact moment he looked down. For a second time, their eyes met and held, but this time it seemed to be in a timeless region where clocks had no meaning. Every jump of the pulse was never ending.

What the hell was going on here? The question echoed over and over again in his head. Ray struggled to remind himself that this was Holly, his lifelong friend, the pal he'd played ball with, learned how to rope young colts with, shared secrets and ambitions with. She knew him better than he knew himself—which right now wasn't hard, he thought because at the moment, he felt like a swirling cauldron of confusion. If he didn't know any better, he would have said that he was reacting to Holly, that he was attracted to her—which, of course, wasn't possible.

If anything, it was the dress. It made her look like a

different person, not good old Doll but some little hottie he hadn't met yet.

He would have blamed his odd, rather intense reaction on the alcohol he'd consumed. Except he hadn't consumed any alcohol yet. Not even so much as a glass of beer. He'd ordered it, then left it standing on the bar when he saw Emma and decided to set his sights on her.

But, while he'd been making his play—and doing rather well, if he did say so himself—he happened to glance in Holly's direction, completely by accident, and saw the uncomfortable and somewhat distressed expression on her face.

He would have hated himself if he'd ignored his best friend's predicament just to win Emma over for the evening—he doubted if anything that happened between them tonight would have led to something with a longer life expectancy than a bouquet of wildflowers.

The band had just stopped playing when someone accidentally stumbled and bumped into Holly, sending her right into Ray. Their bodies, still close because of the dance, were practically sealed together.

Something hot and formless shot through Ray, jarring him down to his very toes, and he reacted entirely automatically.

There was no other earthly explanation for why his mouth was suddenly pressed against hers.

Chapter 6

This was a dream.

It *had* to be a dream.

But, oh, what a lovely, lovely dream it was, Holly thought as her heart hammered in her chest. She'd had this dream countless times before. Usually she was in bed, and visions of what it would be like to have Ray kiss her would seep into her semiconscious or unconscious state.

Sometimes she even had this dream when she was awake. Then, of course, it would be a daydream, most often on megasteroids. She was capable of creating phenomenally real scenarios for herself.

But all the dreams that had come before this magical moment, be they daydreams or ones she'd had while fast asleep at night, had *never* been this vivid, this incredibly breathtaking. Holly felt as if she'd imbibed not one but several very potent drinks rather than actually leaving her first screwdriver untouched.

She felt that light-headed, that inebriated.

This was divinely delicious, and she intended to savor every single second of it.

Rising up on her toes, flying strictly by instinct, Holly leaned into the kiss, weaving her arms around his neck. Any second now, she was certain that she was going to literally fly away.

Especially when she felt his arms closing around her, sealing her away from the rest of the world. He did such a good job that it seemed as if there was no one else inhabiting this microcosm except the two of them.

Damn, what was going on here? Ray's brain demanded silently.

This *was* Holly, right?

He wasn't sure anymore, but even so, he was fairly certain that it really couldn't be. This woman didn't dress like Holly, didn't act like Holly and most of all, she didn't *taste* the way he'd always assumed that Holly would if he ever thought to fleetingly sample her lips.

The Holly Johnson he knew would have smelled of soap and tasted like some kind of minty toothpaste. Holly was practical. Holly was grounded. By no stretch of the imagination was she some femme fatale who got his pulse running like the lead car in the Indianapolis 500 and his imagination all fired up—as this woman did.

Trying to anchor himself to reality, Ray reluctantly pulled back, separating their lips.

Oh, no, oh, no, don't stop. Please don't stop. I don't want to wake up, not yet, Holly's mind cried.

The next moment, the noise around them shattered

the fragile world that had just been created, and reality stormed in.

As subtly as he could, Ray pulled air into his lungs, doing his best not to sound as breathless as he felt. "Thanks for the dance," he murmured.

Holly bobbed her head up and down in response, unable to immediately form any words. Her mouth was far too dry. When she finally could get a few words together and out, she heard herself mumbling the immensely original phrase, "Don't mention it."

Ray regarded her with a mixture of unease and wonder. Aside from her lips having a lethal punch, she sounded a little strange, maybe even disoriented.

There was a lot of that going around, he couldn't help thinking. "You're okay, right?"

"Yeah, sure," she answered hastily, then as her brain stopped revolving at speeds that rivaled the speed of light, she said, "Define 'okay.'"

His eyes never left her face, watching her warily. "I didn't hurt you or anything, did I?"

Oh, you "or anything-ed" me all right, she thought. She was going to remember that exceedingly intimate, wondrous contact for the rest of her life, even if she lived to be two hundred.

"No, you didn't hurt me," she told him with a small, dismissive laugh.

He nodded, taking in her words and trying to find some kind of inner calm for himself. But so far, it just refused to materialize.

What the hell had gotten into him? It wasn't as if he was some oversexed tomcat ready to leap on anything that wandered across his path. He was a decent, fun-loving person who had always treated the women who passed through his life with the utmost respect—and none more so than Holly.

Hell, he doubted he'd ever even been aware of her *being* a woman before tonight. She'd been his friend ever since he'd extended his hand to her the first day she'd come into his classroom, looking like some kind of a lost sheep.

Looking as if she didn't know how to fit in.

He'd felt sorry for her and he hadn't liked the way Margaret Jennings and her girlfriend were making fun of Holly during recess. He'd walked right into the middle of that and offered her his friendship by way of a buffer that day. He'd done it just to be kind—he hadn't counted on really liking her as a pal. But how could he not? They had so much in common. They liked the same things, saw the same movies—and, most important of all, Holly got his jokes.

But never once in all these years had he thought of her as being a girl on her way to womanhood.

Now he couldn't think of anything else.

And he couldn't remember the last time he'd felt even remotely tongue-tied. But right now, words didn't seem to come with any sort of ease.

Instead, they were occurring to him like some randomly shattered mosaic.

"Can I get you anything?" he finally asked, desperate to have something normal to say. "A drink?" he suggested belatedly, latching on to the fact that this was, after all, a saloon.

Holly glanced over toward the table where the grabby wrangler had set her glass down. The screwdriver was still there. She nodded at it now.

"I've already got one, but thanks for the offer."

She took a step toward the table where the drink stood, but Ray shifted so that he was directly in her way.

"I'll get you a fresh one," he told her.

A small smile curved her mouth—the same mouth that had just been beneath his, he couldn't help thinking, staring at her lips.

"It's not exactly like it spoiled, sitting out on the table like that. It's not a cut of beef left out in the hot sun."

Hands on her shoulders, he turned her around to face the bar, then walked toward it himself. "Yeah, but that creep touched it, and who knows where else his hands have been?"

Holly didn't point out that the wrangler had also touched her when he'd tried to get her to dance with him. Instead, she followed Ray to the bar and said, "Thank you, that's very thoughtful."

He laughed, relaxing just a little as they slowly began to slip back into their customary roles. "Well, you know me, Doll, I'm a very thoughtful guy."

"Yes," Holly agreed, her eyes skimming over the back of his head as well as his sturdy, athletic frame. "You are."

She bit her lip, not wanting to drive him away by seeming to be too clingy or anything even remotely like that, but Ray had done what no one else had ever done for her and he'd done it not just once, but twice, if she counted their very first meeting.

He'd come to her rescue, and she would always be grateful to him for that.

"I appreciate your getting that guy to go away," she told Ray with sincerity. "You didn't have to." After all, nowhere was it written that he was obligated to look after her.

"Yeah, I did," Ray contradicted her, waiting for Brett to work his way back across the bar to their end of it. "That wrangler didn't look like the type who was going to be satisfied with just one dance."

She laughed, contradicting *him*. "He would have been once he found out how bad a dancer I am."

She wasn't that naive, was she? Turning from the bar, he held up one finger. "Number one, I don't think that a dance was really this guy's end goal, and number two—" he held up a second finger "—you're not as bad a dancer as you keep saying you are. You've got to quit running yourself down all the time like that, Doll."

"I don't run myself down," she said defensively. "I just know my limitations." She shrugged. "I don't believe in bragging and sending up a smoke screen when it comes to what I can or can't do."

There was such a thing as carrying things too far. "All right, say one positive thing about yourself," he challenged her. "Just one, I dare you. Go ahead," he urged.

She wasn't accustomed to listing her own attributes and it took her a minute before she had something she could offer.

"I'm a very nice person," she informed him. She prided herself on that, on being someone who would go out of her way to help others or to make them feel better about themselves.

She liked helping people.

"That's just a given." As far as he was concerned, that was the very definition of Holly. She was exceptionally nice—to everyone. *Even that grabby wrangler,* he thought begrudgingly.

"Not really," she pointed out. "People aren't just nice

by default." It would be a lovely world if that was true, she couldn't help thinking.

"Well, you get that from hanging around with me," he countered with a straight face.

"Oh, really?" She laughed and then, rather than tease him, since she could most definitely still feel the imprint of his lips on hers, Holly relented and said, "Yeah, maybe you're right, I do get that from hanging around with you."

Ray shook his head slightly, his thick black hair moving just enough to make her fingers itch to touch it. "I'm always right," he told her.

"Tell me," she teased. "Do you ever have any trouble getting through doorways with that swelled head of yours?"

"Nope."

Brett came up to him just then. "What'll it be?"

"One screwdriver for the lady—heavy on the juice," he added, remembering how she took the drink.

"Coming right up," Brett promised.

Ray continued facing the bar, keeping his back to Holly. They were going to have to talk about this someday, about what had just happened between them on the dance floor. But "someday" was not now, and he hung on to that, telling himself that exploring what had just happened—why he'd kissed her, why he'd felt lightning zigzagging through his veins when he had and why his stomach still felt as if it had turned into one giant knot—wasn't going to lead to anything good until he knew what to do with any of the answers he might come up with.

"Here," he said, handing her the fresh screwdriver

Brett had just put on the bar. "An uncontaminated vodka and orange juice."

There hadn't *really* been anything wrong with the screwdriver she'd initially ordered. "I hate being wasteful," she confessed, nodding toward the table where she'd left her drink.

"Oh, it's not going to waste," he assured her with a suppressed laughed.

When she turned around to see what he was talking about, he was in time to see Larry Jones, one of the three town drunks, glance around furtively, then swiftly claim the full glass, wrap his tanned fingers around it possessively and make good his escape by moving toward the end of the bar just off the men's room.

"Looks like the sheriff's going to have a boarder at the jailhouse tonight," Ray commented.

"Not on just one drink," Holly protested. She'd never known Rick Santiago to be a stickler about law enforcement to that degree. In general, as a sheriff, he was rather easygoing.

"No," Ray easily agreed. "Not just on one drink." He looked off in the direction that the heavyset man had taken. "But Larry's fast and he's resourceful. The people here are mostly interested in hearing Liam play and deciding how good he is or isn't. They're not going to have a death grip on their glasses of wine or beer or whatever else they're drinking. And despite his weatherbeaten look, Larry's pretty fast when he wants to be. And he always wants to be when it comes to something with alcohol in it."

"You've studied him?" she asked in surprise. Why would he do that?

But Ray just shook his head. "I didn't 'study' him, but I do get out more than you do—and I notice things."

She certainly couldn't dispute the last part of his statement, given that she hardly ever went anywhere that wasn't either job related or a necessary extension of her home life—such as to the grocery store for food.

"That you do," she agreed. "That you do. So this is what I've been missing?" she asked, gesturing toward the man they were discussing. Even from here he appeared to have a death grip on the glass he'd lifted. "Watching Larry tie one on?"

Ray laughed softly, the sound winding itself directly under her skin. "That and a few other things," he pointed out.

Such as you, she couldn't help thinking. But out loud, she asked, "Such as?" knowing that he expected her to.

"Such as the way the full moon shimmers along the surface of the lake on some very special nights. And the seductive scent of honeysuckle gliding softly on a June breeze."

The images vividly materialized in her mind's eye. Both, she couldn't help thinking, sounded incredibly romantic.

But she was too much of a realist to believe that her best friend was attempting to verbally seduce *her*. He was just talking, saying the first things that came to his mind.

Still she couldn't help teasing him. "Practicing?" she asked.

"What do you mean, practicing?" he asked, looking at her quizzically.

"You know exactly what I mean," Holly told him. When he made no further comment or response, she decided that a little elaboration was in order. "You're using the lines you were going to say to Emma if you hadn't suddenly come to my rescue."

"I don't have 'lines,'" Ray informed her with a degree of umbrage.

Holly pressed her lips together in an effort to keep her smile back. She only partially succeeded. "My mistake. Although," she couldn't resist adding, "I know a few people who might just disagree with you on that little point."

"Like who?" Ray challenged. It was getting increasingly noisy where they were standing at the bar, so he took hold of her arm and guided her over to a slightly quieter corner.

When they stopped moving, Holly obliged him by doing a rundown of the ten women who comprised his latest circle of wistful admirers and would-be girlfriends.

Finished, she asked, "Have I left anyone out? Anyone current, I mean," she specified. "Otherwise, we could probably just pull up an updated census for the town, listing the single women from, let's say, about eighteen to thirty-five—inclusive. That should cover it, don't you think?"

Ray shook his head in wonder. "You have a hell of an imagination, you know that?"

"And you have a hell of a charming manner about you. It makes it all but impossible for a girl to say no to you." Actually, she sincerely doubted that very many had, although it wasn't something she really wanted to find out for herself. This was definitely a case where ignorance was bliss. "You know, you'll make it hard for yourself to ever really settle down if you keep going through the women around here like they were just disposable tissues."

"I don't go through them like they were disposable tissues," he protested vigorously. "And who says I plan to settle down?"

Granted, she'd never heard him say anything close to that. But men didn't always talk about such things—that would involve talking about emotions, a subject most men avoided like the plague and few knew anything about anyway.

"Most men do," she responded.

"I'm not most men," he pointed out.

No, he wasn't, she thought, and Holly knew it was probably wrong to feel this happy that her best friend had just reiterated his intentions to not form any attachments that lasted for more than a week or three.

But if he planned to drift from woman to woman, that definitely meant he wasn't making plans to marry any one of them, and as long as he wasn't married, he was eligible—she thought. And who knew, anything could happen, right? After all, despite all those dreams, waking or sleeping, she would never have thought that Ray would actually kiss her—and boy, had he *ever*.

Granted, the kiss had begun as an accident, but what really counted was that he didn't instantly pull away. Instead, he'd deepened the almost erotic contact that they'd shared and that, by most definitions, had been an actual, very real kiss that they had enjoyed.

Or, at the very least, that *she* had enjoyed.

Chapter 7

Holly stifled a yawn as she turned the diner's front doorknob. It was six-thirty the next morning and she hadn't gotten all that much sleep. She'd been far too wired after what had happened to get more than a few small snatches of sleep in between large chunks of just staring at the ceiling—smiling.

She fervently hoped that the diner wouldn't get too busy until her mind had time to kick in. Part of her felt as though she was sleepwalking. With very little encouragement, she could easily curl up on one of the tables and drop off to sleep in an instant.

But that wasn't going to happen. She had a full day ahead of her.

Taking a deep breath, she eased herself into the diner.

Miss Joan was at the far end, wiping down the already clean counter. It was, Holly knew, an idiosyncrasy of hers. She was hoping the woman wouldn't notice her, but she should have known better. Miss Joan seemed to have wraparound vision and could see three hundred and sixty degrees all around her at any given moment.

At the sound of the door opening, the older woman raised her head and spotted Holly the moment she walked in. With an inward sigh, Holly closed the door behind her.

"So how did it go?" Miss Joan asked.

Holly shrugged out of her jacket, leaving it on the back of a chair for the time being. She got her apron from behind the counter.

"How did what go?" she asked innocently as she tied it around her waist.

The slight frown on Miss Joan's face said she hadn't expected extracting information to be easy.

"Don't get sassy with me, girl. You know what I'm talking about. How did last night go?" Miss Joan asked as she watched Holly intently.

Keeping her mind a blank wasn't working. Miss Joan's question immediately conjured up images of dancing with Ray, of having him hold her in his arms. Most of all, it conjured up that spectacularly magical kiss she'd shared with him.

Just thinking about it now got her pulse moving in double time.

Only extreme focus kept her voice even remotely neutral sounding. "It was okay."

Miss Joan cackled as her eyes narrowed knowingly. "That's not what I heard."

Of course not, Holly couldn't help thinking. This was Miss Joan, the woman who somehow managed to find out everything about everything even before the people who were involved knew about it.

Still, Holly played the innocent a little while longer. "Oh? What have you heard?"

Miss Joan went back to massaging the counter, which was already so clean, it was shining. "That you and that Rodriguez boy were caught up in one hell of a lip-lock on the dance floor right after he got that wrangler to drop his paws off you."

Holly began weaving her way from table to table, filling the sugar dispensers. "Is there *anything* that you don't know?"

Miss Joan never even hesitated in her response. "Well, I don't know why, with that kind of a lead-in, you two didn't just go off and enjoy each other's company for the rest of the evening. Instead, you went home with Laurie and your other friends." The last part sounded almost like an accusation.

Not that Holly had consciously made a choice in the matter, but she was abiding by the rules of proper behavior. "I had agreed to a night out with Laurie and the other girls, so it only stands to reason that I went home with them."

"But you went to Murphy's with Ray," Miss Joan contradicted.

Of course she'd know that, Holly thought. Had it been anyone else except for Miss Joan, she would have been surprised at the extent of the woman's knowledge about her evening. But this *was* Miss Joan, and the woman had eyes everywhere.

"Did you arrange that?" she asked point-blank. When Miss Joan just looked at her, Holly elaborated. "Having Ray pick me up instead of Laurie?"

Miss Joan's expression was inscrutable. "Now, why would I do something like that?"

Holly noticed that the woman didn't deny it, but asked another question, instead, to deflect her attention—or so Miss Joan apparently hoped.

"Oh, I don't know," Holly said loftily. "Maybe for the same reason you sent over that shimmering blue dress for me to wear."

Miss Joan merely nodded, neither denying nor agreeing with her assumption. Instead, she replied, "You're welcome."

Holly knew in her heart that Miss Joan meant well and that the woman undoubtedly knew that she liked Ray, but she didn't like the idea of someone pulling her strings, even if it *was* Miss Joan. "I don't recall saying thank-you."

Miss Joan looked up from the counter, her expression just as unreadable now as it was a moment ago. "But you will, girl," she predicted. "If you've got a brain in your head, you will."

She was being too sensitive, Holly thought. There was no point in pretending around Miss Joan. The woman had a way of being able to see through lies, even small ones.

"The dress really *was* beautiful," Holly finally had to admit.

"No, *you* were beautiful," Miss Joan corrected. "The dress was just sparkly material. *You* brought it into the spotlight, gave it life," the woman insisted. "That Rodriguez boy is just like a horse. You've got to lead him to the watering hole and stick his face in the water before he catches on and does what he's supposed to do."

She was afraid to ask what Miss Joan thought he

was supposed to do. The older woman was just outspoken enough to tell her, and Holly really wasn't sure that she was up to hearing Miss Joan lay out her future for her—a future that hadn't a chance in hell of actually happening.

So instead, Holly asked her, "What's the lunch special for today so I'll know what to put down when I do the menu board?"

"Anything that Angel wants it to be," Miss Joan said matter-of-factly.

The cook had carte blanche as far as Miss Joan was concerned. Angel had been with her a little more than a year now, and Gabe's wife was a veritable miracle worker when it came to creative cooking and working with the ingredients that were available.

"She'll let you know what she's making when she gets here," Miss Joan assured her. "But you're going to have to set up the menu board a lot earlier today because you won't be here for lunch."

Holly looked up sharply. Now what? "Why won't I be here?"

"Because I'm recruiting you," Miss Joan said simply. Then she glanced at her to see if Holly understood. "Don't you remember what today is?"

Holly thought for a moment. "It's December first," she said, watching Miss Joan's face to see if there was something more, something she'd apparently neglected to remember.

Miss Joan sighed and rolled her eyes. "You did forget," she concluded, then proceeded to jar her memory. "It's also the first Saturday of the month. I can remember when you were a little girl and you used to count the days until the first Saturday in December," she said with a touch of sadness.

Holly racked her brain for a moment, trying to connect the dots—and then it dawned on her. "Are you talking about getting the town's Christmas tree?"

"Well, what do you know?" Miss Joan laughed, looking at her pointedly. "You remembered. Maybe there's hope for you yet, girl."

This was the first time that the woman had invited her to come along on the tree-hunting expedition. Holly still wasn't completely sure that she had guessed correctly. "You want me to go with you?"

Miss Joan made a vague half shrug, raising one very thin shoulder and then letting it drop carelessly.

"I thought that maybe it was time for you to make the trek, put that young back into it," she told Holly crisply. "I told the rest of this year's crew to be here by eleven so that we could all set out together. I figure that it's going to be tricky," she added.

Holly knew that each year, Miss Joan would ask a few men she thought to be best qualified for the job to come along. The useful ones she asked year after year. The ones who hadn't measured up to her standards, she left behind the following year.

Just what did she mean by tricky? Holly wondered. "Why?"

Miss Joan looked at her incredulously. "Do you ever *look* out this window, girl?" the other woman asked. As if to illustrate her point, Miss Joan walked to the front of the diner and gestured toward the view that was outside and in the distance. "See anything that gets your attention?" she asked in a tone that was devoid of any emotion other than put-upon patience.

Holly crossed over to where the older woman was standing and glanced out the window as she was told. She didn't see anything out of the ordinary. It was the same barren expanse of land it always was.

"Take in the *big* picture," Miss Joan urged when Holly made no response.

"That's where you're going to get the tree, right?" Holly asked, referring to the mountain in the distance.

"That's where *we're* going, yes," Miss Joan confirmed. Her tone indicated that she was impatiently waiting for the proverbial lightbulb to go off in Holly's head.

"I—" Holly was about to say she didn't know what she was looking for and then she realized what Miss Joan was referring to. "There's snow on the mountain."

"Finally. I was beginning to think we needed to have you fitted for glasses."

It didn't snow very often in this part of Texas, certainly never *in* Forever. But the mountains were up high enough to have received a dusting of it if there was any to fall, which there obviously was.

"Mick's going to have to put chains on the truck tires—if he's got any chains to put on," Miss Joan qualified. "That man doesn't believe in being prepared for any contingencies. He just figures if he needs something, he can get it when the time comes." Miss Joan shook her head. "If he doesn't have any chains, we're going to have to drive up really carefully."

Now that she thought about it, Holly started getting excited about the event. "You really want me to come with you?"

"Thought maybe you'd like a turn. You're pretty levelheaded—most of the time," Miss Joan qualified. "And the town's going to need someone to pick out the tree if I'm not around."

Holly looked at the woman sharply. "Why wouldn't you be around?" she asked, suddenly growing concerned. "Miss Joan, are you feeling all right? There's nothing wrong, is there? Something you're not telling me?" she added, prodding the woman.

"There's lots of things I'm not telling you, girl," Miss Joan said. "But on the subject of my health, there's nothing wrong."

Then what was with the drama? Holly didn't understand. "Then why—"

"Because I'm not going to live forever," Miss Joan said practically. "Nobody does, and after I'm gone, I want to be sure that this town always has the best damn tree that can be found on the mountain every year."

"You're not going anywhere," Ray told the owner of the diner, walking in on Miss Joan's last sentence. "You know that you're just too ornery to die," he reminded the older woman.

Miss Joan turned to look at him. "Well, it's not going to be anytime soon, at any rate." She wiped her hands. "You want the usual?" she asked Ray. When he nodded, rather than getting it herself, she turned to Holly. "Get Ray the usual—it's on the house this morning, seeing as how I'm going to be making use of that strong back of yours," the woman informed him.

Out of the corner of her eye, she noticed that Holly had made no effort to move and fetch Ray either the coffee or his customary jelly doughnut.

"Somebody glue your feet to the floor, girl?" Miss Joan asked.

Holly was only vaguely aware that Miss Joan had

said anything at all to her. Her mind had stopped processing words right after she heard that he was going on the expedition with them.

"You're coming with us to get the tree?" she asked Ray, needing to make sure that she'd heard correctly.

"No, I've decided to take a lover and I'm seducing him with my jelly doughnuts," Miss Joan deadpanned. "Yes, he's coming with us. That's why his breakfast—which is a damn unhealthy one if you ask me, but then, you didn't ask me—is on the house," the woman concluded, then shifted her attention to Holly. "Now, are you going to get his coffee and doughnut or have you taught the doughnuts to come when you call?"

That made her finally come to. Holly turned on her heel and moved quickly across the floor, rounding the counter so she could get to the giant coffee urn and fill up a cup for Ray.

Miss Joan was doing her best to sound gruff, Holly thought, but it didn't matter what she said or how she said it, that quirky woman had just created what had to be the perfect day for her. They were going on the mountain to bring back a giant Christmas tree for the town, and not only was she going to be part of the group that selected the tree—or, more accurately, part of the group that rubber stamped Miss Joan's selection—she was going to be doing it with Ray.

"You grin any wider, girl, it's going to slow down your progress considerably," Miss Joan warned her.

"Yes, ma'am, no grinning," Holly automatically agreed. Right now, she would have been hard-pressed to think of a single thing that Miss Joan could ask her to do that she'd turn down.

"Now, did I say that?" Miss Joan asked. "I said, and

I'm quoting now, 'any wider.' That means keep it to a safe level where you're not catching bugs and working with a windchill factor." Three more men came in and Miss Joan frowned as she looked at her watch. "Can't none of you boys tell time? I said eleven, not seven. I know they rhyme, but they're four hours apart."

Eli, one of Ray's older brothers, slid onto a stool at the counter. He nodded a greeting at the older woman, carefully removing his hat in her presence.

Miss Joan smiled at him. She had always had a soft spot in her heart for Eli. She considered him to be the most sensitive of the Rodriguez brothers.

"Maybe we're just all too excited to wait," Eli told her. "It's kind of like when we were little and waiting for Santa Claus to come. It felt like time just stretched out endlessly before us."

Miss Joan looked down the bridge of her nose at the strapping young man. "If you still believe in Santa Claus, Eli, I think we might just have ourselves a problem here."

"Don't spoil their fun, Joannie. If they want to believe in Santa Claus, let 'em," Harry, Miss Joan's husband, said as he came around to her other side and put his arms around her, then pressed a kiss to her cheek. He'd walked into the diner not more than three minutes ago, slipping in quietly as was his custom. He liked to say that he enjoyed watching his wife in action.

Miss Joan didn't look overly happy as she pulled free of his embrace after a rather long moment. "What did I tell you about calling me Joannie in public?" she asked in almost a snarled whisper.

"You said not to," Harry dutifully recited. "But honey, these boys and Holly—" he nodded in her direction "—are like family. No need to be embarrassed around family," her husband teased.

"A lot you know," Miss Joan quipped. If Laurie had been here instead of late the way she customarily was— she'd assigned the girl to start her shift half an hour earlier than she was actually supposed to, thereby breaking even—her nickname would have found itself posted everywhere. "What are you doing here, anyway?"

"Thought I'd come along," Harry told her. "Help you make up your mind about which tree to bring back. You know, do the kind of things a husband is supposed to do for his wife."

"Said the man who stares at three pairs of black socks in the morning, trying to decide which pair to put on. You're staying here, Harry," she informed him in her no-nonsense voice. "You'll just hold me up and I don't want to have to be worrying about you up there."

"No reason to worry," Harry told her. "I'm as surefooted as a goat."

Miss Joan almost hooted. "An old goat," she specified. "And I want to be sure that you just keep on getting older—and you won't if you fall and break that fool neck of yours. End of discussion. You're staying here."

"Then you are, too," Harry informed his wife mildly. "I can be just as stubborn as you, Joannie."

Rick had joined them at the counter, looking for nothing more than a fortifying black cup of coffee. Holly automatically poured him a cup and set it down in front of him.

"No offense, Harry, but not even God is as stubborn as Miss Joan is," Rick told the woman's husband. "There's no shame in retreating if it's from Miss Joan," he guaranteed. "We've all done it."

"Yeah, but you're not married to her," Harry pointed out.

"And you are, which already proves the kind of steadfast man you are. Now, you can stand here, arguing with her and have her argue back, but we'll be losing precious time because she's not budging and if you don't budge, there's not going to be a tree in the town square until Easter," Holly predicted, throwing in her two cents and hoping to make a difference. "Do it for the town, Harry," she urged. "We need you to back off."

"Don't you be telling my man what to do," Miss Joan declared, her hands fisted at her waist and creating a formidable image despite her thin frame. "You can come, Harry. Just stay in the truck. There's snow on that mountain and I don't want you falling and breaking something I've taken a shine to," she told her husband with a surprisingly sexy smile.

"Whatever you say, darlin'," Harry readily agreed. It was obvious that when she looked at him like that, he lost all desire to argue even for a second.

"Okay, that's settled," Miss Joan declared, relieved. She turned toward Ray and a couple of the other men who had shown up, bleary-eyed and mumbling. "One of you boys go get Mick out of bed and tell him we need chains for our tires. And if he doesn't have them, he damn well better find a way to make them—quick," she warned.

"I'll handle it," Cash volunteered.

"Good." Miss Joan nodded at her stepson and half a second later, was on to the next detail of her very detailed list. The others all listened. Everyone knew better than to interrupt Miss Joan once she got rolling.

Chapter 8

Miraculously, Mick Henley, Forever's resident—and only—mechanic, did have not only one but several sets of tire chains. They were packed away in his storeroom where they'd been ever since they'd made the move with him years ago from his previous shop in Utah. Consequently, there were enough sets of tire chains for Miss Joan's 4x4 and Joe Lone Wolf's truck as well as the flatbed truck that Miss Joan had specially requisitioned and brought in from a Pine Ridge garage the day before.

But getting the trucks' tires outfitted took time. So while Holly waited for the vehicles to be prepared, Miss Joan asked her to continue waiting on the customers who came in to the diner to grab a quick breakfast or to treat themselves to a slow, leisurely one because today was Saturday and they had no place to be.

Holly tried to bank down the excited feeling that insisted on pulsating through her, but she wasn't having all that much luck.

Added to that, it seemed unusually crowded to her for an early Saturday morning, and Laurie was already twenty minutes late.

Holly knew everyone by name as well as by their orders. Most people, she'd discovered shortly after taking this job, were predictable. If they found something they liked, they stayed with it rather than experimenting and sampling other things.

She supposed, as she juggled two orders, that she was the same way herself. In her case, it wasn't food that won her steadfast allegiance, it was love.

Specifically, it was love of Ray.

Looking back over her short life, Holly couldn't remember even having so much as a passing crush on any other boy or man from the very first time she'd laid eyes on the youngest of the Rodriguez clan.

And she sincerely doubted that she ever would.

Every so often, Holly glanced out the side window to see how Mick was doing as he worked at getting the tires fitted with the proper chains. Her mind vacillated between the customers she was serving inside the diner and what was going on just *outside* the diner. She was so preoccupied that she came close to refilling the space next to Gabe Rodriguez's cup rather than aiming the spout of her coffeepot *into* his empty coffee cup.

She flushed when she realized that Ray's brother was moving her hand an inch to the left so that his cup could catch the black liquid that was about to come pouring out.

"Oh, God, I'm so sorry, Gabe," Holly cried, dismayed at what she'd almost done. By not paying attention, she could have easily burned his hand. Damn it, she was usually better at juggling tasks than this, she silently upbraided herself.

"No harm done," Gabe told her cheerfully. "What's got your attention so riveted?" he asked, glancing out the same window she'd just been looking through.

"I'm just waiting for Mick to finish putting chains on Miss Joan's 4x4 and the other vehicles," she told one of Forever's three resident deputies.

Holly had piqued his interest. "Why does Miss Joan need chains? Is she planning on taking a trip?" Gabe asked, this time turning his stool around to face the same direction Holly had been looking, "Oh, wait," he suddenly recalled before he could see exactly what the mechanic was doing. "Today's the day she picks out the town's tree, isn't it?" Gabe's eyes shifted back to the flustered waitress who was hovering over him and he made a calculated guess. "And you're one of the people she picked to go with her this year, aren't you?" When Holly bobbed her head up and down, Gabe asked, "Who else is going this year, do you know?"

She rattled off a few names, then added, "and Ray," doing her best to sound nonchalant, or at least indifferent—and fairly certain that her future did *not* lie in the field of acting.

But if Gabe suspected that she had a crush on his brother, or any feelings for Ray at all for that matter, he gave no indication.

Instead, the deputy continued to make polite conversation. "Dad said Ray seemed to be in an all-fired hurry to be somewhere this morning when he left the house." Specifically, the senior Rodriguez had called him to ask if he knew what was up with Ray and why he'd actually gotten up and gotten dressed so early in the morning without being nagged into it. Of all of them, Ray was the one who liked to sleep in the most.

"So it takes a Christmas-tree expedition to get Sleeping Beauty out of his bed," Gabe marveled. "I would have said that it would have taken nothing less than a shotgun aimed at his toes to get Ray moving before dawn." But even as he said it, Gabe had serious doubts that getting Ray up early actually had anything to do with selecting the right Christmas tree.

From what he'd heard from a couple of his friends who'd been at Murphy's last night, Gabe was far more inclined to believe that his younger brother had actually been motivated by the promise that his best friend was going on the expedition, as well.

The slight noise made by the bell that Miss Joan had hanging at the front door instantly caught Holly's attention. The first thought she had was that someone had been sent in to fetch her.

But it was only Laurie coming on duty.

Good, that meant she could go outside and wait for Mick to finish there.

Her joy was short-lived. The other waitress looked bleary-eyed and seemed as if she was having trouble focusing. Instead of going behind the counter for her apron, Laurie sank down on the closest empty stool and propped her elbows up on the counter. She used her hands in turn to prop up her head.

"Coffee," she called out to Holly. "Please," she added plaintively. "Pour it straight into my veins if possible." As she leaned her head harder against her upturned palm, she made a miscalculation. The next thing she knew, her chin slipped and it all but made contact with

the counter, jolting her into a state of almost wakeful-
ness as her eyes flew open.

Holly was quick to bring her the requested coffee,
black as midnight.

"Hey, careful before you knock yourself out," Holly
warned, witnessing the near collision of chin and counter. She slid the cup and saucer directly in front of the
other waitress.

Laurie eyed her accusingly. "Why do you look so
wide awake?" she asked. Before Holly could say anything, Laurie thought of an answer. "Don't tell me you
actually went into your house when we dropped you
off there last night."

Holly shrugged, not quite following what the other
waitress was getting at. "Okay, I won't," she agreed,
then couldn't help asking, "Why won't I?"

"Because none of us did, that's why." She thought
of her own evening. "Jimmy Evans swung by to pick
me up in his Jeep after I dropped off the other girls."
Laurie managed a wide, wistful smile.

"What time *did* you get in?" Holly asked.

Laurie looked at her watch, trying to focus on the
numbers and finding that her eyes weren't up to the
task just yet. "What time is it now?" she asked Holly.

"You didn't go home at all, did you?" Holly guessed.
"You just stopped off to change before coming here,
right?"

"Nobody likes a smart-aleck," Laurie mumbled. The
next moment, she seemed even worse than when she'd
first walked in. "Take my shift, Holly," she begged suddenly.

"I can't," Holly said, thinking of the afternoon that
lay ahead. She really didn't want to miss being part of

that, especially since Ray was going to be part of it, as well.

But Laurie wasn't ready to give up. "Please? Pretty please?" she begged more urgently. "I'll give you my firstborn."

"Tempting though that is, I really can't. Miss Joan wants me to go with her." And that was the main reason she wasn't going to stay and take Laurie's shift as well as her own. Because when Miss Joan told you to come, you did exactly that, even if there were obstacles in your way.

"Miss Joan wants a waitress who's conscious," Laurie pointed out. Holding her cup with both hands, she all but drained it, then waited for the caffeine to kick in. It didn't. Impatience coupled itself with nervousness. "You *have* to take my shift, Holly. If I don't get some sleep and soon, I'm going to die," she lamented.

"Correction. If you try to palm off your shift onto someone else, you're going to die," Miss Joan said, walking into the diner. As was her habit, she'd zeroed in on the conversation that concerned her most. Her hazel eyes shifted toward Holly. "We're ready. Come outside," she instructed.

She really, really wanted to go, but there was someone in distress right in front of her. How could she have a good time, knowingly abandoning Laurie in this miserable state?

"But Laurie doesn't feel well," Holly pointed out, unhappily resigning herself to take the other waitress's place as well as waiting on customers in her station. "She needs to go home."

"Laurie is hungover," Miss Joan corrected. "What she needs is to man up so she can do her shift as well

as yours." Miss Joan paused to take the other waitress's chin in her hand, closely examined the young
woman's face from both sides, then released it. "You'll
live," she told Laurie crisply. "Nobody ever dies from a
hangover—they just want to," she added with a knowing look. "Now get out there," she said, addressing the
command to Holly. "We roll in less than five."

Holly knew that Miss Joan was as good as her word,
and if she wasn't out there on time as ordered, the small
convoy would head out without her. She didn't want
them to.

Quickly making up her mind, Holly removed her
apron and grabbed the jacket she'd left slung over the
back of an unoccupied chair. Saturdays were casual,
and Miss Joan allowed her waitresses to wear jeans,
which was lucky for her, Holly thought, hurrying into
her jacket and trying to keep up with the older woman
as she walked out of the diner.

"Were you ever in the military, Miss Joan?" Holly
asked, quickening her pace. In the background, she
could hear Miss Joan's husband laughing at her question.

"I tried to enlist once, when I was a lot younger," she
admitted, then deadpanned wryly, "But they told me I
was too tough for them."

Holly could readily believe it.

"Good luck!" she heard Gabe call out after her. She
turned and waved at him just before she crossed the
threshold.

Holly couldn't help wondering if the deputy actually
thought she was going to need luck or if he'd just said
that automatically.

The next moment, Gabe and the possibly cryptic

meaning behind his words were stored away and forgotten.

She saw Ray standing outside the cab of the flatbed truck, holding the driver's-side door open.

"You're riding with Ray," Miss Joan told her in the no-nonsense voice she used when she wasn't about to tolerate the slightest argument or contradiction from anyone about anything. "I told him to drive the flatbed truck. The rest of you have your assigned positions," she declared, looking over the seven other men she had tapped for the job of securing the town's annual Christmas tree this year. "Okay, gentlemen—and Holly—let's roll," she ordered, getting into her own vehicle and waiting for her stepson to climb into the passenger seat beside her.

As she'd predicted, the small convoy of vehicles was heading toward the mountain in the distance in less than five minutes.

Not one of them would have dreamed of keeping Miss Joan waiting.

"Miss Joan is running this like a military operation," Ray commented as they were approaching their destination.

"Miss Joan has a tendency to run everything like a military operation," Holly reminded him.

Ray nodded. "Maybe she was a military brat," he guessed. It was a possibility.

No one in town knew very much about the woman's background before she came to Forever, and Miss Joan wasn't very forthcoming unless she specifically wanted to be—which most of the time, she didn't.

"I think it's more likely that she just likes the precision that the military stands for, so she emulates it. That and she likes ordering people around," Holly added with a grin. "But she's got a good heart, so I guess it all balances out in the end."

It was a known fact that if anyone was in trouble, or found themselves with their back against a wall, Miss Joan would quietly come to their aid, asking for nothing in return.

Holly watched as they came closer to the end of their journey. Her sense of excitement growing, she suddenly turned to Ray and asked, "What's snow like?"

The question caught him entirely off guard. He was sure he hadn't heard Holly correctly. "What?"

She decided to rephrase her question. Maybe Ray hadn't experienced snow, either. He certainly had never mentioned anything about snow to her. "Do you know what snow's like?"

He looked at her as if one of the screws holding her brain in place had come loose. "Of course I do." And then the implied part of her question suddenly hit him. "You don't?"

Holly shrugged. She'd made a mistake asking. But this was Ray and they shared all kinds of thoughts with each other. She knew he hadn't meant to make her feel dumb for asking about snow. She really hoped that he didn't think she was odd because she'd never held snow in her hand.

"No," she answered quietly.

Ray thought she was pulling his leg. He was sufficiently far enough behind Miss Joan's truck not to worry about hitting the vehicle. He looked at his best friend for a second before turning back to diligently watching the road.

He wanted to get this straight.

"You've never touched snow?" he asked her incredulously.

"Never mind," Holly said, waving away her initial question. "Forget I ever said anything." She shouldn't have spoken up. Sometimes she was just too honest, too trusting.

"No," he insisted. "You started this and now you've got me curious. I can't believe you don't know what snow feels like. It's snowed on the mountain before," he pointed out. "I can remember at least a couple of other times when there was a snowfall."

"Maybe." She wasn't about to dispute that part of it, but it had never snowed down here, at Forever's altitude. "But I've never gone up to the mountain before."

He couldn't believe it. How oblivious had he been to have missed this piece of information? He tried to recall if they'd ever talked about anything having to do with snow before and realized that the subject had never come up.

"Why not?" he asked.

She looked at him and realized that he was serious about getting an answer to his question. "Well, from the time I was eight, I was always busy helping my mother. That's when my father—"

"Died," Ray filled in, chagrined. He'd certainly walked into that one with both feet, he thought, annoyed with his lack of tact—and memory. "Yeah, I remember now. I'm sorry."

She never allowed him to beat himself up. "Nothing to be sorry about," she told Ray. "After all, I wasn't the only kid who lost a parent. You lost your mother," she said quietly, just to prove her point.

"Yeah, and you were there for me for that," he recalled.

Looking back, he knew he wouldn't have been able to make it if it hadn't been for Holly. She'd been the one friend he'd unloaded all his feelings, all his anger on. She was the one friend who had seen him cry while he'd kept a stiff upper lip around everyone else, including his own family. Holly knew him better than anyone else.

"You know," Ray admitted contritely. "You've always been a much better friend to me than I've ever been to you."

"It's not a contest, Ray. But if you want to be there for me now…" she said as he brought the flatbed to a halt. Miss Joan had already stopped her own vehicle. The plan was to go on foot from here.

"Yeah?" he asked, waiting for Holly to finish.

She was nervous about walking in snow for the first time. She didn't want to make a fool of herself. "If I start to slip, hold me up so I don't embarrass myself in front of the others."

He grinned at her just before he jumped out of the cab. "I've got your back, Doll," he promised.

Heartened, Holly pushed open the door on her side of the truck and looked down at the pristine blanket of white below her. It looked harmless enough. How bad could it be?

Okay, she thought, here went nothing.

She jumped out. The next second, she felt her boots sinking into the snow, searching for bottom.

The gasp escaped her lips inadvertently.

Chapter 9

"Ray!"

Every fiber, nerve ending and bone in Ray's body went on high alert, galvanizing and becoming hard.

Standing on the other side of the flatbed truck's cab, unable to see Holly, all he had to go on was her voice, and it was half panicky, half bewildered.

Before his imagination had time to go into high gear, envisioning everything from a sinkhole to a lumbering bear or ravenous coyote, Ray had rounded the front of the truck and hurried over to her side.

It wasn't hard to see what the problem was. Holly couldn't sustain a foothold.

Grabbing her hand, he kept Holly from sinking into the snow as well as from falling, face-first, into a snow-drift. Aside from keeping her upright, Ray was also doing his level best not to laugh at the surprised, distressed expression on her face.

Holly hadn't been kidding, he realized. This really was her first experience with snow.

"Takes some getting used to," he told her.

"No kidding," she muttered under her breath, annoyed with herself.

"You two coming, or would you rather keep trying to make snow angels?" Miss Joan called over to them as the rest of the crew gathered around her, waiting for instructions. Every group needed a leader who organized things, and Miss Joan was clearly theirs.

"We're coming," Holly responded, raising her voice. Taking small steps, she held her arms out for balance, trying to get her "snow legs" so that she could move forward without looking like a flailing baby sparrow trying to fly.

"You're getting there," Ray said, encouraging her. He took hold of one of her hands to give her an anchor in hopes of keeping her upright.

"If you say so," Holly answered, not bothering to suppress her own grin.

She supposed that there were some major advantages to the snow after all. Anything that got Ray to make some sort of physical contact with her was definitely not all bad.

"Stick together," Miss Joan instructed. The warning was intended for the group, but she was looking specifically at Holly when she issued the order. "I don't want to have to be the one to ask the sheriff to bring in a search party out here. As long as you make sure you keep a couple of people in sight at all times, you're not going to get lost," she said, then ordered, "Okay, buddy up and let's get busy. Anyone find a tree worth considering, holler for the others. Remember, we need to find this year's tree pretty fast. The last thing we want is to be out here when it gets dark."

With Miss Joan's words ringing in their ears, the men and Holly all fanned out, each pair moving in a slightly different direction than the others.

"They all look so pretty," Holly noted, looking around at all the majestic specimens that reached out toward the sky before them. "How do we choose just one?" she asked Ray. To her, the very first one they looked at seemed perfect.

"Well, in this particular case, size does matter," Ray told her, dismissing the tree she was looking at. He estimated that at its highest point, it was barely ten feet tall.

"Okay, then how about that one?" Holly asked, selecting another, far taller tree.

"Better," he agreed expansively as he approached the one she'd picked.

"And it's certainly tall enough," Holly needlessly pointed out.

"Right," he agreed; however, she'd overlooked something again. "But don't forget," he reminded her. "We've also got to be able to transport the tree back to town."

One glance at the gargantuan tree was enough to make him realize that there was no way it was going to be brought back to town by utilizing the flatbed truck, even if the surface of that flatbed *was* extralong.

"Unless, of course, we find a way to roll it down the mountain," Ray deadpanned.

"Point taken," she replied. They began walking again, searching for a new candidate. "I guess finding the right tree is going to be a lot like the story of the three bears."

Ray stared at her, not having the faintest clue what she was talking about. "Come again?"

"You know," she prompted. "Not too big, not too small, it has to be *just right,*" Holly said in the high-pitched, singsong voice she used whenever she read storybooks to her niece.

"Glad you're getting the hang of this," Miss Joan congratulated them sarcastically as she joined them momentarily to see how they were doing. "Now see if you can find something that qualifies."

"Yes'm," Ray answered for both of them.

He was sorely tempted to salute the older woman but he had a feeling that he'd regret the veiled foray into sarcasm. When it came to utilizing sarcasm, Miss Joan knew no match.

Finding just the right tree turned out to be harder than she would have thought, Holly discovered. It was difficult finding a tree amid all the tall ones that was small enough to be transported, yet large enough for the town square. Predominantly, large enough for everyone who wanted to decorate at least a little of the tree. The one thing that Miss Joan insisted on was that the tree be large enough for everyone in Forever to feel as if it was actually theirs.

Finally, after trudging around for the better part of almost two hours, they found a worthy candidate. Joe Lone Wolf, the sheriff's deputy, was the one who found it in the end, and he called over the others in the group to get their vote.

"No doubt about it, it's a beautiful specimen," Holly told him appreciatively, shading her eyes as she looked up the length of the tree. "It's tall and full," she noted, glancing toward Miss Joan to see what she thought of it. "Just like you specified."

Never one to become effusive even when faced with absolute perfection, Miss Joan nodded casually. "I guess it'll have to do. Okay, boys," she declared, turning toward several of the men she'd recruited who had come up on previous expeditions, "you know what to do. Now get busy and do it!"

"What can I do?" Holly asked, stepping forward.

"Once they chop that baby down, I'll need all of you to load the tree onto the flatbed. As for right now," Miss Joan continued, looking at the waitress, "you can get out of the way—unless you want to risk getting hit by a stray branch."

Ray pulled her back as Cash and a couple of the others returned with the battery-powered saws they'd brought up with them.

"Just watch," he told Holly.

Holly frowned. She'd never liked standing on the sidelines while others did the work, and she wasn't very good at it.

"I feel like a bump on a log," she complained bitterly to Ray.

"Well, you don't look like one," he said with a laugh, tossing her a crumb. "And besides, if you don't do what Miss Joan tells you to, you know she's going to chew you out."

Holly signed. She knew he was right.

The area around the tree that had been picked out came alive with activity as the men set up their workspace. Holly did as she was told and moved back, out of the way. Since more and more seemed to be going on with chips of wood flying every which way, Holly continued to move farther and farther back.

When she suddenly missed her footing, a small cry escaped her lips and she started to fall backward. Hearing her, Ray came to her rescue.

Or tried to.

This time, though, rather than him stopping her, she caused him to lose his balance and when she did fall backward, she took him with her.

Despite tensing his body, Ray wound up falling on top of her.

The wind was knocked out of both of them. So much so that for a split second, all either one of them could do was lay there, two bodies pressed up against each other, their faces less than an inch apart.

But rather than grow colder, lying on the snow the way they were—especially Holly—they grew warmer.

Decidedly warmer.

So much so that Holly was fairly certain that she was sinking deep into the snow, the newly created hole forming thanks to the rise in her body temperature.

"Are you all right?" Ray asked her, still somewhat stunned—and still making no effort to get up.

Holly stared up into his eyes. "Never better," she heard herself whisper. She was surprised that her words were even marginally audible, competing the way they were with the sound of her heart slamming wildly against her ribcage.

"I didn't hurt you, did I?" he asked, concerned.

Her eyes on his, Holly slowly moved her head from side to side. All of her felt as if it was on fire.

Was this what it was like, she couldn't help wondering. What it was like to want someone, *really* want someone?

She had never been intimate with anyone; there never seemed to be a point. She had never cared about anyone enough to get to that incredibly special, incredibly private place inhabited by only two people at a time. Her heart had been lost to Ray at a very young age and she had never even made an effort to reclaim it.

Now she knew why.

Because she would have missed out on this, on the way adrenaline was rushing through her body because they were so wondrously close to one another.

And it felt sinfully intimate.

Ray knew he should get up now, before anyone looked over in their direction and saw this. Before Miss Joan strode over and made one of her wry, cryptic remarks, asking how this helped the process of securing the town's Christmas tree.

Right now, this was still an accident, a result of improper shifting of bodies. If it continued, well, then it was something more, not the least of which would be his taking advantage of the situation.

But the rest of his body was not responding to what his mind was telling it to do. Rather than jumping to his feet, he continued lying over Holly, not to protect her but to savor and absorb the heat of her body seeping into his despite the layers of clothing that were between them. It was almost as if the intense body heat he was feeling was melting away everything that lay in its path.

The next moment, rather than get up, rather than offering her his hand, Ray caught himself framing her face and bringing his mouth down on hers.

If it was possible to experience a Fourth of July moment in the beginning of December, then that was what this felt like.

The taste of her sweet mouth had rockets exploding in the air all around him. The fireworks only made him deepen the kiss, only made him want her more.

Want her?

What was *wrong* with him?

This was Holly he was reacting to, Holly he found himself wanting with every fiber of his being. Holly, who had been like another sister to him, Holly, who he had gone skinny-dipping with a hundred years ago when they were both kids.

And yet, this wasn't Holly at all, at least not *that* Holly. This was someone who stirred him on a level that not a single other woman ever had yet

And it scared him.

Scared him, but not enough to flee, not even enough to immediately pull his mouth away.

At least, not until he heard Miss Joan say, "You find a new way to apply CPR, boy? Or did the two of you forget the right way to make snow angels? If that's the problem, you're supposed to be next to each other, not on top of each other," she reminded Miguel's youngest son.

Ray immediately jumped to his feet, extending his hand to Holly.

Embarrassed, fighting to keep the color of her complexion down to a subdued pink rather than a blazing red, Holly took the offered hand, wrapped her fingers around it and quickly gained her feet.

"I slipped," she told Miss Joan, deliberately avoiding the older woman's eyes.

The latter nodded knowingly. "I can see that," she

commented, her voice pregnant with meaning. "Think the two of you can stay upright long enough to help carry this tree onto the flatbed?" she asked, looking from one to the other.

"Of course I can," Holly said with more conviction than she felt.

Inside, she felt as if she was entirely made of whipped cream.

"Just lead the way," Ray told the older woman, his voice sounding very stiff and formal. He didn't like being embarrassed and Miss Joan had succeeded in doing just that.

"Oh, I can lead all right," Miss Joan assured them. "But can you follow?" she asked, her hazel eyes sweeping over them meaningfully.

"Sure," Holly said quickly.

"No problem," Ray bit off.

Miss Joan laughed under her breath—none too quietly—as if to say, "We'll see about that," but for once she kept the words to herself.

Cash had backed up the flatbed so that it was as parallel to the felled tree as possible. There was enough space all around the specimen for the men and Holly to adequately surround the tree.

Miss Joan ordered everyone to squat down and get one arm and shoulder under their section of the Scotch pine. "All right, everyone, put your backs into it!" she instructed.

The first effort was less than successful, accompanied by a cacophony of grunts and groans. "You call that trying?" she demanded, clearly disappointed with their combined effort. "A bunch of kindergarteners could do better than that."

"Maybe we should wait until you bring them in," one of the men, Gary Walker, grumbled.

"This isn't a dialogue, Walker," Miss Joan snapped. "Unless you want to be the one to tell the kids in Forever why they don't have a tree this year. No? I didn't think so. Okay, now let's see you give it a *real* try this time," she ordered, her sharp gaze taking everyone in. "Get in under the branches, wrap your hand around the section of truck next to you and let's see you do it. On the count of three this time," she said, then proceeded to do a countdown. "One. Two. *Three!*"

This time, the trunk cleared the ground. The tree wavered and looked as if it was going to go back down again, but somehow, between them all, they managed to stabilize it and with a chorus of louder grunts and groans, they finally got the tree loaded onto the flatbed.

Exhausted, the ten people Miss Joan had selected to be part of her crew leaned against the perimeter of the truck.

"I don't know about you, but I just got my Christmas present," she heard Cash say to someone, viewing the Christmas tree with pure satisfaction, as well as relief because they had managed to get this perfect specimen of a tree onto the flatbed without any incident.

"Yeah, me, too," she heard Ray agree softly, but when she looked up, she found that he wasn't looking at the tree. He was looking at her.

A very warm shiver danced down her spine.

Chapter 10

Because the crew Miss Joan had brought with her to select this year's Christmas tree had found the one they wanted to put up in the town square rather quickly, they wound up returning to Forever well before dusk.

Word spread fast, and the town's citizens hurried over to the square to pass their own judgment on the Scotch pine.

As if she was leading a wagon train into the Wild West, Miss Joan brought her own truck to a stop in the center of town, jumped out of the cab and called for a halt of the other vehicles.

"We got another beauty," she announced to the sea of faces that surrounded her. A chorus of agreement met her statement.

Rather than just leave the tree where it was until the following day, Miss Joan decreed that there was enough daylight—and certainly enough willing hands—to get the tree off the flatbed truck and upright in the town square.

"You picked another winner," Harry proudly told his bride, planting a quick kiss on her cheek.

"Save that for later, Harry," she told him. "Right now, I need harnesses and winches. You know the drill," she told her husband.

"Got 'em waiting right behind Mick's garage," Harry told her. He summoned a few men to come with him so that they could bring back the required equipment that would help the process of getting the tree upright and secured in the desired position.

Miss Joan relinquished control of this portion of the operation, allowing her husband to oversee it. Harry happily went to work, employing Cash and a number of the other younger men to get the job done. They worked in harmony, having either done this before or watched it being done year after year.

Ninety minutes after rolling into town with the giant Scotch pine, this year's Christmas tree was up, stable and secure—and ready to be decorated.

Everyone who wanted to, regardless of age, took part in this phase of the event. The only rule was to wait until the lights were put up, which they were in amazingly short order, thanks to the practically military precision instituted by Harry. Beyond that, once the lights were operational, there were no rules to follow other than to have fun.

There was no end to the number of people who wanted to be part of this segment of the ceremony—because it was such a beloved tradition.

Looking around the town square, Ray saw not just

his father—who happen to be Harry's best friend and might have been in town for reasons other than the tree decorating ceremony—but his brothers and sister, as well. Granted Alma and Gabe both worked in town, but standing around in the square, waiting to be able to take their turn at adorning the Christmas tree, was not part of their normal job description.

Just as it wasn't part of Olivia Santiago's job description. Besides being the sheriff's wife, she was also one of the town's two lawyers, having formed a partnership with Alma's husband, Cash. Saturdays were either for catching up at the office or trying to cram in seven days of family life into two. But here she was, with everyone else. Right now, it was hard to say who was the more casually dressed, Olivia or her husband, both of whom were usually so carefully and formally attired.

Ray grinned as he scanned the area. Wearing what looked like their most comfortable clothes, everyone had come out for the occasion that was viewed by many as an unofficial day of celebration.

"You picked a really pretty tree, Holly."

Turning around to the source of the comment, Holly saw that even her mother had come out to join the rest of the town. Or, more accurately, Martha Johnson had been brought out by Ray's brother Eli. Eli and his wife, Kasey, followed by their two-year-old son, had steered Martha's wheelchair to the center of town to await the tree's arrival.

Martha, although exceedingly independent, appreciated the help since she had her hands full at the moment.

Holly saw that her niece, Molly, was comfortably seated on her mother's lap. Seeing Holly, however, the little girl wiggled off her grandmother's lap and made a mad dash for the woman she considered to be more mother than aunt. What she lacked in height she more than made up for with her boundless energy and enthusiasm.

"Holly, Holly, Holly!" the little girl cried with enthusiasm as she wrapped her arms around Holly's legs. "The tree is here!" she declared excitedly.

"I know, Monkey, I helped bring it in," Holly told the little girl with a laugh as she scooped her niece up in her arms. "I take it you like it."

"Very much," Molly answered with a sharp, smart nod of her head, sounding for all the world as if she was an old person trapped in a child's body instead of the age she really was.

"We'll leave you in good hands," Kasey murmured to Martha as Kasey and her husband withdrew along with their son.

"Thank you!" Martha called after the couple.

"Mom, what are you doing here?" Holly asked her mother as soon as she had her attention.

"Same thing everyone else is doing here—waiting to do my part in decorating the tree. Just because I can't get up on my tiptoes anymore doesn't mean I'm ready to be shipped off to the elephant's graveyard just yet. I've still got a chapter or two left in me."

"I know that, Mom, I didn't—" Holly began, only to be interrupted by her niece.

Older in spirit and mind than she was in actual years, Molly looked at her grandmother, a panicked expression crossing her face as she cried, "Don't go to the elephant's graveyard, Grandma. Please don't go. I don't want you to," she pleaded.

Laughing, Holly kissed the top of her niece's head.

"Nobody's going anywhere, Monkey. Your grandmother's going to be around for a very long, long time. Okay?" she asked, looking into Molly's puckered face.

The little girl looked as if she was on the verge of crying at any second.

Then, just like that, the tears vanished.

Molly bobbed her head up and down with such force, Holly half expected it to pop off her neck. But Molly didn't even look dizzy.

Crisis averted, Holly picked up a shiny star ornament laid out on one of the tables that had been brought to the square. There were tables lining two sides of the square so that everyone could have access to the decorations.

"Okay, Monkey, let's see how high you can reach," Holly told her niece, presenting her with the ornament.

Molly examined the star, then, cocking her head, looked up at the towering tree. "You gonna hold me up?" she asked.

"That's cheating," Holly pretended to protest. Molly's small face instantly puckered up again and she looked upset.

"No, it's not. I'm a little girl. I can't reach high without you. Please, Holly?" she pleaded.

"Don't be a bully, Doll," Ray told her, joining the three generations that comprised his best friend's family. He looked down at the little girl. "Would you like me to hold you up, Molly?" he asked.

Molly had developed a king-size crush on Ray in the past month or so and she smiled from ear to ear at her heartthrob's suggestion. She put her arms out to him, wiggling to get free.

"Yes, please," she agreed with enthusiasm.

Because he was taller than Holly, Ray could hold

the little girl up even higher in his arms—and for longer—than Holly could.

The latter ability became very necessary because, as it turned out, Molly had trouble making up her mind exactly where she wanted to hang the ornament. After changing her mind a total of three times, she finally settled on a branch.

Once it was hung and deemed secure on its perch, Ray was allowed to put her down. He did as he was instructed.

"Typical female, can't make up her mind," he said with a laugh.

"I'm not tip-ick-cal," Molly protested indignantly. "Grandma says I'm special."

"And special you are," Holly agreed, ruffling the little girl's hair. Holly turned toward her mother. "Mom, you want to hang up another ornament?" she asked, ready to fetch a second one for her from a nearby table. Her mother had already placed one on a low branch while waiting for Molly to hang hers.

But Martha demurred. She was here to observe and watch over her granddaughter. "No, I'm fine, dear. I just want to watch everyone else decorate the tree, if you don't mind," she said.

Holly didn't like her mother hanging back like this. It wasn't like her. Did that mean that something was wrong? Rather than asking—and receiving a negative answer, as she knew she would since her mother hated complaining—she took another approach.

"I don't mind," Holly told her mother. "But you have to hang at least one more ornament, Mom. Those are the rules, you know that. If you show up, you have to hang up," Holly said, quoting the rule Miss Joan was said to have made up years ago.

"Tell you what, Mrs. Johnson. You pick one out and I'll get you in close so you can hang it up a little higher," Ray offered cheerfully.

Martha nodded. "I'd like that, Ray."

"You do have a way with the Johnson women," Holly said to him, lowering her voice to a whisper.

He flashed a grin her way just as he guided her mother's wheelchair toward the tables where the decorations were laid out.

The tree wouldn't be fully decorated today, not by a long shot. It was never completely decorated within one day's time, and they were already working with an abbreviated day, but at least they had gotten a good head start on the job.

The town's tallest ladders—housed the rest of the year in Silas Malcolm's barn because it was the closest large space to the town square—had been put up against the tree so that, in addition to stringing up the lights, people could decorate the top portion of the tree.

Holly stood back and watched as people took turns—in some cases just once, in other cases as many turns as they could squeeze in—using the ladder and dressing the tree until evening finally blanketed the square, robbing it of much-needed light.

"That's it for today," Miss Joan announced as she called a halt. "We'll get started tomorrow just after first light," she said, more out of habit than necessity, since the rules were never changed.

And neither did the ritual that came next.

"All right, coffee and pie for everyone," she declared. Hooking her arm through her husband's, she briskly led the way to the diner. The coffee was intended for all the participants who were fifteen and over. Those who had joined in and were younger received glasses of milk to wash down their servings of pie—or cookies, if they preferred.

"I love this time of year," Holly confided to her mother as she got behind the wheelchair, ready to push the woman to the diner, which was located only a few blocks away from the town square.

"So do I," Martha agreed, but her voice sounded a little weary to Holly. If she had any doubt, her mother's next words confirmed her thoughts. "Listen, I'm a little tired—and apparently Molly is even more so." Martha nodded at the little girl who was sleeping curled up on her lap. "We're going to go home."

"Okay," Holly said without a single word of protest, turning the wheelchair in the opposite direction.

"No, Holly, by 'we' I mean Molly and me, not you," her mother clarified. "I want you go on to the diner with the others."

She had no intention of letting her mother push herself all the way home. "That's okay, Mom, I—"

"No, it's not okay. I insist," Martha said firmly, cutting in. "And I know what's running through your mind," she added. "Don't you treat me like an invalid. I'm perfectly capable of taking my granddaughter home and putting her to bed. There's no need for you to cut your evening short just to hover over me," her mother informed her.

"Especially if she has help," Miguel Rodriguez Sr. said, gently edging Holly out of the way as he took over the handles on the back of her mother's wheelchair.

Martha twisted around in her chair to look at this

new champion she'd attracted. "Miguel, I don't need your help, either."

Ray's father nodded understandingly. "I know," he replied in his soft, accented voice. "But perhaps I need to do something gallant and this would be a very nice opportunity. Do not spoil it for me, Martha. Let me pretend to come to your rescue," he told her. "And this way, you can use both your arms to hold your granddaughter on your lap instead of trying to balance her and keep her from falling off as you go around corners, yes?"

Martha surrendered with a sigh. "If you insist."

"That I do," Miguel told her, then looked over his shoulder at Holly just before he began to push the wheelchair in the direction of the Johnson house. He winked at Holly, looking at that exact moment for all the world like his youngest son, Holly couldn't help thinking.

"Go, enjoy yourself a little bit," he encouraged her. "You do not do that nearly often enough—and you really should."

"He's right, you know," Ray said, putting his hands on her shoulders and physically turning her toward the diner. "You don't relax nearly often enough anymore. I can remember you had a lot more fun as a kid."

"Kids are supposed to have fun," Holly pointed out, but she was walking in the direction he'd steered her. "Adults are supposed to work."

"Okay, I'll give you that—in general. But nowhere is it written that work has to be twenty-four hours a day, every single day," he pointed out. "Even machines wear out like that."

Holly stopped walking and turned to face him for a moment. Did he forget?

"I took today off," she reminded him.

"No, you didn't," he contradicted. She opened her mouth to protest, but he talked right over her. "You didn't put in a full day at the diner—but you did work up a sweat," he pointed out. "That's work."

Holly shrugged away his comment. "There are lots of ways to work up a sweat that don't have anything to do with work."

The way he looked at her told Holly that he had attached a very particular meaning to her words, a meaning that she hadn't necessarily intended.

She could feel herself blushing again, damn him.

"Did you blush this much when we were younger?" Ray asked her teasingly. "I can't remember, but I don't think so."

Holly deliberately picked up her pace, walking fast so she could get ahead of him and he wouldn't be able to see her face.

"Hurry up, slowpoke," she urged. "Let's get going before all the pie is gone."

"As long as we get to the counter before Big Jim Zucoff claims a spot, we're okay," he told her, picking up his pace nonetheless. "That man'll eat anything that doesn't eat him first, and I've never seen anyone with a bigger sweet tooth than Big Jim."

"Miss Joan will keep an eye on him," Holly assured him. The other woman liked to keep things fair and equal, making sure that no one had an unfair advantage over anyone else, and Big Jim could eat faster than anyone she'd ever met. "Remember, she did last year."

"But he's bigger this year," Ray pointed out with a laugh. "I don't think anything'll succeed in reining him in, short of throwing lassos around him, tethering him and staking the ends of the lassos in the ground."

"Well, if anyone can do it, Miss Joan can," Holly bantered back, but her mind wasn't really on the man they were talking about, or the coffee and pie Miss Joan was giving away or even the Christmas tree she'd worked so hard to help bring back into town.

No matter what words came out of her mouth, Holly's mind was stuck in third gear and totally focused on those few precious moments when time had stood still and Ray's mouth had found hers again.

Except that this time, though she wouldn't have thought it was possible until she'd experienced it, had been even more intimate and stimulating than the first time that Ray had kissed her.

The way she saw it, there was nothing she could find under her tree come Christmas morning that could possibly come close to competing with what she'd already experienced.

As far as she was concerned, she'd already had her Christmas miracle—and it would last her for many Christmases to come.

Chapter 11

Sitting in front of her outdated computer, Holly felt her eyelids drooping. She struggled to keep her eyes open. But it was definitely not easy.

She'd gotten up early—as usual—to put in some study time. Exams were coming up soon and she needed to be ready for them if she was ever going to achieve her goal and become a nurse. However, getting up early, staying up late and working her study schedule around her workday as well as the needs of her mother and Molly was definitely challenging.

But then, she kept telling herself over and over again, if it wasn't challenging—if all this phenomenal amount of juggling were easy for her—then life would have been extremely boring with a capital *B*. It was in her nature to work hard, and she'd always *liked* challenges.

It was just a wee bit difficult to work *this* hard and be

this challenged. Holly had to admit that she would have welcomed being a little less challenged once in a while.

"Damn it," she muttered under her breath. Her eyes had closed again. She had to stop doing that or she was going to flunk.

Unless, of course, she found a way to absorb all this information by osmosis.

Fat chance.

"Are you asleep at the computer again?"

Holly's eyes flew open as she heard her mother wheeling herself into the small bedroom that had been converted into Holly's study area. She'd thought that her mother was still in bed. Just how long had she been asleep anyway?

"Nope, not me," Holly denied cheerfully. She pressed her lips together to suppress the desire to yawn. "Just resting my eyes, that's all."

"Uh-huh," Martha murmured, clearly skeptical. "You should try resting the rest of yourself once in a while, as well." Her mother shook her head disapprovingly. "You go on burning the candle at both ends this way, one day you're going to find that you're not going to have any candle left. You know that, right?"

Holly closed down her computer. It was time for her to go to the diner and work.

"Sure I will, Mom." Holly turned from the darkening monitor and lightly brushed a kiss against her mother's cheek before she got up. "Now if you'll excuse me, I've got to get to work."

"Why don't you call in sick and go catch up on your sleep?" her mother suggested.

"Because Miss Joan doesn't pay me for being beautiful, Mom," Holly said, tongue in cheek. "She pays me for showing up and working."

Striding to the front of the house, Holly rummaged through the hall closet, found her jacket and put it on. The temperature had dropped in the past couple of days and it was actually rather chilly in the morning. She supposed that since it was December, she really shouldn't be complaining. A lot of the country was dealing with record snow storms, so a little temperature drop was a small thing in comparison.

"She also doesn't pay you for being dead on your feet," Martha pointed out.

"Who's dead on her feet?" Holly asked, feigning confusion.

Martha frowned. "Don't play dumb, Holly. You could never pull that off. Even as a baby, you were always alert, always quick to look as if you understood what was going on."

"And you're not prejudiced in any way, right?" Holly laughed.

Martha lifted her chin as if she'd just been unfairly challenged. "Of course not."

Holly grinned. "Maybe you're giving just a little too much credit to a toddler, Mom—even if that toddler was me."

Martha sighed, throwing up her hands and resigning herself to business as usual as far as her daughter was concerned. "I don't know why I keep hitting my head against the wall like this. You never listen to anything I say anyway."

"Sure I listen, Mom. I just reserve the right to pick and choose which advice I want to follow and which I want to put away for another time," she answered tactfully. They both knew that the second kind of advice wasn't being put off for another time but being put away into cold storage, to be ignored for *all* time. "I'll be fine, Mom, really. Please stop worrying. I'll cut back on this hectic pace soon, I promise."

"Right, when you land in the hospital in Pine Ridge."

"Ever the optimist, Mom." Holly laughed, shaking her head.

"No, what I'm being is a realist, Holly. You simply can't keep going like this without some sort of consequences."

"And I won't keep going like this," Holly promised. She was going to be late, but she couldn't just leave when her mother was this upset with her. She needed to put her mother at ease as well as make her understand that right now she needed to keep up this pace a little longer. "I'll be graduating in less than six months—provided I pass my tests—and with any luck, new worlds will open up for me. For us," Holly amended, smiling warmly at her mother.

Martha appeared far from convinced. "If you haven't worked yourself to death by then."

"Never happen, I promise," Holly said, raising her right hand as if she were taking a solemn vow. "I won't let it."

Her mother murmured something under her breath about it not being all up to her, but Holly was determined to leave while she was still ahead in the game—or at least even. She dearly loved her mother, but Martha Johnson could talk a person to death once she got going on a subject. And right now, Holly thought, she had only so much energy to work with and it was all she could do to stay awake and functioning.

There was a whole day stretching out in front of her. If she spent time arguing with her mother, that would take up energy she needed for work, for studying tonight and for giving Molly a little quality one-on-one time, as well.

And what about you? When do you get some me *time?* a little voice in her head demanded.

The thing Holly had discovered about little voices was that she could ignore them if she chose. It was all mind over matter, properly applied.

"Hold down the fort until I get home, Mom." She kissed Martha's cheek again. "We'll talk about this then."

"No, we won't," Martha predicted as Holly left the house.

Right you are again, Mom.

Holly walked briskly to the diner. She passed the town square and the lovely Christmas tree, which now stood in all its finery like a giant, well-dressed sentry. All the decorations had been hung—if not all with the greatest of care, then at least with the greatest of affection.

She smiled to herself as she hurried by it. To her the tree was a symbol of the harmony that existed in Forever. She dearly loved living in a town that had traditions such as this one. From the bottom of her heart, Holly felt sorry for the people who were living in big cities, people who passed their neighbors on the street without a clue as to who they were or what kind of people they were.

Wax poetic later, Holly. If you don't pick up your pace, you're going to be late.

That's what she got for falling asleep in front of her

computer, Holly berated herself. She was going to have to go over those last few pages she was supposed to have covered. Attempting to summon them now, she was drawing a blank. If those pages turned up on the exam, she was going to wind up failing it.

Shadows accompanied her through the streets, marking her path as she made her way to the diner. Dawn had yet to crease the horizon with the promise of first light.

Though she'd promised herself not to, Holly glanced at her watch. Five minutes after six. Not bad as far as being late went. Miss Joan was undoubtedly on the premises already. If it wasn't for the fact that she knew the woman lived with her husband in Harry's house, she would have sworn that Miss Joan slept in the diner so she could be there 24/7.

But when Holly arrived at the diner she found that the door was locked.

She looked at it in surprise.

Well, what do you know? She'd beaten Miss Joan in. That was definitely a first.

Holly fished out her key and unlocked the door. Miss Joan had given her her own key on the outside chance that she arrived first, but neither Miss Joan nor Holly had ever thought that was going to happen.

Holly caught herself hoping that everything was all right. Stripping off her jacket as she walked into the diner, she dropped it on the back of one of the chairs and went directly to the coffee urns. She had to get the first pots of coffee going.

She was filling the last urn with water for brewing tea when she heard the door to the diner opening behind her. Glancing over her shoulder in that direction, she saw Miss Joan in the doorway. The expression on the woman's face was somewhat bemused.

"You beat me in," she said.

Relieved that Miss Joan looked to be all right, Holly cheerfully replied, "Had to happen sometime."

"No, it didn't," the older woman retorted.

"Okay, I can leave and come back in again," Holly offered.

Miss Joan scowled at her as she deposited her purse behind the counter then shrugged out of her coat. "Don't patronize me, girl."

"I'm not patronizing you," Holly protested. "I'm just trying to guess what you want."

"Not even God can do that," Ray told her as he came into the diner himself.

Clearly not expecting anyone in this early, Miss Joan turned around and looked him over. "Well, look what the cat dragged in," she commented. "It's practically the middle of the night—at least for you. What are you doing out of bed so early, boy?"

Ray shrugged carelessly, as if he hadn't really noticed that he was the first customer at the diner, a fact he was acutely aware of.

"Thought I'd get an early start for a change," he told Miss Joan, carefully avoiding looking in Holly's direction—the old woman was a mind reader and he didn't want her thinking that he was here on account of Holly. He wouldn't even allow *himself* to think that. "Got a long list of things to do today."

"Like sitting on a counter stool, listening to your hair grow?" Miss Joan asked, tying on her apron. "Or are you here to watch my waitress work?" She gestured toward Holly.

"I'm here to have some of your excellent coffee and sample one of those fantastic raspberry-jelly donuts," Ray informed her.

Miss Joan laughed, shaking her head. "Well, I'll say one thing for you, boy. Your lies are getting smoother and rolling off your tongue with more charm. What do you think, Holly? Is Ray here becoming a more skillful liar than he used to be?"

Holly's early morning routine at the diner had become second nature to her and she could initiate it in her sleep—which some mornings was rather fortunate. But there was no sleepwalking through a morning that contained Ray. She was aware of every single movement she made—as well as every single one of his.

"I think he's just as attached to your jelly donuts and your coffee as he always is," Holly answered, waiting for her pulse to settle down to its normal irregular beat whenever Ray was anywhere around.

Miss Joan looked from one young person to the other. "You've been handling the donut orders for the past two years and as near as I can remember, you're the one who makes the initial pots of coffee in the morning, as well. Sounds to me like you're the one who should be garnering those compliments—or malarkey—from this boy and not me."

Ray sat down at the counter, taking the stool that was closest to where Holly was working. "Coffee ready yet?" he asked her, since as far as he could tell, the urn was still in the process of making its loud brewing noises.

"You're in luck," she told him. "The first urn just finished brewing." The other two urns were still going through their paces.

Holly poured the midnight-black liquid into a cup, placed it on a saucer and took it over to Ray. Setting the cup and saucer down on the counter, she selected a raspberry-jelly donut from the center of the box that had been delivered late last night and, placing that on a plate, put it beside the saucer on the counter. She put the creamer on the other side.

Within a moment, Ray had made short work of the cup of coffee. The rate he was consuming it made her think he needed it to wake up.

Ray exhaled, pure pleasure on his face as he looked her way. Two thirds of the coffee was gone when he set the cup back on the saucer. "Makes me feel like a new man," he declared.

"Nothing wrong with the old one," Holly heard herself saying before she could think her comment through and keep it to herself.

Surprised, Ray smiled at her while Miss Joan laughed shortly and said, "You're obviously not a very good judge of character, Holly. But you'll learn." Turning to Ray, she asked, "How's that wedding coming along?"

Startled, because his mind was clearly elsewhere, Ray looked at the woman with more than a little nervousness and asked, "What wedding?"

"Your brother Mike's wedding," Miss Joan specified, her eyes all but pinning him to the wall. "That's not off, is it?"

Of course she was talking about Mike's wedding. What other wedding would she have been referring to? Ray upbraided himself. Ever since he'd kissed Holly, his mind—not to mention other parts of him—had been playing tricks on him, making him wonder about things that he'd never wondered about or even contemplated before.

"No." And then he cleared his throat, repeating the word with more conviction. "No. As far as I know, it's still on."

"What else do you know?" Miss Joan asked with a strange, sly smile on her lips. A smile that made him fidget inside.

"About the wedding?" Ray asked, not sure if they were still on the same topic.

Miss Joan sighed and shook her head. "No, about how long panda bears live. Of course about the wedding. Are they still planning on inviting the whole town, or have they come to their senses and decided to elope?" She spared Holly a glance, saying, "Eloping is really the best way. Just you and your intended and the good Lord—and a preacher, of course."

Holly said nothing, but that definitely did sound good to her. Anything sounded good to her, as long as it included Ray.

Ray laughed at Miss Joan's suggestion. "Well, I know that Mike would probably like that idea a lot, but seeing as how Samantha doesn't really have any family to speak of, I think she kind of likes the idea of having a big wedding with lots of people around. And Mike likes seeing her happy, so yeah, they're still having the whole town at the wedding."

Pouring her own cup of coffee, Miss Joan leaned over the counter, fixed Ray with a very intense look and asked, "Anything else?"

He had no idea where Miss Joan was going with this—or even if the woman had a destination in mind.

With Miss Joan, he'd learned a long time ago, nothing was what it seemed.

"Like what?" he asked innocently.

"Like are you part of the wedding party?" Holly asked, getting into the general inquisitive mood that seemed to be permeating the diner this morning.

"Me? Hell, no," Ray laughed, waving away the mere notion. "That would mean I'd have to put on a monkey suit."

"You could always go in that lovely outfit you have on," Miss Joan deadpanned, gesturing at the sheepskin jacket, plaid shirt and worn jeans that he was wearing.

But Holly had a serious question that she raised now. "You mean you wouldn't put up with a little discomfort in order to stand up for your own brother?"

Ray became somewhat defensive. "Hey, it's not like he's my only brother, and you wouldn't call it 'a little' discomfort if you'd had to put up with it like I did for the last wedding, when Rafe married Val. Or the one before that when Angel and Gabe did the same thing," he recalled.

Now that he'd gotten started, it was like opening up a floodgate. "Then there was Eli and Kasey. And Alma and Cash started the ball rolling when they got married." He'd been there for four of his siblings. That, as far as he was concerned, was above and beyond the call of duty. "Way I see it," he told her, "I've done my time."

"So you're bailing out on Mike?" Holly asked.

The way she said it sounded like an accusation, Ray thought. But rather than take offense, he just shrugged. "It's not like he'll miss me," Ray said glibly.

"The hell he won't," Holly countered. "I've seen all of you together. You all act tough, like you could take the rest of your family or leave it, but deep down, that's not true and you know it. You all love each other and there's not one of you who wouldn't go to their grave defending the others."

Ray stood up. "I've got to get going before you start charging me for this little head-shrink session," he quipped, digging into his pocket for money. Taking it out, he laid several bills on the counter.

"Keep it," Miss Joan said, pushing the money back at him. "It's on the house. You're going to need the money to rent that pretty little monkey suit you were just complaining about."

After a beat, Ray picked up the bills and shoved them back into his front pocket. "Thanks," he murmured.

Holly noticed that he didn't bother contradicting what Miss Joan had said. It looked as if Ray was going to be in another wedding party. Which meant that she had another opportunity to see him looking better than any man had an earthly right to be.

She didn't realize that she was smiling as she went about her work.

But Miss Joan did.

Chapter 12

As the diner door closed behind Ray, Miss Joan turned around to look at Holly. "Well, you seem to have things under control here, so I'm going to go over some of the order forms," the woman told her. "If you need me, I'll be in my office."

Holly nodded. She moved faster through her routine when she was alone. "Okay. I've got plenty to keep me busy out here."

She heard the front door opening again after what seemed like only a couple of minutes had passed. Holly didn't bother turning around when she asked, "Forget something?" She'd just assumed that Ray had doubled back to the diner for some reason.

She should have known it wasn't him when the hairs on the back of her neck didn't stand up the way they always did whenever he was in the vicinity.

"Yeah," a feminine voice said. "What my feet look like." The words were accompanied by a deep, heartfelt sigh.

Startled, Holly swung around to see Alma making her way to the counter at the pace of an arthritic snail. Holly glanced at her watch out of habit.

"You're early," she commented. The past couple of months, Alma had taken to coming in every morning like clockwork for a large container of herbal tea to go. But she usually came in closer to nine, not seven.

"I know." Alma pressed her hand to her spine, no doubt trying to relieve an ever-present ache. "I thought if I showed up early at the sheriff's office, I could leave early, as well."

"To go home and put your feet up so you could get more comfortable?" Holly guessed, returning to the counter and rounding it in order to begin preparing the deputy's container of herbal tea.

Alma's laugh was short, harsh and dismissive. "Holly, I'm eight-and-a-half-months pregnant with a giant elephant—there *is* no comfortable position I can possible get to without first being knocked unconscious."

Holly gave her an understanding smile. "You have my sympathies. The usual?" she asked even as she got the pot of hot water.

"The usual," Alma echoed as she attempted to sit on a stool and redistribute her bulk in some sort of balanced fashion. But her eyes widened in distress before she could actually make satisfactory contact with the stool. "Speaking of usual," she said with a huge sigh, completely abandoning the notion of sitting. "Looks like I've got to pay a visit to yet another bathroom. I swear, I should just pick a bathroom stall and have all my mail forwarded there. It feels like I've got to go every three and a half minutes." She frowned at she looked down accusingly at her protruding abdomen. "Either this kid is spending all his or her time sitting on my bladder or my bladder has mysteriously shrunk down to the size of a pea."

"Maybe it's a little of both," Holly speculated helpfully. She'd picked up Alma's ambiguous reference to gender. "I take it that you still don't know what you're having?"

Alma shook her head. "I want to be surprised," she said as she began the slow journey to the rear of the diner where the restrooms were located.

"Well, you certainly have a lot more willpower than I do, Alma," Holly acknowledged. "If it were me, I'd want to know."

Alma flashed a weary smile in her direction. "I really like surprises." She winced a little. "Better make that an extralarge container, Holly. I need something to settle my stomach. I've been feeling really queasy since yesterday morning."

"Maybe you should go in to see the doctor," Holly suggested.

"I am, this afternoon. Right after my shift," Alma told her as she disappeared around the corner. "Until then, I need tea."

"One giant-size tea coming up, Deputy," Holly called out, reaching under the counter for one of the oversize cups that Miss Joan kept there.

Holly placed it on the counter, took two tea bags from the vacuum-packed canister where Miss Joan kept the herbal tea and deposited both into the cup. She then took it over to the urn and carefully poured the hot water over the tea bags.

While the tea bags were steeping, Holly went back to what she'd been doing to get the diner ready for the morning crowd that would begin arriving within the hour, looking to have breakfast.

Almost ten minutes had passed before she remembered to check on the tea.

When she did, Holly frowned. The tea was darker than the way Alma usually drank it. But then, she *had* asked for a larger container, so maybe she wouldn't mind that the tea was stronger, as well.

"Hope you like your herbal tea strong, Alma," Holly said, addressing the comment to the woman she assumed had stopped to look at something at the rear of the diner after she'd left the restroom. When she didn't receive even a grunt back, Holly glanced over her shoulder. "Where are you anyway?" she asked, half directing the question to the absent deputy, half to herself.

Maybe I should check on her, Holly thought, growing a little concerned.

Rounding the counter, she made her way to the rear of the diner, expecting to walk headlong into Alma at any moment.

But she reached the restroom door, and still no deputy.

Cocking her head, Holly paused for a second, listening to see if she heard any sort of movement on the other side of the door.

She didn't.

She was becoming uneasy. Alma was taking too long. Something wasn't right.

"Alma, are you in there?" Holly asked, raising her voice.

There was no answer.

Why?

She knew that Alma couldn't have left the diner without her noticing. There was only one way in or out, and the deputy would have had to pass the counter in order to leave. It wasn't as if there was a crowd she could have blended into.

Had she gone to see Miss Joan for some reason? Holly wondered. The woman was her mother-in-law and maybe there was something Alma wanted to share with Miss Joan.

But even as Holly came up with the excuse, it just didn't sit well with her.

Something was wrong, she could feel it in her bones.

"Alma?" she called through the door. "I'm coming in, okay?"

Very slowly, Holly pushed open the outer door with her fingertips, giving Alma every chance to call out and tell her to stay outside. When she didn't, Holly pushed the door open all the way.

That was when she saw her.

Alma was lying facedown on the floor. She appeared to be unconscious. Oh, God, had she fainted?

For a fleeting second, Holly thought of running for help, but she just couldn't move. Maybe she'd already allowed too much time to go by and this was one of those times where every second was critical. The thought all but froze her in place.

Rather than leave Alma, Holly shouted as loudly as she could, *"I need a little help in here!"*

Holly dropped to her knees beside the unconscious

pregnant woman—which was when she realized that she was kneeling in something damp.

Alma's water had broken.

Her hand on Alma's shoulder, Holly tried to gently shake her awake.

"Alma? Alma can you hear me?" she asked urgently. "Alma, it's Holly. Can you tell me what happened?"

Since Alma was still lying facedown on the tiled floor, all she could make out was one eyelid fluttering slightly. It was enough to give her hope.

"That's it, Alma, wake up. You can do it. C'mon, try to sit up for me," she coaxed.

Angling, Holly slipped her arm under the older woman's shoulder—which was when she heard Alma's involuntary cry.

Alma's eyes flew open—and immediately filled with pain. "No, I can't… It's…the baby… The baby's… coming," she cried in an unnatural panic, each syllable sounding as if it was physically being wrenched out of her throat.

"I've got to get you to the doctor," Holly told her, doing her best not to panic herself. This was a natural process, a perfectly natural process, right? Women had been giving birth, with or without help, for centuries, right?

But when she tried to move Alma, the other woman clutched tightly on to her arm, trying to stop her from doing that.

"No, I can't… I *can't*."

Holly regrouped. "Okay, you don't have to get up." She started to rise. "I'll go get him to come—"

Holly never got the chance to say *here*. Alma caught her wrist in what felt like an iron grip. "No…stay…

please," she pleaded. "Now... Coming... *Now!*" she cried between firmly clenched teeth.

Holly took a deep breath. This was *not* going well. "Okay, I'll stay, Alma. I'll stay," she promised. With effort, Holly centered herself. And drew on what she knew. She offered Alma an encouraging smile. "And don't worry, you're actually not my first. I brought Molly into the world."

For a second, she recalled the utter chaos of that night, with her brother yelling orders at her and his girlfriend crying and screaming. And there she'd been, caught up in the eye of the hurricane, praying she didn't mess anything up.

Molly had arrived in less than a heartbeat—and she was perfect.

"Jill went into labor three weeks early and there was no time to get her to the doctor, either. And I know more now than I knew then because of those nursing courses I've been taking, so everything's going to be all right. Trust me."

She was doing her best to put Alma at ease, but apparently she wasn't being too successful. Alma still looked scared.

"But, Alma, I'm going to need my hand," Holly told her gently. The words didn't seem to register with the pain-racked deputy. "Let go of my wrist, Alma," Holly requested a little more forcefully.

Belatedly, Alma opened up her hand, then instantly dug her fingertips into her own palms. The pain was almost making her pass out.

"Sorry..." Alma breathed.

"Nothing to be sorry about," Holly said soothingly. "I get it."

Stripping off her apron, Holly did her best to slide it under the deputy's writhing body. From this new position, Holly got a better look at Alma's face. There was a fresh cut, still bleeding, right above her right eye. It wasn't very hard to figure out what happened. Alma had to have hit her head on the edge of the sink when she fainted.

But right now, that was of secondary importance. Bringing this baby into the world, healthy and sound, was her first priority.

"This…is…*awful*…" Alma cried.

"It'll be over soon, I promise," Holly told her.

With determination, she folded back the bottom of Alma's oversize blouse and then tugged down the khaki-colored elastic-waist slacks she had on, taking them off the deputy.

"This is where it gets personal, Alma," Holly muttered. "But like I said, it'll be over with soon." *It just won't feel so soon until it's over,* she added silently.

One look told her that not only was the baby crowning, but that this baby was coming whether or not either one of them was ready for its arrival.

"Very soon," Holly told her.

"Holly?" Alma cried uncertainly.

Holly heard everything she needed to in Alma's voice. She knew what the deputy was asking her.

"The baby's coming, Alma. I need you to bear down and push," she instructed. "I'll do the catching." Alma screamed as a fresh pain ripped through her. The sound vibrated through Holly's head, all but making her deaf. "Well, you've certainly got that part down. Now *push!*" Holly ordered in a voice that would have made a drill sergeant envious.

The door directly behind her swung open just then. "I heard that all the way through the diner. What the hell is going on here— Oh, my God!" Miss Joan cried out as the sight of her daughter-in-law lying on the bathroom floor and what that meant registered. "Alma, baby, are you all right?"

"She's fine, Miss Joan," Holly told her, trying to keep her voice calm. "You're about to become a grandmother. If you're not busy," Holly added drolly, "could you get behind her, please, and support her shoulders?"

For one of the few times in her life, Miss Joan appeared indecisively torn. "I'll go run to get the doctor—"

"There's no time," Holly snapped impatiently, cutting Miss Joan short. "Get someone else to go. I need you to get down behind Alma, Miss Joan. *Now!*"

Without another word, Miss Joan did as she was told. Hurrying out, she called to the only other person in the diner, Angel, and dispatched her for the doctor. Rushing back into the bathroom, she knelt down directly behind her daughter-in-law and propped Alma's shoulders up against her own body before adding her hands to the effort. She pushed Alma into a forward position so that she could do as Holly instructed.

"Okay, Alma," Holly said, focusing entirely on the deputy. "Now push again. Harder."

"I…*am*…pushing…*harder*."

"Again!" Holly ordered.

The next moment there was the sound of another voice, far higher, joining in.

Crying.

"It's a girl, it's a beautiful, beautiful baby girl! You

have a girl, Alma," Miss Joan said, sobbing as she remained leaning forward, propping Alma up.

Holly, holding the brand-new life in her hands, offered the infant to her grandmother.

Miss Joan was shaking as she accepted the baby and wrapped her arms around it. "Perfect," she pronounced, never taking her eyes off the precious life she was holding.

Rocking back on her heels, Holly exhaled a ragged breath. That had been the most nerve-racking, exhilarating experience she'd had in a very long time. She recalled the thrill of holding Molly in her arms after coaching her transition from womb to world. It was a heady feeling.

She began to get up. "I'm going to go get a knife to cut the cord," she told Alma.

A feeling of déjà vu all but blanketed her when she felt Alma grabbing her by the wrist again, her eyes once more wide with pain that went on to etch itself on her face.

"Holly?" Alma cried, bewildered yet certain at the same time. "I'm not done yet. I'm having twins."

Rocking back on her heels again, Holly was about to ask her what she was talking about, but then the next second, there was no need. Back to her initial position on the floor beside Alma, she saw that there was another head pushing forward, struggling to come into the world.

Twins?

"What's going on?" Miss Joan cried, looking from Alma to Holly. Given where she was, sitting directly behind Alma's head, the older woman didn't see what was happening.

"Cash and I didn't tell anyone. We…wanted to… keep…it our…secret…"

"You really do like surprises, don't you?" Holly marveled, looking at Alma. "Okay, here comes number two!" she announced, hunkering down. "You know the drill, Alma. Push!"

Alma did as she was told. She pushed.

Holly offered what encouragement she could, urging Alma to push at regular intervals. After enduring what felt like the longest minutes of her life, Holly found herself helping ease Miss Joan's *second* grandchild out into the world.

Alma's scream was almost muted in comparison to the scream that had initially brought Miss Joan running to the restroom.

Holly held the second baby close to her. The warmth that worked its way all through her had little to do with the infant's body temperature.

"It's a boy, Alma," she said, looking at the worn-out, brand-new mother. "You got one of each." As gently as possible, she laid the second infant in Alma's arms. "No offense, Alma, but I sure hope that you're finally closed for business now," she said, nervously eying Alma's lower half.

This time, there was no explosive follow-up.

For a second time, Holly started to rise to her feet. Unlike the first time, she made it.

"I'm going to get some clean dish towels to wrap around these babies," she told Miss Joan and Alma.

She sincerely doubted that either woman heard her. But that was okay, as they were otherwise occupied, Holly thought, smiling to herself as she stepped out of the restroom—

And right into Ray.

"What the hell happened to you?" he asked, staring appalled at the state of the front of her uniform.

For the first time since she had met him, her Ray-dar, as she secretly referred to her ability to feel his presence wherever he was, had failed to go off and alert her to the fact that Ray was around.

Collecting herself, she stepped back.

"I just got a frantic call from Cash saying that Alma wasn't answering her cell phone and the sheriff said she should have been there half an hour ago. I know she picks up her tea here first so I thought I'd ask if you'd seen her."

The words came out in a rush as he went on staring at the blood on her uniform.

Holly nodded numbly. "Alma's in the ladies' room at the moment."

Sensing the blood he was looking at wasn't Holly's, he asked, "Is she okay?"

Holly took a deep breath, trying to center herself and calm down. "She is now. Oh, by the way, congratulations." Her eyes crinkled as she grinned at him. "You're an uncle."

As far as he knew, Alma wasn't due for another couple of weeks. The doctor had calculated that the baby was to arrive right after Christmas. He stared at Holly blankly. "What?"

"Alma just had her baby," she enunciated slowly, then corrected herself. "Her babies."

Ray was still working his way through the first part of the sentence. "Here?" he cried.

She nodded. Opening a drawer located off to the side, she took out several fresh towels. "They couldn't wait."

"Wait— What? They?" Ray repeated, clearly confused. He stared at Holly, trying to decide which of them had lost their minds. "What do you mean they couldn't wait? Who's they?"

"They are your new nephew and niece. Alma gave birth to twins," she told Ray. "Seems that she and Cash were holding out on us. Apparently, only they and the doctor knew. Speaking of which, where is he?" she wondered out loud. "Miss Joan sent someone to go get him."

Meanwhile, Ray was apparently not listening. He'd stopped at the mention of the word *twins*. She'd never seen Ray turn pale before.

Chapter 13

"Twins?" Ray repeated. "Two babies?" He stared at her as if she'd just told him that aliens from Mars had landed. "Are you sure?"

It was amazing what men decided to question. Didn't he think she could count?

"I brought them into the world one at a time, so yes, I'm sure. What would you call two babies born a few minutes apart?"

"A shock," Ray answered automatically. "Oh, my God, Cash doesn't know she gave birth already, does he?"

"Not unless there's a spy camera inside the ladies' room. Can you go get him?" she asked. "And see what's keeping Dr. Davenport, too," she added. "I'd go myself but I'm a little bushed right now," Holly confessed.

"I'm an idiot," Ray suddenly realized, saying the

words by way of an apology. He'd been so stunned by the information she'd given him and so concerned about his sister, he'd completely ignored the fact that Holly had been there for Alma when his sister had needed someone the most. "Can I get you anything?" he asked, glancing around to see what he *could* get for her. His familiarity with the diner ended on the other side of the counter.

Ray's question surprised her. And touched her. She waved away his offer even as she secretly held it close to her heart.

Most likely, Ray probably didn't know how sweet he was being, she thought. But that was okay. She knew, and that was all that mattered.

"No, I'm okay," she told him. "Alma did all the work. I just coached her. But if you could get the doctor and Cash here, that would really go a long way to ensuring Alma's well-being on all fronts. She looks healthy enough, but hearing Dr. Davenport say so will make all concerned happy."

Ray nodded and was halfway to the door when he suddenly spun around on his boot heel and doubled back to her.

Surprised, she looked at him uncertainly. "Something wrong?"

"Nope, not a thing." And then he grabbed her by the shoulders and planted a very enthusiastic kiss on her lips. "You're the best!" he declared with equal enthusiasm.

Then he released her shoulders and made it through the diner's front door in less than two thuds of her accelerated heart.

If her knees hadn't felt weak before, they certainly did now.

But, before, it was all due to tension. Granted she knew what she was doing and, thanks to her studies, and because of Molly, she had more experience than the average person when it came to helping a woman through the painful process of giving birth. But there was always the danger of something going wrong, some unforeseen element throwing the equation out of kilter.

In contrast, her knees now had the strength of over-cooked spaghetti because Ray had just kissed her and told her she was the best.

She knew the reason any of it had happened was because Ray was both relieved that his sister was all right and grateful that she'd been there for Alma and hadn't just gone to pieces the way someone else might have—especially when confronted with the need to deliver two babies, not just one.

But whatever the reason, he'd kissed her and said those magical words. Words that made her feel absolutely special, if only for a few fleeting moments.

"You forget where the linens are, girl?" Miss Joan asked, suddenly appearing next to her. Startled, still embedded in her temporary euphoria, Holly gasped in surprise. Dropping her tough-as-nails facade, Miss Joan asked in concern, "Are you all right? You've been gone long enough to have gone to the emporium for those fresh towels."

"I'm fine," Holly was quick to assure her, then explained why she hadn't come back. "Ray was just here, looking for Alma. I sent him to get Cash and see what happened to the doctor."

"Good thinking. I'll go get those towels, you go keep

that crowd in the restroom company," Miss Joan said, nodding toward the rear of the diner.

Holly waved the other woman back. "No, I got this. You just go back to Alma and visit with your grandbabies."

She expected Miss Joan to turn on her heel and return to the restroom, but instead, the woman looked at her and in an unexpected moment of tenderness, Miss Joan brushed a kiss on her cheek.

When Holly looked at her, stunned, she murmured, "Thank you."

Holly shrugged self-consciously. "Like just I told Ray, Alma did all the work."

"But you got her through it," Miss Joan pointed out. The next moment, she turned on her rubber-soled heel and disappeared around the corner, heading toward the restroom.

As if coming out of a trance, Holly snapped to it. She rushed off to the linen closet to finally get the fresh towels she'd come out for.

A minute later, Cash, looking far more stressed than she had ever seen him, came sprinting in like a man trying to outrun a cattle stampede. Seeing Holly, he cried, "Where?"

"Restroom," was all she said, pointing.

Cash had no sooner disappeared into the back to greet his new family than Ray and Angel returned with the town's only physician.

"Sorry," Dan apologized. "I was setting Zack Riley's broken arm and I couldn't just leave him. I've got to get another doctor out here with me," he told Holly wearily. "So where's my patient? Or should I say patients?" Dan asked, glancing around.

"Alma and the babies are in the restroom. So are Cash and Miss Joan."

"Looks like I'll need a shoehorn," the doctor commented as he began to make his way to the back, as well.

"Doc?" Holly called after him. When he stopped and looked at her over his shoulder, waiting for her to continue, Holly held out the towels she'd fetched. "You might want to take these in with you. I've got the twins wrapped up in aprons right now."

Dan took the towels from her. There was admiration in his eyes as he said, "You are one resourceful young lady, Holly Johnson."

Again she shrugged, as if to physically deflect the compliment. She was accustomed to hanging back, to being in the background, not being noticed for any outstanding reason. "You just learn to make do in an emergency," she said by way of diminishing her accomplishment.

Because there were no noises coming from the back of the diner, Dan allowed himself to pause for a moment longer. "Ray told me you're studying to be a nurse and that you'll be finished with your courses within six months. Is that true?"

She was surprised that Ray had paid that much attention to what she'd told him. Usually their conversations were either about him, or the new woman who had caught his fancy. On those rare occasions when the conversation turned to her, she just assumed what she said went in one proverbial ear and out the other, scarcely registering.

"That's right," she replied, refusing to let her imagination go.

Dan smiled. It looked as if he was finally going to

have a little help. "You can put this down under interning. I'll be happy to write a letter for you, and if you need more in the way of hands-on experience to graduate, come see me later and we'll arrange something. I could certainly use a good nurse in my practice."

It was Holly's turn to stare. She would have pinched herself, but she didn't want to run the risk of being woken up.

"I will," she told him, feeling as if she'd suddenly been completely recharged and could go on for hours.

Ray flashed her a grin and gave her a thumbs-up sign as he followed the doctor to the restroom.

If she thought she would have more time to dwell on and possibly savor this new development in her life, she realized she was mistaken. Behind her, she heard the noise of people walking into the diner. Hungry people who started their long days by having breakfast at Miss Joan's diner.

Turning around, Holly scanned the incoming faces, looking for either Angel or Eduardo, Miss Joan's short-order cooks. Energized or not, Holly knew she wasn't going to be able to take down orders and serve the customers after first cooking those same orders.

When she saw Eduardo coming in, Holly all but grabbed him and pulled the thin man toward the kitchen. "Oh, thank God."

The silver-haired cook, who had been verbally sparring with Miss Joan for as long as anyone could remember, looked at Holly and laughed.

"I have had many women say that when they saw me, but I am afraid that you are a little too young for my tastes, *chica*."

"And you're too young for mine," Holly countered,

getting a second laugh out of the man. "But we're really shorthanded this morning and I need you to man the kitchen."

"Do I not always?" he asked, going behind the counter and opening the swinging door to the kitchen. "By the way, where is our grumpy boss?" he asked, looking around.

For now, she thought that keeping quiet about what had transpired in the restroom was for the best, so she said evasively, "In the back. She's busy. It's just you and me running things right now."

"Ah." He nodded his head knowingly, pleasure highlighting his features. "Good," he declared with a wink, then disappeared into the kitchen.

Squaring her shoulders and bracing for a long day, Holly went to take the order of the table at the far end of the diner.

Holly began to feel as if the day was just never going to end.

Miss Joan eventually came out to help in the diner, once Alma and the twins—over Alma's protest—were taken to Pine Ridge to be thoroughly checked out.

Knowing that, despite Miss Joan's nonchalant act, the woman was concerned about Alma and the babies' well-being, Holly told the older woman that she was free to go along with her daughter-in-law. Not surprisingly, Miss Joan waved away the words.

"They need a little alone time right now—although alone time is what got them into this mess," Miss Joan commented, smiling to herself. Taking a deep breath, she took a slow look around the diner. "I see you're holding down the fort pretty well."

"Didn't have much of a choice," Holly told her, rushing by with three orders of pancakes and juice. "And besides, Eduardo's here to help, so it's not as bad as it could be." If she'd had to cook as well, everything might have come to a grinding halt indefinitely.

"Where's Laurie?" Miss Joan asked, scanning the diner a second time. Laurie was the other waitress on this morning shift.

Holly looked away as she answered, "She phoned in to say she was going to be late."

Miss Joan looked at her closely. "She didn't call, did she?"

Holly frowned. The only thing she hated more than lying was being caught lying.

"No," she admitted, "but Laurie'll be here. She always is."

"Let me give you a very important little life-saving tip," Miss Joan said, pausing to put an arm around her shoulders, forcing her to stop moving for a moment. "Don't ever play poker, girl. You have a really lousy poker face."

Still holding a full tray, Holly nodded. "I'll try to remember that," she said wryly. "Right now though, I'm busy trying to remember who gets what at table number four."

"Doesn't matter. That cocky little guy with the silver moustache back there can cook up boots nice and tender—and if you ever tell him I said so, you're fired, got that?" Miss Joan asked, giving Holly a look that penetrated clear down to her bones.

"Got it," she assured Miss Joan.

"Okay, then," Miss Joan said, releasing her again. "Get back to work."

"That was my intent, Miss Joan. That was my intent," Holly murmured under her breath, hurrying over to table four.

It felt as if she'd been going nonstop and full steam ahead all day long. Added to that, in the middle of it all, Miss Joan had suddenly left her in charge and taken off with Harry to visit Alma at the Pine Ridge hospital.

It had been decided by all involved that Alma deserved to spend a night in the comfort of a hospital bed, being looked after and cared for before she began the hectic existence of being the mother of twins, which, some had already hinted, was like being thrown headfirst into roaring rapids.

After calling her mother to tell her to put Molly to bed because she wouldn't be home for several more hours, Holly stayed on for the third shift as well as her own first two.

Holly's extra shot of adrenaline was completely depleted by the time she finally closed up for the night. Dragging one foot after the other, it was all she could do to walk to the door, flip the switches and lock up. But once it was done, she breathed a sigh of relief.

Just as she turned away from the locked door, she heard someone knocking. Part of her felt like pretending she hadn't heard a thing and just keep going until she reached the back office.

But it was against her nature to turn her back on anyone. So, despite the fact that the other waitresses, as well as Angel and Eduardo, had left and she was all alone in the diner, Holly turned around to head back to the front door. Prepared to let in this night owl, she was going to warn him—or her—that all that was available was half a pie and the last of the coffee.

When she saw Ray standing on the other side of the door, her pulse accelerated as it always did, but not for the usual reason. Ray had been gone for most of the day, visiting at the hospital along with the rest of his family. Seeing him here could only mean one thing, Holly thought.

"Something wrong with Alma or the babies?" Holly asked breathlessly as she threw open the door to let him in.

He looked at her a little oddly as he walked in. "Not that I know of. Why?"

She stared at him, stumped. "Then what are you doing here?"

He laughed. "I thought that maybe the woman of the hour might like a ride home. Near as I can figure it, you've been going nonstop since about six this morning."

"Five," Holly corrected. "I've been up since five." God, but that seemed like a lifetime ago. "But then, who's counting?" she cracked. She stopped moving and stared at him again, as stunned now as she had been a second ago when she'd first heard him tell her why he was here. "You really came to give me a lift?" *Not that you don't do that every time you turn up near me,* she added silently.

"Sure," he said expansively. "Why not? You're my best friend," he reminded her. "And you went over and above the call of best-friend-dom today," he added with a wide grin. "So I thought that maybe I'd do something nice for you for a change."

As she sighed, she allowed herself to relax for a

moment and feel the full weight of her exhaustion. It seemed endless.

"I do appreciate your offer," she told him. "Because now that I've stopped moving, I feel just about wiped out," she confessed. But even though he said he was just doing payback, Holly felt she needed to offer him something in exchange for his being so thoughtful. "Would you like to have some dessert and coffee?" she asked, nodding toward the chocolate-cream pie that was still on display.

Ray nodded with enthusiasm. "Pie and coffee would be great—as long as you join me."

Holly was about to demur out of habit, then thought better of it. After all, it *was* after-hours. "Sure. But give me a minute."

Then, as he watched, she moved around the diner, turning off the lights in one area after another except for the light near the rear of the diner, which was completely out of view of the front door.

"What are you doing?" he asked. If he didn't know better, he would have said that she was setting a romantic scene rather than apparently locking up for the night.

"The diner's closed for the night, so if anyone looks in, I don't want them seeing the lights on. It might make them think that it's still open. They'll knock harder, expecting a response, and I'll feel guilty about not letting them in. It's a lot easier if I just turn off all the lights except that last one," she said, nodding toward the table in the far corner.

He laughed. It was all just so typically Holly. "That sounds like you, all right." He rounded the counter, going to the coffee urn. "Tell you what, let's have a division of labor. You get the lights, I'll get the pie and coffee," he offered.

"That's okay, I can—" But Holly didn't get a chance to finish.

"Don't argue," he told her, interrupting her protest. "It's about time someone served you for a change."

She had no idea how to answer that.

So she didn't.

Chapter 14

"How's Alma?" she asked once she'd joined Ray at the table. She knew that he'd gone earlier today, along with the rest of his family, to Pine Ridge Memorial Hospital, to see his sister and the new twins.

Aside from wanting to know how things were going for the brand-new mother, Holly was also desperately trying to keep her mind on something other than the fact that the diner had suddenly become a very romantic-looking place, what with all the lights out except the one close to the table she and Ray were occupying.

The only way it could have been even more so was if there had been candles in place of the overhead light. And that would have completely spelled her doom.

"Restless," Ray answered. "You know Alma, she has trouble taking it easy, but she's fine," he told her, then added, "thanks to you."

Holly shifted. Maybe coffee and pie was a bad idea. All sorts of thoughts were crowding her head, none of which had anything to do with the immediate conversation and everything to do with the man she was having it with. "I already told you, Alma did—"

Ray rolled his eyes. "Will you learn how to take a damn compliment, already?" he said, raising his voice as he cut her off. "Nobody's going to think you're getting a swelled head or an inflated ego if you just say thank-you when someone says something positive about what you did."

Holly blew out a breath, then surrendered and murmured a small, "Thank you."

The corners of Ray's mouth curved as satisfaction entered his light brown eyes. "There. Was that so hard?" he asked.

Was it her imagination, or had the space between them at the table somehow gotten smaller? It had definitely grown more intimate.

"No, but—"

"Uh-uh-uh." Ray wagged a finger at her, deliberately calling a halt to anything further she might want to say. "I want you to quit while you're ahead." His whole family wanted to thank Holly, and he wasn't about to let her just dismiss what she'd done for Alma. "Besides, Alma told us that she'd felt faint, and from that gash on her forehead, I'm guessing she must have hit her head on the rim of the sink when she went down. If you hadn't found her, who knows how long she would have been out?"

Granted, she'd shaken Alma awake, but there was no way the woman would have remained unconscious for long. "Most likely until the first really strong contraction seized her, would be my guess," she told him.

It was his turn to shrug off a comment. Holly was just too damn modest for her own good, he thought. In this one area, she was the complete opposite of him. He liked to grab attention; she was apparently happier in the shadows. They could each stand to learn from each other, he decided—especially he from her—although he had no intention of admitting that. At least, not right now.

"All I know is that Alma said she wouldn't have gotten through it as well as she did if you hadn't been there for her. By the way," he threw in nonchalantly between forkfuls of pie, "Alma and Cash would like you to be the twins' godmother."

Holly dropped her fork to her plate as she stared at Ray, for once not undone by the heart-melting handsomeness she saw there but by what he'd just told her.

"What?"

"Godmother," he repeated slowly, enunciating each syllable. "You're not familiar with the concept of godmother?" he asked, tongue in cheek.

"No, of course I am," she retorted. "It's just that— wouldn't she want someone who's closer to her to be the twins' godmother?"

"Right now," Ray said, laughing, "the only being closer than you is God. My dad wants to adopt you. And Cash asked me to tell you that he'll be your attorney for life—for free. According to Alma—and Miss Joan—you stayed calm and collected throughout the whole process, from start to finish." Then he added, "That went a long way in calming Alma down."

He was looking at her strangely, Holly thought. Now what? Was there something he wasn't telling her? Her mind scrambled around, attempting to discover an answer. She came up empty.

"What?" she asked him.

He hadn't been aware that he was staring at her. He supposed that he was.

"I'm just impressed, that's all. I still kind of think of you as that skinny little kid I went swimming with at the lake every summer." And then he grinned at her. *Really* grinned.

She couldn't take her eyes off Ray. When he grinned like that, it went straight to the very core of her. Something was up. Something that went beyond her helping Alma give birth.

"Now what?" she breathed.

"I just remembered," he answered mysteriously.

It was like pulling teeth with this man. "Remembered what?"

The grin was turning downright sexy and just winding itself all through her system. She found it increasingly difficult to sit still and not fidget.

"That a few of the earlier times," he told her, "we went skinny-dipping."

"We were eight and nine," she reminded him. "There weren't any differences back then." At least, none that she'd felt self-conscious about. Exactly.

"Oh, there were differences, all right," he countered, a sexy, mischievous look entering his eyes.

She drew herself up, trying her best to look indignant and knowing that she couldn't quite pull it off. "You're just saying that to get under my skin and embarrass me." But she could hold out only so long. "You noticed?" she asked in a hushed whisper. As clearly as she could remember, they were just eager to get into the water and cool off.

"As I recall, I was a red-blooded little boy." He nodded. "I noticed." Ray saw the color spreading through her cheeks at an amazing rate. "You're going to blush now? Fifteen years after the fact?" he asked incredulously.

Really embarrassed now, Holly shrugged, looking away. "I didn't think you noticed," she mumbled.

"If I didn't, I should have," Ray told her, finally coming clean.

"Then you *didn't* notice," she concluded. A sigh of relief escaped her.

"Maybe not," Ray conceded. It wasn't his intention to embarrass her over something so far in the past. However, the present was a different matter. He'd have to be blind not to notice her attributes now.

How was it that he hadn't noticed until that evening he'd picked her up to go to Murphy's?

His eyes swept over her, lingering on the tempting swell of her breasts as she struggled to regulate her breathing.

"But I'm noticing now," he told her quietly.

She could have sworn his very words were dancing along her skin, making her feel unseasonably warm. Had the air shut down in the diner when the lights had been turned off? She couldn't tell.

"Maybe it escaped your notice, but we're not exactly skinny-dipping at the moment," she pointed out, congratulating herself for getting the words out when her throat and tongue were drier than the Texas Panhandle in the middle of a July heat wave.

"But we could be," he told her. "We're not too far from the lake."

"It's the middle of December," she said. Nobody thought about swimming in the lake in December.

"Water stays warmer than the land," Ray reminded her, his eyes never leaving hers.

Why hadn't he ever noticed before now just how really beautiful she was? Or had she gradually become that way, right under his nose, without his having been aware of her subtle metamorphosis?

He wasn't sure. All he knew was that he was noticing all that now, and it was hitting him where he lived, twisting his gut so that he could hardly catch a decent breath.

"I'm too tired to go skinny-dipping in the lake," she told him. Besides, the last thing she wanted was to come off like some desperate, clingy female, eager to take any crumbs he was willing to toss her.

"Rain check, then," he replied so seductively, it was really hard for her to concentrate.

Holly was barely aware of nodding her head. "Rain check," she echoed, feeling light-headed again and disconnected from the rest of herself.

She forced her mind to focus on her surroundings, on conducting herself as if it was business as usual with Ray, and what was usual was that his attention was *never* focused on her.

But it was now.

Holly looked down at his plate and saw that he had eaten the slice of pie she'd served him. Automatic pilot kicked in, causing her to ask, "Would you like to have another slice of pie?"

His eyes remaining on hers, Ray moved his head

slowly from side to side. Then, just before he reinforced his reply verbally, he reached across the table and took her hand, stopping her as she began to rise.

"No," he answered, "I don't want more pie."

Why did that sound like a leading line? And why was she having trouble breathing, as if the very air in her lungs had turned solid and she couldn't draw in any more air to sustain herself?

Don't say it, don't say it, Holly cautioned herself. It would just be setting herself up for a fall.

And yet, despite her self-warnings, she heard the words coming out of her mouth.

"Then what do you want?"

He rose then and for a split second, she thought he was going to leave.

But he didn't.

Instead, he took her hand in his and silently coaxed her to her feet. Holly rose from her chair like someone caught in a trance, never taking her eyes away from him. Her heart began pounding so hard, she was surprised that she even heard him when Ray softly responded, "You."

She swallowed, doing her best to unglue the words from the roof of her mouth. "I'm not on the menu," she finally said through lips that were barely moving.

Ray smiled then, smiled right into her eyes as he said, "Good, because I like ordering things that are off the regular menu."

A shiver shimmied up her back, then down again.

It made no sense, and yet, somehow, it did.

But she had no time to try to puzzle it out because the very next moment, Ray had framed her face between his hands and brought his mouth down to hers so softly at first, that she thought she was fantasizing, creating the scenario by allowing her mind to drift right into a vivid daydream.

And as her blood began to heat in her veins, the warmth of his lips penetrated her very being, making her head spin as wildly as if she was on a merry-go-round. She knew what she was experiencing was real. Moved by gratitude or opportunity or just reacting to happenstance, Ray was kissing her. Kissing her and simultaneously unraveling life as she knew it.

Going with the moment, she leaned into him, into the hard outline of his body as she wrapped her arms around his neck and gave herself up to the wild sensation roaring through her.

And the more she did so—the more she did so. Each step, each moment, led to another and another.

This, she was certain, would only happen once, and then Ray would come to his senses, apologize and they'd never talk about it again. She knew that as well as she knew her name—but she didn't care.

All she cared about, all she wanted, was to have this one time, to allow it to turn into a memory that she could revisit again and again when she was feeling lost or alone, just so that she could experience the indescribable surge she was feeling right at this moment.

Holly groaned when his hands skimmed along the sides of her body, melted as his kiss deepened and then moaned when his lips trailed along the sides of her neck, weaving an array of soft, sensual kisses along every part of her that he came in contact with.

She could feel her very core quickening, yearning for his touch, for the union, however brief, that would forever have her belonging to him, no matter where life took either one of them. From this evening forward, she would indelibly be his.

Without being completely conscious of her actions, Holly began tugging at his shirt, her fingers nimbly working the buttons free from their confines, all the while kissing him with as much passion as she was receiving.

Engulfed in a heated haze, Holly felt him coaxing her back, guiding her out of the dining area and toward the rear of the diner, toward the one place that contained an overstuffed sofa.

The office where she did her inventory, where Tina Davenport, the doctor's wife, worked on the accounts and out of which Miss Joan ran the whole business.

Holly knew they shouldn't be in here. And they definitely shouldn't be doing what they were doing in here, but as she undid his belt buckle and pulled his belt free of the loops on his jeans, she knew that this time, decorum was *not* what she was after. Before something happened to call a halt to it, she wanted to have Ray make love with her once, just once.

And after thinking it was never going to happen, that he would always be chasing other women and never her, it was finally, finally happening.

He wanted her.

She was breaking down his resistance as if it was constructed out of wet tissue paper, crumbling apart on contact.

Not that he had much resistance. He never really had, at least, not when it came to the fairer sex. But this was Holly. Holly, his friend, his pal, the keeper of his secrets…and, he just now realized, all this time she'd had a big secret she'd never even hinted at, never shared with him.

He had never guessed that there was a hot, smoldering woman just beneath the calm, precise surface. A woman he would never have *dreamed* existed.

But she did exist. And he found her exciting beyond words.

One thing was leading to another as if by some unseen design, and before he knew it, Ray realized that he'd removed the light blue uniform he had grown so accustomed to seeing Holly in. As it dropped to the floor, it unveiled a body that both stimulated him and, in a strange way, humbled him.

"You're right," he whispered against Holly's ear, as he brushed more ardent kisses along her skin. "You *have* changed since we went skinny-dipping. Changed a great deal."

The tone of his voice brought joy rushing through her heart to a degree she hadn't thought remotely possible. If she'd loved him before, she was insanely *in* love with him now.

Rather than answer or say anything at all, she began to kiss him with the passion she had tried to hold back, the passion she'd struggled to restrain all these years whenever she talked with him.

There was no holding back anymore because, as his hand brushed along the more sensitive places on her body, eruptions began to happen, one after the other, one feeding into the next until she thought she'd just die from the exquisite ecstasy of it all.

Twisting and turning into his touch, wanting more, not certain if she could really *withstand* more, Holly opened the eyes that she hadn't realized until this moment she'd closed and whispered with effort, "Make love with me, Ray. Make love with me *now*."

His grin went straight to her heart as he pushed her back onto the sofa. "I thought that was what I was doing," he said in a teasing voice.

But his eyes were serious as he loomed over her. Balancing his weight on elbows that framed either side of her on the narrow sofa, Ray drew his hardened torso along her damp body, first lowering his mouth onto hers, then lowering his body, sealing it to hers as he entered her.

The brief moment of resistance he found there had him stunned. His first inclination was to draw back, and he would have had she not wrapped her legs around him and held him in place.

It forced him to go forward rather than retreat.

And then, there was no place for thought, no place for hesitation or noble efforts. There was just the all-consuming flame of desire.

Responding to the way she moved beneath him, he undertook an ever-increasing tempo, his hips prompting hers to go faster, faster, until he was all but panting as they raced up to the very top of the peak.

The magnificent release engulfed him.

He didn't even feel pain when Holly bit down on his lip in response to the wild surge that coursed through her veins.

And as he descended, his pulse continued to beat erratically. It took a while for his head to stop spinning.

And throughout it all, he held Holly close to him, afraid she might disappear if he didn't, even as disbelief at what had just transpired echoed through his brain.

Chapter 15

Euphoria still had a very tight hold on her as Holly's pulse hit a more rhythmic, steady beat.

But despite the incredible, lighter-than-air euphoria, reality was beginning to elbow its way into her consciousness.

And reality was tightly bonded to fear.

Fear of the future, of what lay ahead as far as her friendship with Ray was concerned.

They had never been members of the "friends with benefits" club, at least not in the standard manner. The benefits that could be garnered by having her for a friend were that she would go to the limit and beyond in any capacity that was necessary *when* it was necessary, strictly to help him, with no thought to her own well-being.

This, however, wasn't part of that package or even

remotely implied as a "benefit." Much as making love with Ray had thrilled her, she was terrified that the very act had brought irreversible consequences with it. Consequences that would ultimately spell the loss of his friendship.

Trying to blot all of that from her mind for just a little longer, Holly curled up against him, treasuring the warmth radiating from his body to hers. She gloried in the sound of Ray's heart beating not quite calmly beneath her cheek. She wished with all her heart she could find a way to just freeze time, to make it stand still at this moment indefinitely. This was the absolute perfect high point of her life. It was not going to get any better than this, and most likely, Holly felt, it would only go downhill from here.

"You didn't tell me." Startled, she both heard and felt Ray say the short, accusing sentence.

Her mind scrambled around quickly, desperately trying to put a clearer meaning to his words, but she couldn't. She kept drawing a blank. Fear was holding all her thoughts prisoner.

"Tell you what?" Holly finally asked.

Again she felt his words rumbling against her cheek. "You know."

Holly raised her head to look at him. He wasn't teasing her or playing some guessing game. He looked serious and—unless her perception was off—uncomfortable, as well.

She knew it.

She just *knew* that when the heart-racing frenzy had lifted, Ray would be uncomfortable around her because they'd been intimate.

Was she going to lose his friendship because of her misstep?

Oh, God, how did she turn this around?

"If I knew," she said, her voice hardly above a whisper as she measured out her words, "I wouldn't be asking you what you meant. I don't play games, remember? How long have you known me?"

She was trying to use the time factor to her benefit, to remind him that they had been friends for years and years, and lovers for under an hour. With her head clearing, she didn't want to sacrifice their friendship for an exquisite hour of pleasure, no matter how wonderful it had been—and it had been *really* wonderful. But wonderful or not, she wanted Ray in her life beyond tonight.

Then you should have gone home, she upbraided herself angrily.

"How long have I known you?" Ray repeated. "I don't know. An hour, maybe less."

Now he had really lost her. *Was* this some game after all? "What are you talking about? You've known me for years and years."

"I *thought* I knew you for years and years," Ray corrected. "But obviously, I never did. This is a whole new side of you that I don't know. And you never once broached it," he pointed out.

"Broached *what?*" she cried. That she loved him? That she wanted to be with him? That she couldn't stand listening to him talk about other females when she ached to be the one in his arms? The one he made love with and wanted to have children with?

It took him several tries to tell her. Each time he began, it was as if his tongue went numb. "That you—

That you were— That you were a virgin." He all but expelled the final word.

She stared at him. Was he complaining about her lack of experience? Had she wound up disappointing him in the end? Was *that* what this awkward conversation was about?

Exactly when did he think she should have announced that little piece of information? "Not exactly a conversation starter," she bit off as she struggled to sit up. Once upright, she reached for her discarded uniform on the floor. "I'm sorry I disappointed you."

"Disappoint—" He swallowed the rest of the word, stunned. "That's *not* what this is about," he told her, frustrated and angry at the same time. Frustrated with her for not telling him she was a virgin, angry at himself for what he'd just gone and done.

"Then what *is* this about?" she asked.

Didn't she understand? Why did he have to spell it out this way? "Damn it, Doll, I *took* something from you," he shouted. "I took your innocence, your virginity," he specified helplessly.

He wasn't feeling disappointed, he was feeling guilty, Holly suddenly realized.

"You didn't 'take' anything I didn't want to give you," she insisted. Taking a breath, she let her voice drop a couple of decibels. Maybe he just wanted her to sweep it all under the rug. She could oblige him—or pretend to.

"Look, what happened here happened. We'll just move on," she told him, praying that they could, that he wouldn't just distance himself from her the way he had from the other women he'd been involved with.

"Don't you understand?" he asked her, struggling

not to take out his anger on her. "You should have told me you were a virgin."

Let it go, Ray, let it go. "In case you hadn't noticed, we weren't doing all that much talking at the time. Look, if you feel like you wasted your time, I get it. No words needed—"

"Wasted my time?" he repeated. "Holly, I wasted yours. Your first time should have been special."

She looked at him, knowing she was risking everything by what she was about to say to him. But knowing, too, that she had to be truthful with him. Being truthful was the definition of who and what she was. If she turned her back on that, she would be turning her back on her soul, as well.

Her eyes met his as she said, "It was."

She totally disarmed him. He had no idea what to say to her. All his fancy speeches, the charm he could pour on so effortlessly, it all deserted him, leaving him tongue-tied and totally confused.

She was his best friend. He'd just made love to his best friend. And he didn't even have a whisper of intoxication to blame it on.

This, he knew, was going to require a great deal of sorting out in the morning. And who knew if it *could* be sorted out? But right now, they were here, in this tiny back room, with nothing between them except the heat they'd just generated.

This wasn't the time to be going by the rule book. This was a time to start making up new rules.

"Miss Joan ever come back here after she's left for the night?" he asked her.

Holly thought for a moment, then shook her head. "Not that I know of," she confessed. "I've only closed up a couple of times before. She's never mentioned coming back. When she leaves for the day, Miss Joan spends the rest of the night with Harry. She's mentioned a couple of times that she feels like she's shortchanging him by working all those hours." She cocked her head as she looked at him. "Why?"

"Well," Ray responded, picking his words slowly— almost as slowly as he feathered his fingers through her hair, "I just wanted to be sure that we weren't going to have to go scrambling for our clothes because she's come back to the diner to get something."

"Well, there is always that chance, I suppose," she guessed, doing her best to hide the amused smile that rose to her lips.

It was going to be okay, her heart sang.

"How about it? Do you feel lucky?" Ray asked. He searched her face, trying to read her expression and match his words to it. But he couldn't quite delve beneath the layers. Was she teasing? Or serious?

"The way I see it," she told him, "I already am lucky."

"Okay." There was pure sensual mischief in Ray's brown eyes as he said, "So how about it? One for the road?"

"The road," she told him, bringing her mouth closer to his, "can take care of itself."

The next moment, there was no more room for words.

He wasn't clear if he'd started to kiss her or if she had made the move first and kissed him. All he knew was that their lips were suddenly, pleasurably, sealed to each other's.

Again.

Ray could feel himself instantly wanting her again,

wanting her with an overwhelming desire that he'd never experienced to this heightened degree before. He knew, because of the circumstances, that this time around he should be more gentle, more tender with her, but he was more ravenous.

And all the while, a small, unbidden voice kept whispering over and over again, *This is Holly, your best friend, Holly. How long has this been going on without you suspecting it was there?*

Ray had no clue, and right now, he wasn't up to solving the mystery. All he wanted to do was to make love with her again, until he was finally, permanently satisfied, the way that he always had been before.

He wasn't going to get his wish, Ray thought darkly several days later. He wasn't going to be finally sated, finally satisfied so that he could just move on. The fact was becoming all too clear to him.

Because every time he made love with Holly—and they had managed to find a way to make love at least once every day since that first evening—all he wanted was to do it again.

And again.

And when he couldn't, he could only think about when he could.

What the hell has happened to you? he silently demanded, bewildered and frustrated as he tried to work off his tension by baling hay behind the main barn.

That was where Rafe found him.

Rather than yell out a greeting, Gabe's twin brother stood in silence for a few minutes, watching a man who strongly resembled his carefree youngest brother take out whatever was bothering him on the bales of hay.

"The hay do something to offend you, brother?" Rafe finally asked as he stepped forward to join Ray.

Ray paused, the pitchfork grasped in his hands suspended in midthrust. He slanted a dismissive glance in Rafe's direction. "What the hell are you talking about?" he asked, struggling not to snap the words out at Rafe.

"Well," Rafe began expansively, "you're wielding that pitchfork as if you're intent on stabbing each bale of hay before it gets the drop on you. I was just wondering if they did something to offend you—or if you've been nipping at your own private stock of whiskey a little early today."

Ray was having enough trouble dealing with his feelings and this unfamiliar situation he found himself in— he'd never wanted a woman *more* after having her. It had always been the law of diminishing returns for him, not this. Having to put up with Rafe's off-kilter sense of humor was just asking too much of him.

"Don't you have anything better to do than watch me pitch hay?" Ray demanded.

"No, not at the moment. This is pretty entertaining," Rafe confessed. And then he became serious. "Something bothering you, Ray?" he asked.

Ray glared at his brother. "Other than you?"

His brother inclined his head. "That was implied, yes."

"Then no," Ray bit out. The next hard thrust sent not just the hay flying, but the pitchfork, as well. Ray swallowed a curse, then sent another glare in Rafe's direction. "Not a word," he warned.

"Just an observation," Rafe couldn't resist saying. "You get more done if you hold on to the pitchfork."

Stomping over to where the pitchfork had landed,

Ray snatched it up and stomped back to where he'd been working.

"Maybe I'll get more done if I use it on you and get you to shut up."

"That's not going to solve your problem, Ray."

"*You're* my problem, Rafe," Ray snapped.

"No," Rafe contradicted, then explained to his brother, "I'm what my wife calls 'the Greek chorus.'"

Rafe spared him another annoyed look. "What the hell is that?"

"Some kind of a writer's device they used back in the day. It's to summarize for the audience what's going on in case somebody who's watching loses track. They put things into words."

"You ask me, you're already using too many words as it is," Ray snapped, turning his back again.

Rafe shifted so that he was standing in front of his youngest brother, not letting him avoid eye contact.

"Look, we don't spend enough time together anymore, and pretty soon there'll even be less time available, what with all of us getting married and such. Don't waste what little time we have by pretending everything's okay with you. Word is that you're not tomcatting around anymore. Wanna tell me what's up?"

"Not particularly," Ray said coldly, trying to ignore Rafe again.

"Tell me anyway." This time, it didn't sound like a request so much as an order.

Tempted to tell his brother what he could do with his suggestion, Ray reined himself in and just barked, "I'm busy."

"You were *never* too busy for female companionship,

even when you were in first grade. Now, what's up?" Rafe demanded, looking at his brother more closely.

"You've met somebody," he suddenly realized. "Somebody serious," Rafe concluded. "And you're scared to death."

"Now who's drinking?" Ray asked, even as he turned away from Rafe. His brother was getting too close to the truth, and Ray had no desire to go into it at length or even just discuss it fleetingly.

But Rafe circled so that his youngest brother couldn't avoid him. "Look me in the eye and tell me there's nobody serious."

Ray pressed his lips together, anger flaring in his eyes. "There's nobody serious," he bit off.

Unconvinced, Rafe shook his head and declared, "Liar."

Fed up, Rae thrust the pitchfork handle at his brother. "Since you're here and you seem to have all this time on your hands, *you* pitch hay for a while."

"While you go visit your mystery lady?" Rafe asked.

"No," Ray countered. "While I go and look up the name of a good head shrinker in Pine Ridge, because you clearly are in need of one." With that, he stormed off in the direction of the house.

"Who are you bringing to Mike's wedding?" Rafe asked, calling after him.

"Holly." The answer came spontaneously, before Ray could think things through and realize the trap that he'd just walked into.

"Damn," Rafe cried, stunned. And then he grinned from ear to ear. "Holly, huh? I'm slipping. I should have realized it sooner."

Ray squared his shoulders like a man about to do battle, but instead, he forced himself to just keep walking. "Nothing to realize," he snapped out, trying to sound indifferent and detached.

But it was too late. Rafe saw through the smoke screen. "If you say so, Ray."

He heard Rafe laughing to himself. Ray picked up his pace. Protesting what Rafe was alleging would only make things worse.

For everyone.

Chapter 16

She wasn't sure, until he turned up on her doorstep, whether or not Ray *would* come to take her to his brother Mike's wedding.

Unofficially, of course, the whole town was invited, and she could have gone to both the ceremony and the reception without any problems. No one would have said anything, especially after she'd delivered Alma and Cash's twins.

But Ray had talked about their going together before they had become lovers, and she didn't know if, after their relationship had taken this unexpected turn, he would still want her there, or if being with her in public would make him feel awkward somehow.

And, as much as she wanted to attend the ceremony and reception, and as much as she cared about all of his siblings, she didn't want to be there if Ray didn't want her there.

So when she heard the doorbell ring, Holly froze before the mirror on her closet door, unable to make a single move because her knees had suddenly ceased functioning.

"I'll get it!" Molly called out, the sound of her little feet rushing across the living room to the front door reinforcing her declaration.

"No, you won't, young lady," Holly heard her mother call out, then order, "You stop right there."

Granted, this was Forever and doors were left unlocked because everyone knew everyone else. But obedience was as highly prized here as anywhere else, and Molly had been taught not to open the door unless either her grandmother or her aunt was with her.

Martha pushed her salt-and-pepper hair out of her eyes. Moving quickly in her wheelchair, she reached the door just as Molly came to a skidding halt. The little girl looked at her grandmother, shifting impatiently from foot to foot, her little fingers wrapped around the doorknob.

"Now Grandma? Can I open the door *now?*"

The still youthful-looking woman maneuvered her wheelchair, bringing it to a halt right by her granddaughter. Only then did she say, "Now."

Molly yanked the door opened with both hands. "Aunt Holly, it's Ray," she called out at the top of her four-year-old lungs. "He looks really pretty, too," the little girl added, punctuating her statement with a giggle she tried to stifle with her hands.

"Well, thank you," Ray said in his best courtly manner. "This is for you," he added, holding out a gaily wrapped package. "I just passed this jolly-looking little fat man in a red suit and he asked if I could give it to you." Ray looked at her solemnly, as if he was quoting chapter and verse of a legal statement. "Said you were extragood this year so he couldn't carry all your presents at once. Told me he'd be back when you were asleep with the rest of them."

Molly's mouth dropped open as her eyes grew huge. "You saw Santa Claus?" she asked in hushed disbelief. "Really?" Disbelief turned to delight as she eyed the gift Ray had in his hands.

"Was that who it was?" Ray asked, looking at her in surprise. Then he nodded his head, as if he'd reviewed the evidence in his mind. "I guess it was, at that. Those prancing reindeer he had with him should have given it away, huh?"

"He had his reindeer with him?" Molly echoed, beside herself with excitement. She looked as if she was going to begin jumping up and down at any minute. "What did they look like?"

"Like their pictures," Ray answered, smoothly getting out of offering a description he wasn't prepared to render.

"Aunt Holly, Aunt Holly," Molly called out when she apparently heard Holly coming down the hallway. "Look what Santa Claus gave me. A present! Can I open it, *please?*" she begged.

But it was Martha who answered when she saw Holly wavering. "You know the rules, Molly. Any Christmas present you get goes under the tree until Christmas morning."

Molly sighed mightily, as if the weight of the world was on her shoulders, forcing her to behave like a responsible adult even when she didn't want to.

After another sigh, she finally agreed. "Okay, I'll wait." Molly looked far from happy about having to follow through with the statement.

"That's a good girl," Martha told her, lightly patting Molly's head.

Neither Molly nor Martha looked as if they were dressed to attend the ceremony. Ray looked from one to the other before asking, "You two ladies aren't going to the wedding?"

Martha shook her head. "Between the ceremony and the reception, we'd wind up coming home way passed Molly's bedtime. And besides," she interjected, "I don't want Holly spending all her time at the wedding wheeling me around." Martha slanted a warm look at her daughter, then shifted her eyes from Holly to Ray. "She deserves to have a little fun instead of being stuck playing nanny to someone twice her age."

"Pushing you around in the wheelchair isn't a hardship, Mom," Holly protested.

"Well, it certainly doesn't come under the definition of having fun," Martha insisted. "Ray, would you please get her out of here before she starts to badger me?"

"You heard your mother," Ray said, pointedly offering Holly his arm.

Aware of every single one of Ray's actions as if they were transpiring under a high-powered magnifying glass, Holly slipped her arm through his, feeling as if she was moving in slow motion.

"Have fun, you two. That's an order," Martha Johnson instructed as she wheeled herself to the door in their wake and closed the door behind them.

"You look really, really good tonight," Ray told her as he held the passenger door of his freshly washed truck open for her.

It was dusk, and Holly was extremely grateful that

the partial darkness hid the annoying blush that she could feel speedily taking possession of her cheeks. She was *really* going to have to work to get that under control, she lectured herself. She wasn't a starry-eyed twelve-year-old, she was a woman, and women didn't blush in this day and age. Even women who were wildly head over heels in love.

"Thank you," she murmured. "So do you." Getting in, she buckled up and waited for Ray as he rounded the hood and got in on the driver's side. "I wasn't sure you were going to come pick me up."

"Why not?" he asked, puzzled as he started up the truck. "I said I would." Pulling the truck away from the front of the house, he turned the vehicle around and stepped down on the accelerator.

Holly avoided his eyes, looking instead at the knotted hands in her lap. "I know, but that was before."

"Before?" What was she talking about? For the most part, he and Holly understood one another—mainly because she didn't retort to *female speak,* something he'd found most women did when they wanted to utterly confuse the man they were talking to. "Before what?"

"Before you and I…" Holly paused, searching for the right, delicate way to word this. She finally settled on, "Got close."

She was obviously not getting through because, in all innocence, Ray reminded her, "We've always been close."

"Not *this* close," she stressed.

The light finally dawned in his head and Ray laughed as he drove them to the church where the wedding ceremony was to take place.

"You have a point, but that still doesn't change the fact that you're my best friend and after the way you came through for Alma, my father would probably skin me alive if I didn't bring you to the wedding—or if I turned out to be the reason you decided not to show up." He glanced in her direction. "You do want to attend, don't you?" he asked. "I mean, what's going on between us isn't going to make you feel uncomfortable going to the wedding, right?"

It had never occurred to her that Ray might see the situation from her perspective, thinking that *she* might not want to be around him rather than the other way around.

Could Ray possibly feel...insecure?

It hardly seemed likely. And yet, how else could she explain that the man whose relationships lasted only slightly longer than the life expectancy of a fruit fly was concerned that *she* might not want to continue this part of their relationship because it made her uncomfortable to be around him?

"No," Holly replied quietly but firmly. "What's going on between us doesn't make me feel uncomfortable around your family. I just don't want to cramp your style," she told him for lack of a better way to phrase her reason for thinking he might not come for her.

"My style," he echoed, the corners of his mouth curving at the phrase she'd used. "About that," he began, then paused.

"Yes?" she asked, silently urging him to continue even as she wondered if she'd ultimately regret finding out what he meant.

She was well aware that once things were said, they

couldn't be unsaid. And, as long as they *weren't* said, she could go on pretending that everything in Paradise was just perfect. Even though "perfect" was a condition that in all likelihood didn't really exist.

Oh, God, when had life gotten so very complicated? Holly couldn't help wondering.

"Just exactly what is my style, Holly?" he asked.

She shrugged, fidgeting inside. "You're the charmer, the smooth talker, the one who all the unattached— and not so unattached—women gravitate to." He knew that, didn't he? Why was he asking her to spell it out? "What's the matter, Ray, your ego need a boost? Is that why you're asking me to define your style? You afraid that lingering with me might disturb some sort of equilibrium you have going out there in the universe?"

"What the hell are you talking about?" he asked her, completely confused.

Holly was being honest with him. She'd known Ray far too long not to be, and besides, she didn't know how to be anything else *but* straight. There wasn't—and never had been—a single conniving bone in her body.

She ran her tongue along exceedingly dry lips before she told him, "I'm waiting for the shoe to drop."

"What shoe?" he asked, no clearer now as to her meaning than he had been a moment ago.

"*The* shoe," she emphasized. Didn't he get it? "The proverbial shoe."

"What the hell is the proverbial shoe? Those online courses you're taking scrambling your brain?" he demanded, clearly frustrated that he didn't understand what she was trying to say. "I'm a plain man, Holly, talk plain."

She opened her mouth to answer him, and then shut it again as she stared at Ray. Holly. He'd called her Holly. Not Doll the way he usually did, but Holly. She couldn't remember the last time she'd heard him use her given name.

Was that a good sign, or should she *really* be bracing herself for something serious?

Something bad?

"The proverbial shoe," she repeated, then went on to add, "Everything that goes up must come down. For every good, there's a bad. If there's a high point, there has to be a low—am I making myself clear?" she asked, her voice rising.

Almost at the church, he suddenly pulled over so that he could focus completely on this conversation that wasn't making any sense to him. Maybe if he wasn't distracted by driving, it would become clearer.

"If by clear, you mean do I notice that you're talking in clichés as well as going around in circles, then, yes, I get that. I also know that of the two of us, you're supposed to be the optimist and I'm the one who's supposed to shoot down all your red balloons or the bluebird of happiness, or whatever it is that pessimists fantasize about doing to optimists to get them to reverse their opinions. But I'm not feeling any of that," he insisted, then quietly admitted, "I am, though, feeling a little confused because I've never been on this path before."

"You're going to have to be more specific than that, Ray," she told him. "What path?"

He'd already said too much, Ray upbraided himself.

He would have laughed if it wasn't all so damn ironic. Normally, this was a conversation he'd be having with his best friend—with her—about the way he was feeling about the woman he was currently seeing. But in this case, his best friend and the woman he was currently seeing were one and the same, making all of this immensely complicated for him.

He'd always laid his soul bare to his best friend, but never to the woman he was dating.

Ray sighed, dragging his hand through his hair, trying hard to sort out his thoughts. It really didn't help.

He started up the truck, fully aware that Holly was staring at him. Waiting for him to continue.

He was going to have to handle and sort out this problem himself. Later.

"Never mind," he said, tabling the subject indefinitely. Focusing, he suddenly realized that they were almost on top of the church. "We're here," he announced, making it seem that he wasn't going to go into any lengthy explanation about what was going on inside his head because they had arrived at his brother's wedding. "Don't want to be late," he added quickly as he got out of the truck.

By her watch, they were a good fifteen minutes early, but she wasn't about to point that out. The last thing in the world she wanted to do was to come across as pushy. She was going to do her damnedest to continue being his best friend—except even better, she thought.

And what? He's going to get so overwhelmed by you, by how great you are, and so carried away by Mike's wedding that he's going to propose to you? Wake up and smell the rejection that's coming, Holly. It's the only way you're going to survive.

But she knew that she didn't want to survive. Not *just*

survive. She wanted to be his best friend *and* the woman he came home to at night—or, at least, the woman he wanted in his bed.

Dream on, an annoying little voice in Holly's head mocked.

That was probably the right term for it, she thought, making her way into the church beside Ray. A dream. That was all she had and all she ever would have.

No matter what she wished to the contrary, Ray Rodriguez was not the marrying kind. He'd told her only a few weeks ago, when Mike said he planned to marry Samantha on Christmas Eve, that he thought his brothers were surrendering their freedom one by one and he considered Mike to be the last bastion of bachelorhood With Mike's fall, he was the very last standard-bearer.

Standard-bearers did *not* get married, not when they considered themselves the epitome of bachelorhood. Besides, it was a known fact that Ray always had too much fun being single and in demand. What man who had all that going for him would want to give it up for just one woman?

She knew the answer to that.

No man would. At least, not Ray. And she really couldn't fault him for it.

Which meant she was going to enjoy this interlude she was sharing with Ray and have absolutely no expectations, cast no webs, twine no strings.

This was what it was: decidedly wonderful—and, in all likelihood, decidedly fleeting.

With that in mind, she stood up in the pew, brought to her feet by the beginning strains of "Here Comes the Bride."

And as she listened, she tried very hard to suppress the tears that rose to her eyes due to the sharp, painful realization that this song would never be played for her.

Chapter 17

Because the weather promised to be colder than they had originally anticipated, it had been decided the day before the actual wedding to shift the site of Mike and Sam's reception to the Rodriguez ranch.

Those guests who were hearty enough not to be bothered by a little drop in temperature celebrated outside, directly behind the ranch house, where several canopies were set up—brought in for the occasion thanks to Rafe's wife, Valentine, and her connections with the movie industry where the use of canopies on location shots was commonplace.

Guests of a slightly more delicate constitution celebrated the wedding indoors, easily filling the house to overflowing with their bodies and their laughter.

Faced with the choice, Holly stayed outdoors, where a blanket of stars made the evening seem even more special than it already was. That, and the fact that Liam Murphy's band had set up outside—close enough to the house to be heard inside, but really resonating outdoors.

To her surprise, rather than mingling and disappearing, Ray had stayed with her for the entire evening, despite the blatant efforts of more than one woman to catch his eye.

It was, all in all, an enchanted evening as far as Holly was concerned. But even fairy tales ended, so this evening had to, as well. She had somewhere to be after midnight.

"You keep looking at your watch," Ray noted as he brought her another glass of punch. "Is there something I should know?"

She'd really tried not to be obvious about it, and she hadn't thought that he'd even noticed. The man was more aware of things than she gave him credit for.

"Like what?" she asked innocently.

"Like that you turn into a pumpkin at midnight. You know, the Cinderella thing," he prompted with a grin. He felt himself getting nervous, wondering if maybe he'd misread the signs after all. Was she anxious to leave the reception—and him?

"No," Holly said, "I'm not turning into a pumpkin, but I do want to be home around that time so I can get the rest of Molly's presents under the tree before she wakes up. Christmas Eve, she sleeps with one ear open, trying to catch Santa Claus in the act," she told him with a laugh. "By the way, that was a very nice thing you did, bringing Molly that gift and telling her it was from Santa."

He shrugged casually, dismissing the deed. "Well, I'm a very nice guy."

You don't have to convince me, Holly thought. *I've always been your biggest fan.*

Out loud she said, "You didn't have to do that, you know."

"I know." The truth of it was that he enjoyed it. "There's just something magical about that age, about believing in Santa Claus and an old man who can bring toys to everyone in one night."

"To all the kids in one night," Holly corrected.

About to continue, trying to warm to his real subject, he stopped abruptly. "What?"

"You said *to everyone,*" she pointed out. "Santa is just supposed to bring gifts to the kids."

Ray frowned, his brow furrowing. "Is that written down somewhere?" he asked her, looking so solemn that for a second, she thought he was serious.

And then she realized that he was just pulling her leg, the way he always did, and she laughed. "It must be."

"Well, I never saw it written anywhere," he continued as if they were having a philosophical discussion. "And until I do, I'll keep on believing that Santa Claus is supposed to bring gifts to everyone."

Holly shook her head. "Just how much beer and wine have you had tonight?" she asked.

He looked at her for a long moment. The noise around them seemed to fade into the distant background as he told her quietly, "Just enough to make me see things a little more clearly than I normally do."

He was dragging this out a little, but she just *knew* there was going to be some kind of a punch line at the end.

"Uh-huh. You just keep thinking that." Holly glanced at her watch again. It was getting really close to midnight. She had to get going before she was completely dead on her feet. "Well, it's been a lovely night and a beautiful ceremony, but I'm going to have to ask you to take me home. Or better yet," she said, looking around the immediate area, "maybe I'd better ask one of the Murphy brothers to do it."

"One of the Murphy brothers?" Ray echoed, frowning. "Why?"

Granted, Ray didn't smell as if he'd been drinking, but something was off. He wasn't acting like himself tonight, and she just assumed it was because he'd had a bit to drink. She didn't want him taking any chances.

"Well, Brett and Liam don't seem to be drinking," she told him, "and even if we're not anywhere near the heart of Dallas, it's still safer to face the road stone-cold sober—especially at night."

Ray caught her hand, threading his fingers through hers. When she looked at him quizzically, he told her, "There's still plenty of time to get you home," he assured her. "A few more minutes won't make a difference in the grand scheme of things." The next moment, as she began to open her mouth in what he anticipated to be protest, he coaxed, "Dance with me."

"There's no music," Holly pointed out.

Ray held up his free hand. "Wait for it," he told her, cocking his head and following his own advice.

If she'd only had herself to consider, she would have stood right here beside him until the world ended. But she had Molly to think of and that changed everything. "Ray, I really have to—"

"See? There it is," he told her as Liam's band, returning from their fifteen-minute break, began to play again. It was a slow, bluesy number that Ray thought was just perfect. "You just have to be patient," he told her, drawing her out onto the dance floor that he and his brothers had just constructed for the occasion yesterday. It had taken all of them working together to make it a reality overnight. But that was the kind of thing he and his brothers did—the impossible in a short amount of time.

He took comfort in that now.

"Now that's funny," she said as she began to relax a little and follow his lead.

Ray looked intently into her eyes, allowing himself to get lost there just for a moment. "What is?"

"You telling me to be patient." *I've been patient all my life, Ray, waiting for you to notice me for just a little while.*

His mouth curved a little, despite his attempt to sound as if he was serious when he asked, "Are you hinting that I'm impatient?"

"No, not hinting," she countered with a laugh that filtered into her eyes. "Saying it outright."

"Maybe I was," he allowed magnanimously. "But that was the old me. The new me is very patient," he informed her.

Yeah, right. Never happen. But for the sake of peace, she played along. "And what is this 'new you' being so patient about?" she asked, doing her best not to laugh at him saying his name in the same sentence as the word *patient.* Everyone knew he was mercurial and the very definition of impatient.

She'd understand better afterwards, he decided. "Why don't we get back to that later?"

"Okay," she agreed, convinced that when "later"

came, he will have forgotten all about it, which would have been typical Ray. Charmingly absentminded.

It wasn't that he was deliberately telling a lie, he just wasn't able to keep track of everything that he'd said. That was part of who he was and she accepted that, accepted it all, just as long as she could have these precious moments with him to savor and relive later in her mind until she had worn off all the edges on her memories.

I'm never going to forget any of this, God. Thank You, she thought.

"It's almost Christmas Day," Ray told her, as if searching for the words that he needed.

"I know," she told him quietly. "I pointed that out to you. That's why I need to get home."

"You don't open presents until it's Christmas Day, right?" he asked her out of the blue.

"It's a tradition," she explained. "When you don't have much, you like to stretch out the drama a little, stare at your gift and imagine what it could be." She wondered if he was asking why her mother had told Molly to put his gift under the tree rather than allowing her to open it right then and there. "Mom and I both spoil Molly, but it won't hurt her to wait a bit, the way I did."

"I never realized that you were actually poor," he confessed.

"I didn't feel poor," she told him quickly, not wanting him to think this was some sort of a ploy for sympathy. "It was just in hindsight, looking back over everything, that I realized I didn't have as much—materially speaking—as some of the other kids. But on the plus side," she added, because she always tried to find the positive in any situation, "it made me stronger and less materialistic."

"So presents don't matter?" he asked her innocently.

She laughed. If there was one thing Ray wasn't, it was innocent.

"Now, I didn't say that. They matter," she admitted freely. "Because I'm not expecting them and because no one has an obligation to give me anything." There was something in his eyes she couldn't fathom. She didn't like not being able to read him. "What's all this talk about gifts?" she asked despite herself. The right thing would have been to allow him to talk and then drop the subject when he stopped. But her curiosity had gotten the better of her.

What if he's feeling you out and wants your advice about giving some girl a gift at midnight? An important gift at midnight?

Rather than answer, he went on dancing with her, raising his eyes to the old clock that was mounted on the back wall of the ranch house as they spun by.

The music ended just as the clock struck twelve.

"It's midnight," she told him needlessly.

He glanced over his shoulder at the clock out of habit. "Yes, it is."

"Now can I go home?" she pressed. As much as she loved being in his arms, dancing like this, she had to tear herself away—before she couldn't.

"In a minute," he told her. "I need to show you something."

Holly struggled to suppress the sigh that rose within her of its own accord.

She was right.

He had a gift for some other girl and wanted her

opinion on it. She needed to leave. Why hadn't he shown it to her earlier?

Seriously? Is that what you would have really wanted? To spend the entire evening knowing that he was here with you like this just out of friendship, and the woman he really wanted to spend time with was going to get a special Christmas gift while you found your own way home?

"Where are we going?" she asked as he walked beyond the canopies. Within moments, they had left the reception behind them.

He wanted to keep going until they were all alone. But then they would also run out of light because, as star filled as the sky was, it still didn't afford that much actual light. And he wanted her to be able to see what he had to show her—as well as wanting to see her expression when she saw it.

He hoped to God that he wasn't going to regret this.

"Here," he told her, stopping. "We're going here."

She looked around. They were practically out in the open field. She looked back at him uncertainly. "What's here?" she asked.

"We're here," he told her simply.

"I kind of figured that part out," she told him, waiting to hear just what was going on. When he hesitated, she looked at him with concern. He'd never had trouble telling her anything before.

Was this going to hit her hard? she suddenly wondered, bracing herself. Whatever it was, anticipation was making it far worse. She wanted to get it over with, like ripping a Band-Aid off an open wound.

"Is something wrong?" she asked, her throat so dry she was having trouble talking.

"Well," he said slowly, "that all depends."

"On what?" she asked him, surprised that she could actually get the words out despite the fact that they were sticking to the inside of her throat.

His eyes held hers. Time seemed to stand still, he noticed. "On what you say."

She stared at him. Since when did her opinion matter *that* much? Oh, he usually asked her what she thought, but the truth was he was his own man and did whatever he wanted to in the end.

Her saying no wasn't going to matter, so why was he going through this charade?

But she played along. "Okay," she told him gamely. "I'm ready."

"I hope so," he replied, only managing to compound her confusion.

Before she could ask him what that was supposed to mean, he put his hand into his pocket and pulled out something small. "Here," he said, thrusting out his hand and opening it.

She stared at the small square velvet box in the palm of his hand.

"Here what?" she whispered. She willed herself not to cry, but even now she could feel her eyes sting. Having her approve a ring for someone else was downright cruel.

"Here," he repeated more urgently. "Open it."

She felt her heart plummet to her toes. Her moment with him was over. She wasn't ready for it to be over, but it was. Just like that.

Forcing herself to take the ring box from him, she opened it. Inside was the most beautiful diamond ring she'd ever seen. It managed to capture the moonlight, defusing it through the cluster of small diamonds, bouncing it off the large marquis shape in the middle.

"Well?" he asked impatiently. It clearly had taken her breath away. Why wasn't she saying anything?

"It's beautiful," she whispered in a very shaky voice.

"But?" he asked, hearing the slight note of hesitation in her voice.

She looked at him, mystified. "But nothing. It's beautiful," she repeated. Taking a long breath, she raised her eyes to his again. "Who's it for?"

His jaw almost dropped open. "You're serious?" he asked, stunned.

Her eyes were stinging more than ever. It was only a matter of time before the tears began falling. She needed to be out of his sight by then.

"Please don't play games with me, Ray. Yes, I'm serious. Who's it for?"

"You, you idiot." *How could she not get that?* he couldn't help wondering.

"I'm not being an idiot," Holly shot back indignantly. "I'm— Me?" she cried as his words suddenly registered and sank in. She stared at him, her jaw slack. "You're giving *me* the ring?"

Why did she think he'd handed it to her? "Yes," he insisted.

Anyone else would have been jumping up and down for joy, assuming that the ring was for them—but she wasn't anyone else, and neither was Ray. Everything needed to be spelled out before she allowed any of her feelings to emerge.

"Why?"

She *still* needed explanations? This was harder than

he'd thought—but then, Holly was worth it. "Because I thought you'd want to be traditional about this."

"This?" she asked, still refusing to embrace the obvious out of fear of being humiliated and hurt.

Ray could only stare at her. He wasn't being vague— Why was she giving him so much flack?

"Why are you making this so difficult?" he asked. "I'm asking you to marry me."

She almost lost the ability to talk just then—but then it came back to her. "No, you're not. What you are is confusing me. There's been no mention of marriage." Her head began to spin wildly as her heart beat so hard, she thought she was just going to pass out. "You're actually asking me to marry you?"

"Yes!" he shouted. "Finally!" he added with relief. He was beginning to think she was never going to get his meaning.

"Why?"

The question was almost as bad as her not getting it. "What do you mean why?"

"Why?" she repeated. "It's a perfectly clear three-letter word. Why are you asking me to marry you?" she asked. "Did you have too much to drink, or do you have some kind of bet going that you could get married at midnight, or—"

"It's because I love you, damn it," he shouted at her. "I love you and I realized these past couple of weeks that I've been wasting my time, going from woman to woman when I've got all the woman I'll ever need right here next to me."

He held her gaze for a moment, his eyes searching hers, looking for some sort of a sign of commitment, a note of validation.

"You're my best friend and I can't stop thinking about you. I don't *want* to stop thinking about you. Ever," he emphasized. "Marry me, Holly."

He was asking her to marry him. He was *really* asking her to marry him. This wasn't a dream. "When?" she asked.

"Whenever you're ready. Now, if you want me to go get the preacher," he told her eagerly, ready to pull the man out of his home behind the church.

"Wait, wait, this is going too fast." Part of her still expected to wake up at any second. "At the risk of ruining something I've wanted ever since I first saw you, I have to tell you something." She took a breath before adding, "You need to know that you're not just marrying me."

"I'm not?" Just exactly what was she getting at?

"No. I've got responsibilities, Ray. I've got Molly to take care of. I can't just turn my back on her."

Was that all? He got a kick out of the little girl. For one thing, he could talk to her. That wasn't always the case with kids Molly's age. "Not asking you to."

"And then there's my mother," Holly went on nervously. She didn't want to chase him away, but her responsibilities were what they were. "She's independent and stubborn, but I can't just leave her on her own."

"I know that." He grinned. "I like your mother. I know that she kind of likes me, too. And she said you'd be stubborn about this, but to keep after you until I wore you down."

"Wait." Something wasn't making sense here. "You talked to my mother about this?" she asked, stunned.

"Yeah." The conversation had been lengthy. "Why do you think she didn't come to the wedding? She didn't want you distracted, taking care of her, looking after

Molly. I've got her blessing, by the way," he told her. "What I need now is yours."

Did he really think he had to ask? "You've had that all along," she told him. Without a need to restrain them, her tears fell freely.

"You're not supposed to cry when you say yes," he told her.

"Says who?" she sniffed.

"I don't know. Sounds like a good rule, though." He took her into his arms. "You're my everything, Holly, and I'm finally smart enough to realize that." It damn well took him long enough, he thought.

"If you're so smart, why haven't you shut up and kissed me yet?" she asked, challenging him.

"Just getting to the good part," he told her, bringing his mouth down to hers.

And it was the good part. The very best part of all. And he vowed that it would always remain that way.

Epilogue

Holly couldn't wait to tell them.

Couldn't wait to get home and tell her mother and Molly that she was going to marry the man she'd dreamed about marrying for most of her life.

Of course, there was a part of Holly that wanted to walk into her house and pretend that she'd decided to turn him down as a way of making her mother pay for having kept Ray's pending proposal a secret from her.

Her mother should have told her the second she knew.

But then she supposed she could see the argument for allowing Ray to be the one who actually asked her face-to-face. After all, it was his question, so he had to be the one who got to surprise her.

Hearing it come from his lips had kind of made the proposal rather perfect, Holly decided.

So she abandoned the idea of getting back at her

mother by pretending that she had turned Ray down. For one thing, she truly doubted that she could fool her mother. She really wasn't *that* good an actress, especially not when her mother knew just how crazy she was, and always had been, about Ray.

Because she wanted to tell both her mother and Molly at the same time, Holly knew that meant she needed to get home fairly early.

When she broached the matter to Ray to get his input, she was surprised by what he said.

"We don't have to leave the reception," Ray told her. "At least, not permanently, not if you don't want to."

"You mean, we should wait until morning to tell Mom and Molly?" she asked.

"No, I mean we can leave the reception temporarily. Take a break, like commercials being shown during some episode on TV. Just a quick break. It's not like we have to cross the state line to see your family."

Holly still hesitated for a moment, torn. After all, this was Ray's brother's wedding and she didn't want to seem rude or run the risk of offending anyone in his family. "You don't mind?"

"I don't mind anything that makes you happy," he told her simply.

Now that he had admitted to loving her, part of Ray couldn't help wondering what had taken him so long to come to his senses. What had taken him so long to see what was right in front of him.

He supposed that he should stop beating himself up about it and just be glad that he finally saw the light. End of story.

Or maybe, he couldn't help thinking with a grin, just the beginning of a new story.

"And your family won't mind?" she wanted to know.

"My family loves you, remember? You're the hero who brought Alma's twins into the world. *You* can do no wrong in their eyes."

He'd convinced her. "Okay," she said, taking Ray's hand in hers and leading him out toward where he'd parked his car. "Let's go."

Her heart rode shotgun in her throat all the way to her house, even though the trip seemed to be over in the blink of an eye.

The second Holly put her key into the front-door lock, it swung open. Martha was on the other side of it, her eyes bright, her expression a portrait of anticipation.

"Well?" Martha demanded, looking from one to the other expectantly. "Did you say yes?"

"Yes to what?" Molly wanted to know, hanging on to one of the wheelchair handles and attempting to swing herself to and fro. She was just small enough in weight and stature not to throw Martha off balance.

"You mean you don't know?" Holly asked with a laugh, stroking the little girl's hair.

"Uh-uh," Molly confirmed, then started chanting, "Tell me, tell me, tell me."

She told Molly gladly. With only minor coaxing, she would have yelled it out on a rooftop. "Ray and I are getting married."

The little girl surprised them all by looking very quietly and very solemnly from Holly to Ray, as if actually weighing what she'd just been told and subjecting that information to a number of criteria that she kept in her little head.

"Do you want to?" she finally asked Holly.

"Yes, I do. Very much," Holly told her niece.

Molly then looked at the man standing beside her aunt and rather than ask the same question, asked instead, "Are you going to be moving in with us?"

"Looks that way. Is that okay with you?" he asked her, one adult to another, an attitude that Molly greatly appreciated.

When he asked her about her feelings on the matter, *that* was when her smile finally came out, a smile as big as a sunburst.

A smile that closely resembled the one he'd seen time and time again on Holly's lips.

"Yes!" Molly declared. "'Cause I really like my room and it would make me sad to leave it behind if I had to move away."

Ray dropped down to one knee to be on Molly's level. "Well, you're not going to be sad because we're not moving."

"Yeah!" Molly cried as she enthusiastically threw her arms around Ray's neck. "Can you marry us tomorrow?" she asked, turning it entirely into a family affair.

"It doesn't work that fast," he explained to Molly, talking to her as if he was talking to an adult. "But as soon as I can, I will."

Molly's eyes were shining as she nodded her approval. At the same time, she struggled to stifle a yawn. She was unsuccessful in the latter.

"Time for you to go to bed, young lady," Martha told her granddaughter. Just before she started to herd Molly from the room, using her wheelchair as effectively as any cowboy used his cattle pony, Martha glanced over at her daughter and her future son-in-law. "And why don't you two get out from underfoot and make your-selves scarce?" she ordered with a broad wink.

Ray took Holly's hand in his again. "I believe we've got a wedding reception to get back to," he said to her.

"You took the words right out of my mouth," Holly replied.

He grinned as they walked out of the house again. "Get used to it. I plan on doing that kind of excavation a lot."

She looked at him quizzically as the door closed behind them. "I don't think I understand—"

Rather than explain, he showed her by pulling her into his arms and sealing his mouth to hers. And just before he did, Holly, in a small, knowing voice, uttered an enlightened, "Oh."

The sound was muffled against his lips—which she could have sworn were smiling.

* * * * *

Cathy Gillen Thacker is married and a mother of three. She and her husband reside in North Carolina. Her mysteries, romantic comedies and heartwarming family stories have made numerous appearances on bestseller lists. A popular Harlequin author for many years, she loves telling passionate stories with happy endings and thinks nothing beats a good romance and a hot cup of tea! You can visit Cathy's website, cathygillenthacker.com, for information on her books, recipes and a list of her favorite things.

Books by Cathy Gillen Thacker

Harlequin Special Edition

Texas Legends: The McCabes

The Texas Cowboy's Quadruplets
His Baby Bargain
Their Inherited Triplets

Harlequin Western Romance

Texas Legends: The McCabes

The Texas Cowboy's Triplets
The Texas Cowboy's Baby Rescue

Texas Legacies: The Lockharts

A Texas Soldier's Family
A Texas Cowboy's Christmas
The Texas Valentine Twins
Wanted: Texas Daddy
A Texas Soldier's Christmas

Visit the Author Profile page at Harlequin.com for more titles.

A TEXAS SOLDIER'S CHRISTMAS

Cathy Gillen Thacker

Chapter 1

"It certainly looks like Christmas came early for you, Nora!" ninety-year-old Miss Sadie said.

Nora Caldwell regarded the ladies gathered in the Laramie Gardens community room. All were grinning and merrily nudging each other. Not sure she *wanted* to know what was causing such hilarity, she slowly turned toward the portal. What she saw in the doorway was enough to stop her heart.

United States Army Lieutenant Zane Lockhart, the love—as well as the bane—of her life. And it wasn't even Thanksgiving yet! Her knees went weak as she took him in.

Breathing a huge sigh of relief, Nora noted that the Special Forces officer did not show any new battle scars.

Clad in desert camouflage shirt and pants and utility boots, his six-foot-three-inch frame was as broad-shouldered and solidly muscled as ever. His ruggedly hand-some face bore the perpetual tan she knew so well, his sensual lips the same knowing slant. It didn't appear he had done more than run a hand through the thick layers of his wheat-gold hair, but it didn't matter—the cropped shiny-clean strands looked good no matter which way the wind tossed them.

Resisting the urge to throw herself into his arms, she deliberately met his gaze, while his dark silver eyes roamed her frame every bit as hungrily as she surveyed his. And still, neither of them moved. He was here. Alive. Safe. A feat that, as always, felt almost too good to be true, given the types of dangerous missions he went on.

"Oh, my!" Retired librarian Miss Mim fanned her face, her face turning as red as her auburn hair while Zane and Nora continued to silently size each other up. "Is it *hot* in here or what?"

It was definitely steamy, Nora thought. But then, wasn't that always the case when she and Zane were in the vicinity of each other? Sparks flew, even as duty and honor and strong wills tore them apart.

"If this is the result of serving in the Army Nurse Corps, I wish I'd done a tour or two," Miss Patricia teased.

Not, Nora thought, if your heart had been shattered as often and surely as hers had by this gorgeous hunk of a man.

Oblivious to the admiring glances of the three dozen women gathered in the community room, Zane asked, "Sorry to interrupt, ladies, but may I have a word with you, Nora?" His expression abruptly becoming inscru-table, he added, "Privately?"

Where was his usual wide-as-all-Texas grin, the easy charm he managed to exhibit no matter what, Nora wondered, acutely aware he could be about to give her bad news about one of their fellow soldiers.

Oblivious to her worry, the ladies promised in unison, "Go ahead. We can handle the rest of the holiday planning session."

Breaking eye contact with Zane, Nora drew a deep enervating breath and said to one and all, "I'll be in my office if you need me." Shoulders stiff with tension, she led the way down the hall to the door just off the formal entry.

Zane read the bronze plaque next to the door. "Are you just the director, or the director of the nursing staff?"

"Both." Although she imagined he, like her brigadier-general mother, did not view her current position with the same high regard as her previous assignment in one of the premier military hospitals in the world.

He followed her inside.

Nora spun around to face him, still tingling all over. Zane shut the door behind him. Ignored the chair she offered.

She sat down behind her desk anyway.

"Why didn't you tell me what was going on with you?" he said plainly.

He wanted to talk about their ill-fated off-and-on-again romance? *Now*? Over a year after it had finally ended? With an insouciance she couldn't begin to feel, Nora waved an airy hand. "I didn't think my resignation from the Army was relevant to you, given the way our relationship ended."

Zane's gaze narrowed all the more. "How about your

private life?" His square jaw jutted out. "You didn't think I had a right to know about *any* of that?"

Why was he acting so weird? Like a man on a mission? It wasn't as if he hadn't known she intended to return to the small West Texas town where she had grown up when she ended her career in the military service.

Laramie was home to her.

Laramie was comforting.

It had been to him, too, as a child, when he had left his wealthy life in Dallas and visited his much more rustic paternal grandfather's Laramie County ranch in the summers.

But now he clearly wasn't thinking about their closeness back then.

Doggedly, he persisted, "You didn't think you should at least write or call me and let me know of your plans?"

Feeling even more baffled, Nora shrugged. "Ah. Not really."

His expression changed. Became almost rueful. He sat down and leaned forward, his muscular forearms on his spread knees. He speared her with his gaze. "Did I really disappoint you that badly?"

If he only knew. Hurt filled her heart. She swallowed and tried again to explain, "I told you…it wasn't you. It was never you." Zane had been clear about who and what he was from the very start. "It was me," she admitted in a low, strangled voice. "I'm the one who couldn't handle the intensity of our affair." The fact that every time he left she had to contend with the fact she might never see him again.

He straightened, squaring his broad shoulders. "So you came here?"

It was the only thing in her life at that time that had

made sense. Especially with everything else she'd had going on, familywise. "My sister, mother and I all still jointly own a home here, the one my grandparents left us." The one she had grown up in.

Nora swallowed around the parched feeling in her throat. "After serving in field hospitals and military trauma centers—" helping the sometimes mortally wounded "—I needed something low-key."

He squinted, displeased. "That doesn't explain why you didn't tell *me* about your future plans."

Actually, Nora thought, it pretty much explained everything. Sharing in his obvious exasperation, she glared right back at him. "We weren't in touch after we ended things." And hadn't been for the last year.

"Actually, Nora, *you* ended things," he jumped in to correct. Sounding a little angry and resentful now.

Guilt flooded her. "Okay, yes, I did. And I told you then that it wasn't your fault. You handled the dangerous aspects of your military service just fine. It was me who couldn't take the not knowing where you were, or what you were doing, or if you were okay. It was me who couldn't take you just showing up hurt, repeatedly, in the military hospital where I was assigned."

It had gotten to the point where she couldn't eat or sleep, or even smile when he was deployed, he was on her mind so much.

That was when he had begun to worry about her, too.

And being distracted like that, they both knew, could get him killed. So she had ended it, and a few months after that, exited the armed service honorably.

He rose and paced the office for several long moments. Stopping abruptly, he leaned against a wall, arms folded in front of him, and locked his steely gaze on her. "Okay, I get all that. What I can't fathom is why you didn't think I had a right to know!"

She huffed in frustration. Demanded finally, "Know what?"

"That you had our baby."

Zane had braced for a lot of different reactions from Nora Caldwell. Defiance, anger, resentment, even heartlessness. He wasn't prepared for shock. And dismay.

Nora pushed back her chair and shot to her full five feet nine inches. Her hair, always a beautiful chestnut brown, now sported sunny golden highlights and fell past her shoulders in the kind of loose, sexy waves military regulations never would have permitted. Beneath her elegant cheekbones, her soft luscious lips clamped down on an O of surprise, while her sky blue eyes radiated a resentment that seemed soul-deep.

Still glaring at him furiously, she propped her hands on her hips. In a pair of black scrubs, with a long-sleeved light blue T-shirt underneath, she was as lithe and physically fit as ever.

Frowning, she demanded, "What in heaven's name are you talking about?"

So. She was going to carry the ruse on to the end. Another disappointment. He'd thought she was better than that.

He met her glare equably. "Our son?"

Her delicate brow furrowed. "You and I don't have a baby!"

"Your Facebook page says differently."

"First of all, you and I aren't Facebook friends."

"And now I know why. Because you didn't want me to know about the baby."

She drew a deep breath and shoved a hand through her hair. "Obviously, you are referring to all the photos of Liam I've posted since I adopted him three months ago."

Adopted!

Zane paused. "You didn't say anything about that in any of the photos."

"Maybe because I didn't need to!" Flushing, she turned away. "Maybe all I need to know—all anyone needs to know—is that he is my son and I love him with all my heart, you dumb son of a gun!"

She was swearing at him again.

That meant she still had *some* feelings for him, right?

"Hey." Still holding her gaze, he aimed a thumb at his chest. Not ready to give up on what he had assumed up to now to be true, he shot back, "The timing fits." Too well for comfort, if you asked him. "We broke up a year ago. The kid was born three months ago."

Looking as if it were taking every ounce of self-control she possessed not to slug him, Nora nodded. "So naturally he had to be yours. Right, soldier?"

She hadn't slept with anyone else. Of that he was certain. She was as much a one-man woman, as he was a one-woman guy.

Hence, there had been only one conclusion to jump to. Still could be. Aware there was a very good reason—in her mind anyway—for him not to be named the little tyke's daddy, he folded his arms across his chest. "Let's just say that there was a definite probability."

Just as there was a definite probability their on-again, off-again relationship was about to be right back on.

Her brow lifting in disdain, she huffed, "Which is the only reason you showed up here like this! So you could do your duty and honorably acknowledge paternity!"

He wanted to say it wasn't true.

But he couldn't.

The minute their mutual friend had showed him the social media pages, he had started making plans, arranged for long-overdue leave and hopped a flight back to the good old US of A, figuring Christmas had come early for him, too.

Nora Caldwell, however, apparently had other ideas.

Ideas that apparently did not include a welcome home hug and kiss. Or anything else of a friendly nature.

She clamped her soft, kissable lips together tightly. Looked him up and down, finding nothing but fault. "I see."

Did she?

Because as far as he was concerned, adoption or no adoption, this was their big chance. Maybe their *last* chance. If they could go back a step and start this reunion over. Something that again did not appear to be in *her* game plan.

"Well. Nice seeing you again, Lieutenant." She whipped her hands off her hips and shoved him none too gently toward the portal.

He dug in his heels. Once again, he had blown it with her, without meaning to. He lifted both hands in abject surrender. Not a usual acknowledgment on his part. "Nora…"

His heartfelt plea fell on deaf ears.

"Don't let the door hit you on your way out!" She gave one final shove to the center of his chest, and then he was standing on the other side of the portal. Her office door slammed in his face.

The first thing Zane noticed was the fact he wasn't alone. In fact, quite a crowd of senior men and women had congregated in the hallway. The expressions on their faces indicated they had heard at least part of what had transpired.

The second thing he saw was a young woman dressed like a student, in jeans and a community college T-shirt. She had a diaper bag slung over her shoulder, a baby boy cradled in her arms.

Liam.

Zane had spent enough hours poring over the social media photos, while on the flight home to Texas, not to recognize this little angel. The tiny fella was again dressed all in blue. He had a cute little face and the same long-lashed sky blue eyes as his mother. The hair peeking out from beneath the cap was light, too.

No wonder Nora had called him the love of her life. Zane was completely captivated by him, too.

As were all the smiling seniors.

"Umm…is Nora available?" the young woman asked. "She usually collects Liam when she gets off work, which should have been about ten minutes ago. And I've got to go to class…"

The office door swung open. Nora stood there, a light jacket thrown over her uniform, car keys in hand. "Hey, Shanda. Sorry if I kept you waiting."

"No problem." With a smile, Shanda handed little Liam over.

Zane stood there. Ready to apologize again. Nora sent him a look. "Don't even…"

The circle of seniors seemed to agree it would be a bad idea to talk to her now. So, cursing the circumstances—which always seemed to be against them—Zane left.

* * *

"Well, that's a relief," Nora murmured to Liam as she ducked back into her office, gathered up their belongings and walked out to her red minivan. He cooed as she put him in his car seat. "I wasn't sure Zane was going to exit so readily."

Liam stared up at her, listening intently.

"It's a long story," Nora reassured her baby boy. Finished buckling him in, she shut the door and climbed into the driver seat. "The bottom line is, Zane would not approve if he knew exactly how and why you came into my life. He would tell me that letting someone else out of their familial obligations and adopting you was a big mistake that could only hurt me in the end. And he would be wrong." Nora drew a deep breath as she turned off Spring Street and onto Wildflower Lane, then into her own driveway. "Because I know firsthand how a child needs at least one parent in his or her life. Every day. I know what it feels like when they're not," she said, putting her minivan in Park. "And I am going to be there for you, my darling baby boy." *Whether Zane likes it or not.*

Liam chortled in agreement.

Nora grinned at her son's happy acknowledgment, then got out to begin their evening. As always, it began with a leisurely postworkday play session. She read him a few stories—on the premise that it was never too soon to start loving books—then followed that by giving him a relaxing bath. When he was cozy in his pajamas, she sat down in her rocking chair to feed him a bottle.

He drank it readily, burped like a champ and then fell asleep to the sound of his favorite lullaby. She was just about to ease him out of her arms when a knock sounded at her front door.

Wondering who it could be, she set her sweetly snoozing son gently down into his Pack 'n Play. She moved soundlessly to the portal. Opened it. And sighed.

"You again," she said.

Chapter 2

"**I** thought we should start over," Zane Lockhart said, capturing her gaze in that intent way that always made her catch her breath.

Nora wasn't surprised to see the handsome soldier on her doorstep so soon after their argument. She knew he'd been taught to rectify mistakes, ASAP. Whereas she'd grown up, picking herself up, dusting herself off and pretending whatever had hurt her didn't matter, because time healed all wounds.

But sadly, in this case, the passage of months hadn't fixed anything and might never.

Keeping her guard up, she stepped out onto the porch opposite him. Across the street, smoke curled from the chimney of a neighbor's home, scenting the air with burning oak.

Wary of letting him back in her life in even the

slightest way, she stared up at him coolly. "And I think we should leave things as is." Frustration curled the corners of his lips. "Come on, Nora." He pressed a brightly wrapped present and a bouquet of flowers into her hands. "Hear me out."

She supposed she owed him that much, after all they had once been to each other.

She set the gifts on one of the rockers on the front porch. Trying not to notice how strappingly handsome he looked in the soft glow of her porch light, she turned back to him and folded her arms in front of her. "I'm listening."

His expression sobered. "First, I apologize for any conclusions I might have jumped to."

About time, she thought.

He held her eyes for a long moment. His voice dropped a compelling notch. "And second, I want to congratulate you on your new son."

His words were so sincere she couldn't help but respond. Figuring peace was better than conflict any day, Nora drew an enervating breath. "Thank you."

Regret tautened the chiseled lines of his face. "I should have known if Liam were mine, you would have told me."

"You're damn right about that," she said fiercely, trying not to think how much she had always longed to have his baby.

And perversely, she still did. But that wasn't happening any more than a reconciliation, so the best thing to do was end their disagreement, and hence his reason for pursuing her.

"Thank you for coming by to say that." Nora shivered in the cold November air. "I accept your apology."

"Does that mean I get to come in long enough to see Liam again and watch you two open the baby gift?"

It'd be rude not to have him come in for a moment.

Aware she was practically shaking she was so cold, Nora picked up the gift and flowers. Turning toward the door, she led the way inside.

Acutely aware of him following lazily behind her, she glanced over her shoulder, frowned. "Why is it if I give you an inch you take a mile?"

He held the door for her. "Must be my easy Texas charm."

She made a face and quipped right back before she could think. "It's definitely something."

He had changed into his civilian clothes since she had last seen him. The tweed sport coat and light blue shirt hugged his broad shoulders and muscled chest. Worn jeans cloaked his hard thighs, sturdy Western boots covered his feet.

Eyes twinkling, he followed her into the living room, where Liam still snoozed contentedly in his Pack 'n Play.

Zane paused to regard her son with a mixture of longing and tenderness that further stirred her emotions.

Nora set the flowers on the coffee table, then perched on the edge of a chair, the present on her lap. She gestured for him to have a seat on the sofa.

"Going to guess what it is?"

She couldn't—wouldn't—make too much of this. Ignoring the faint flutter of her heart, Nora tilted her head to one side. "Something the clerk at the baby boutique in town picked out for you?"

He flashed a cheeky grin. Not the least bit put off. "I'm more invested than that."

She certainly hoped not. Because to have him invested in her life—in Liam's—was the path to heartache, all over again. Doing her best to keep her guard up, Nora undid the ribbon.

Inside the box was a completely adorable red velvet Santa outfit, complete with cap and knit booties that looked like little black boots.

Zane turned his attention to the Pack 'n Play. Observing Liam, his expression grew tender once again. "I know Liam is a little young to know what the holidays are all about, but seeing as how this is his first Christmas—" his voice roughened slightly "—I figure he ought to celebrate it up right."

Nora knew as an adoptive parent, versus a biological one, she should not be having postpregnancy hormonal shifts. But having Zane back in her life, even temporarily, was causing a seismic shift. She jerked in a quavering breath, still not daring to look her ex in the eye. "It's lovely," she murmured back huskily. "Thanks."

He reached across the chasm of space between them, clasping her delicate hand in his rougher one. "So we're good?"

Yes, Nora thought, her pulse racing despite herself. And no...

Luckily for her, she was saved from having to answer that by the ringing phone.

She rose to get it.

The news on the other end was not good.

"You have to go back to work *now*?" Zane asked.

Aware she had no time to don her scrubs again, Nora grabbed a belted cardigan-style jacket instead, looped the chained badge over her head and settled the ID between her breasts. She paused to pull on her favorite pair of Western boots. "It's an emergency with a new resident. Unfortunately, I don't have time to wait for a sitter to get here…so I'm going to have to take Liam with me."

He followed her back to the Pack 'n Play. "Is that going to be a problem?"

Gently, Nora eased her son into a fleece jacket and cap. "No. He goes to Laramie Gardens with me every day." It had been part of her employment deal, and the only way she would go back to work so soon. "I just usually have a sitter there with me. To keep an eye on him between feedings." Which she usually did herself.

"Want me to go along and help?" Zane asked.

An extra pair of hands was always helpful, particularly when an infant was on the scene. Nodding, Nora collected the diaper bag and her purse, then gathered her son in her arms. "Actually, yes, if you wouldn't mind. At least until I can get reinforcement."

Together, they hurried out to the drive. Luckily, Liam seemed more dazed than unhappy to be woken up. Not always the case.

The pickup truck Zane had driven forever was parked behind her. "I'll follow you over there," he called.

Short minutes later, the two of them were walking into the home for senior citizens. Just before they entered the doors, Nora handed Liam, who was still strapped snugly into his infant carrier, off to Zane.

And not a moment too soon, it appeared. At the other end of the hall, a determined Russell Pierce was slapping a jaunty brown felt fedora on his head. In a safari shirt, khaki cargo pants and a worn leather jacket, he bore a striking resemblance to Harrison Ford. With a physical vigor belying his eighty-five years, he was arguing with the night charge nurse, Inez Garcia. "I'm telling you, nice as this visit has been, I have to go close up The Book Nook, and then get home to have dinner with Esther and the baby."

Wordlessly, Nora directed Zane to take Liam into the community room, where help awaited him. "Hey, Mr. Pierce," Nora said, sauntering closer.

"Well, hello there, young lady!" he said. "I was just about to call you. The rest of your special order came in."

"Great." Nora smiled and gently took his arm, attempting to orient him. "Do you know where we are?"

He looked around. Suddenly confused.

"Laramie Gardens, Home For Seniors," she said.

He squinted, uncertain.

"Will you let me walk you back to your room so we can take your blood sugar and talk a moment?"

Mr. Pierce hesitated. "I still need to get home to Esther," he said more urgently than ever.

"I know you miss her and want to be with her," Nora said softly.

He nodded. Tears glistened.

Nora fought the lump rising in her throat. She put her arm through his, and together, they walked back toward his room.

An hour later, all was calm.

Nora went in search of Zane and the baby, hoping they were still in the community room. Only to hear sounds of what had increasingly become the norm.

"Yes, but it isn't fair," Wilbur Barnes said.

"All the activities are female oriented," complained Kurtis Kelley.

"We want an equal-opportunity holiday around here!" Buck Franklin reiterated gruffly.

"Hey! We gave you fellas ample time to weigh in on the scheduled activities," the always-elegant Miss Sadie said.

"You all refused," retired librarian Miss Mim pointed out.

Nora crossed the threshold.

Zane stood in front of the fireplace, a wide-awake Liam cradled in his arms. The two of them were a picture of contentment. Leading Nora to secretly wish for the impossible...

"What do you think, Zane? You've got enough distance to lend perspective," Darrell Enlow, the resident peacemaker, said.

Zane squinted at the group gathered around him. "I'm not sure you want to hear what I have to say."

"Yes, we do!" everyone cried in unison.

Zane looked at Nora. Figuring it couldn't hurt to get an outside opinion, she encouraged him with a nod.

He drew a breath, his attention focused solely on the thirty or so seniors gathered around him. "Well, when I hear you argue about whether hand-painting ornaments is an appropriate activity for guys I can't help but think about all my fellow soldiers stationed around the world right now who are away from their families, who would give anything to be home with their loved ones. In fact," he admitted, in a low, gravelly voice, "they'd be so damn grateful, they wouldn't care what they were expected to do as long as they could spend time together."

The ache in Nora's throat came back, full force.

This was the Zane she had loved.

The big, strong guy with the heart as vast as the Lone Star State. The man who never let her—or anyone else who was depending on him—down. The soldier who was always ready and willing to render aid to someone else in need.

Who was helping her out with her son, even now.

Several throats cleared. More than one resident dabbed their eyes.

"You're right," Wilbur Barnes said finally. "We can do better."

Zane shifted Liam a little higher in his arms. Her son reacted by resting his blond head contentedly against Zane's broad chest. "Which isn't to say I don't understand your frustration," he continued empathetically. "The holidays are a time when it's just as easy to think about what you don't have as it is to count your blessings."

How true, Nora thought, aware right now she was acutely cognizant of how much she had missed him. And maybe always would...

"I also know that you-all would feel a lot less lonesome if you were helping someone else," Zane concluded, his gaze softening as Liam yawned sleepily and cuddled even closer against him.

Smiling down at him, Zane stroked Liam's downy soft head.

The moment so affectionate, so unexpected, it brought tears to Nora's eyes.

Zane continued in a tone that was both pragmatic and gentle, "And I've got just the idea on how to make that happen."

"That was brilliant, getting them involved with the West Texas Warriors Assistance nonprofit," Nora complimented Zane, as they walked out to the parking lot. Aware this was beginning to feel like a date, when it most certainly was not, she forced herself to put aside her increasingly warm feelings for the sexy soldier.

He opened the door for her, then stepped back to give her room to settle the sleeping Liam back in his car seat. "My family and the others running it can use the help, especially this time of year."

Nora straightened and shut the door. To her relief, Liam continued sleeping.

Tilting her head back, she looked Zane in the eye. "I know Bess Monroe, the nurse who runs the rehab unit. I'll call her tomorrow and see what we can do to set things up between us."

Zane flashed another flirty grin. "I can help with that, you know."

Awareness swept through her. Fighting the urge to touch him, Nora took a step back. "I appreciate your Good Samaritan spirit."

"But?" The street lamps brought out the wheat-gold hue of his hair.

Resisting the urge to run her fingers through the thick strands, Nora frowned. "I can't go down this road with you again, Zane." And working closely with him, on anything, would lead to just that. A fact he seemed to know all too well.

He regarded her with barely veiled bemusement. "Our relationship doesn't have to end badly. In fact—" he shrugged his broad shoulders laconically "—it doesn't have to end at all."

Nora tossed her bag into the car. "I think, given the very different things we want in life, that it already has," she said, casting him a probing sidelong glance.

"In any case, Thanksgiving is tomorrow. It will be a very busy day at Laramie Gardens, with all the guests and family coming in."

"I'm guessing it won't be a happy occasion for everyone."

Nora dipped her head, acknowledging wearily this was true. For every happy heart, there would be a broken one to mend. "I'm going to need all my energy to see them through it. So we better call it a night."

Apparently not quite ready to give up just yet, he watched her climb behind the wheel. "Sure you don't need my help getting Liam in the house, or seeing you get some dinner?"

Need?

No. She could do whatever was required all by herself.

Want was a different matter entirely.

"I heard my dad had another episode last night," Lynn Russell informed Nora the next morning.

Nora ushered the sixty-year-old noted actress into her private office. Although currently filming a television series in NYC, the glamorous redhead had flown back to enjoy the holiday with her dad.

"He suffered a period of brief confusion last night."

"Wasn't that the second time since he's been here?"

"In the course of two weeks. Yes."

Lynn settled in a chair on the other side of Nora's desk. "Do you know why?"

"We initially chalked the first incident up to simple fatigue. He was exhausted by the plane ride and long drive here. Neither of which is easy for someone his age."

"And the one last night?"

Nora regarded the medical chart in front of her. "We're not sure. He hasn't had much of an appetite since he moved in. So his blood sugar was a little off. We got the levels back to normal after he finished eating his dinner. And it was normal again this morning."

"So that's not likely it."

"Probably not. But with folks his age, we keep a close tab on that just the same. He could also have been sundowning a little."

Lynn turned off her phone and set her bag on the floor. "What's that?"

"It's a type of confusion that occurs later in the day. It can be an early symptom of Alzheimer's or dementia. But I've also seen it brought about simply by a change in environment in an elderly person."

"So, if it's just the move back to Texas causing this…?"

"Then his occasional disorientation will ease as he adjusts to life here at Laramie Gardens and everything becomes more familiar to him."

Lynn tapped her fingers, thinking. "And if not?"

Nora sobered. "Then treatment might be required. Which is why we have a geriatric specialist, Dr. Ron Wheeler, coming in tomorrow morning to go over his medical records and examine him. But not to worry, your dad is in fine spirits this morning. So you should have a nice holiday together."

Her expression regretful, Lynn walked with Nora to the door. "I wish I could have convinced Dad to stay with me in New York City and continue to have home care help to assist him in my absence. But he was insistent he return to the place where I grew up and he and my mother spent their entire married life."

Together, they moved down the hall. "I can see where that would be comforting."

Lynn shook her head sadly. "He's never gotten over losing her two years ago."

Nora recalled Esther, who had worked side by side with her husband at the Laramie bookstore they founded. A kinder, more devoted couple could not have been found. "How long were they married?" She paused just outside Mr. Pierce's door.

"Sixty-three years." Lynn smiled and waved at her dad, who was standing in front of a bookcase of leather-bound classics. *Treasure Island, Moby-Dick, A Christmas Carol, Gunga Din, The Catcher In the Rye, Don Quixote*... Mr. Pierce had quite the collection. And he was deeply attached to them all.

"Wow," Nora said. "I can hardly imagine what it would be like to be married that long."

"I know." Lynn grinned as she headed in to see her father. "Not many couples make it that long these days."

Certainly, Nora thought, not she and Zane.

"Is Lieutenant Lockhart coming for the feast this evening?" Miss Mim asked.

"We invited him to attend," Miss Sadie said helpfully.

Nora cradled Liam against her shoulder, all the while keeping an eye on the dining room, where places for all one hundred and fifty residents, and the hundred special guests also in attendance for the buffet dinner at 4:30 p.m., were being set up.

Nora shoved aside her own need to see the handsome soldier. "I expect he's with his own family today."

"Ah...think again..." chimed in Miss Mim, who'd

been matchmaking for the two of them since they were kids who hung out together every summer, when Zane visited his paternal grandfather.

Every nerve end tingling, Nora turned.

And there came Zane striding toward her in an olive green shirt, tie, blazer and jeans. He had a huge sheet cake in his hands. "Did your sister, Sage, make that cake?" Buck Franklin asked.

Zane chuckled. "She did. And she even put the great big turkey on it, just like I asked." He held it out so everyone could see the decoration adorning the vanilla frosting.

Nora couldn't help but compliment, "That was so nice of you and Sage." His sister was a fabulous chef, as well as café bistro owner.

Zane grinned and regarded Nora mischievously, his eyes alight with interest. "Consider it the Lockhart family's contribution for the feast today."

It was something, all right.

Oblivious to the sparks flying between Zane and Nora, Wilbur Barnes stepped in to relieve Zane. "Thanks, son."

Miss Patricia led the way across the dining hall. "I'll make room for it on the dessert table."

Suddenly, the world narrowed once again. Zane regarded Liam, who was looking around with a slightly perturbed expression on his cherubic face. "Not to worry, little fella," he said, patting Liam's head. "You'll have a chance to have cake when I bring it next year."

As if Zane would be there with them next November, Nora thought irritably. The practical side of her laid down odds he would not. Which meant for all their sakes she had to keep her guard up.

As the seniors gathered around them eased off to give them a little privacy, she nodded at the brash fabric knotted around his neck. "Where did you get that tie?" she quipped. "Pick it out yourself?"

He held out the brown, orange, gold and green silk. Then gazed admiringly at the upside-down design. "Neckwear sporting a traditional cornucopia is hard to find."

Nora rolled her eyes. "I'll bet."

He chuckled, knowing—as always—he was doing a great job of getting under her skin.

Figuring she had no choice but to brazen her way through this situation, Nora cleared her throat. She had a job to do here, and her first order of business was getting rid of him. "Seriously, it was nice of you to drop by, but doesn't your family want you to spend the holiday with them?"

Stubbornly refusing to take her hint, Zane shrugged his broad shoulders. "Mom served her dinner at noon. She didn't want any football games interrupting the family meal."

Trying not to think how much his nearness disturbed her, Nora returned, "I thought Lucille didn't allow *any* televised sports at holiday get-togethers."

One corner of his sensual lips slanted up. Dark silver eyes glittering warmly, he leaned closer and teased huskily, "I like the way you remember every little thing about me…"

She recalled way too much all right, Nora thought, flushing self-consciously.

Like the way he kissed and touched her. The way he smelled when he first woke up, or was fresh out of the shower. The way he looked at her when he thought she wasn't aware, like he wanted to hold that moment in his heart forever.

A riptide of sentiment swept through her. Followed swiftly by a physical longing that was just as intense.

"This particular memory was about your mother," Nora fibbed, lifting a nonchalant brow.

He chuckled at her sassy tone. "Yes, well, Mom's softening a bit in her old age. She allows a game or two to be on as long as we all have dinner together—uninterrupted—first."

Nora let her gaze rove over his tall, solidly built frame. Told herself she wasn't affected. Nope. Not one little bit. "Ah."

"Anything we miss, she figures can be recorded and watched later."

She didn't want to kiss him again, either. Not today. Not tonight. Not ever. "Smart woman."

Oblivious to the ridiculously out-of-bounds nature of her thoughts, Zane sighed and shook his head.

"Who, unfortunately, understands very little about the superstitious nature of sporting events. Luckily for me, the guys here *do* know how much viewer participation it takes for any team to win," he announced, grinning when Nora groaned. "So they have told me, they are all in, and will be ready to cheer on my teams with me."

Which meant Zane would be here for hours. As would she, since she was pulling a double today. It was all Nora could do not to stamp her foot in dismay.

"Just don't let things get too rowdy," she warned.

Zane grinned in all innocence and gave her a once-over that quickly had her tingling from head to toe. "Who, me?" he said.

Chapter 3

Nora didn't know what was worse. Having Zane underfoot during the Thanksgiving feast, paying attention to her. Or having him underfoot, blissfully unaware she was even around.

All she knew for sure was that he was a hit at the table he was sitting at during the meal. Even from the other side of the dining room, she could hear the bursts of laughter in response to whatever stories he was telling.

And he was an even bigger hit in the TV room, watching the football games. Enough of a man's man to appeal to all the guys and enough of a charmer to appeal to the ladies.

Luckily, she had a lot to concern herself with. Three bottle feedings and a number of diaper changes for Liam. A lot of families, and lonely residents, to speak with. By the time her second shift ended at eleven that evening, she was worn to a thread.

Aware the last football game was just about over, she decided to duck into her office and wait until Zane bid adieu to his new pals and departed. With a sleeping Liam snuggled safely against her chest in his BabyBjörn carrier, Nora sat down on the love seat in the corner of her office and let her head fall back against the cushions.

The next thing she knew she was snuggled against something big and solid and warm, struggling to wake up.

Blinking, she looked down. Liam was still snoozing in his BabyBjörn. It was to her left that...

Oh, my heaven!

She struggled to sit up.

Not easy when she was cuddled snugly into the curve of Zane Lockhart's tall, strong body. But somehow she managed. Turning toward him, she leaned forward and watched his eyes open. Refusing to get lost in the mesmerizing depths, she declared, "You can't sleep with me in my office!"

Night supervisor Inez Garcia loomed in the open doorway. "I totally agree." She shook her head at Nora and Zane. "You-all ought to go home. Pronto!"

"There's no need to be embarrassed," Zane said, stepping outside with her. The chill from earlier in the day had faded into an unusually balmy warmth. The night air was scented with approaching rain. "I'm sure it's nothing your nurse-colleague hasn't seen before."

Irked to find the weather shifting as erratically as her moods, Nora stumbled slightly under the weight of the baby still strapped to her chest, his diaper bag and her own shoulder bag. "That's not the point," she grumbled.

Zane reacted as swiftly as usual, easing a palm beneath her forearm, the other around her waist. As soon as she steadied, he tenderly searched her face. "You okay?"

"Yes," Nora fibbed, "I'm…"

He took the diaper bag from her resisting fingers, slung it over one broad shoulder and moved in even closer. "Barely awake?"

The sad truth.

She eased away from the hand beneath her elbow. "It was a long day." A very, very long day.

He fell into step beside her. Staying close enough to assist her if need be, far enough away not to crowd her. His every action as perfectly gallant as always.

"Let me drive you both home."

When even the gruff sound of his voice had her tingling all over? Not wise. Wishing she hadn't parked quite so far away from the door, Nora kept her eyes on her waiting minivan. "It's only two miles."

Zane tilted his head at her and Liam. "Plenty of time for you to fall back asleep, jump a curb and hit a tree."

She hated it when he was right. A sixteen-hour shift on a holiday, while simultaneously caring for her infant son, was too much. He, on the other hand, looked chipper as could be. But then Special Forces soldiers were trained to get by on very little shut-eye and still perform at optimum ability.

Using what felt like the very last reserves of her energy, she picked up her pace. "Then how are you going to get to your pickup truck?"

One half of his mouth quirked up in a smile. "I'll run back. I haven't worked out today. It'll be fine."

The wind gusted. With one hand, Nora held back the hair that had blown into her face. Maybe he did want a good run. In any case… With a sigh, she reluctantly gave in. "Fine. If you're sure you don't mind."

"I don't."

Not daring to look him in the eye, she used her firmest voice to let him know, "Once we get there, I'm not asking you in."

Out of the corner of her eye, she saw him shrug, his expression inscrutable. "Not asking you to."

She turned her head to face him. They locked gazes. Damned if he didn't look serious about that, too.

With a sigh, Nora traversed the last ten feet to her minivan. Unlocked it via the keypad, then handed him her keys at the same time Liam finally woke.

Her little angel was not happy about being eased out of his cozy baby carrier, and into his car seat. He let his discontent be known with loud howls all the way home. And Liam was still crying furiously as Zane unlocked her front door.

"How can I help?"

Stubborn pride made her want to refuse. However, three months of experience had taught her self-reliance only took a new mom so far. If she wanted Liam to be as happy as possible, and she did, she had to let others assist her in situations like this.

With a reluctant sigh, she asked, "Do you know how to change a diaper?"

"Yep."

She regarded Zane skeptically. She knew they did not cover that in the military training he'd had.

His expression deadpan, he explained, "I've got five nieces and nephews in the infant and toddler stage. Three brothers, a sister and various in-laws, none of whom are shy about asking me to lend a hand when I'm in town."

Which probably meant he knew a lot more than she had given him credit for. "Okay then," she acquiesced, watching while he followed her and Liam across the threshold.

She paused to hand over her squalling son. "The nursery is upstairs, next to the last room on the right. His pajamas and a clean diaper are already laid out. If you can get things started up there, I'll warm a bottle for him and be right up."

Liam, who had miraculously slowed down his crying during their exchange, stared worshipfully up at Zane, tears still glistening moistly on his rosy little cheeks.

She understood the abruptly spellbound attitude.

Zane had that effect on a lot of people.

Even on her.

Zane smiled down at Liam, as fondly as if he were her son's daddy. Nora's heart gave another leap.

"Atta boy," Zane soothed, running a hand over Liam's back. "We'll get you into your jammies in no time..." He headed up the stairs, Liam now quietly compliant in his arms.

Trying not to think about how nice it would be to have Zane here helping her all the time, Nora went into the kitchen. Three minutes later, she joined them.

Zane was standing over the changing table, laughing, a big, gentle hand placed over Liam's bare chest. "Nice shot, fella. You have a future as a comedian."

Nora edged closer.

Saw, too late, the damp arc across Zane's sport coat, holiday tie and shirt. Smelled the urine. *Oh, no.* She sucked in a breath of embarrassment and regret. "I'm so sorry."

"Really?" Zane chuckled, stepping back to let her take over, as promised. His eyes twinkled merrily. "Because I would've thought you would feel it was what I deserved for hanging out on your office sofa, waiting so long for you to wake up that I fell asleep myself."

Why did Zane have to possess such a great sense of humor? Take everything in stride? Even the news that this darling little baby wasn't his, after all.

Nora lifted an airy hand. Ignoring her mounting desire for him, she professed, just as humorously, "One of the hazards of raising a boy, I have learned."

He shrugged out of his sport coat, unknotted his tie, set both aside. "You've taken incoming, too?"

"Oh, yeah. The worst time was my first day back at work when Liam was six weeks old. I was trying to get him changed before we headed out the door. And bam, he hit me with everything he had. I ended up having to completely change both of us."

While she finished dressing Liam, Zane unbuttoned the first couple of buttons on his shirt and rolled up his sleeves. "Do you always take him to work with you?"

Nora nodded. "It was part of my condition for returning so early, that I have Liam nearby. I hire student-sitters during my shift to help out with him. But I try to do all his feedings myself, even if it means I stay a little longer to finish up my work."

Overhead, without warning, a soft staccato sounded. Was that…?

Catching her frown of dismay, he confirmed, "It's raining."

Nora gathered Liam in her arms. She looked up at Zane, achingly aware how cozy this all was. How right it felt. And would have been if only Liam were Zane's baby, too.

But he wasn't. The sound of the rain overhead picked up, thundering against the roof. Nora peered outside and frowned. "How are you going to get back to your vehicle?"

Looping his soiled garments over his arm, Zane shrugged nonchalantly. "I think I can handle a little precipitation. Besides—" he held out the stained fabric of his dress shirt and the T-shirt beneath "—maybe the downpour will help rinse out some of the smell."

Nora grinned.

Only Zane would be able to find the bright side in that.

Together, they walked downstairs.

The rain came down even harder. Nora hesitated. Only a heartless woman would send a soldier home on leave out into torrential downpour at one in the morning. Reluctantly, she insisted, "You have to stay."

He shook his head stubbornly, shrugged on his damp jacket and turned up the collar against his neck. "I don't think so." Zane opened the front door.

Another wave of guilt and anxiety swept through her. Followed swiftly by a soul-deep emotion that was even harder to rein in. "But…" she protested.

Their gazes clashed as surely as their wills. His scowl deepening, he said huskily, "You'll only resent me in the morning."

She put out an arm to stop him from shrugging on

his jacket. Her hand curled over the flexed muscles of his bicep and she felt a jolt of electricity skitter through her. Face flushing self-consciously, she looked him in the eye, determined to clarify this much. "I didn't mean in my bed."

He regarded her with mounting amusement. Eyes gleaming mischievously, he said, "I didn't think you meant in your bed."

She dropped her hand. "Then…"

His sensual lips formed a sober line. "I showed up at Laramie Gardens today because I promised Miss Mim and Miss Sadie and all the guys that I would. It wasn't because I wanted to annoy you."

She fought back a sigh. "You didn't."

He clearly didn't believe her for one second. "Uh-huh." Another silence fell, fraught with tension. Gently, he continued, "I came by your office after the last game ended to tell you that."

And then he had stayed to rescue her. Lending a hand, showing her all over again what a great guy he was.

Nora released a wistful breath.

Why did he have to make everything so simultaneously hard and wonderful? "So now that I have…" He released her, turned, and swung open her front door again. Another blast of wet air flowed in. A sudden yellow zigzag of light filled the sky, followed immediately by a clap of thunder loud enough to make her jump. "I'll be on my way." He stepped onto the porch.

Like heck he would. Feeling very glad he was there, despite herself, she caught his arm, her palm curving around the swell of his bicep and tugged him right back inside. "You're not going anywhere, soldier. Not in a thunderstorm."

He turned to her, his shoulder nudging hers in the process. "There's no need for you to babysit me," he insisted.

Her palm tingling as badly as the rest of her, she dropped her hand.

Rocking forward on his toes, he hooked his thumbs in the denim loops on either side of his fly. "I'll wait out the worst of it on the porch. Then go." Their eyes met and held, and another jolt of awareness swept through Nora. Letting her know just how very much she had missed him.

She hesitated, unsure.

"I'll be fine." His tone was both conciliatory and deadpan. So why was he suddenly looking as if he were thinking of kissing her again? Why was she feeling the same way?

Nora winced and ducked as another sharp zigzag of electricity lit up the sky and thunder rumbled half a second later. Wow, that was close. Dangerously so.

A fact that left her no choice.

She had a duty and responsibility here to maintain his safety, just as he'd done for her half an hour prior.

Her heart racing, she countered in exasperation, "No, you won't," she said.

He quirked a brow.

She dragged in a bolstering breath, then stepped closer, determined to try and talk sense into him. "You know how it is in Texas, Zane, particularly this time of year. This storm could go on for hours." She gave him a long level look. "There is no reason to huddle out here on the porch, never mind risk life and limb, waiting for a reprieve that might not come until dawn. I have a guest room. You can bunk there tonight." She waved an amiable hand, deciding if she was in, she might as well be all in. At least when it came to reluctantly hosting. "I'll even wash your pee-soaked shirt."

He waved off her offer of aid, then cupped her shoulders warmly. "I can do that if you point me toward the laundry room. You look ready to collapse on your feet."

She was.

"So how about you go on to bed?" he suggested, seemingly oblivious to the way the casual contact was affecting her. With another brief companionable squeeze, he let her go. "I'll start the washer and close up down here."

Had she acted too hastily? Could they still actually be friends?

Savoring the possibility, she reluctantly gave in. "Okay. Thanks."

He nodded at her, like the Texas gentleman he'd been raised to be. "See you in the morning."

His innate gallantry brought forth another slew of memories. Time seemed to be suspended. Suddenly it was just the two of them again, their only duty and responsibility to each other.

Her heart racing, she jerked in a steadying breath, inhaling the brisk masculine fragrance of his hair and skin. It had been hours since he had shaved, and the stubble of new beard on his jaw only enhanced his raw sex appeal. "You know which one the guest room is?"

He cocked a brow, his gaze drifting over her lazily. "The one on the other side of the nursery, with the silver comforter on the bed?"

Trying not to wonder if his mind was traveling down

the same forbidden paths as her own, Nora smiled. They were both adults. They could handle this.

"That's the one," she confirmed lightly. "There are towels, washcloths and soap in the hall bath, extra toothbrushes and toothpaste, if you need that."

Thunder roiled, even louder.

He nodded again. "Thanks."

She felt him watching her as she headed upstairs, realizing that despite everything, even when they were moving apart, fate kept throwing them back together again.

Nora fell asleep listening to the sound of the rain still drumming on the roof and thinking about Zane. She woke to the sound of an even softer rain and Liam starting ever so gently to fuss.

By the time she had changed her son's diaper and put him in a new playsuit, the sumptuous smell of breakfast cooking filled the air.

She went downstairs, not all that surprised to see Zane standing at her stove, making himself completely at home. Bare-chested, with his jeans riding just below his navel, he looked sexy as hell. It was all she could do not to run her fingers through his rumpled hair and rub her cheek against the morning beard lining his square jaw.

He smiled warmly at her and the baby in her arms. "I'll be out of here as soon as my shirts are dry. In the meantime I thought you might be as hungry as I am."

She was.

Trying not to think how often he had made breakfast for her in the past, never mind how often they had made hot, passionate love to each other after that, she eased past him. Retrieved a bottle of formula from the fridge. "What are you making?"

He looked in the pantry, emerged with a bag of tortilla chips. "Migas."

Her favorite.

And he'd brewed coffee and poured juice, too.

This was all so cozy. Too cozy.

She put Liam's bottle in the warmer, still cuddling her son close, then looked out the window at the water pouring down.

He followed her glance. "Yep, it's still raining."

She had hoped it would have stopped by now, but that did not look very likely, given the gloomy skies overheard.

Zane cast a glance at her drenched shrubbery and lawn. "No thunder, though." He beamed as Liam offered him a toothy grin. Reaching out, he gently touched her son's cheek. Liam chortled softly in response.

Zane slid his little finger into her son's tiny fist.

Liam held on tight.

The way Nora wanted to hold on…

Oblivious to her forbidden thoughts, Zane regarded her son, then lifted his glance to meet her gaze. "I forgot to ask you last night. Do you have to work today?"

Acutely aware of how wonderful it would have been if Liam had been Zane's child, Nora shook off her wistful mood. She swallowed around the sudden parched feeling in her throat and forced herself to meet Zane's eyes. "No. I've got the day off."

Liam jerked on Zane's hand. Grinning at the mingled demand and curiosity in her son's baby blue eyes, Zane stepped closer still. His smile widened as Liam chortled happily.

Zane nuzzled Liam's knuckle, eliciting another happy gurgle, then smiled again and turned his attention back to her. "Any plans?" he asked, that charismatic intensity solely focused on her now.

He smelled like toothpaste and soap. And pure, primal man.

Blushing at the memories the tantalizing fragrance elicited, Nora turned her attention away from Zane and plucked the bottle out of the warmer.

Working to corral her escalating feelings, she sat down at the table to feed Liam. "My sitter is coming at ten o'clock. I was going to go get a Christmas tree, but with it raining, I don't know that it's the best time to try and pick one out. I wouldn't be able to bring it inside until it dried out anyway, so I'll probably get a jump on my holiday shopping instead."

Still listening, he crumbled chips in his fist, and stirred them into the pan of scrambled eggs and cheese.

Nora drew a deep breath as the Tex-Mex aroma filled the room. "In any case, not to worry," she continued, giving him a look to let him know this meal would not be followed with the usual passionate lovemaking. "I can drive you over to get your pickup truck and drop your jacket off for cleaning on the way."

Zane flashed a sexy smile. "Actually, I'll take care of the dry cleaning if you do me a favor." He spooned up a plate of migas and a side of salsa, and carried both over to her.

Curious, she met his eyes. It was unlike him to drive a bargain. Usually he gave, then walked away. Thereby keeping control of the situation. But now he clearly wanted something from her. Something he seemed unsure she would be willing to give.

Aware this was a first, she looked at him, waiting.

He grabbed his breakfast and sat down opposite her, their knees touching briefly beneath the table. Then, his emotions suddenly as fired up as hers, said, "Come out and see the ranch my father left me in his will. And give me your unvarnished opinion about what you think I should do with it."

Chapter 4

Nora told herself the only reason she was following Zane out to his ranch was because she was interested in seeing exactly what he had inherited from his late father.

Well, that, and it had been a good way to get the sexy soldier out her door, back to his pickup truck and on his merry way as fast as possible. Before she started wanting to make love with him again... Which, she promised herself resolutely as she followed him out of town in her minivan, she most certainly did not.

Being completely alone with him without her son as an emotional shield, however, proved more challenging than she had expected. Luckily, they had the No Name Ranch he had inherited to focus on.

The two-thousand-acre spread was surrounded on all sides by barbed wire fence and covered with scrub vegetation and the occasional strand of trees.

In the center of the long-neglected land, a half mile back from the road, there was a newly renovated A-frame ranch house with a raised wraparound deck. Inside, everything from the wood floor to the open kitchen-family-living area and big masculine furniture on the first floor bore the same neutral brown and gray color palette as the exterior.

Zane's king-size bed and a luxurious bath with steam shower dominated the loft-style second floor. A lone duffel sat on the floor in the wide-open space, reminding Nora just how light Zane traveled.

She headed back downstairs, determined to stay just long enough to be polite before getting back into her minivan and heading out to Christmas shop, as planned. "Your brother and sister-in-law did a nice job on this for you. Did Molly and Chance pick out the furniture, too?"

"Actually, I told them not to furnish it, since up until a few days ago—"

When he'd learned about Liam, Nora realized uncomfortably. And jumped to the erroneous conclusion her child was his...

"—my intention was to sell."

Made sense, she noted, since he was rarely in Texas. "And property with a move-in-ready home fetches a much higher price," she guessed, shivering a little.

"Right." He strode to the thermostat and made an adjustment. The furnace kicked on with a purr.

She looked around, trying not to feel disappointed he was already on his way out of her life. Again. "Well, your stagers did a remarkable job here."

He stood, looking over at her, hands braced on his waist. "Actually, I didn't plan on doing that, either." He tossed her a fond look. "All the furnishings, down to the dishes and towels, are an early Christmas gift from my mother."

A rueful smile curving his sensual lips, he walked into the kitchen and began making a pot of coffee. "She wanted to make the No Name Ranch house so cozy I'd never want to leave."

Nora slid onto a stool at the island. "Did it work?"

His gave her a long look that spoke volumes. Finally he leaned toward her and with an even more intimate look, said, "It's not the decor that interests me here."

Oh, dear.

She pulled in a stabilizing breath, clasped her hands in front of her and tried again. "In any case, it's a really nice bachelor pad." For whoever eventually wanted it.

He leveled an assessing gaze on her, kept it there.

"Yeah, well—" he shrugged and turned away "—my dad never expected me to want to marry or settle down."

No one did.

In fact, she was pretty sure they still didn't.

She breathed in the delectable scent of freshly brewed coffee. Aware her knees weren't as steady as she wanted them to be, she slid onto a counter stool. "So he left you the ranch as an investment?"

Nodding, Zane lounged on the other side of the island, his arms folded over the hard muscles of his chest. "And a place I could crash while on leave and still be close to the rest of my family, who also all inherited property here."

And yet Zane had still, by his own admission, been thinking of selling the property. A move she sensed the rest of the close-knit Lockhart clan would not have taken well.

The coffeemaker gurgled as it reached the end of

the brewing cycle. She searched his face, wishing for some chink in Zane's emotional armor, some sign that he was capable of more than fulfilling his pledge to defend their country. "Did your dad expect you to ranch?"

With a brief shake of his head, he filled two mugs and pushed one her way. He got the peppermint-mocha creamer from the fridge and handed that, along with a spoon, to her.

"No. Dad knew I don't have an ounce of rancher blood in me. He suggested I do something more outside the norm with the land."

"Like...?"

"Set up a skydiving school, shooting range, ninja-warrior-type obstacle course or outdoor physical fitness training center."

Interesting. Frank Lockhart always had been a visionary. With the hedge fund and charitable foundation he created. As well as his wife and five kids...

Nora took her mug and, feeling the mood inside his home had gotten a little too intimate for comfort, walked back outside. He followed suit.

The rain had finally stopped but the ground and deck were still soaked. Hence, she had to be careful not to touch or lean against anything. Especially him.

She traversed the length of the deck, overlooking the property, thinking, considering. "Any one of those ideas would work if you marketed to city slickers looking for a little adventure. Although—" she tossed him a teasing look over her shoulder "—the property would need a new moniker."

He chuckled and sauntered closer, filling up the space, making her all the more sensually aware of him. "You don't like the one it's got?"

He shook his head, his eyes drifting slowly over her face, before returning to her eyes. "No," he said gruffly. "Not at all."

Nora looked up at him. For a guy who'd planned to sell the property, he suddenly seemed proprietorial. "How did it become the No Name Ranch?"

"The husband and wife who owned it before me were never able to agree on much of anything," he replied with an affable shrug. "Including what to call this land, which they used as a vacation-home-slash-investment. So they jokingly called it the No Name, decided they liked that better than anything either of them was suggesting and eventually even made up a sign."

"That's actually a kind of cute backstory, Zane. You could probably use it in whatever you decide to do with the property." *Even if it's just as a way to eventually sell the place.*

He moved closer. "Maybe."

Or maybe not, Nora thought, judging by his unenthusiastic tone.

Not surprised Zane wasn't interested in doing anything he saw as that frivolous, even if it could benefit him financially, Nora took another sip of her coffee. "What does the rest of your family think you should do with the property?"

Disappointment glimmered in his eyes. "Just what you'd expect. My brother Wyatt thinks I should board and train horses, like he does on his ranch. Chance wants me to start a cattle breeding operation to supply quality mama cows for his bucking bull breeding and training operation."

No surprise there. His two middle brothers were absolute cowboys and always had been, from the time they had first set foot in Laramie County, visiting their paternal grandpa when they were kids. "And Sage?"

"Thinks I should find something adrenaline fueled to do for a living, then use the No Name as a private retreat where I can recoup from my new and exciting yet somehow less risky profession."

"I like the way your only sister thinks," Nora quipped, before she could stop herself.

Zane set his empty coffee cup on the railing. "So does my mom, except she doesn't want me to do anything the *least bit* dangerous anymore."

I see her point. Suppressing her desire to protect him, too, Nora pushed on, "What about Garrett?" His brother, a highly skilled physician, had served in the Army, too, before resigning to lead the family charitable foundation.

Zane sobered. "He wants me to help separated and current military at West Texas Warriors Assistance, here in Laramie."

"Like you're doing with the holiday gift basket drive."

"Except on a more permanent basis."

"But that doesn't appeal to you, either?" she asked curiously.

Zane exhaled. "I'm happy to volunteer. But as for a career, I see myself in a more physically active role, whatever it is."

"You could join local law enforcement." They took a lot of ex-military. And Lord knew their life was full of challenges, Nora thought.

He nodded as if he had expected her suggestion. "I've got an appointment to talk with the Laramie County sheriff's department next week."

"Good!"

"Don't get your hopes up." His lips twisted. "I'm not sure that will be a good fit."

But he was looking into it. That was something he'd never been willing to do before. "You never know." He was certainly selfless and heroic enough for the job.

"No. You don't," he agreed, taking her coffee cup out of her hands and setting it aside. "And I'm going to have to do something when I leave the military," he murmured as he drew her into his arms. "So I might as well look at all my options."

Nora caught her breath as one palm slid down her spine, flattening her against him, and the other hand eased through her hair, tilting her face up to his. "What are you doing?" she gasped, way more turned on than she wanted to admit.

Eyes warming, Zane looked down at her. He rubbed his thumb across her lower lip. "Making amends with you."

Nora splayed her hands across his solid, muscular chest, holding him at bay. Not the least bit surprised to suddenly be so flustered. It happened every time they were together.

He'd come striding in and give her one of his "I can't get enough of you" looks, and she'd start feeling the same way. As if there were no one else on earth who was ever going to affect her the way he did. Excited. Enthralled. And ready for so much more. "Hey…" she chided softly, her heart already racing, as he held her flush against him, buried his face in her hair and breathed in, "I said we weren't going to make love again."

He moved closer still and her body registered the heat.

"At your place last night." He dropped a string of butterfly kisses from her temple to her cheekbone, the lobe of her ear and the nape of her neck.

As she felt the pounding of his heart, the depth of his desire, tingles swept through her. She melted against him, her insides fluttering even as she struggled to keep her feelings in check.

Grinning seductively, he slid his hands down her hips to cup her against him. Softness to hardness. "We didn't say anything about today…"

The turmoil inside her increased as his lips parted hers. Her knees went ever weaker. She jerked in another quick, bolstering breath, the kiss deepening, their warm breaths mingling. "Zane…"

Over and over his tongue plunged into her mouth, stroking and arousing. "I've missed you, Nora." His lips covered hers. He kissed her hotly, ardently. Until she kissed him back. Until her arms were wreathed about his neck and there was nothing but need and yearning, and more need…

He kissed her the way he always kissed her, slowly, purposefully, demanding everything she had to give. Until he wasn't just taking but giving. Inundating her with the heat of him, his masculine strength. Filling her heart and soul with everything she had ever yearned for. And still the clinch continued. His mouth moving expertly over hers, his arms wrapped tight around her, plastering their bodies together. And lower still, she felt the searing pressure of need. His, hers. And she gave herself over to the thrill of being loved by him once again. Then, finally, when she thought she could bear it no more, he lifted his head. Drew back. Said gruffly, "And the way you just kissed me back says you've missed me, too."

And then some, Nora thought, trembling.

"So why don't we give each other a little early Christmas gift and make love. Here," he rasped. "And now."

Nora knew all the reasons why she should say no. Zane was never going to put her ahead of his commitment to country. He didn't love her the way she needed to be loved. As if she—and now Liam—were his entire world. And given the fact that he was a soldier first and foremost, he probably never would.

But she did care very much about him. Always had and always would. And now that he was here with her again, wrapping his arms around her and holding her close, all she could think was she needed to make up for all those long, lonely days and nights. Needed to do something to assuage the ever-present fear that something would happen to him and she would never see or be with him again.

So, if that meant she threw caution to the wind once again and let him into her life for just a little while, then she would. She could worry about being sensible later. When he eventually left Texas again. As she knew, deep down in her soul, that he would.

Zane hadn't expected Nora to give in so easily, but he couldn't say he minded the enthusiasm she showed as they kissed their way through the downstairs of his A-frame and all the way up the stairs.

It had been a long time. Too long, since he'd had her in his arms. Too long since he'd felt the sweet give of her lips beneath his, or the soft swell of her breasts nestled against his chest. And it had definitely been too long since he had seen her naked.

Easing his hands beneath the hem, he lifted her sweater over her head. Her silky camisole top followed. Beneath the lace of her bra, her nipples jutted impudently. A familiar thrill soaring through him, he bent his head to kiss her again and rubbed his thumbs across the crests. His body tightened all the more as he felt her impatience and heard her moan, soft and low in her throat.

"You next," she insisted throatily. Unbuttoning his shirt, guiding it off, then tugging his T-shirt over his head, she caught her breath. "This is new." She kissed an angry red scar on his upper arm.

And the last time he'd be wounded while participating in a covert military mission, he wanted to promise her. But couldn't. Not just yet. Not and have her believe him. So instead, he admitted to the injury with a shrug, tugged off her boots, jeans, bra and panties, and tumbled her onto his bed.

Hand beneath her head, she struck a sexy pose. Grinned and watched him strip down, too. Aware they were probably moving way too fast—as usual—he joined her on the bed. Naked, too. "Now…where were we?" he murmured.

To his delight, she cupped him in her hand. "Right here, I think…"

Eager to please her, he shifted her onto her back and slid between her thighs. Kissing his way across her breast and belly, he mused playfully, "I think it might have been here…" Gasping, she clung to him. Determined to make it last, he caught her hips in his hands and went lower still.

"Oh, Zane..." she whispered, her response honest and passionate and uncompromising.

Driven by the same frantic need, he explored. Caressed. Loved. Until fire pooled in his groin. She quivered and arched her back. When she would have hurried the pace, he held back, making her understand what it was to feel such intense, incredible yearning.

Closing her eyes and fisting her hands in his hair, she gave herself over to him. His heart full, he savored the heat and taste and feel of her. The way she opened herself up to the moment and the passion they shared.

Suddenly, he wasn't the only one shuddering with pent-up need. Aware he'd never had more reason to proceed with care, he paused to find protection. Then, easing his hands beneath her, he lifted her, touching her with the tip of his manhood in the most intimate way. She arched against him, her mouth hungry, her soft breasts pressed against his chest. With a low moan, she wrapped her arms and legs around him, clasping him close, taking him into her, giving him everything he had ever wanted and ever needed.

She was all woman, and she was *all* his, Zane thought possessively, as they succumbed to the inevitable swirling bliss.

As Zane had expected, it didn't take long for the regrets to come. With the two of them, there were always regrets when the intensity of their passion faded and reality returned.

As their shudders faded, Nora extricated herself from beneath him and rolled onto her side, facing away from him.

He shifted onto his side, too. Moved in close enough

to spoon with her. And although she didn't move away, not yet, her slender body tensed.

Outside, it began to rain again, the precipitation slamming hard against the glass. The interior of his bedroom was shrouded in a wintry gloom not unlike her mood.

He ran a hand over the silky warm skin of her hip, lightly down the delicate line of her thigh. There was only one way they'd get close again.

"Tell me what's on your mind," he urged quietly.

Nora sighed, her gaze still on the view of the ranch outside the triangular-shaped floor-to-ceiling window. "I was just wondering if your father knew about us before he passed away." She bit her lip and briefly closed her eyes. "If that's why he gave you the property here, because he knew my family home—the one my mother, sister and I inherited from my grandparents—was here, too. And he thought…hoped…" Her voice trailed off sadly.

Zane fell silent, reluctantly reminiscing, too.

Nora had come with him to see his dad before his father died, five years ago. She and Zane had been off again at that moment, so they'd declared themselves just friends.

They hadn't really fooled anyone.

Even when he and Nora were off again, their feelings were always intense. Forbidden. Romantic.

Nora shifted to better see his face. Reluctantly, he admitted, "Dad and Mom both said you were the one for me, but they also knew you deserved better than what I was willing to give you."

Which, he admitted ruefully to himself, wasn't much, back then.

He forced himself to continue matter-of-factly, "So they understood completely why you wouldn't have wanted to actually date me."

She scoffed, as acutely aware as he that they hadn't ever bothered to formally court each other. Even when they were together, it was all about whatever moment they were in. Like now. Because they knew it could all end in a heartbeat. If just one thing during a mission went wrong. So they had just celebrated the rare moments they were together by staying up all night talking and tumbling in and out of bed.

The barriers around her heart went all the way up again. "Smart parents…"

He rolled her flat onto her back. Bent to kiss the curve of her shoulder. "Hey, it's not just my folks who disapprove of a liaison between us," he reminded her wryly. "Your mom doesn't like me, either."

Nora shrugged and wiggled out of his grasp before he could sideline their argument by making love to her all over again. Rising, she bent to snatch up her clothes. "That's because 'The General' doesn't want anything or anyone interfering with my military service."

Except Nora wasn't in the military right now.

Was she getting pressure to return? The way most valued members did?

Zane watched Nora pull on her panties, slip her bra over the sumptuous curves of her breasts. When she struggled to fit hook in eye, he rose and stepped behind her to fasten the clasp. Then he shrugged on his boxer briefs.

Curious, he asked, "What did your mom think about Liam, then?"

Nora went still.

Avoiding his gaze, she put on her sweater, then her jeans.

He pulled on his pants, too.

Finally, he guessed what her silence meant. "Are you serious? She didn't want you to adopt?"

Nora turned away and drew another deep breath. "It's complicated."

He moved closer, still buttoning his shirt. "Because you're single?"

Nora sat down on the edge of his bed to pull on her socks. "Because becoming Liam's mother cemented my decision to permanently leave the Army Nurse Corps."

He watched her stretch out her long lissome legs to pull on her boots. "Your mom does want you back in the military, then?"

Nora leaped to her feet and breezed past him. "She's career Army, Zane, a woman who spent her entire adult life rising to the rank of brigadier general." Swiftly, she descended the staircase, leaving him to follow. As she reached the first floor, she tossed the words over her shoulder, "So of course she wants me back in uniform, just like my sister, Davina! But it's not going to happen," she vowed heatedly.

"You're not going to continually leave your child to be deployed, the way your parents left you and your sister."

"No. I'm not," Nora said firmly. She plucked a brush out of her bag and ran it through her hair. Tilting her head, she met his probing glance and admitted thoughtfully, "That is the one thing 'The General' likes about you, though. Your dedication to service."

He sat down to pull on his own boots. "Somehow that doesn't sound like a compliment."

Nora shrugged. "In her view, it is."

But not yours, he thought, watching Nora cover her lips with gloss, then drop the tube back into her purse, too. Hands on her hips, she spun around, looking for her rain jacket. "As for what you should do with this ranch…"

He blocked her path to her coat. Lifted a brow. He might always be departing to serve his country, but she was always shutting down discussion whenever things got too intimate or intense.

"Deft change of subject," he drawled.

Ignoring his gentle rebuke, she lifted her chin and speared him with a testy gaze. "If you want to know the truth, I think my opinion is unnecessary, because you *already know* what your plan is regarding this ranch."

Damned if she didn't know him through and through.

"You're just not willing to share whatever that is with anyone yet."

Also true.

Color flooding her cheeks, she blew out a frustrated breath. "But it should be whatever *you* want, long-term, Zane, not what *your family* desires."

On that much they totally agreed. He promised her gravely, "It will be."

"Oh, and for the record…" Still looking deliciously tousled, she waved an airy hand toward the bedroom. "I'm not sure what this was just now, except for more reckless behavior on my part." She stepped closer, her hands fisted at her sides. "But I am certain about one thing."

"And what's that?" he countered gruffly, feeling another exit speech coming.

Her lower lip trembling, she announced with a great

deal of wariness, "I can't do this with you again, Zane. This whole bit where I feel like we're really starting to become a couple, only to discover that nothing has really changed, after all."

He knew that, too. "I've already told my commanding officer that I'm not reenlisting. When my tour is over January 15, I'm out."

She surmised sadly, "But between now and then, you'll have to go back."

He helped her put on her rain jacket. "On December 27, yeah, I will have to rejoin my unit. But only for a couple of weeks."

Nora stiffened. "So you say now."

He caught her wrist before she could bolt. "I mean it now, Nora."

Hurt shimmering in her eyes, she pulled away. "You meant it four years ago, too, when you told me you were resigning your commission."

Her icy rebuke stung.

He followed her out onto the porch, where the rain was coming down hard. Grimly reminded her, "You know what it was like back then. The danger a lot of our troops and diplomats were in!"

Oblivious to the pouring rain, she shook her head. Sighed sadly. "There will always be turmoil somewhere in the world. Always someone in need of rescue, Zane."

Frustration churning through him, he folded his arms in front of him. "Why won't you believe me?" She had to know he had never lied to her. Never pretended to want or need anything he didn't.

Looking as piqued as he felt, Nora took a deep breath and tilted her face up to his. "Because, Zane, if I know anything, it's that duty-driven soldiers like you never change." Her soft lips thrust out stubbornly. "If they did—" she paused to look him in the eye and let her harsh words sink in "—Liam wouldn't be my son. He'd still be my *nephew*."

Chapter 5

Zane blinked in surprise. "What the hell are you talking about?"

Nora passed a hand over her eyes. What was it about this man that had her spilling her guts every chance she got? Especially when she had sworn to keep the circumstances surrounding Liam's birth private!

She slumped against the porch railing, knees weak, hands clamped tightly on either side of her. "My sister, Davina, is Liam's biological mother."

Zane took her by the hand and led her back inside his house. The next thing she knew he was taking off her coat and leading her over to the sofa. Sitting next to her, he wrapped an arm about her shoulders and clarified with gentle astonishment, "And your sister gave him over to you to raise?"

Nora nodded. "Yes." It was a relief to finally talk about this with someone outside her family.

"But why?"

"Because Davina couldn't bear to leave the Army."

Zane stood and went over to light the fire in the grate. "She could have remained a military linguist and still been a mother."

"True." Nora watched the logs flame. "But she wouldn't have been able to sign up for the extremely demanding assignments she favors. Not with a clear conscience, anyway."

Zane replaced the screen, then came back to her. "What about Liam's biological father?"

"He's in military intelligence. And was no more interested in becoming a parent or leaving the military than Davina was, but they both knew I wanted a family." She sighed. "So they asked me if I was interested in adopting. Otherwise, they were going to give the baby over to a private agency, right after birth, and let them find loving parents and a good home."

Zane walked into the kitchen, returned with two fresh cups of coffee. "So you said yes."

Noting he'd added just the right amount of flavored creamer to hers, Nora took a long, enervating draught, let the beverage warm her from the inside out. "Not right away. To tell you the truth, I kept thinking my sister would change her mind. Especially when she was confronted with the reality of meeting her newborn infant for the first time. In any case, she stayed at a friend's place in Pittsburgh during the last four months, while she was on medical leave, and I flew up to be with her when she gave birth to Liam."

Sensing—correctly—that Nora needed her physical space, Zane lounged against the mantel. "Your mom?"

Restless, she stood, too. "Was in meetings in South Korea at the time."

Zane watched her pace to the windows. "So 'The General' didn't come back?"

Nora swung to face him and took another sip. "She Skyped with us. Met her new grandson that way. And told us both we were doing the right thing."

Zane gave her a bluntly assessing look. "Davina wasn't upset by your mother's absence?"

Strangely, no. Nora shrugged and with a great deal of effort met Zane's penetrating gaze. "She didn't want to make a big deal over Liam's birth, either. Although they were both happy for me."

"And that was it? Davina didn't have any second thoughts? Then or since?"

The unselfish part of Nora only *wished*. "She loves him like a distant aunt. That's all. Davina's real passion is for her work with the Army, just like my mom. Everything else pales in comparison."

Zane ambled over to join her at the window. Gently caressed her cheek, then said philosophically, "Sounds like Liam may have dodged a bullet, then. 'Cause it's clear you adore him."

At the mention of her son, Nora's heart filled with love. "I do."

"I can see why." Zane's lips curved into an empathetic smile. "He's a really cute little fella."

Another silence fell and they walked back into the kitchen. Zane offered Nora more coffee. Declining, she drained her mug and put it in the sink. He set his mug next to the coffeemaker.

"What was your mom's reaction to becoming a

grandmother?" He was standing so close she could feel the heat emanating from his powerful body.

Nora shrugged, doing her best to hide her deep disappointment about this, too.

She couldn't help but compare her every-woman-for-herself family to Zane's much more close-knit brood. To her consternation, he seemed to be doing the same.

"As usual," she replied, standing with her back to the counter, her arms clamped in front of her, "The General was more concerned about the *logistics* of care than the emotions involved." She sighed wearily. "From the first, she wanted to ensure that our duty and responsibility to the new life was met. A solution found that would best suit all of us."

Zane regarded her sympathetically.

Aware he was going to be very hard to resist if he kept caring for her this way, Nora replied matter-of-factly, "It was actually her idea that I take over the familial obligation and raise Liam myself."

He moved closer still and lounged next to her. "Like your grandparents brought up you and your sister in your parents' absence."

Nora nodded, aware that although she had never lacked for love from her mother's parents, she had acutely missed the day-to-day attention of her own.

His expression turning even more serious, Zane pivoted to better see her face. "And Davina was on board with that idea, too?"

Nora nodded, lifting her chin to meet his empathetic gaze. "She was the one who wanted to take it a step further, make it official and have me actually *adopt* Liam."

Zane did not appear surprised by any of this. Maybe because he knew both her sister and mother, and how unmaternal they both were. He walked over to pour himself the very last of the coffee. "So Davina would be clear of any future parental responsibility?"

Reluctantly, Nora admitted, "That, plus Davina knew how hard it was for us kids, having parents who chose active duty over us, year after year after year. Even when Dad died in that training accident, when we were in our teens, Mom refused to request in-country assignments. She was on track to be brigadier general. And nothing was going to stand in her way of achieving her goal."

Nora fought the tide of emotion rising inside.

Swallowing hard, she forced herself to continue, "The General envisions the same bright future for Davina, if she stays on track. And my sister intends to do just that. Now that this 'blip' in her rise to success has been dealt with, anyway."

Zane's gaze narrowed, his expression grave. "Is any of this common knowledge?"

"No. Davina and my mother were both afraid if word got out, some of her fellow soldiers would think less of her, and it would hurt her chance for promotion, and garnering the plum assignments she has come to really enjoy."

"Like being the assigned interpreter for some of the top brass, overseas?"

Her breath hitched in her throat. "Right."

Zane leaned over to put his empty mug in the sink, next to hers, his broad shoulder brushing hers in the process. "And you agreed with this part of the plan, too?"

That was much harder to quantify.

Noting the rain was diminishing once again, Nora confessed, "I want to protect Liam. Make sure he feels safe and loved and wanted and has the kind of good, stable home every child deserves."

He straightened slowly, his big body blocking any easy exit she might have made. "Are you ever going to tell him the truth?"

Nora raked her teeth across her lower lip, shivering as Zane tracked the movement. "When he is a lot older, if need be. If, on the other hand—" *as I really hope* "—Liam demonstrates no curiosity about what his biological origins were, then…" She let her voice trail off.

Zane clamped a hand on the counter on either side of her. His expression turning even more brooding, he said, "Okay, I get why you did what you did for the little guy, even if you've put yourself at risk for tremendous heartache down the road."

Nora stiffened, wanting to deny the potential for hurt was there. She couldn't—not in good conscience, anyway. So she met his gaze, aware her emotions still felt pretty raw. "If you're worried the adoption won't become final in three months…"

Apparently, he was.

With a short exhalation of breath, she flattened a hand over the center of his chest and slipped out of the cage of his arms. "You needn't be. Davina is not going to say one thing only to later do another."

Zane shot her another intuitive glance. "Why do I suddenly think you're comparing me to your sister?" he asked, deadpan.

Maybe because she was?

He waited. Expecting—no, *demanding*—she explain what she was thinking and feeling.

Deciding far too much soul-baring had been done for one day, however, Nora went in search of her coat and bag once again. "Look, I get it, Zane," she said over her shoulder. Then she swung back to face him.

"I've even felt a tiny fraction of what you and my mother and my sister and a whole host of other soldiers feel about putting your service to your country above all else. Including family. And it's admirable, I know." Aware she was suddenly on the verge of tears again, she shrugged on her rain jacket, lifting her hair out of the collar, then zipped it up. "Because without people like you the world would be a much less safe place for the rest of us."

Once again, he saw far more of what she was thinking and feeling than she would have wished.

Shoulders stiff with tension, Zane walked her to the foyer. "Except you'd never turn your back on loved ones in order to go off and rescue someone else."

She opened the door, then paused in the portal. With difficulty, she met his probing gaze. "I'm not sure I'd put it quite that way," she returned. "But you are right. Now that I have a son I love more than life, I couldn't leave him behind for weeks and months at a time for any endeavor, no matter how noble."

She paused to let her words sink in. Ignoring the telltale wrench of her heart, she added resolutely, "Liam has to come first. Ahead of my work. My duty to others. And most definitely my personal life, Zane."

He studied her with a look that was maddeningly inscrutable. Finally, he palmed his chest. "So where does that leave us?" he asked gruffly.

Nora drew a deep breath, her emotions in complete turmoil once again.

If only Zane were going to be around for more than a few weeks. But he wasn't, so...

She threw up her hands in dismay. "I don't know, Zane. I'm going to have to think about it."

"So what do you think, Liam?" Nora cooed late Saturday morning, as she situated her son in his stroller, a short distance away from the driveway.

The previous day's torrential rain had left the Texas skies sunny and clear and briskly cold.

"Are you ready to see Mommy take our Christmas tree off the roof of our car?"

All bundled up, Liam gurgled happily.

"Then here we go!" Nora said.

The only problem was that the twine the lot attendant had secured it with was awfully tight. So tight, it was hard to get the utility scissors between the metal and pine. But finally she managed and with a sigh of relief, grabbed on to one of the thick branches and gave the tree a tug. It didn't budge at all.

She turned to see what her son was doing. He had his head tilted to one side, a cloth-covered rattle clutched in one hand. "I'll get it," she promised cheerfully.

Figuring it might go easier if she snipped the twine on the other side, too, Nora walked around. Cut again. To no avail.

The big tree still wouldn't budge from the center of her minivan roof.

"Need a hand there, darlin'?" The deep masculine voice sent a thrill up her spine.

Nora turned to see Zane jogging up the sidewalk toward her.

It wasn't surprising he was out for a run. Active duty military worked out daily. Nor was she surprised that he was on her street. He could run up and down every avenue, business or residential, in the town limits and still barely get in his usual six miles. What was disconcerting, however, was just how happy she was to see him. They'd only been apart twenty-four hours, yet it felt like so much longer.

Especially because they'd left things so up in the air.

He squinted, grinning, awaiting a response.

Embarrassed not to be able to handle this chore by herself after all, she came back around to see Liam, who was still watching patiently. Then she decided, why look a gift horse in the mouth? "Sure," she told him, "if you think you can get it down."

He reached over the minivan roof. Tall enough to grasp the center of the evergreen, he lifted it up and over and down, standing it upright. It was a foot and a half taller than his six foot three inches and almost twice as wide among the lower branches as his extended arm.

He gave it an admiring glance. "Nice tree."

As well as a fair sight bigger than she'd realized. But that was okay, she thought, since her home had high ceilings.

His gaze drifted fondly over her. "Do you have a stand for it?"

Nora felt an answering warmth. "Inside."

"I'll carry it in for you."

The assumption she couldn't handle that, either, rankled almost as much as her ever-resurging feelings for him. She wanted to be friends with him, at the very least, but she wasn't sure she could limit it to that. And that could mean trouble. For both of them. "I've got it," she announced cavalierly.

He lifted a brow. "Sure?"

Reminding herself she had decided to take a time-out

to decide what kind of relationship they should have in the future, she nodded and grabbed hold of the middle of the tree. He made sure she had it, then let go.

The weight of it sent her reeling backward.

He caught it with one hand, her waist with the other, then flashed the kind of wolfish grin that said he always knew best. "Why don't you let me give you a hand?" he asked quietly.

Figuring the fastest way to have him on his merry way was to acquiesce, Nora drew a deep breath. "Thank you." Spine stiff, she extricated herself from his protective grip. Taking hold of Liam's stroller, she led the way to the door and put her baby boy inside, in the corner of the living room, well out of harm's way. Then went back to hold the door for Zane.

He carried the tree in and over to the stand.

Short minutes later, it was upright and secured into the bottom of the base. Unfortunately, it practically scraped the ceiling with its height. And was clearly bigger and fuller on one side than the other. Flushing, Nora turned the evergreen one way, then the other. To no avail. It still looked almost-comically lopsided.

Grooves deepened on either side of his mouth. "You could put it in a corner with the skimpy side hidden from view," he suggested. "That's what my mom always does."

"Lucille has this problem?" Hard to imagine. His mother was so elegant, so pulled together. Competent in all the cozy nesting ways her own mother was not.

"You can never really tell what you're getting on the lot, with all the trees bunched together like that. That's what makes it fun." Zane moved the tree around. "See?" He pushed it back. "It looks fine now."

Surprisingly, it did. If you didn't look too closely, that was.

From his stroller, Liam kicked his feet and gurgled happily, albeit a little impatiently.

Aware what was really important was finding a way to embrace the Christmas spirit and do everything in her power to make her son happy, she turned back to Zane.

Perhaps their next step was to simply try and be friends… "Want to stay and help us decorate it?" she asked impulsively.

Regret flashed in his eyes. "Love to." He hunkered down to fondly brush her son's cheek. "Just can't do it today. Which is why I came by."

He straightened to his full height, his tall, physically fit frame towering over her more petite one. He regarded her for a long careful moment.

"I need to talk to you about the gift baskets for soldiers."

"Okay." Nora ignored the sudden racing of her pulse.

"Miss Mim and the others wanted to help with that, but if the presents are going to make the next transport, the Army needs them by Monday noon. So we're going to have to get them all put together tomorrow afternoon. Is that going to be doable on your end?"

"Sure," she replied, knowing there was nothing her senior patients liked more than still feeling needed. Working to hide her disappointment she and Zane wouldn't be spending any more time together today, she moved close enough to inhale the lingering woodsy scent of his aftershave. "How many gift baskets are we talking about?"

"West Texas Warriors Assistance has pledged to provide ten thousand."

Nora staggered dramatically backward, a hand to her heart. Zane laughed, as she meant him to.

"Not to worry." He grasped her wrist lightly and reeled her back to his side. "We've got four churches, three civic organizations and a big group of high school students working, too. So if Laramie Gardens can't handle their allotment of a thousand," he said, letting her go once again, "some of the other organizations can pick up the slack."

Oblivious to the way her skin was still tingling from his touch, Zane sobered. "Just let me know what to expect, so I can make sure the supplies are all where they should be by the time we get started."

She nodded, doing her best to concentrate on the requisite logistics instead of the ruggedly handsome man opposite her. "I think we can do it." Nora walked over to get her son out of the stroller. "When will you be bringing the stuff by?"

"Just before we get started tomorrow. I'm heading to Dallas and Fort Worth with my brothers and a few other WTWA volunteers shortly to pick up a lot of the donated materials."

Once again, she had to work to hide her disappointment. She tore her eyes from the sinewy contours of his chest. "Then Liam and I won't keep you," she promised.

Even if she, at least, really wanted to. Even if he had only twenty-seven days of leave left.

Not, she reassured herself firmly, that she was counting.

Chapter 6

"Okay, does everyone understand what we're doing?" Zane asked the one hundred seniors assembled in the Laramie Gardens dining hall, the next afternoon. "Everyone has five baskets in front of them, and some sheets of red tissue paper that you can use to line the bottom."

He turned to Nora and waited for her to demonstrate. Trying not to notice how sexy he looked—both in and out of uniform—she did.

"While you're all doing that, we'll come around and pass out the items that go in the baskets." He walked over to hand her the items. "Then we'll put the holiday cards the elementary school kids made for the soldiers on top of that." Their hands brushed as he gave her one. "And wrap the baskets."

Intoxicated by his genial, take-charge nature, Nora

again showed the seniors how to proceed. Securing the cellophane overwrap with a snap-on bow.

Smiling, Zane turned his attention back to the crowd. "Once we finish the toiletries gift baskets, we'll start on the food ones and use the same process. Okay?"

Resident Kurtis Kelley cupped his hand around his mouth. "We got it, Lieutenant! So get moving already!"

Everyone laughed.

Zane took a pushcart. The younger volunteers he'd brought with him to help out—mostly ex-soldiers and their wives or husbands—followed. Nora took up the rear.

Perhaps because it was so well organized, the process went remarkably fast. Three hours later, each senior had put together ten gift baskets. The younger volunteers put them in shipping boxes, which would then be loaded onto trucks.

Yet few seemed ready to disperse as they filtered out into the community room while dinner was being set up by the kitchen staff. Nora didn't want to leave, either, with Zane still there. So she retrieved Liam—who was still sleeping soundly in his stroller—from his sitter and returned to find the handsome soldier standing next to the fireplace, holding court.

"So tell us, Lieutenant, did you always want to be in the Special Forces?" Miss Sadie asked.

Interested in the answer, too, Nora parked the stroller in a distant corner of the room and took a seat next to her son.

Zane lounged against the mantel and shot her a surprisingly intimate look, which caused her to blush in return. "I definitely wanted to do something adventurous."

"Because your grandfather was career military?" Miss Mim pressed.

Several people turned to see what had so thoroughly captured Zane's attention.

He let his gaze drift over Nora one last time, before turning back to the crowd. "That, and the fact I had so many conditions put on me while I was growing up. For example—" one half of his sensual lips crooked up ruefully "—I was permitted to jump out of an airplane, but only once, on my eighteenth birthday, and only with a skydiving instructor of my parents' choosing. After much instruction."

Miss Patricia scoffed. "Sounds kind of reasonable."

Zane frowned, the way he always did when he felt boxed in. "From their point of view, maybe. Not mine. By the time I was sixteen, I was already visiting a recruiter."

Nora remembered. Even as a kid, Zane had been determined to one day be the kind of person who made a real difference in this world. He still was, she thought admiringly.

"The sergeant took one look at my grades and convinced me I had what it took to be in the officer corps and lined me up with a ROTC scholarship at the college of my choice, which happened to be the University of Hawaii Warrior Battalion."

Grins all around. Kurtis Kelley mimed the hula. "Because of all the pretty island girls?"

Nora rolled her eyes, recalling how jealous she had been then. For no reason, it had turned out. Zane only had eyes for her, and she him.

"Well…" Zane drawled with a flirtatious wink that had the ladies tittering. "That, and it seemed like one of the most challenging programs to get into and graduate from. And I thought it might be fun to learn to surf while I was in college."

Everyone chuckled again.

Moving to stand closer to Nora, Zane related casually, "And then of course, once I was in, I had to go for the maximum challenge, the Special Forces."

The former town librarian, who'd known them both as kids, looked from Nora to Zane. "Any regrets?" she asked him.

Getting Miss Mim's point, Zane's eyes briefly met Nora's. He knelt down to protectively survey the sleeping Liam. "Not about my chosen career, no."

Silence fell.

She had the feeling Zane was about to ask if she needed any help getting Liam home, when the vivacious and no-nonsense Betty Blair asked, "Nora, why did you go into the Army Nurse Corps?"

"To please my mother and honor my late father."

"And...?" Miss Sadie pressed.

Nora shrugged. Determined to lighten the mood, she quipped, "Ah...take care of the men who love danger?"

Everyone laughed again.

"How come you didn't marry one of them while you were in the corps?" Kurtis Kelley asked.

Dear Lord, how had they gotten into this? "It's complicated," she said, squirming uncomfortably.

Zane tilted his head to one side, amusement curving his lips. He aimed a thumb at the center of his chest. "I'd like to hear more," he said, a wickedly sexy gleam in his dark silver eyes.

Not surprisingly, from the women in the room, there were swoons all around.

Figuring if she didn't put a stop to the matchmaking now, they'd be producing strands of mistletoe at any minute, Nora drew a breath and set everyone straight. "The truth is, I've never wanted to date anyone who was actively serving in the military, because I grew up with two parents who were always deployed, and I don't like being left behind all the time."

The quizzical regard in the room deepened.

"I find it difficult to believe a woman like you didn't revere your fellow soldiers' commitment to country, honor and duty," Buck Franklin scolded.

That was the hell of it.

Nora nodded, accepting the criticism. "The noble part of me did value that then, and I still do." She turned to look at Zane, wanting him to understand this much, even if it hurt his opinion of her.

"It was the selfish side of me that felt abandoned and distraught every time someone I cared about was deployed. And believe me—" she held up a staying hand, confessing, even as guilt racked her soul "—I know that's wrong. And that in turn makes me feel like I've hurt and betrayed them way more than they've ever hurt me by leaving."

There was a murmur of understanding from the women in the room. The men, however, seemed to struggle with her candid revelations.

Turning away from Zane, and the sharp rebuke in his expression, Nora pushed on, "Plus, I knew those kinds of emotions weren't something any couple could build a life on. So I tended not to go there in the first place."

Or at least she had *tried* not to go there.

Zane had managed to cut through her barriers time after time after time.

Often to their mutual regret.

Which was why they had been off-again as much as they had been on-again.

"Surely, some of the men must have asked you out anyway," the hopelessly romantic Miss Sadie persisted.

All eyes turned expectantly to Zane.

"I won't say she wasn't chased. And chased with enthusiasm." Zane comically waggled his brows. "But she was hard to get."

Recalling exactly what he was talking about, Nora flushed.

"I bet you could have won her over if you tried," Betty Blair insisted.

Zane shrugged and reached out to affectionately pat Nora's shoulder. "Actually," he conceded playfully, to all, "I'm still trying."

"Why did you have to say that in there?" Nora chided, the moment they retired to her office.

Zane shrugged, refusing to apologize for publicly staking his claim on her. "First, it's true." Hands shoved in the pockets of his jeans, he ambled closer. "Second, everybody here knows I have a thing for you. And vice versa."

Her heart skittering in her chest, Nora drew in another whiff of his tantalizing aftershave. "How could they know that?" she demanded as she set the brake on the stroller.

He flashed a mischievous grin. "The way you look at me and the way I look at you."

Heavens! Nora knelt down to remove her son from his stroller. She handed Liam to Zane to hold, then went to get the diaper bag. She moved to set up a changing pad on the love seat. "You are incorrigible—you know that?"

Zane pressed his cheek against the top of Liam's downy soft head. "This little guy doesn't seem to think so."

The sight of her son cuddling contently against Zane's broad chest generated a wave of warmth.

"You're right," she admitted softly, watching Liam gaze adoringly up at the lieutenant. And Zane return the affection tenfold.

If only the two had been father and son! How wonderful would that be?

But they weren't, so...

It was time she came back to Earth.

Nora cleared her throat. Fresh diaper out and ready, she reached for her son.

As Zane carefully handed him over, Nora looked into his eyes, serious now. "Thank you for involving our residents in the charity work today. It really helps them to feel needed and appreciated."

He lingered close by while she changed her son. "It was my pleasure. So what next? When do you get off work?"

"Two and a half hours ago," Nora admitted ruefully, putting her baby boy in his fleece jacket and matching powder blue cap.

Although she could have left, she'd wanted to stay and lend a helping hand with Zane's charity project, too.

He sent her an admiring glance. "Got any plans for dinner?"

"Not yet." Nora stood and handed off Liam once again, so she could put her own coat on. "I'll figure something out after I get this little guy fed and in bed."

He shifted his gaze to her lips. "Want to figure something out together?"

She felt herself floundering. "Um… I can't go out tonight."

He came closer. "I'll bring something in."

The idea of not having to cook was almost as irresistible as the notion of spending the evening with him. Yet there were inherent dangers in doing so, too.

She could fall for him all over again.

Be tempted into making love with him again.

Thereby paving the way for even more brokenheartedness than they had already suffered at each other's hands.

They could also become strictly platonic friends.

Learning how to enjoy each other's company without passionate complications.

The amorous look on his face indicated that was a long shot.

She grinned and shook her head. "You are persistent."

He winked flirtatiously. "And you're resistant."

Nora groaned at his play on words.

Brushing the back of his hand across her cheek, he bent to kiss the top of her head. "That doesn't mean we can't have a good time together, sharing a meal."

He seemed serious now, in the way that meant he wanted the two of them to get closer. The heck of it was she wanted that, too.

Zane held the door for her. He accompanied her and Liam as they walked through the foyer and out into the fading light. "So is that a yes, or a maybe, or a…?" His voice cut off abruptly.

Nora paused at what they saw, too. Mr. Pierce wandering through the cars, before stopping next to her minivan, one hand on his thinning silver hair, the other rested on his waist. To her dismay, the older gentleman wasn't wearing his leather jacket or his fedora. He also looked perplexed, and then some.

"Problem?" Zane guessed.

"I don't know." She handed her son over to him. "Would you mind coming with me, just in case…?"

"Sure."

"Hi, Mr. Pierce!"

The older gentleman turned. "Nurse Nora!"

Nora sighed with relief. Thank goodness he knew who she was! She strode cheerfully toward him. "What are you doing out here?"

"Actually—" Russell Pierce massaged the back of his neck thoughtfully, watching as she removed her car keys from the outside zipper pocket on her bag "—I'm not sure. I know I came out here for something… I just can't recall what."

"That happens to me all the time," she said lightly. With the keypad, she electronically unlocked and opened up the side door.

She paused to put her purse and Liam's diaper bag inside the cargo area. "I run up the stairs at home looking for something, then get up there and can't for the life of me recall what I was going to get and run back down the stairs, only to remember what I was going to get."

Mr. Pierce chuckled.

Zane chimed in, "I think it happens to all of us."

"I imagine so." Mr. Pierce turned back to her vehicle and ran his hand over the gleaming red surface. "Is this your minivan?"

"Yes, it is."

"It's a beauty. Esther and I had one just like it. We got it a couple of years before she passed." He paused affectionately, reminiscing, "She used to really love driving it, and so did I."

"I can see why." Nora and Zane both smiled. "I love mine, too." Aware the elderly resident was shivering without his coat, she slipped her arm through his.

"I still can't figure out why I came outside, though," he said, perturbed.

Nora patted his arm gently. "I'm sure it will come to you later. The way it always does me. Usually when I least expect it!"

They all chuckled.

She regarded Mr. Pierce intently. "In the meantime, they've started serving dinner in the dining hall. And I know you don't want to miss that."

"No, I do not," Russell Pierce said with enthusiasm. "Fried chicken, isn't it?"

"With all the trimmings. Is it okay if I walk in with you?" Nora asked, still holding on to his arm. "I think I left something in my office."

She handed her minivan keys over to Zane, suggesting cheerfully, "If you want to get the heater running…"

He nodded at her, looking completely natural with her baby boy in his arms. "No problem."

By the time she returned, Zane had Liam strapped into his car seat, the minivan snug and warm. Her son had Zane's little finger clasped tight in his little fist and was staring up at him adoringly, as Zane sat next to him in the back seat and sang "Santa Claus Is Coming To Town" in a soft mellow baritone.

She opened the driver side and stuck her head in. "Hey, thanks for doing this."

Reluctantly, he disentangled his hand from Liam's, and stepped out of the rear passenger seat. "Glad to help out." He waited as she climbed behind the wheel. "Mr. Pierce okay?"

"He is." Loving the way she could always count on Zane to help out, whenever he was needed, she asked, "So, did you still want to do dinner?" After that false alarm, and the even-longer day, she could use the company.

He looked over at her, as protective as ever. "As long as you let me provide it."

Nora exhaled. Sometimes it was good to be taken care of. Especially by an incredibly kind and sexy man. And it was Christmas, after all.

The season for giving. And taking. And giving…

"You're not going to get any argument there."

His gaze swept over her, lingering briefly on her lips before returning to her eyes. "Meet you in an hour, then?"

"Sounds good." *Really good*, she thought, as another spiral of heat swept through her.

Attempting to keep her mind on the mundane, instead of the sizzling chemistry between them, she asked, "What are we having?"

He flashed a mysterious smile. "That, Nurse Nora, is a surprise."

Nora had just gotten Liam to sleep and into bed for the night when the doorbell rang. She walked back downstairs.

Wishing she'd had time to change, spruce up her hair. Something. But then that would have made it feel like a date, and it wasn't a date. It was just dinner between two old friends.

She opened the door.

Zane strode in, dressed as he had been before, in a crew neck sweater and jeans, a large take-out bag from the Dairy Barn in his arms. She gazed at him, refusing to be taken in by the blatant desire in his gaze. "You didn't..."

His grin widened. "Our favorite craving when we were overseas."

She set the bag on the dining room table and pulled out the various containers with all the delighted surprise of a kid on Christmas morning. "Chili dogs, root beer and onion rings."

"And dark-chocolate peppermint ice cream!"

Wow.

"I gather you're pleased?"

Was this what it would be like to be taken care of by him, all the time? "Very."

Her heart fluttering in her chest, she stashed the ice cream in the freezer and got out the plates and utensils. He looked so darn good here.

So right.

Together, they loaded their plates with hot, fresh food. "What do you think they put in their chili anyway, that makes it so damned good?" Zane asked, as they began to eat.

Nora shook her head. She was no slouch in the kitchen, thanks to the many lessons her grandmother had given her when she was growing up. Zane was pretty competent, too. But the recipe for this stymied them both.

She savored the spicy, cheesy goodness. The crisp

crunch of an onion ring. "No clue." She met his intent gaze and smiled. "All I know is that no matter how we tried to duplicate it when we were deployed overseas we could never really get close. It was always missing something."

He nodded, looking relaxed. Happy. Powerfully masculine… "I remember."

Nora remembered, too. So much. Their happy reunions. The worry she'd had whenever he had been hurt on a mission. The joy they'd experienced when they were together. The heartbreak and loneliness they'd felt when they were apart.

She wasn't sure she could go back to that kind of topsy-turvy life. But the truth was, Zane filled up her heart and her soul the way no one else ever had. Or ever would.

And much as she might want to discount that, she couldn't.

Gratitude for all he'd done for her that day increasing even more, she rose to clear the table. "Thank you. This really hit the spot."

He moved to help her, his gaze moving over her lingeringly, as if he were already mentally ending this evening by making love to her. "What can I say?" he drawled, as he joined her at the sink. "I aim to please."

Her phone rang. The caller ID said Laramie Gardens. "I'm sorry… I have to take this." She picked it up to answer, but to her dismay, the report was not good. "You're sure you can handle it?" she asked the night supervisor. "Call me if you need my help. Thanks."

"Problem with Mr. Pierce again?" Zane asked when she joined him at the sink.

"No." Nora bent to put their dishes in the dishwasher.

"He's fine. Another resident just got news her daughter's family is not going to be able to be with her for Christmas or New Year's this year—they are going to see the son-in-law's parents." She sighed, her heart going out to the wonderful senior citizen. "So she's very upset."

She grabbed two spoons and the container of ice cream from the freezer and headed into the living room.

Zane settled beside her on the sofa. "I guess in that situation you have to take turns."

Nora sat close enough to share, her thigh nudging Zane's. "I think Miss Isabelle would be fine with having them with her every other year." She worked off the lid and offered him first dibs. "But they never spend any of the holidays with her. It's always his folks. And since her husband died last year, they are the only family she has left."

Zane used his own spoon to offer her the first bite. "Not nice."

The decadent treat melted on Nora's tongue. "No," she sighed, offering Zane a taste from her spoon, too. "It's not."

Their eyes met. Held.

Zane fed Nora another bite. "I don't suppose you could interfere?"

Aware they hadn't done this since the last time they were together, Nora did the same.

"No," she said. "Much as I'd like to call Miss Isabelle's daughter and give her a piece of my mind, I can't. Not that it would do any good." She shrugged unhappily. "From what I've observed in situations like this one, the kindest souls are always the ones who lose out."

Zane regarded her steadily, no more willing to give

up on this than he was on the two of them. "Is there anything I can do to help?" he asked softly.

"Well…" Nora paused, smiling as her next idea hit. "Now that you mention it…maybe there is!"

Chapter 7

"Adopt a grandparent?" Miss Isabelle repeated in consternation late Tuesday afternoon.

While Nora watched, Zane stood in the doorway of the elegant older woman's suite and explained, "I've been tapped to do some kid sitting for my nephew Braden after school today while his parents do some Christmas shopping. I also promised Nora I'd help her get the garlands hung around the community room, so… since Braden likes to draw and color, and you used to teach art at the local high school, I thought maybe you could help us out a little?"

Twin spots of color glowed in the older woman's cheeks. "Just for today," Miss Isabelle clarified anxiously.

"Actually, if it goes well," Nora cut in, "it might become a new volunteer program at Laramie Gardens for anyone who's interested."

"And this is because you two feel sorry for me?" Miss Isabelle asked pertly. "Because I won't have any family with me at Christmas?"

Never one to run from potential conflict, Zane looked Miss Isabelle square in the eye. "I've been in the military ten years. In that time, counting right now, I've only been able to be with my family for four of the Christmas holidays."

And he and Nora had never been together on Christmas Eve or Christmas Day, she thought sadly.

Until this year.

This year held potential.

"So, yeah," Zane admitted candidly, running a thoughtful hand across his jaw, "I know that being separated from loved ones this time of year totally sucks. And in that sense, I'll admit it. I do feel for you."

Miss Isabelle arched an elegant brow in Nora's direction.

"My parents were in the Army and were seldom home for holidays, too," Nora put in with a commiserating glance. "It hasn't gotten much better since I've grown up."

Zane folded his arms in front of his chest and continued, "But we also know that there are a lot of kids who—for a variety of reasons—are in similar straits. So, if we can pair the older with the younger and expand everyone's sense of family and make them all happy, why not?"

Why not indeed? "And if you're willing to be the test case for the proposed program…?" Nora began.

"How old is your nephew?" Miss Isabelle cut in.

Zane smiled fondly and walked over to show Miss Isabella a picture. "Braden just turned six. And though he's lucky enough to have plenty of family, he's also got a six-month-old baby brother..."

Miss Isabelle smiled knowingly. "So in other words, he's now having to *share* the spotlight."

"And though Braden loves Josh a lot, I think he could do with a little special attention."

"But," Nora put in, holding up a palm, lest they get ahead of themselves, "if you don't feel up to it, Miss Isabelle, or choose not to participate at this time, we both understand. We don't want you to feel pressured."

The former art teacher stiffened indignantly. "Of course I want to meet this adorable young man!" She handed the photo back to Zane. "When did you say he would be here?"

Zane looked at his watch. "Thirty minutes."

Miss Isabelle rose. "Then I better get ready."

Zane and Nora thanked her. Together, they exited the room and walked companionably down the hall, toward her office. "Good job," she told him.

He slid a hand beneath her elbow, then used the leverage to stop her in her tracks and turn her toward him. "It was your idea."

She reveled in their brief moment of privacy. "You sold it."

He leaned down to whisper in her ear. "*We* sold it."

Nora sucked in a breath. "Now, if only all our problems were that easy to solve," she said.

Zane exhaled, the weight of the world suddenly in his eyes. "No kidding," he said.

"You two make a really good team," Miss Mim complimented Zane and Nora an hour later.

Having promised a group of seniors she would let

them all have a turn cuddling Liam, before she left for the day, Nora settled her son in Miss Mim's arms. Zane, who'd been regaling some of the men with his exploits, hovered nearby. He turned, showing none of the worry he had briefly evidenced earlier. With a charming grin, he asked, "In what way?"

Nora could think of lots of ways.

At work.

At home.

In bed.

Betty Blair nodded discreetly in the direction of one of the craft tables. "You got Miss Isabelle to come out of her suite and smile again."

Nora and Zane turned. Evidently as pleased as she was to see that Miss Isabelle and Braden were still chatting and coloring diligently, Zane lifted a staying hand. "Don't credit me for that. The proposed program had been on Nora's mind for a while now."

"But you made it happen, Lieutenant," Miss Sadie said.

That he had, Nora thought with glowing admiration.

With all she had on her agenda during the holidays, she likely wouldn't have had the time or opportunity to do anything like this until after the New Year.

"Nora, dear," Miss Patricia pleaded, "give the poor fella another chance."

The group of seniors around them nodded, in full matchmaking agreement.

Buck Franklin winked flirtatiously. "If I were another forty years younger, I'd give you a run for your money, soldier."

Nora blushed at all the attention while Zane chuckled. "Good thing you're not, then," he drawled, stepping in to wrap a possessive arm about Nora's waist.

Russell Pierce furrowed his brow. "Does that mean you're still determined to win her back? Because you don't have much time left, if that's the case…"

Twenty-three days, Nora thought. Not that she was keeping track or anything…

With a glance directly into her eyes that telegraphed otherwise, Zane told the group, "We're concentrating on being just friends."

His good-natured assessment was not met with glee. Miss Patricia knitted her hands together. "Then, Nora, *you* do something!"

Exasperated, Nora stepped out of the warm arc of Zane's embrace. "Like what?"

All eyes went to one thing she had yet to notice, prominently placed in the center of the community room.

Mistletoe. Nora flushed at the implication. "Whoa now. I'm working."

Miss Mim gave Miss Sadie a turn with Liam. "Actually," Betty Blair said, keeping track of everything, as per always, "you were off half an hour ago."

"I need to get this done." Nora gestured at the box of stockings, meant for the community room fireplace.

Miss Patricia relieved Nora of the decorations. "It's your own tree that needs trimmed, Nurse Nora."

She huffed. "I put it up." She just hadn't had time to do much else.

Darrell Enlow looked at Zane. "You should be a gentleman and help her with that."

Molly and Chance Lockhart walked in to pick up Braden.

Catching the tail end of the conversation, Zane's sister-in-law agreed. "That's exactly what his brother and I are thinking! Don't let this golden opportunity go by... especially when it comes to a once-in-a-lifetime love."

Nora felt the blood rush to her face. "Who said anything about love?" she couldn't help but blurt out.

Liam was shifted to Miss Patricia. "We all see it, dear."

Zane gave Nora a smug look. "Don't you start!" Nora warned.

He shrugged. "Doesn't seem like I have to."

Disliking the expectant way everyone was looking at them, Nora glowered at the entire group, "Well, you-all are going to have to get over your disappointment because I am *not* going to kiss him."

Zane ambled closer, a devilish look on his face. "Then I'll guess I'll have to kiss you."

Nora gasped, as he bent her backward from the waist. Afraid if he kissed her again, she really would lose herself in this moment—this man—to disastrous result, she spread her hands across his broad chest. "Zane Lockhart," she warned as their eyes met, held, "don't you dare!"

Dark silver eyes shuttering to half-mast, he dared in a low husky voice that further stirred her senses, "Tell me that again five minutes from now, sweetheart, and I'll believe you. Until then..."

He lowered his lips to hers and delivered a kiss to end all kisses. Sweet, tempting. Adoring and tender. Passionate, yet incredibly restrained, too...

It was, Nora realized as she surrendered the way she always inevitably surrendered to Zane, the kind of ultraromantic kiss that ended a wedding ceremony and began a marriage. The kind of kiss that spoke of the days and weeks and months and years to come. The kind of kiss that forever linked two hearts and souls.

When it finally ended, Zane lifted his head and gazed into her eyes. The silence in the room such that you could have heard a pin drop.

"Tell me," he whispered.

That she didn't want him to kiss her like this? That she didn't want him in her life? Dear Lord… Her knees went weak. She couldn't speak. Couldn't deny him any more than she could deny herself.

With a look of immense satisfaction, he lowered his mouth again. Kissed her even more tenderly, Longing swept through her, and then all was lost in the heart-pounding passion engulfing them both.

Zane hadn't really thought she'd let him kiss her. Not in front of an audience. But now that she had, the soft press of her body against his, mixed with the sweet give of her lips, was enough to nearly send him over the edge.

Whatever happened next, however, was not destined to happen here. Reluctantly, he lifted his head and ended the soul-shattering kiss. Dimly became aware of the claps, gasps and whistles.

"Hallelujah!" Wilbur Barnes said.

"Finally!" Darrell Enlow chortled.

"About time the two of you came to your senses!" Zane's brother Chance declared.

"I agree about the last," Nora muttered beneath her breath, struggling to regain her balance.

Gallantly, Zane brought her upright. She sent him a withering look, not about to let his actions go unchallenged. "I can't believe you just did that!"

He could. He'd do it again, too.

Taking in Nora's resentment-filled glare, Buck Franklin elbowed him. "You've got your work cut out for you, buddy!"

That was okay. Zane chuckled. He knew he was up to the task.

Nora wasn't surprised when her doorbell rang at six-thirty that evening. Liam in her arms, she went to answer it. Zane was on her doorstep, a shopping bag in each hand.

Liam grinned up at him.

"Hey, little fella," Zane said, bending down to buss her son's forehead. "I'm happy to see you, too." His amused glance drifted over her. "Can't say your mommy feels the same enthusiasm about my presence, however."

She did and she didn't. And yet time was already passing, too fast... She propped her free hand on her hip and huffed, "Are you here to apologize for kissing me?"

He flashed a grin as wide as Texas. "Never, darlin'! That clinch made my day! Hell, my week! My year, my life...!"

She couldn't help it; she laughed and ushered him inside.

Expression sobering, he crossed the threshold and removed his coat, looping it over the stand next to the front door. Picking up the bags, he carried them over to the sofa table in the living room, so she could see. "I am sorry for embarrassing you in front of everyone. So I brought you and Liam a present, in way of apology."

She peeked inside the bag. "Cool-touch Christmas lights." Excitement zinged through her. There were enough boxes to really light up the unadorned tree in her living room.

Zane mugged at Liam, who was still staring raptly at their visitor. He was then rewarded with a slow smile and an infant gurgle of delight. Zane tucked his little finger inside Liam's tiny fist, as had become their custom. The baby tugged on Zane's hand excitedly.

"Miss Sadie told me the ones your grandparents used to use, years ago, weren't as safe as you'd like."

Enthralled by the bond Zane and Liam had already established, Nora nodded appreciatively. "That's true. Luckily, the ornaments are all still really nice." She pointed to a red storage box next to the tree. "Unfortunately, you can't put the ornaments on until you have the lights on."

Zane turned to survey the task. "I can help with that if you'd like."

Before she had a chance to answer, Liam let go of Zane's finger. Then, surprising them all, he reached for Zane, grabbing hold of his sweater, and tried to propel himself into the lieutenant's arms. Zane acted fast to catch Liam and hold him against his broad chest.

Nora gasped in wonder. "That's the first time he's ever done that!"

Liam chortled happily and tightly grasped Zane's cashmere sweater. The big guy grinned. "Finally, I'm in the right place at the right time," he boasted.

"Apparently." Had the two ever looked more like father and son than at that moment, their eyes sparkling happily, blond heads together? Nora didn't think so.

Zane cuddled Liam closer. "He's never done that for you?"

"No," she admitted, a little hurt.

"I'm sure it's just because he doesn't have to hurl himself into your arms. You always take him immediately and hold him when you see him after the two of you have been apart."

That was true, Nora admitted. It did not however in any way diminish the special relationship Liam and Zane were forming.

Zane handed Liam back to Nora, but Liam immediately reached for him again. When Zane hesitated, Liam let out a rebel yell.

Amused by her son's strong will, Nora smiled, suggesting, "How about you hold him for a while, and I'll unspool some of the lights?"

Zane sat down with Liam in the rocking chair and turned the baby so he could see his mom, too. Swayed him gently while she draped lights from the bottom of the tree, upward. She had just reached the middle of the tree when she noted Liam was fast asleep.

"We really should put him down in his crib upstairs," she said. "It's his bedtime."

"We?" Zane whispered, looking slightly alarmed by the prospect.

Nora ambled closer, unable to help but note once again how sweet the two men in her life looked. "Well, you're holding him," she whispered back. "And the less we transfer him around, the less likely he is to wake up."

Zane straightened cautiously. "Only one problem," he quipped, as the two moved smoothly toward the stairs. "I don't really know how to do that."

Nora curved a hand around the swell of his bicep. "I'll teach you."

Together, they went upstairs into the softly lit nursery. Nora put the side of the crib down.

"Okay," she directed in a hushed voice, "put one hand behind his head, use the other to support his spine. Then slowly lower him down to the mattress. Set him down, wait a minute, then ease your hands out from under him."

As Zane finished, Liam sighed drowsily.

Nora took Zane's big hand in hers and placed it gently over Liam's chest until they were sure that Liam was fast asleep once again, then carefully withdrew their touch. Ever so quietly, Nora eased the safety rail up and clicked it back into place.

She turned on the monitor. Taking Zane's hand again, she nodded to the door and they quietly exited the room.

"You make it all look so easy," he complimented her when they reached the first floor once again.

Nora thought of the way she had struggled to make everything work when she'd first brought Liam home from the hospital. And then, several weeks after that, home to Texas. How different things would have been if only she'd had Zane here to share that time with her. "Ha!"

He put his hands on her shoulders. "I'm serious."

She knew that. It's what made their situation all the more poignant and intense.

"You really seem to know what you're doing. From what I understand, that's not always the case."

Nora led the way back to the tree. She picked up the strand of lights where she'd left off. Zane grabbed the other end. "Well…all nursing students do rotations in maternity and pediatrics. So I learned how to handle babies there."

"But…?" They moved in tandem around the tree.

Finished with one, they added another strand and began decorating the top half of the tree. "Being a mom, 24-7, is a lot more demanding. There's so much you have to learn. Luckily, most of the women at Laramie Gardens have cared for infants, so I've gotten a lot of helpful tips. Plus, assistance holding and rocking him during what is otherwise his fussiest time of the day."

"Early evening."

"Mmm, hmm."

Her cell phone rang. Nora looked at the caller ID. "It's Davina."

"Want me to step outside?"

Nora shook her head, already answering. "Hey, sis. Still in Qatar?"

"Roger that," Davina retorted happily. "Although I may be moving back to AFRICOM in Stuttgart, Germany, soon." Davina went on to tell Nora a little bit about her latest assignment, which sounded both challenging and exciting...

When it was her turn to talk, Nora said, "I just put Liam down, but if you want to FaceTime so you can see how big he's getting, I'll wake him..."

"No, don't do that." Davina's response was adamant.

"Or I could just take the phone up there, and let you see him sleeping?" Nora hated the desperation in her voice.

The ever-present need for a familial connection that never really seemed to come.

"Just send me a photo when you have time," Davina went on briskly. "Listen, I got your note about Liam's Christmas gift. You can get him anything you want from me. Just put my name on it. And send me the bill. And you may want to do the same for Mom.

You know how bad The General is about remembering stuff like that."

Really bad, Nora acknowledged miserably.

Still, she tried again. "You sure you don't want to at least help pick out the gift? I could send you a few choices."

"I don't have time," her sister retorted, "and anyway, I'm sure you know best. Got to go. I'll call again soon. Okay? And if I don't talk to you before then, merry Christmas!"

Nora choked out, "Merry Christmas to you, too." Doing her best not to cry, she cut the connection.

"Everything okay?" Zane asked, as Nora put her cell phone back on the charger. Briefly, she explained.

"You were hoping for a different outcome," Zane guessed sympathetically.

Nora nodded, as tears began to fall.

The next thing she knew, Zane's arms were around her. He held her close while the storm inside her raged.

He stroked a hand through her hair. "Davina's disinterest doesn't have anything to do with Liam," he said.

"I know that." Nora sniffed.

He pressed a kiss to the top of her head. "Then what's gotten you so upset, darlin'?"

She'd held her worry inside for way too long. She had to confide in someone. Nora swallowed around the ache in her throat. "What's going to happen to Liam if anything ever happens to me?" She drew back to look into Zane's eyes. "Is my little boy going to end up like Miss Isabelle? Deserted by those who should love him and be there for him, but just won't…for whatever reason?" Selfish reasons.

Zane carefully wiped away her tears with the pads

of his thumbs. Briefly, he looked as miserable as she felt. "I'd like to say no, but…" His voice trailed off. He searched her face for a long moment, then frowned in concern. "You don't have a guardian lined up?"

Guilt rolled through her with the force of a tsunami. Reluctantly, she shook her head. "I know I should. The lawyer who handled the adoption advised me to get one, but…no. I don't."

"Then how about me?"

Chapter 8

Nora stared at Zane in amazement. "You want to be Liam's backup guardian?"

Actually, he wanted to be the little fella's daddy, but afraid that he'd scare Nora off again, he said, instead, "Yes. Especially if it will help give you peace of mind."

Her sky blue eyes narrowed in consternation. "But if you're not here, then..."

He had already told Nora he was not reenlisting. Obviously, she did not believe him. No one who knew him did. Figuring she'd realize how serious he was when his actions bore out his promise, he reminded her, "I was prepared to step up and take paternal responsibility for him—when I came back."

"Yes!" She threw up her arms and began to pace the length of her cozy living room. "Yes. When you thought Liam was your child."

He tore his eyes from the flattering red corduroy shirt and jeans she'd put on after work. The shirt buttoned all the way down the front, curved in at the waist and hugged her body in all the right places, just like her dark denim jeans.

"He still could be."

Pretty cheeks flushed, she spun back around to face him.

She took a step closer, looking more beautiful and impassioned than ever before. "In a worst-case scenario."

The doubt in her voice made him want to reassure her.

"And best case, too." He flashed a grin, but his heart lurched when she just stared blankly at him. "Unless you can see someone else as his daddy?" Zane pressed.

"Whoa now, soldier." Hands up in surrender, Nora took a deep breath and backed away. "Now we're really getting ahead of ourselves."

Not in his view. He wanted her to be able to count on him. The way she'd never been able to count on anyone else.

"Not necessarily," he reiterated gruffly, closing the distance between them and taking her hand in his. "I've always felt connected to you, Nora. From the time we were kids and spent summers hanging out together." They'd had something special from that first moment. A shimmer of awareness. An undeniable bond. It was still there. Would always be—if he had anything to do with it.

She gazed down at their entwined hands. Let out a quavering breath. "I've always felt connected to you, too," she confessed softly.

Seeing a chink in her emotional armor, he pointed

out, "Our dual stints in the military only intensified that."

She disengaged their palms and moved away. Her eyes locked on his. "Except now I'm out, Zane. For good."

And he still had to go back. For a few weeks, anyway.

Refusing to let that be a roadblock, he moved closer. Continued resolutely, "I was prepared to leave the service for Liam as soon as I heard about him. I'm *still* ready to do that."

Nora looked at him as if none of what he said computed. Peering down at her, he took in the tousled state of her hair and her flushed cheeks. "You need to know that Liam will always be taken care of. That he'll have family and be loved, whether you're here or not," Zane said practically. "You need to know that there will be a rock-solid backup plan for him." Without warning, his voice grew unaccountably rusty. "I want that for the little guy, too."

Nora's lower lip quavered.

Her vulnerability broke his heart. Resolutely, he continued, promising firmly, "If you let me step up here, you'd never have to worry that Liam would end up alone or be forgotten."

Nora stared up at him, thinking, considering.

Zane paused to let his words sink in. "No matter what, he'd have the *whole Lockhart clan* there for him. My four sibs, their spouses, my mom…"

"That's quite an offer," she said, her voice abruptly turning rusty, too.

And one that came straight from his heart. He studied the soft shimmer in her eyes. "The question is," he rasped, inhaling the sweet lavender scent of her, "will you take me up on it?"

* * *

Nora didn't know what to say to that.

She knew what she wanted to say, of course. Yes, yes, jingle bells all the way, yes! But if this was a pity ploy…

She folded her arms tightly in front of her. Challenged him emotionally, "It all depends. Are you doing this out of some misplaced sense of duty or honor?"

He stepped close, his brow furrowed. "Because I'm not Liam's biological daddy but could have been?"

He radiated pure masculine strength and his nearness made her want to kiss him again. Nora swallowed around the parched feeling in her throat. "Because of the way things ended between us the last time we called a halt to whatever-this-has-always-been," she said with difficulty, staring into his eyes. "Because you made promises to me before. About quitting…"

"That I ended up not keeping," he interjected grimly.

"Yes."

"I hadn't thought about it that way. But I do want to make it up to you, for all the things I've done backward or badly in the past."

Nora sighed and shook her head. "You don't have to do that. I was at fault, too. I wanted to keep both feet out the door every bit as much as you did."

"True." Crinkles appeared at the corners of his eyes. "But I could have been more traditional about it from the first. Made sure that you felt like the fine Texas lady you are."

She knew what he was getting at, but she had never felt used. The two of them had both gone into their tempestuous affair with their eyes wide-open. They'd both known what they were risking and chosen to take the leap anyway.

She went back to decorating the tree. "I'm an independent woman, Zane. Always have been. Always will be."

He followed and began to help. "An independent woman who still needs a backup plan for Liam." Their fingers brushed as they draped the end of the light strand near the top of the tree. "Because you know the way life is." They stepped back, to view the gorgeously lit tree.

Zane caught her hand, clasped it warmly in his. "If you have insurance of any kind, you'll likely never need it." He shook his head. "The minute you don't..."

Nora sighed as she pivoted to face him. "You find yourself in one heck of a mess."

"Right." Zane wrapped his arms around her. Gently, he smoothed the hair away from her cheek. "So think of my stepping in as a way of guaranteeing that Liam's future—and yours—is every bit as happy and wonderful as it deserves to be."

Nora splayed her hands across Zane's chest. Beneath her fingertips, she felt the steady thrumming of his heart.

She wasn't surprised he was protecting her.

He was always rushing to rescue someone.

It was in his nature.

"This won't change anything between us." It wouldn't make him fall in love with her, in the boundless way she wanted to be loved. "This agreement won't change who and what we are."

His eyes darkened. "I know that."

She studied his sober expression. "You don't care?" Because a part of her did. Very much!

A corner of his mouth quirked up. "I wouldn't say that," Zane drawled in the sexy timbre she loved.

He lowered his head. Kissed her lightly. And his eyes smoldered all the more. "I wouldn't say that at all."

He deepened the kiss, and need swept through her. Taking his head in her hands, she rose on tiptoe, and then with an aggression she had never let herself unleash before, she pressed herself against him and poured every bit of passion and longing she had into the steamy embrace.

Zane groaned, his unbridled hunger coming through loud and clear. The years of wanting and needing, coming together only to separate again, accumulated into a soaring, desperate yearning.

"I want you," he muttered.

Nora gazed breathlessly up at him. "I want you, too."

Taking him by the hand, she led him upstairs, to her bedroom. Instead of heading for the bed, she backed him up against the wall. And then all was lost in the thrilling press of mouths and bodies.

He kissed her like he'd never get enough of her. She kissed him back in exactly the same way, sliding her hands beneath the hem of his sweater, moving her palms up and over the width of his shoulders and the satiny smooth muscles of his back.

She kissed his neck, his jaw, each corner of his lips. Felt him shudder in response.

Lower still, there was a tsunami of desire. Pressing against the front of his jeans. Dampening hers…

The next thing she knew, her shirt and bra were coming off. Their positions were reversed. It was her back against the wall, and his sweater was coming off. They came together once again, her breasts nestled in the soft mat of hair sprinkled across his chest, her breath catching.

He bent his head, ravishing her lips again, using the flat of his palms, then the pads of his thumbs to tease her nipples into aching crowns. When she could stand it no more, his touch drifted lower still, unfastening her jeans, sliding inside the satin of her panties. Finding her there. His fingers exploring the slick folds, sliding inside her. Making lazy forays. Moving in and out and in again.

"I thought I was supposed to be in charge here," Nora gasped.

"In due time..."

He drove her crazy with his touch, making her feel more womanly and wanton than she ever had in her entire life. Until her body ignited and she was so consumed with wanting him inside her she could barely breathe.

Needing to give as well as receive, she tried to wrestle free. He held fast. Lowering, delivering the most intimate of kisses. Thrilling, she slipped right over the edge, into ecstasy.

When the delicious shudders had finally ceased, she kicked completely free of her jeans. Divested him of his. And then, her heart brimming with feeling, knelt to show him just how talented she could be. Flush with victory, she discovered the hardness of his body, the fierceness of his desire. Sending him right to the brink.

He lifted her up. She rolled on his condom and he possessed her with one smooth stroke. Awash with sensation, she clamped her legs around his waist and rose up to meet him. He lifted her, going deeper, slower, stronger. Bringing them closer, making them one. And then there was nothing but the hot, melting bliss.

The two of them clung together for long moments. Knees weak. Hearts pounding.

"About this," Zane said finally. "About us…"

Nora had no idea what he was going to say. His expression was so inscrutable.

She knew what she wanted, however.

"How about we take it one day at a time?" she suggested recklessly. "Just…" She inhaled a quavering breath. "Let what happens…happen…"

For a moment, she thought he was going to ask for something else. What, she wasn't exactly sure.

Then, to her immense relief, he smiled and nodded. Threading his hands through her hair, he lowered his head and delivered another soul-stirring kiss. "Sounds good to me," he muttered gruffly, inciting her passion all over again. "And what I'd like now…" He lifted her in his arms and carried her to her bed. Following her down, he stretched out beside her. "Is this…"

And "this," as it turned out, was more than good enough for her. More than good enough for both of them.

Two days later, Zane sat at his dining room table, surrounded by mounds of paper. Résumé, credit report, income tax returns. Financial and bank statements. A half-finished business plan and lists of assets still needing to be purchased, facilities built.

Hearing a car in the lane, he put the lengthy application he was working on aside. Groaned at what he saw.

Not about to let his mom see what he was currently working on, he grabbed his jacket, the big box of outdoor holiday decorations and the toolbox she'd brought over to him the previous weekend. "Hey, Mom. Great timing. Want to help me put up the lights?"

Lucille made her way up the walk, looking elegant as ever in a designer wool coat, scarf and heels.

"Ah… Not really."

Zane held out a cushioned deck chair for her. "You can sit and keep me company then."

Lucille looked longingly toward the inside of his ranch house. "It's a little chilly out here."

"Hang on." Zane dashed inside and returned carrying a velvety lap blanket with a shearling underside. "So what brings you out here?"

Lucille pulled a pair of fine leather gloves from her pocket and inched them on. "I wanted to know if it was true. Have you been making the rounds to the West Texas Warriors Assistance, the sheriff, fire and EMS departments, as well as the local airstrip, talking about employment?"

Not about to jinx anything at such a precarious stage, Zane pounded a few nails in, above the windows. "Just checking out my options, Mom. I'll have to do something when I do get out of the military."

Lucille paused, the way she always did when she was about to jump ahead to what was really on her mind.

"Is the misunderstanding about Liam's paternity the only thing that brought you back to Laramie for the holidays?"

Zane moved the ladder a little farther down. "No." He had already planned to return to Laramie when he was on leave, because he knew Nora had settled here. He had wanted to see if they could somehow make a go of it again. Not wanting to get into all that with his mother, however, he resumed hammering and said, "I also wanted to see you and the rest of the family."

Lucille tucked the blanket more closely around her. "Is Liam the only reason you were even considering not reenlisting in January?"

Initially. Zane strung snowflake lights across the windows, above the doors, then moved his ladder to the other side. "If he had been my biological son, it would have been the right thing to do."

"And now that you know he's not your child?"

For a whole host of other reasons, it was still the right thing to do.

He squinted at his mother. "I don't appreciate the inquisition, Mom."

Lucille turned up the collar on her coat. "If I didn't pry just a little, I would never know anything about your life."

True, but there were some things she didn't need to know about. Zane regarded his mother steadily. He knew he was the baby of the family, but she had to let him grow up sometime. "Maybe we should change the topic," he suggested.

She watched as he resumed his hammering. "Fine. We'll talk about all the time you've been spending at Laramie Gardens, then. I hear you're quite popular around there."

Grinning, Zane moved his ladder down the porch again. "I like it there. Reminds me of the summers I spent with Grandpa, when I was a kid. Plus I knew a fair number of the residents, like Mr. Pierce, the former owner of the Book Nook, and Miss Mim, the town librarian back then, too."

His mother smiled. "So you're fond of them."

Zane nodded. He went back to stringing snowflake lights. "Their various life experiences give them a valuable take on the world. They're constantly reminding me that life is short. You've got to grab it with both hands while you can."

"I thought that's what you've been doing with the Special Forces."

Zane knew his mom hated what she saw as his way-too-dangerous-occupation. "It is." But Nora and Liam had been teaching him there was more to life than just protecting and serving their country, too.

"Is that what you are also back to doing with Liam's mother, Nora Caldwell? Living in the moment? Grabbing life with both hands?"

Briefly, Zane dropped his head. "What happened to the ultradiscreet mother I used to have?"

Lucille got up and walked over to him. "She vanished in the wake of the Lockhart Foundation scandal that rocked Dallas a few years ago."

Zane knew that was true. His mother had gone from trusting too much to challenging everything.

She looked him in the eye. "I'm going to be direct with you, son. You have to quit treating your never-ending love affair with Nora Caldwell like it's some dirty little secret!"

Wow. Talk about a shot right to the heart. "Mom! Seriously!"

Lucille held her ground. "Laramie is a small town. Where everyone knows everyone else, and watches out for everyone else. When your pickup truck is parked in front of her house every night, sometimes all night, like it has been the last few evenings, people notice. Even when the two of you keep declaring to one and all that the two of you are not officially dating."

Zane had never liked being backed into a corner. He liked it even less now.

"It's none of their business, Mom." Although he'd made it clear to the matchmaking residents of Laramie Gardens that Nora had won him over long ago.

"Maybe not, but everyone sees the sparks between the two of you. They have for years now."

Zane exhaled roughly. "So?"

"So the two of you are both thirty years old. Why have you never gotten married or even engaged? Why do the two of you keep pretending to others there is nothing much between you?"

Because Nora had always wanted it that way. And when it came to public perception of them, he chose to honor her wishes. "It's complicated."

Lucille waited.

"When we were teenagers there really was nothing to report. We were just very good friends." Who secretly lusted after each other, yet feared doing anything that would potentially impact their friendship.

Lucille's expression gentled. "And when you were in college?"

Zane went back to stringing lights. "We were thousands of miles apart. Our contact was limited to email, phone, text messaging." Although they'd both burned up the wires doing that.

Lucille watched him retrieve an additional strand. "And once you each graduated and went on active duty?"

Reality and fantasy, want and need, had all begun to blend. "With her in the armed services, too," Zane reflected, "our relationship became even more complicated."

Lucille followed, her high heels tapping across the deck. "Because?"

Zane paused to remove the new strand from the packaging. "There are military regulations, Mom. Fraternization, especially between nurses and their patients, is frowned upon."

"She only cared for you personally once, that time you injured your shoulder on a mission and had to have surgery in Germany."

"Yes, but I've been in and out of the military hospitals where she's been on the nursing staff multiple times."

"With gunshot and shrapnel wounds," Lucille recalled with an unhappy shudder. "That one horrible concussion…"

"It wouldn't have been appropriate for Nora to care for me." Because she had been too emotionally involved with him. And he with her.

"Mmm, hmm."

The innuendo in his mother's low tone prompted him to rush to say, "Plus, Brigadier General Caldwell wouldn't have approved if it had been anything more."

The General had wanted Nora to have only one love—the upward trajectory of her career in the Army. Hence, they'd kept their increasingly intimate on-again, off-again relationship as private as possible.

"And you know this how?" Lucille demanded.

Zane looked his mother in the eye. "The same way

I know you don't approve of what is or is not going on with me and Nora right now."

"First of all, you don't know what I approve of or not because we haven't discussed it. But, you're right. I am upset to hear via the WTWA grapevine that you're thinking about becoming Liam's guardian, when your relationship with Nora is still so...casual."

"*Backup* guardian, Mom," Zane corrected. "The person who steps in, in the event of an emergency or life-altering circumstance." Which was why he'd had to go over to the West Texas Warrior Assistance and get information on military benefits for active and separated military. Find out what, if anything, Liam would be eligible for. Answer? The way things stood? Not much. Not that he intended to leave it at that, in any case. "We signed the papers at Nora's attorney's office this morning. So it's already official."

"I'm guessing you volunteered for this."

Well, he certainly hadn't been drafted. "Yes."

"Why?"

His mother's near-constant disapproval rankled. "Because Nora needs me. And so does her son."

"If you were seriously dating...or even engaged," his mother continued, frowning, "it might make sense—"

"It makes sense *now*, Mom," he interjected. "Nora doesn't have anyone else to call upon to be there for her son."

"What about her mother and her sister?"

He scrubbed a hand across his face, his patience wearing thin. "Davina isn't the least bit interested in kids. She's all about her career. As far as her mother, The General wasn't there for Nora when she was a kid, and she still isn't."

"Are you?" Lucille asked emphatically.

I'm sure as hell trying to be. As much as she'll let me. Aware his mother was still watching him carefully, he said, "Liam is special."

"I agree."

He wondered at the reason behind her disapproval. Usually, his mother was all out when it came to helping others. It was why she and his late father had poured most of their fortune into a charitable foundation. "But...?" Zane prodded.

"It's fine to promise Nora all this now, when you are home on leave. But once you're deployed again, you won't be available to either her or her son."

Except he *wasn't* reenlisting. Knowing his mother wouldn't believe it any more than Nora or his siblings did, however, he merely said, "We'll make it work, Mom. Now, and in the future. That's the good thing about both Nora and I. We can adapt."

Something akin to respect glimmered in his mother's eyes. "I can see you're determined," she said finally.

"I am."

"Then behave the way you were brought up," she urged kindly but firmly. "Treat them like the family they are to you. And bring them to dinner at my ranch with the rest of your siblings and their loved ones."

And get even more of the third degree? Zane went back to hanging decorations. "Nora's pretty busy right now."

His mother retrieved her car keys from her purse. "I'm sure she can find time before Christmas. I'll send you a couple of options. If those dates don't work, tell me which one will. Or we could both call her right now..."

As if on cue, Zane's phone went off. It was Nora. Texting SOS—the private code they had used when they were kids. She hadn't used it in years. And she had never once used it lightly.

"Thanks for stopping by, Mom, but I've got to go." Zane escorted Lucille to her car, then rushed off.

Chapter 9

Twenty minutes later, Zane strode into Laramie Gardens. Nora met him at the door of her office. "What's up?" he asked. Definitely something. The normally unflappable woman he adored looked harried and upset.

She stepped closer and he caught the scent of her lavender perfume. "Mr. Pierce wants you there for his meeting with Dr. Wheeler, the geriatric specialist in charge of his case. Is that going to be okay with you?"

Zane paused. "Instead of his daughter?" Who could probably be available by conference call or Skype?

Her delicate hand lightly cupping his elbow, Nora led him down the hall. "Mr. Pierce will explain his reasoning. But if you're okay with this, I'll have him sign the necessary privacy forms that will allow you to be informed of his medical issues."

"Sure."

Zane followed Nora into the conference room. Russell Pierce was sitting across the table from Ron Wheeler, a genial-looking young man not long out of medical school. The two seemed to be in some sort of standoff.

Zane shook the hands of both men while Nora presented the necessary HIPAA forms to Mr. Pierce, who signed with a shaky hand.

"Thanks for coming, Zane," the dapper older man said, as Zane took the seat next to him. "I need someone I can trust to put their emotion aside and help me decide what's right."

Zane nodded his assent. "So what's the issue?"

Mr. Pierce pointed at the doctor and nurse on the opposite side of the table. "They want to have hospital tests run on me…"

"MRI, EEG, CT," Dr. Wheeler said.

"It's all outpatient," Nora explained, "and could be done over a couple of days."

Although time-consuming, none of the tests were painful or invasive. Zane leaned forward intently. "So what's the issue?"

Mr. Pierce grimaced. "Say I am in the early stages of a brain tumor or a degenerative disease like Alzheimer's. At eighty-five, I'm too old and frail to have major surgery. And it's my understanding the medicines they have for a lot of the more debilitative neurological conditions don't really work all that well. Bottom line, if there is something really wrong with me, I'm not sure I want to know. Especially at Christmastime."

Zane met his glance equably. "I can understand that," he said. He turned back to Nora, and Dr. Wheeler, lifting a brow in silent inquiry.

"It's true—we could get bad news from the tests," Dr. Wheeler acknowledged. "But we could also get information that would allow us to properly diagnose the reason behind this confusion and disorientation you're now having most evenings."

"Is that guaranteed?" Mr. Pierce persisted.

"No," Dr. Wheeler reluctantly admitted.

"But it's better than doing nothing, while your symptoms slowly but steadily worsen," Nora put in.

Mr. Pierce looked at Zane.

He had to ask. "Does your daughter, Lynn, know about any of this?" From what he had observed, she was very caring.

"No," Mr. Pierce replied stubbornly. "And I don't want Lynn to be informed right now because she'd put me on a plane back to New York City and have all sorts of doctors doing every test imaginable on me. And I don't want that. I want to stay here in Texas. Where my home and heart and late wife and friends all are."

That made sense, too, Zane noted.

"So if I were your parent," Mr. Pierce persisted, looking straight at Zane, "what would you want me to do?"

He returned the older gentleman's straightforward look. "I'd want you to find out the truth behind your condition, if you could, via any test that is not too invasive or uncomfortable for you," he advised kindly.

"And then…?"

Zane continued, "Weigh your treatment options against any probability of success. And then concentrate on the quality of life. Because at the end of the day," he asserted firmly, meeting everyone's eyes, "if you're not really present every minute of every day, then you're not really living."

* * *

Grateful for Zane's compassionate, steady presence, Nora walked Zane out to the front of the building. The cold, crisp winter air was a welcome respite from the sometimes stifling heat of the seniors' living facility.

Aware they were being watched by many of their matchmakers, she paused beneath the portico. Keeping a respectful distance from Zane, said, "Thanks for helping out today and volunteering to accompany Mr. Pierce when he goes to the hospital the next couple of days. We could have sent a staff member, but I think he feels more protected, knowing you're going to be there."

Noticing she was beginning to shiver, Zane removed his fleece jacket and draped it over her shoulders.

The warmth of his body, and his woodsy scent enveloped her as surely as one of his hugs. His glance cut to the ladies swooning behind the glass windows of the community room. He shook his head at the lack of privacy, then returned his attention to her face. "Because I'm part of the Special Forces?"

"No," Nora replied, forcing a smile. "Because you're you." Suddenly, inexplicably on the verge of tears, she jerked in a bolstering breath and worked to cover the building emotion within her. Try as she might, the worry over what she was going to do, how she was going to cope when Zane left again in a few weeks was always at the back of her mind.

She whisked an imaginary piece of lint from the hem of her uniform top, teased with a blatant wink. "But you're right, there is something prestigious about taking you anywhere."

He chuckled and shoved his hands in the pockets of his jeans. "Nice to know, sweetheart."

Nora ignored the men now standing at the windows, eating popcorn. It was all she could do not to blush. "Listen. I kind of feel I owe you for this afternoon." She dared almost asking him for a date. "So if you want to come over for dinner later…"

Zane hesitated. "I'd love to," he admitted, his glance drifting affectionately over her face, "but I've got some stuff back at the ranch I have to take care of this evening. Particularly if I'm going to be going to the hospital with Mr. Pierce the next three days."

Doing her best to hide the hurt of rejection, Nora nodded. "Of course."

Had she asked too much? Put too much domestic pressure on Zane? Hard to tell from the suddenly inscrutable expression on his handsome face. Had she somehow made him feel hemmed in, or forced too much upon him, asking him to sit in a hospital for hours on end, cooling his heels when he could be out protecting their country and/or saving the world?

He reached out and gently took her hand. "But there is something you could do for me in return."

"Anything," she said, swallowing hard.

"My mother's having a family dinner on Sunday afternoon. She'd like us both to be there. And of course, she wants you to bring Liam, too."

Stepping back out of view of their cheering section, Nora held Zane's gaze. "What would you like?"

Understanding precisely what she was doing, he moved with her. "To not be put under the familial microscope?"

Nora laughed, as she knew he meant her to.

Guaranteed a few seconds of privacy, he brushed the hair from her temple. "Seriously, I know we promised we'd keep it casual and take it day by day while I'm on leave." A coaxing smile lifted the corners of his sensual lips. "But I'd really like it if you would be my plus one. And Liam my plus two since he is now sort of a member of the Lockhart clan."

The thought of having family standing by for them warmed Nora as much as his jacket. Enthusiasm building, she asked, "What time?"

"I'll pick you up at four. And Nora—" he hugged her briefly and trailed his lips across her cheek "—thanks for this."

Zane wasn't surprised Nora and Liam both received a warm welcome at the Circle H Ranch that weekend. Although his family had once been as disconnected as Nora's, his father's illness and death, coupled with a scandal at the family's charitable foundation, had not only made them work as a team, but forged close and loving bonds.

Now, with all four of his siblings married to the loves of their lives and raising families of their own, the pressure was on him to do the same.

Hence, they barely had their coats off before the subject of his romantic future came up. "I can see why you wanted to be this little guy's guardian," his brother Chance remarked, watching as Nora shifted her son to Zane so she could refrigerate the bottles of formula she'd brought.

"Backup guardian," Zane corrected, lounging against the counter, Liam cradled snugly in his arms.

Wyatt and Adelaide grinned at the way Liam was clinging to Zane's collar and cooing adoringly up at him. Each was holding one of their twin toddlers, and they shifted slightly so Nora could take her place beside Zane. "Doesn't look like Liam is differentiating," Wyatt observed.

Unable to help himself, Zane grinned back down at his tiny charge. Darned if the little guy didn't feel like his son. Nora, the woman he was meant to spend the rest of his life with...

Garrett and Hope sauntered over to greet Liam, too, their arms full of their own two boys, almost-two-year-old Max and his newborn brother, Jack. "He definitely seems to know when he's got it good," Garrett observed with the gravity of their oldest sibling, as well as the first among them to actually settle down.

I'm the one who has it good, Zane thought to himself, aware for the first time he didn't have to envy his siblings' happiness.

Sage pushed her way in to offer their three-month-old guest a cloth covered candy-cane-shaped baby rattle, while Nick followed with their six-month-old son, Shane. "I agree. Nora's little boy is absolutely darling!" She mugged at the infant until Liam mugged back, then tucked her index finger into his tiny fist, declaring, "If anyone can bring Zane back to Texas for good, it's this little fella."

"And his mommy," Lucille added, beaming with enthusiasm.

Zane felt Nora stiffen almost imperceptibly beside him.

Lest she feel pushed into something she wasn't ready for, Zane lifted a staying hand. "Okay, everybody, let's not get ahead of ourselves here."

Nora relaxed, ever so slightly, her shoulder brushing his arm.

Ever the romantic, Sage palmed her chest innocently,

and said, "Hey, calm down, bro. We're just saying you-all make a cute family."

Nick elbowed his wife, letting her know with a glance she needed to back off a bit, lest she jinx it. "In the loosest, most casual definition of the word," he clarified.

Although she was still smiling dutifully, Zane knew Nora couldn't be happy about the direction the conversation was taking. At this rate, his family would have them hitched, Liam adopted by him, too, and Nora pregnant in no time.

And although *he* might be ready for all that, Nora had given no sign that *she* was. "I thought we were going to make Christmas cookies for the residents of Laramie Gardens this evening."

Braden piped up. "I promised Miss Isabelle I'd bring her some when I went over to color pictures with her again."

To Zane's relief, his mother got the hint. "Then we better get started," Lucille said.

"You've got to take it down a notch," Zane told Sage, a few hours later, when they went out to the grill, behind the Circle H bunkhouse.

She adjusted the controls on the state-of-the-art gas grill with the precision of the professional chef that she was. "I'm sorry. I'm excited."

Wishing he hadn't had to go to his older sister for business advice, Zane stood by, large glass dish in hand. "I don't want Mom or Nora to know what I'm doing until it's all ready to go."

"Understood." Sage lifted the plastic wrap, and

checked on the marinating skirt steak. "How are things going, by the way?"

A helluva lot slower than expected, Zane thought in frustration. "I still need an appraisal and survey done." Along with a substantial small business loan.

"Did you contact Raquel Morrissey at First National, as I suggested?"

"On my list." *My very long to-do list.*

"Listen, Zane, I love the businesspeople here in Laramie. But for a project the size and scope of what you're trying to do, you need to go back to Dallas. And take advantage of all the connections we had growing up."

Garrett joined them. He carried a second dish. This one contained boneless chicken. "Mom says the crew is getting hungry."

"We're hurrying." Sage placed meat on the grill. She looked at the cooking platform and smacked her forehead. "I forgot the veggies. Can you guys handle this for a second?"

Garrett and Zane shrugged in unison. "Sure."

Hands on her hips, Sage regarded them skeptically. "Don't flip anything until I get back. Just make sure it doesn't burn—by turning down the flame, if necessary."

Zane's phone went off. He checked it, then put it back in his pocket without answering.

"Someone from your unit?" Garrett guessed.

Zane exhaled. The only other person who could understand how hard all this was for him was his eldest brother, who had also spent years in the military, as a physician, before resigning to marry and raise a family with Hope. Casting a glance behind him to make sure they were still out of earshot, Zane nodded. "How did you know?"

Garrett shrugged and turned his attention back to the grill, same as Zane. "I figured you would be under a lot of pressure to reenlist."

No joke. He sipped his beer. "They're offering me everything they can think of."

"Like?"

"Promotion, higher salary. Choice of assignment."

"Yeah, well—" Garrett turned and clinked his own bottle against Zane's "—do us all a *very big favor* and don't mention a word of this to Mom until right after Christmas. She deserves a good holiday." Garrett took a drink and shook his head in silent remonstration. "And if she thinks you're leaving again…"

A throat cleared behind them.

Zane turned, expecting to see his sister. Instead, Nora stood there, a half dozen grilling utensils in one hand, two pot holders in another. Her eyes weren't quite meeting his; her face was a blotchy pink and white.

Stepping forward, she flashed both men the kind of impersonal grin she gave Laramie Gardens residents when they were being a pain. She thrust the items at him and said, "Sage will be right out."

Giving him no chance to reply, she turned and fled.

"Are you going to talk to me?" Zane asked, hours later, as they turned onto the lonely country roads back to Laramie.

Nora kept her eyes on the countryside. "It was a long day, Zane. I'm really wiped out."

He imagined that was so. She'd been acting as if nothing at all were wrong for several hours now. Ignoring all his subtle attempts to get her alone for a private chat while they were still at the Circle H ranch. "Then how about we stop by the No Name?" he asked casually, not about to let her call it a night with this misunderstanding still lingering between them.

Her slender shoulders slumped in defeat. "I—"

He reached across and briefly squeezed her hand before letting it go. He returned both hands to the steering wheel. "It won't take long. I have something to show you." Something he really hoped she liked.

He wrinkled his nose as a very particular odor filled the compartment of his pickup truck. "And from the scent of it, Liam needs a little break, too."

Nora thought she'd been embarrassed before. Having walked in on what was obviously a private conversation between the only two brothers in the Lockhart family who had served in the military. A conversation that had seemed to point the way to Zane reenlisting, as she had always expected he would.

But now...

As the odor emanating from the infant seat in the back seat worsened, she realized it wasn't just a little excess tummy air. Cringing, she turned to Zane. "You smell that, too?" Nothing like a three-month-old baby to take the romance out of an equation! But maybe that was what they needed—a smelly, soiled diaper to bring them back to earth, fast.

And out of this fantasy world she had been living in...

The fantasy world where Liam had not just an in-case-of-emergency-guardian, but a mommy and a daddy and a big, wonderful, loving extended family to go with it...

Zane cast her a look as Liam, in his car seat, waved his arms and kicked his legs and noisily worked on evacuating the last of his dinner.

"In fact," Zane teased with a laugh, "the way our little buddy is going, I think everyone for ten miles is soon going to smell it. And since there is no place to stop for a diaper change between here and town…especially after dark…"

Nora couldn't help it as her son kept up his antics. She laughed, too. "Okay, okay!" She put up surrendering hands. "You win. Your ranch, it is."

Which, truth be told, was where she wanted to be anyway.

She and Zane hadn't had a moment alone all day. And call her crazy, but she missed having her one-on-one time with him. Desperately.

As they drove up the lane, Nora caught the first sight of the No Name ranch house. The A-frame had been completely outlined with twinkling white snowflake lights, making the ranch house stand out majestically against the moonlit fields surrounding it. Her only lament was the fact her son was a little too young to really enjoy the Christmas sight.

"Oh, Zane." Nora pressed a hand to her heart. "That is absolutely gorgeous!"

Grinning, he got out to help her and Liam out of the minivan. "Goes with the wreath on the door, don't you think?"

Nora grabbed her diaper bag, while Zane lifted Liam and his carrier out of the safety seat base in the rear seat. "Is this why you've been so elusive this week?"

Gallantly, he escorted her up the walk. "What do you mean?" He flashed her a stymied look, then paused to punch in the security code on the pad next to the front door. "We saw each other every day at some point. Always had lunch or dinner together." And on three of the four days found time to make love, too.

Nora pointed out curiously, "But then you came back out here, to work on things." Things he had never exactly explained. But that had kept him awfully distracted and busy.

His broad shoulders emanating as much strength as the rest of him, Zane led the way inside. He hit the switches that turned on the lights across the entire first floor of the A-frame, then nodded at the laptop computer, printer, scanner and stacks of folders on the desk behind the sofa. "I've been getting caught up on a lot of paperwork, too."

It certainly looked like it.

Aware the job of changing Liam was going to be a "roll up your sleeves and try not to breathe in" task, Nora eased out of her coat. She tossed it on the sofa. As merry as the exterior was, it still seemed like a total bachelor pad inside. "No tree?"

He inclined his head in a way that seemed to indicate he didn't plan on messing with that.

His eyes twinkled merrily. "But there is something even better," he promised, "that I'll show you once we take care of the little guy." He unstrapped Liam from his carrier, slid his hands beneath and gently lifted her son out.

Too late realizing that Liam's sleeper was damp with leaking brown liquid that soaked into his shirt.

"Oh, no!" Nora grabbed the closest thing—a roll of paper towels from the kitchen—tore off a half dozen and pressed them against Zane's rib cage to mitigate the damage and keep the moisture from leaking down to his pants.

Seeing what was going on, Zane laughed and shook his head at their tiny charge. "Got me again, fella! Good one!"

Liam gurgled, and now that his little intestines were blissfully empty, relaxed against Zane's broad chest.

Nora took in the smelly, awful disaster. "I am so sorry, Zane!"

"Not to worry," Zane chuckled, unperturbed. "He's just initiating me. Letting the 'new man in your life' know who is really boss in this equation." He bussed the top of Liam's head. The baby cooed contentedly and snuggled closer.

Nora rolled up the sleeves on her shirt. "I'm going to have to put him in a bath." Upstairs, Zane had only a steam shower. Which left few options. "Do you think we could use the kitchen sink? I'll sterilize the whole area after."

"Sure." He gave her a leisurely once-over. "What do you need me to do?"

"Crank up the heat down here and grab a few big fluffy towels." She held out her arms. "But first, let me relieve you of your charge."

"You're going to get this on you, too."

"It's okay. I don't wear anything that's not machine washable these days."

The transfer was made.

By the time Zane returned with the towels, Nora had filled the sink with about six inches of warm water and removed the last remaining clean sleeper, packet of travel wipes and baby wash from her diaper bag.

Zane watched her lay Liam down on the first towel. "I hate to say this, but you're covered, too."

Nora made quick work of unsnapping Liam, getting him out of the soggy, soiled diaper and wiped down cursorily as best she could. "All three of us smell delightful."

Zane stripped off his shirt and undershirt. Luckily, the offending goo hadn't reached his skin. Nora laid Liam in Zane's arms, briefly. "Just give me a second to strip down, too." She took off her fitted corduroy shirt, then noting her camisole was damp, too, took that off. Clad in her bra and black skirt, she reached for Liam and gently lowered him into the waiting water.

He grinned with delight as she washed him down, first with a cloth, and then with the liquid baby soap that Zane warmed between his hands before spreading it over Liam's chest, back, arms and legs.

They rinsed him again with the cloth, then brought him out of the water. All nice and clean and smelling of lavender.

Nora placed her son on another clean towel, then dried him off with a third. By the time he was diapered and dressed, he was yawning mightily.

Nora handed him off to Zane. "If you could just walk him around while I tidy up this mess. And…is it okay if I use your washing machine?"

"Please do!" Zane said, so fervently she laughed.

As they wandered off, with Zane softly singing "Good King Wenceslas," Nora made short work of starting the laundry and restoring his kitchen to its former immaculate state.

By the time she returned to Zane's side, Liam was cuddled against his chest, fast asleep. He turned to her and smiled. "Ready to see my surprise?"

Chapter 10

Nora was ready for something, all right.

The close proximity to Zane, coupled with their half-dressed states, had her thinking all kinds of wild things.

With a fast-asleep Liam still snuggled in his arms, Zane led the way up the stairs to the second floor of the A-frame. It was just as she recalled, with one exception. The full-size crib, rocking chair and changing table in one corner. She stared in shock. "You set up a nursery?"

Zane shrugged amiably. "I thought Liam might appreciate a comfortable place to be when he is out here on the ranch."

"It's...amazing." And definitely not the actions of a man who had one foot out the door.

He turned to her, exuding the thoughtfulness she so admired. "If you want, we could let him test it out right now."

"You want to put him down?"

He smiled at her incredulous look. "For the night. If you'd like to stay."

Nora edged closer, trying not to let on what his low, sexy voice did to her. Her heart did *not* melt, her insides did *not* turn to mush just listening to him!

"I don't have any nightclothes." It was one thing to make love on impulse and have him stay on for a few hours, holding her in his arms, and then slip out before dawn. That was simply taking their relationship moment by moment, a feat they had done many times before. But it was something else entirely to plan so deliberately to bring her—and Liam—into his day-to-day life.

He stepped closer still, inundating her with his steady masculine warmth. "You can borrow something of mine to wear." Leaning down, he continued softly, persuasively, "I've got diapers and Liam's formula, too."

Aware how very close she was to falling all the way in love with him, she released a reluctant, admiring sigh. "You really are prepared." *And kind and thoughtful. Capable and commanding...*

"Hopeful, always, when it comes to you, and now Liam. And yeah, darlin'—" he paused, a determined, sexy glint in his eyes "— I am. So what do you say?" he asked huskily, "Want to spend your first night ever at the No Name?"

At the moment, Nora couldn't think of a better Christmas gift to herself. And him. "Yes," she whispered back, knowing no matter what the future held, there would never be a man more perfect for her than Zane.

She tiptoed closer to the crib. Beckoned Zane to follow. Her gaze fell to her contentedly drowsing son. Although she knew firsthand there was no cozier place to be than snuggled against Zane's warm body, she also knew her son would sleep more soundly in a crib. "Let's put—" *our son*, she almost said "—*Liam* to bed."

Oblivious to her near mistake, Zane lowered Liam slowly to the mattress and eased his hands out beneath him. With her at his side, he kept the other resting ever so slightly on her son's tiny chest until he was sure that Liam was still snoozing.

Contentment flowing between them, they backed away.

Zane took Nora's hand in his. Soundlessly, they moved to the other side of the spacious moonlit loft. "Now what?" he asked, drawing her close.

She caught a whiff of his chest, then her own. She wrinkled her nose comically. "I think," she whispered back, wanting to rid them of the lingering noxious scent, "we should both hit the shower."

He reached behind her to undo the zipper on her skirt. "Together?"

She splayed her hands across his chest and felt his heart thud against her palm, in tandem with hers. She fit her lips to his and kissed him seductively. "It will save water."

It wasn't the first time they had stripped down and climbed into a stall together. But it was by far the most intensely passionate, Nora thought, as they lathered each other from head to toe, and then stood together under the spray to rinse.

"I'm sorry I was ticked off at you earlier." She slid her arms around his back and pressed him intimately against her, inhaling the spicy scent of his soap and the even-sweeter fragrance of his hair and skin.

He kissed her fiercely, evocatively, until they were both groaning for more. He turned her so she was facing the tiles, her hands splayed out in front of her. He pulled her back against him, one hand exploring her breasts, the other moving across her tummy, downward. Her hips rocked restlessly against him as his lips made a thorough tour of the sensitive place behind her ear, the vulnerable slope of her neck.

"Nothing has changed since the last time we talked about my commitment to the military," he murmured, as her soft, pliant body surrendered all the more. "My siblings just don't want me talking about it to my mother."

Her whole body was quivering with sensation when he turned her to face him. Aware she hadn't ever wanted him this desperately, Nora looked up at him. "They think she won't believe you?"

The large glass enclosure filled with steam as the water sluiced down over them. He fit her against him once more. Hardness to softness. All the need she had hoped to see was reflected in his gray eyes, and it set her body on fire.

He cupped her head between his large hands and kissed her languidly at first, then with building ardor, rubbing against her, driving her to the brink. "You didn't."

Her erect nipples ached as she surged against him once more. Going up on tiptoe, she wreathed her arms about his neck. A shuddering sigh escaped her lips. "I'm beginning to."

"Good." He lowered his mouth to hers. Kissed her deeply. Then more and more rapturously.

"Because I want you to know how much I care," he rasped against her mouth, finding her with his fingertips, possessing her, body and soul. Until she felt it, too. In every kiss and caress. Needing and giving. As lovers, as equals, as friends. And maybe even, she thought, as he continued to make sweet love to her, as something even more…

An hour before, Zane hadn't figured the evening would end as he wanted, with the two of them in each other's arms. Never mind in his shower. But as they rolled on a condom and settled onto the teak bench against the wall, Nora straddling his lap, kissing him as if it were an end in and of itself, he knew things were changing.

She was opening herself up to him in a way she never had before. Drawing out the moment. Celebrating the occasion. Taking everything he offered. Possessing him, as well. Until there was nothing in the world but the two of them and this all-encompassing bliss. And he knew if she continued to let him into her life, and heart, if they continued to grow closer, by the time Christmas arrived, their every dream would finally come true.

An hour later, they headed for the kitchen. Zane got them both some water, then pulled out a package of peppermint and white chocolate pretzel crisps. As they settled on the sofa in front of the fire, his gaze drifted over her, taking in every well-adored inch. "You look ravishing."

Nora fluffed her tousled hair and swept a hand down her still-tingling body and bare legs. "I think you mean *ravished*." Playfully, she let her eyes move over his bare chest and low-slung pajama pants. "Where did you get these anyway?"

He was wearing the Black Watch plaid bottoms of

a pair of men's pajamas. She was wearing the notch-collared, buttoned-front top. Nice as they were—and they were made of the finest, softest flannel—they didn't seem exactly his style.

Zane opened up the bag and offered her first dibs. "My brothers gave them to me a couple of Christmases ago. Said that since I'd probably be an old man before I settled down, they wanted to go ahead and give me the appropriate nightwear."

"Cute."

He shook his head at the joking antics of his brothers. "Speaking of settling down, though, I do have something important I want to talk to you about."

As their eyes met and held, Nora felt a shimmer of tension between them. "Okay."

He sifted a hand through her hair. "Finding out about Liam was a wake-up call for me."

Doing her best to maintain a poker face, Nora ran a fingertip across the inside of his wrist. "In what way?"

He continued to study her with his steady gaze, as if trying to figure something out. Admitting finally, "I guess I always thought we would get back together again eventually. Even after our last breakup."

So did I, Nora thought on a wistful sigh.

He lifted her hand to his lips and pressed a kiss into the center of her palm. "Seeing you move on without me, creating a new life here, a new family, forced me to realize you weren't going to wait for me forever." His voice took on a husky undertone. "And I'd been a fool to think you would."

His heartbreak engendered her own. Nora shook her head. Why go back to that, if all it was going to do was hurt them both? "Zane…"

His eyes gleamed with undecipherable emotion. "Let me finish, Nora. Anyway, I didn't—don't—like the idea of you moving on without me." His voice dropped a husky notch. "And I especially don't want Liam to grow up without a man in his life he can count on."

Nora regarded Zane in shock.

Please tell me he's not going to propose out of some misguided sense of duty or honor...

As he gazed over at her, Nora had the strong sense he was thinking of kissing her again. But he did not.

Which was good. Because kissing would lead to touching and touching would lead to lovemaking, which would lead to even more confounding emotions than they already had.

He traced her lifeline with the pad of his thumb. "And I really don't like the idea of you and Liam ever wanting or needing anything."

Palm tingling, she reiterated softly, "We don't." *Especially now that you're in our lives.*

"So I'm stepping up here. I started working on figuring out what to do with the inheritance my dad left me. As well as my will."

Oh, dear God. "Zane..." She knew how superstitious soldiers could be. Sometimes just preparing for death could lead them to believe the end was imminent.

"I've changed the beneficiary to my personal life insurance policy, and the one I get through the military, to benefit you and Liam. And when I get the stuff with the No Name all sorted out, I plan to add that to the inheritance, too."

Nora turned to face him directly. She gazed at him in consternation. "Does your family know this?"

He shook his head somberly. "Only the lawyer I hired in town. Plus, of course, the insurance people."

Nora lifted a trembling hand. "Zane. I appreciate the thought. But—" she gulped "—this is crazy."

Exuding his trademark confidence, he shifted her over onto his lap and cuddled her close. "Actually—" the corners of his lips quirked up "—I think it's the sanest thing I've done in a long while."

Worry combined with her guilt. "I don't want your money." She'd done nothing to earn it.

"Too bad." He buried his face in her hair, breathed in deeply. "Because I want you and Liam to have it."

Nora closed her eyes, too, praying for strength. "But your family..." How were they likely to take this? Yes, they welcomed her now, but if they thought she was a gold digger, how would they react?

"My family does not need any money from me." Zane stroked a comforting hand down her spine. "They all have enough, on their own."

"That's really not the point," Nora murmured miserably.

"Yes," Zane countered, "it is." He cupped her chin, lifting her face to his. Gazing deep into her eyes, he said, "They want me to be happy, Nora. They know that you and Liam make me happy."

He made her happy, too.

"And since you are the closest thing to family outside the Lockharts that I have, let me honor that connection by looking after you and Liam. And in turn, you can take care of me." He kissed her tenderly.

"Through sex," Nora guessed, pulling in a stabilizing breath.

"That's one way." He leveled an assessing gaze on

her and kept it there. "There are other ways, too, that are just as important."

She swallowed around the sudden ache in her throat. "Like…?"

"Just be there for me," he replied hoarsely, in a way that made her heart skip first one beat, then another. "Know I have to go back to active duty for a couple of weeks, after Christmas. But then I'll be home for good."

Unless, Nora thought, something happened somewhere in the world that required his services. But Zane wasn't allowing himself to entertain that possibility. Not in his mind. Not in his heart. Not yet.

Recklessly deciding to let the specter of reenlistment go, at least for now, she said softly, "And when you return?"

His expression turned even more sincere. He kissed her again, then advised, "Greet me with open arms, and an even more open heart."

Zane and Nora made love again, through the night. They got up at 4:00 a.m. with Liam, fed and diapered him, and then all went back to bed for another two hours' sleep. But then it was time to get up and figure out what they were going to do for the rest of the day.

"Since you're the one who is working, while I'm the one on R & R, you should probably get first dibs on the choice of activity during your day off," Zane said.

Nora sat with Liam on her lap. Still clad in his oversize pajama shirt and a pair of his thick wool hiking socks, she looked sexy and at ease. "Does that mean you're volunteering to come with?"

"I am." Zane paused to read the back of the pancake box. After a thoughtful squint and some mental calculating, he poured in half the packet of flour mix into the bowl.

"Do you want to measure that?" Nora asked, her hair tousled, cheeks still pink with sleep. She snuggled her son against her with a maternal tenderness that made something raw and elemental twist in his gut.

"Nah. I'm good." He broke two eggs into the bowl. Added a splash of milk and a couple spoonfuls of melted butter.

The truth was, he loved having them here. Knew the No Name would forever feel lonely without them.

But he was working on that. Hopefully, when Christmas got here, he would have everything in place.

In the meantime, he had two hungry "family members" to feed. He paused, looking at the fruit bowl on the counter and the containers of fresh berries in the fridge. "Blueberries or bananas?"

Nora smiled, as if enjoying the show. When he caught her admiring his physique, a faint blush stained her cheeks. "Blueberries."

Glad she wasn't as immune to him as she sometimes pretended to be, he sauntered closer. "Maple syrup or berry?"

Her sky blue eyes glowed happily. "Maple."

He walked over to brush a brief kiss on the top of her head, another on Liam's, then went back to the stove and turned on the griddle. "Back to what we were saying… about what you'd really like to do today?"

Nora sobered. "Well, although I've ordered a few things on the internet, I haven't had time to do any in-person shopping for Liam. So shopping would be nice."

"Consider it done." Zane poured her a glass of juice and handed it to her. "How far away do you want to go?"

She sent him a hopeful glance. "There's a new mega toy store in San Angelo. And they usually have a Santa Claus at the mall there."

The coziness factor in the room increased tenfold. "Sounds fun."

Her brows knit together. "What do you want to do?"

Aware he could really get used to this, Zane sent her a sidelong glance. "Whatever you want to do. The day is yours. And Liam's." He gave her a long meaningful look, then promised playfully, "My mission is seeing to your every need."

And what an adventure it turned out to be.

By the time they arrived at noon, the line for Santa was over an hour long. Zane looked at the fussy, impatient children and their equally out-of-sorts parents. "Want to come back?"

Nora bit her lip. "I don't think I'm going to get another chance."

Zane could see she really wanted to do this. "If you want to wheel Liam around in the stroller, I'll hold our place in line."

"You really don't mind?" she asked, coming intimately close.

He inhaled her lavender perfume. "I really don't mind."

And as it turned out, Zane didn't. Mostly because it gave him a little time to field two phone calls from Sage—who wanted to know if he had contacted her friend Raquel yet. Zane hadn't. And a couple of fellas from his unit, who demanded to know if he'd come to his senses. He had. Just not in the way his teammates wished. And last but not least, he used the time to research the hottest new toys for three-month-olds that holiday season.

Finally, it was almost their time. Zane looked around, spying Nora, waved her on over. They got Liam out of his stroller just as their turn came up. Beaming with excitement, Nora handed her son over to Santa.

Liam took one look at the big burly man with the snowy white beard and glasses, screwed up his face and let out a howl loud enough to alert the entire shopping center.

Nora rushed in to comfort him. To no avail.

"Maybe if you hold him up next to Santa," the woman dressed as Mrs. Claus mouthed.

Again, no dice. Liam was having none of it.

Nora gestured for Zane to try, too. That didn't work, either, so the photographer took several shots of the squalling red-faced baby in Santa's arms. They stayed long enough to pay and collect their freshly printed photos, and then moved off into the mall.

As soon as Santa's village was out of sight, Liam quieted.

Nora, however, remained frustrated and distraught. "Maybe it just wasn't the day for it," he soothed.

Nora's spine stiffened, even as she nodded.

"But we can still get in some shopping we wanted to do," Zane said, beginning to understand why some of the young families they saw all around them seemed so tense and out of sorts.

Luckily, by the time they got to the toy store, Liam was drowsy again. "Why don't you let me carry him while you shop?" Zane suggested.

She sent him a grateful glance. "You're sure?"

He admired the sunny highlights in her chestnut hair,

the way the loose sexy waves just brushed her shoulders. "Actually, I'd really enjoy it." Having Liam in the BabyBjörn, nestled against his chest, made him feel like a dad. Liam's dad. And, Zane noted, there was no feeling better than that. Unless you considered also getting an idea of what it would be like to be Nora's husband...

"Well, that went better," she said, when at last they had finished at the toy store, and were loading their bagged purchases into the back of his minivan. She reached up to curve a gentle hand against Liam's cheek. Zane caught the brief, wistful look in her eyes. "Do you think we bought too much?"

Given the fact that, for every item she had purchased, he had insisted on getting something else?

He leaned down impulsively and bussed the top of Liam's head. Wrapping an arm around Nora's shoulders, he pulled her affectionately against his side. "Hey, I'm ready to go back in and clear out the rest of the store!"

She laughed, resting her head against his shoulder. Peering up at him contentedly, she reflected, "It's exciting, isn't it?"

More than Zane ever could have predicted. "I can only imagine what it's going to be like when he sees all his new toys."

Nora turned to him, a mixture of surprise and wary expectation on her lovely face. "You are going to be there with us. Aren't you?"

Chapter 11

"I'd sure like to be there with the two of you on Christmas morning," Zane said huskily, helping Nora settle Liam in his safety seat. Together, they buckled him in and directed his attention to the travel toys within his reach.

As they straightened, Zane caught a whiff of her lavender perfume and the sweet essence that was unique to her.

Nora tucked her hand in his and turned to him with a smile. "Maybe you could spend Christmas Eve with us, too? I mean," she added hastily, lest she overstep, "I imagine you have things you want to do with the Lockhart clan, too."

Aware this was what had been missing in his life, Zane leaned down and pressed his forehead to hers. "Nothing would make my family happier than to have you and Liam there with me, too."

Stepping back, she searched his face in relief. "What about you, soldier?" Her teasing tone held an undercurrent of uncertainty.

Was she kidding? He brought her to him, and kissed her tenderly. "I'm happier than I've ever been."

Nora snuggled against him. "Me, too," she whispered.

From inside the passenger compartment, Liam chortled loudly. Zane and Nora broke apart, laughing. "I think our tiny chaperone is telling us to get a move on," he remarked ruefully.

"I think you're right," Nora concluded, handing Zane the keys to her minivan.

He climbed behind the wheel. They were almost back to Laramie when Nora's phone chimed. She listened with what appeared to be a frown of concern. "Yes, I can be there. Zane, too. Probably fifteen minutes. See you then." She punched the end call button.

Zane tossed her a brief, concerned glance before returning his attention to the road. "Problem?"

Nora moaned. "The Ugly Sweater competition rules are going to be read during the dinner hour this evening. Our presence is requested."

Zane paused. "Why is that a big deal?"

Nora ran both her hands through her hair, then let them fall to her lap. "You only ask that because you haven't heard the rules."

Unable to help but note the way the tousled sun-streaked strands caught the winter light, he said, "Oh, man…"

She nodded, already exasperated. "Exactly."

"What else?" he prodded curiously.

She bent her head as she checked the messages on her

phone. "Mr. Pierce's test results are in, and Dr. Wheeler wants to meet at Laramie Gardens ASAP to discuss them. So, if you can spare the time to sit in for that…"

"I'll be there as long as I'm needed."

"Thanks." She texted a reply. "I appreciate it."

He reached over and squeezed her knee. "No problem."

Twenty minutes later, Liam was being tended to in the community room by a doting Miss Mim, and Zane and Nora and Mr. Pierce were seated in the conference room with Dr. Wheeler.

The geriatric specialist had his laptop open and was showing them the MRI and CT scans. "As you can see," the doctor concluded, "there are no abnormalities."

"So I'm not ill?" Mr. Pierce asked incredulously.

The physician handed over a paper copy of the results. "We had two different teams look at the results. Neurology and geriatrics. The conclusion was unanimous. There's no evidence of stroke, tumor or disease. No diminished blood flow, or any other evidence of anything that would cause mental confusion."

Mr. Pierce slumped in his chair. "So why am I still having periods of confusion and disorientation? Short-term memory problems?"

Good question, Zane thought, as unsatisfied as the man he'd been drafted to support.

"That, we don't know yet," Dr. Wheeler said kindly. "All we can verify right now is that there is no underlying biological or physiological condition evident."

Which meant what? Zane wondered. That a time would come when they would find something nefarious in Mr. Pierce's brain?

The older man sat up straight in his chair. "What

about medication? Isn't there something I can take that would help? I see advertisements all the time."

Most of which were quack cures, even Zane knew. Marketed and sold to the truly desperate.

His manner firm yet soothing, Dr. Wheeler replied, "We're not recommending adding anything else to your daily regimen at this point. We'd rather focus on other options like occupational therapy. Daily physical activity and memory exercises. Perhaps a better, much more specific daily schedule to keep you on track."

"I can make arrangements to get you started on all that tomorrow," Nora put in.

Mr. Pierce traced the buckle on the classic leather-bound copy of *Treasure Island* in front of him. He looked up warily. "And if that doesn't work?"

Dr. Wheeler frowned. "Then we'll have to consider *at least discussing* moving you to a place that focuses specifically on memory care."

While Nora stayed behind to speak with Dr. Wheeler, Zane walked down the hall with Mr. Pierce. His heart went out to the eighty-five-year-old. "Not exactly what you wanted to hear?"

Mr. Pierce shook his head, disappointed. They continued on a moment in silence. "You know what I did last night? I spent an hour looking for my wallet."

"Where was it?" Zane asked.

"In my trousers pocket," he related, embarrassed.

Zane clapped a hand on his shoulder, empathizing. "We all do that. I can't tell you the number of times I've lost my sunglasses only to find out they were on my head."

As they entered his suite, Mr. Pierce continued grimly, "You know what I did at *midnight* on *Friday*?"

Zane shook his head, waiting for the older man to enlighten him.

"I called the owner of the Rare Books Store in Wichita Falls, a colleague I've known and worked with for thirty years, and berated him for not having sent Esther's Christmas gift, which was a gold-leaf embossed leather-bound edition of *Little Women*. Sort of like this one." Mr. Pierce held up *Treasure Island*. "Only without the buckle."

Zane took the seat Mr. Pierce suggested. "What did your colleague do?"

He shelved his book with the other classics in his vast collection. Then returned to sit in the armchair opposite Zane. "Well, at first my friend thought I was joking, since he knows as well as I do that Esther is in heaven. And then when he realized I wasn't, he played along with me. And then called Lynn in New York City."

"I'm guessing your daughter then called you?"

"Yes. Hearing her voice snapped me out of it, and I told her I thought I'd been sleepwalking."

"Lynn doesn't know the problems you've been having?"

Russell Pierce frowned. "Nurse Nora informed her about my occcasional confusion the first couple of weeks that I lived here. Lynn was so concerned I haven't let anyone here tell her anything since."

Which was his right, Zane knew, under medical privacy laws.

"But if this keeps up, my daughter will figure it out. Perhaps sooner rather than later, since she is planning to come down for Christmas to visit me."

Zane looked him in the eye. "How can I help?"

"That's just it. You can't." Russell frowned. "If I'm going to snap myself out of this foggy mess I've been living in, I'm going to have to do it myself."

"Is Mr. Pierce okay?" Nora asked worriedly as Zane caught up with her and Liam. She watched the elderly gentleman walk into the dining hall and take a seat at a table with Wilbur Barnes and Darrell Enlow. He seemed alert and aware. Determinedly cheerful. As if his private talk with Zane had helped somehow. Nora knew how that felt. There was just something so kind and reassuring about him. She always felt better, just being with him.

He turned to Nora, gave her shoulder a squeeze.

"I think so." Zane paused in obvious concern, relating quietly, "He's frustrated, of course."

Nora sighed. "We all are. I had hoped the tests would show something really minor that could be fixed instead of just…nothing." She shook her head.

"Maybe the memory therapies you are setting up for him will help."

Glad she had Zane to lean on in that moment, Nora bit her lip. "Maybe. I just can't help but think we're letting him down somehow, though."

Zane met her gaze. "What else could you have done?"

That was just it. She shook her head in silent admonition. "I don't know." She swallowed around the knot of emotion in her throat. "I'm going to have to think on it some more. Talk to Dr. Wheeler again." She gestured to the front of the dining hall, where Betty Blair and Miss Patricia were waving at them. "In the meantime, I think they've reserved some seats for us."

Zane grinned. "We better get up there then before someone has a conniption."

She ran her gaze over his tall, muscular frame. In jeans, boots and a charcoal crewneck sweater that brought out the dark silver of his eyes, he was the epitome of rugged masculinity. "It's your fault. If you weren't so genial and capable, you wouldn't be so popular."

He tossed her an amused glance, then tilted his handsome head in the direction of her adorable baby boy, currently commanding a similar amount of feminine attention. "Actually, I think it's Liam they're after, darlin'."

Nora chuckled. "Could be."

A cute infant was a hot commodity in a seniors' center.

They made their way and sat down, just as Miss Sadie took the podium. "Okay, everyone, we're going to run through the rules for the Ugly Sweater contest," she announced, as papers stating the same were passed out by the dining hall aides.

"Every sweater must be a base color of green or red."

From the look on Zane's face, it was all he could do not to moan.

Nora nudged his knee beneath the table.

Gave him a look that said *behave*.

Mischief glittering in his eyes, he nudged her knee right back.

"Homemade decals or decorations must adorn the front and/or the sleeves, while the backs of the sweaters are to be left plain."

As Miss Sadie went on, with the exact dimensions and type of fabric or material permissible for each decoration, Zane's eyes began to glaze over a little. He looked distracted. Restless. Worse, Nora couldn't blame him for being bored.

This was a little much.

Even more so for someone in the Special Forces, where high stakes, fast action and adrenaline were the norm.

His phone chimed softly. Looking stoked for the interruption, he removed it from his pocket and put it down on his thigh, where only he could see the screen.

Frowning, he discreetly texted something back. Then put the phone back in his pocket.

It went off again, ever so softly.

And then again.

He answered briefly—twice—then put it back in his pocket.

Nora was curious. And so was Betty Blair, who was seated on the other side of him.

Was it someone from his unit? Nora wondered, as the texts continued nonstop. His family? And why did Zane suddenly look so completely engrossed and businesslike…? As if he had the weight of the world on his shoulders?

Oblivious to whatever was going on with Zane and the messages he was receiving, and the way Betty Blair was practically breaking her neck trying to figure it out, too, Miss Sadie concluded, "So those are the rules. And just like last year, we'll have three impartial judges from the community, unless there are any objections." She lowered her bifocals. "Yes, Betty?"

"I think Nora needs to participate this year." Betty paused to give Zane a long, meaningful look. As if blaming him for his complete lack of attention during this very important holiday event. "Zane, too."

A murmur of assent went through the hall. What was the older woman up to? Nora wondered. More match-making? Or simply an attempt to draw Zane more fully into life at Laramie Gardens.

Nora lifted her hand. "Actually, I don't think it would be fair for me to compete against any of the residents."

This time, Zane nudged her foot with his. "Actually—" he looked at her, his preoccupation with his texts fading, a mischievous twinkle in his eyes "—I think it's only fair you do compete, Nora."

Everyone chuckled.

"Liam could enter, too!" Miss Patricia said excitedly.

Which would really make it seem like the three of them were officially a family. Suddenly, life in Laramie was getting far too complicated.

"If I do it, and Liam does it, you have to do it, too, Zane Lockhart," Nora declared, just as emphatically, wondering how in the world she was going to find the time to make two sweaters before the deadline the following week. Never mind compete with Zane!

The incorrigible lieutenant folded his arms across his broad chest and flashed her a hallelujah smile. Then he leaned toward her and winked, as if he couldn't wait. "You're on!"

"So now do you see what you got yourself into?" Nora asked, several hours later, after Liam was finally asleep in his crib.

Sighing dramatically, Zane studied the contest regulations with a jaundiced eye. "That's a lot of rules," he said finally.

Nora continued putting ornaments on her tree, aware at the rate she was going, her house would not be fully decorated for the holidays until Christmas Eve. But she couldn't really say she minded her slow-as-a-turtle pace, given the reason behind it. All the time spent with Liam. And Zane.

Trying not to dwell on the fact that his R & R was now more than half over, Nora continued her mock scolding, "Which you would have known had you been paying more attention when Miss Sadie was reading them." *Instead of managing whatever it was you were overseeing on your cell phone.*

Zane put aside the competition explanation, then ambled toward her. He picked up several ornaments and began placing them on the branches. The faint restlessness he'd evidenced all evening was still there. Only now it was directed right at her. "What happens if you don't follow the contest rules?" he asked slyly.

Or, she wondered, *you find you can't handle the much-slower pace of a small Texas town, after all?*

Their shoulders brushed as they both moved in the same direction at once. Nora worked to still her racing pulse and stepped back so they were no longer touching. She met his gaze equably. "You get disqualified."

And I get my heart broken all over again, just as I sort of always knew I would.

"How about that," Zane murmured, grinning as if he'd just found a way out of the situation he didn't really want to be in.

Hoping the Ugly Sweater contest wasn't a metaphor for the situation they always eventually found themselves in, Nora frowned. "You need to take this seriously, soldier, now that you've gotten us all in it," she warned, going back to the box for more ornaments.

Because she would be here, living in Texas and working at Laramie Gardens, long after he had left again.

If he reenlisted again.

He *said* he wouldn't.

She knew he *wanted* to believe that. And most of his current actions pointed to that. But she also knew what had happened before, when he'd been needed by his country. He'd gone off to serve. The possibility he might do so again remained, whether either of them wanted to admit it or not. Because there was always a crisis somewhere in the world, an American citizen or soldier who needed rescuing. Always a need for his elite Special Forces unit. And within that, a need for a talented soldier like Zane.

"You can't duck out of this competition," she said sternly. "Not after promising to be in it."

Abruptly reminding her of the way he and his fellow elite operators liked to blow off steam, he regarded her in all innocence. "Not planning to."

Yeah, right. He was formulating a strategy. Most likely an ornery one to liven up what otherwise had the potential to be a very nitpicky and tedious event. She peered at him suspiciously, demanding, "What are you planning?"

Zane picked up the last of the colored glass bulbs. He placed his on the highest branches, filling in the places she had thus far been unable to reach. "I'm going to surprise you."

Exactly what she feared. She needed predictable. She needed safe. She needed him here, with her and Liam.

Smile widening, he clasped her wrist and reeled her in. "And speaking of surprises…"

She quirked a brow, prompting him to elaborate.

"Now that we finally have your tree decorated," he said in that deep, husky voice she loved, "do you want to wrap Liam's presents tonight?"

Something else they'd put off.

Something else that would make them feel even more like a family. One that, despite all her secret hopes and dreams, she wasn't sure was going to last.

"On one condition," Nora countered, before she could stop herself, recalling how elusive and distracted he'd been most of that evening.

Zane's brow lifted the way it always did when unsolicited conditions were put on him.

"You tell me who Raquel is."

Chapter 12

Zane stared at Nora. "How do you know about Raquel?" he asked incredulously.

"Betty Blair was reading your text messages all through dinner. You seriously didn't notice?"

He shrugged. "I only had eyes for you and Liam."

"And your phone," Nora couldn't resist adding.

"True," he said a bit sheepishly.

She held his gaze. Waited.

He came closer. Reluctantly admitted, "Raquel is a friend of Sage's. Someone from our family's Dallas days. She's agreed to help me out with an estate matter."

Nora knew, from her own grandparents' passing, how complicated and seemingly unending the legal matters could be after the loss of a loved one. And given his family's extensive wealth, it was probably even more so.

She flushed, embarrassed to have put him on the spot like that. "Oh."

Gently, he cupped her face in his large, warm palm. "So there really is no need for you to be jealous."

Nora released an uneven breath. "I'm not!"

His brow lifted in a way that said it was his turn to await a response. Unfortunately, Nora couldn't explain it in a way that would not make her sound overly mistrustful. She just had a nagging feeling Zane was holding something back from her.

The clandestine talk with his brother during the dinner at the Circle H, with Garrett requesting Zane not speak to their mom about Zane's plans until after Christmas Day. The big stack of papers Zane was trying to go through, at long last. His changing the beneficiary on his life insurance policies to make sure she and Liam were taken care of, in the event of anything happening to him.

It was all a little too much. All seeming to point to one thing. He was likely going to reenlist for another tour, leave her again for months at a time and let his service to his country dictate the terms of his life.

He was being noble. Courageous.

Whereas she was worried and upset. With effort, she pushed her anxiety away. What good would it do to fret about any of this now, when he only had some twelve days left before he returned to finish his tour? They still had Christmas together.

Maybe it was time she started doing what she had promised herself and start living more in the moment, too. Give him the space he needed to really figure out just what he was going to do next, and then simply support him. Instead of always agonizing about what lay just beyond the bend.

Maybe it was time she dug deep to find a wellspring of courage and selflessness, too.

"I'm sorry. It's been a long day." She swallowed around the ache in her throat. "I'm just exhausted."

Holding her gaze, he rubbed his thumb across her lower lip. "Do you still want to wrap presents, then, while Liam's asleep, or call it a day so you can go on to bed?"

"Actually," Nora said, taking him all the way in her arms. "What I'd really like to do is this."

Zane grinned as Nora tugged off his sweater, then took him by the hand and up to her bed. With a sweeping gesture, she invited him to sit on the edge while she began a slow and seductive striptease.

Apparently, it was his turn for Christmas to come early. He watched her undress, the sight of her extraordinarily intimate and immensely pleasurable.

Tempestuous need glittered in her eyes, as clad only in a very sexy red silk bra and panties, she drew him to his feet and slowly removed his shirt. "I thought you were tired."

Her hands divested him of the last of his clothes, then closed over his pulsing hardness. "Not that tired."

Playfully, he drew the bra straps down over her arms, exposing her erect nipples. "So I see."

She stretched out, facing him on the bed. Smiling as he eased his fingers beneath the elastic and found her damp, silky, waiting. Wanting. Bent to kiss the curve of her bare shoulder. Grinning lustily, she observed, "You're not too tired, either."

"I'm never too tired to make love with you." He'd never stop wanting her, needing her, either.

Determined to make this lovemaking more memorable than anything they'd ever had, he eased the lingerie from her body and rolled so she was beneath him. Positioned himself between her thighs. She came up off the bed as his lips lowered, suckling gently. Her thighs fell even farther apart as he kissed and stroked. Until she shuddered and fell to pieces in his arms.

And only when she could stand it no longer did he slide inside her, in one smooth languid stroke. She clenched around him as he filled her completely, taking him and making him hers. Letting him possess her, hold her and love her, until there was no more denying how much she wanted and needed him in her life. Until the future was theirs, too, for the taking.

All he had to do, Zane thought, as their shudders ended, and they lay together, cuddling, was complete the mission he had embarked on this Christmas.

The mission that would bring both Nora and Liam into his life from here on out.

Unfortunately, there was still a lot to do to make it all happen, he thought, as he stroked a hand through her hair. "I probably should go," he said.

"Stay," she murmured, pressing a string of sleepy kisses across his chest. "Just a little while longer…"

He didn't have to be asked twice. Reveling in the feel of her lissome body entwined with his, Zane shut his eyes. The next thing he knew it was midnight. He had stayed past the time he should. And the bed beside him was empty.

He rose and pulled on his pants. Went down the hall to the nursery. Liam was still sleeping peacefully in his crib. There was no sign of Nora.

He found her downstairs sitting on the sofa, her laptop in front of her. Clad in a long-sleeved, red T-shirt and matching flannel pajama bottoms, her chestnut hair falling in a loose braid over one shoulder, her lips still swollen from their kisses, she looked gorgeous, well-loved. And worried.

Tamping down the desire to draw her into his arms and make love to her all over again, he sat down next to her. "Everything okay?"

She turned a troubled glance his way. "I couldn't sleep. I keep thinking about Mr. Pierce."

Zane wasn't surprised. The elderly man had been on their minds a lot lately. "Still feel like you're missing something?"

Nora nodded. "There's always a reason why symptoms appear. We can't always find it or identify it, but it's usually buried somewhere in the patient's medical history."

"I thought you and Dr. Wheeler had been all through this."

Nora exhaled. "Numerous times. The signs all point to sundowning, and perhaps the very, very early signs of dementia or Alzheimer's."

"But you don't agree?"

"No." She tapped her index finger against her lips. "And I don't know if it's my gut instinct kicking in, the fact I knew Mr. Pierce all those years growing up, that is making me think his intermittent confusion and disorientation is caused by something else that is eminently treatable."

She shook her head miserably. "Or if it's because I *am* so fond of him that I am refusing to accept what could, in time, become a hopelessly demoralizing and discouraging diagnosis."

Denial was tough. He had been in his own form of

it for years now. He took her free hand in his and lifted it to his lips. "So what next?"

Nora reluctantly shut the lid of her computer. "I talk with Mr. Pierce tomorrow. Go over what we know and see if I can find something we might have inadvertently overlooked."

"Is Zane coming in today?" Miss Isabelle asked the following day, while Nora passed out the morning medications to the residents already in the dining hall for breakfast.

"No," she said, recalling how passionately they had made love before he left. "He had to go to Dallas for a few days."

"So close to Christmas?" Miss Patricia frowned.

"I bet it has something to do with that Raquel person." Betty Blair glowered.

Actually, it did. But, not about to go into that with them, Nora simply smiled. Trying not to feel defensive, even though Zane was still keeping an awful lot from her, she said, "Let's not forget Zane did grow up there and still has a lot of friends living in that area," she pointed out reasonably. "Second, whatever Zane's reason, it's his business, don't you think?"

"As long as he comes back in plenty of time to spend Christmas with Liam and you, Nora," Miss Sadie said with an elegant smile.

The constant matchmaking was both heartwarming and exasperating. Knowing, however, the LG residents only had her best interests in mind, Nora reminded everyone gently, "He has plans with his family, too."

"Are you invited?" Miss Mim inquired hopefully.

"Yes." She blushed, trying not to make too much of

that. Although she could see everyone else was. "And I'm sure he will also find time to swing by here to wish everyone a merry Christmas, too."

"What about the Ugly Sweater contest?" Betty Blair asked.

"He was reading the rules for it just last evening."

"So he is going to enter!" Miss Patricia swallowed her meds.

He was going to have to, since he had also roped Liam and Nora into it. "Absolutely," Nora promised. Then headed down the hall to check on Mr. Pierce.

He was still in his pajamas and wearing slippers. His robe was hanging over the back of the chair next to his bed. Not particularly good signs. "Are you cold?" Nora asked, wondering why he had his winter coat on, too.

"No." Russell Pierce patted his empty pockets. "Just looking for my car keys."

Oh, dear, he was confused again. In the morning, too! Usually he was fine in the morning. Nora gently touched his arm. "You don't drive anymore, Mr. Pierce. Remember?"

"Sure I do. Our minivan is in the..." He stopped. Looked at his clothing and sat down on the edge of the bed. He picked up the leather-bound edition of *Great Expectations* and idly fingered the clasp. Muttered something heartfelt that Nora was just as glad not to be able to decipher.

She poured him a glass of water from the pitcher at his bedside table and handed him the plastic cup holding his morning medications.

He took them.

"Is this a good time for us to talk?"

Mr. Pierce nodded.

Nora pulled up a chair. "First, I want you to know that the occupational therapist who is going to be working with you on memory exercises is coming at four this afternoon. The physical therapist will be here tomorrow. And we hope to have your more structured daily routine in place by the end of the week."

Looking oriented again, Mr. Pierce nodded. "Thank you, Nora. I appreciate all you're doing."

"You're welcome. Do you mind if we discuss your medical history for a moment? I was going over your pharmacy records last night, and I had a few questions."

"I'll answer anything I can."

"I appreciate that." She referred to the notes on her clipboard. "The last time you had any changes in your medication was last summer, when you started a new daily antihistamine. Do you remember why you made the switch from the one you had been taking? You were in New York City at the time."

"I had a couple of sinus infections earlier in the year, related to my pollen allergies. So the doc there thought the newest latest greatest thing might be the ticket to get rid of them."

"How did you react to it?"

"Fine."

"Have you had any sinus infections since?"

"Not a one."

Nora made another note. "And nothing else has been prescribed for you?"

"No. The doctors figure with my cholesterol, blood pressure and allergy medications, I've got enough going on."

"And when did your memory issues start?"

He grinned. "I can't recall."

Nora paused. "Are you joking, or...?"

Russell Pierce sobered. "Actually, I don't really know. Esther always said I only remembered the things I wanted to remember, and she was right. I only half listened most of the time." He looked sad again.

"And your move to New York last summer? What prompted that exactly?"

"I had locked myself out of my house a couple of times and misplaced my wallet and lost all my ID, and my daughter didn't want me living alone anymore."

Nora paused. Aware this wasn't in her records. "So you were having memory issues before the move?"

"Yes, but—" briefly his expression became prickly "—no more than I had always had. I tended to do that a couple of times a year anyway. But Lynn was concerned and wanted to spend more time with me, so I let her talk me into it."

Nodding, Nora wrapped up with a few more questions.

Satisfied Mr. Pierce was alert and aware again, she left him to dress unassisted and went back to her office.

The rest of the day was very busy. By the time she finished up for the day and collected Liam, the excitement over the Ugly Sweater competition was at full pitch.

"You better have something really wild to show everyone," Nora said when Zane called her from Dallas that evening.

"I don't know about wild. How about simply *memorable*?" he teased.

Nora groaned, still wishing he were here with her, instead of over one hundred and fifty miles away. "I hope your sense of humor matches the Laramie Gardens residents', soldier."

He chuckled. "How was Liam this evening?"

"Good."

"I missed seeing him."

"He missed seeing you." Her son had gotten used to having two adults around at bedtime, to help with the bathing and feeding, rocking and cuddling and story time.

Zane exhaled. The sound seemed to carry all the loneliness she was feeling. "I missed seeing you, too," he said.

Same here, was on the tip of Nora's tongue. But something, some inner vulnerability, wouldn't let her say it. If she got all emotional, she could start crying and really feeling sorry for herself.

And that would not be good.

For either of them.

"When will you be home? I mean," she corrected hastily, "back in Laramie County?"

He let her remark go unchallenged. "Thursday morning," he said cheerfully.

"The day after tomorrow."

Which meant another day and night, and maybe day alone.

How was she going to survive without seeing him, being with him, making love to him every day?

"What you're doing must be complicated," she said, opening the door for him to tell her more.

To her frustration, he chose not to elaborate about that. Instead, said with his usual cheerfulness, "As long as I am in Dallas, however, I was wondering. Nora, what did you ask Santa for this year?"

Zane. With a big red bow on him. And a lifetime

guarantee. Glad he wasn't there to see her blush, Nora fibbed, "Mmm. I don't know."

He chuckled, deep and low.

Her entire body tingled in response. And missed him all the more.

"Everyone should have *something* to open on Christmas morning," he said.

She knew that. And yet... Nora looked at her beautifully lit and decorated tree, struggling to contain her emotions. "We've never been really big on presents in my family."

His voice took on a more determined edge. "Maybe it's time that changed."

Nora couldn't contain a self-effacing laugh. "Good luck convincing Davina and The General of that." She paused as the silence drew out, wishing Zane were there with her and could take her in his strong arms and offer all the comfort and joy she needed right then.

Nora dragged in a calming breath. "Did I tell you that I heard from my mom, via text message, and Davina was right? Our mom wanted me to buy and wrap something for Liam from her, too."

"She's not planning to come down for Christmas at all?" Zane did not sound happy.

Nora shrugged and tried not to feel bitter. "Maybe in the spring, she said."

Zane was silent. They weren't FaceTiming, so she couldn't see his expression. And for once she was glad of that. She didn't want to view his pity. It was enough to hear it in the awkward silence still stretching between them.

"Jewelry?"

"What?" she said, her mind still on the gregarious

warmth of his family. He was so lucky to have the Lock-harts in his corner. She wondered if he knew it.

"I need you to give me a *category*," he said.

A frisson of fear trickled through her. Presents would make everything seem traditional, and they both knew their relationship was anything but the norm. "You really don't have to do that," she returned.

"I really *want* to do that." His voice dropped a sexy, affectionate notch. "So...jewelry? Don't all women love jewelry?"

They loved wedding and engagement and eternity rings.

But she couldn't say that, either. Not without boxing him into a corner. And they both knew how much he hated that.

No, if Zane ever wanted to be with her and Liam, he would have to decide to do so on his own. Not be regimented into it. In the meantime, she needed to work on changing her own attitude. Becoming all that she could be in the mom and not-quite-a-girlfriend, not-quite-a-wife, but-a-heck-of-a-lot-more-than-a-simple-friend-or-lover category. "Maybe something Mom-ish," she said finally.

"Like a locket?"

Or a wedding ring.

She really had to stop this. Wishing for the impossible. Even if it was Christmastime! "Or a broach with birthstones," Nora said, "like my grandmother used to wear."

She could almost hear him smile. With pleasure. Or was that relief? "Liam would probably like that," Zane said.

He'd like us married even more, Nora thought.

But that wasn't likely to happen. Not with Zane leaving again. And even if he did ask, she wasn't entirely sure she could say yes. Even if it was what she wanted, deep down. Not when she knew he was just going to walk out the door. Not when she knew being married to him was only likely to leave her feeling even more lonely and disappointed when he did the inevitable and reenlisted.

"Nora…?" Zane prodded.

"Liam probably would like that. Very much. The question is, soldier, what do you want?"

"You, Nora," he said in that husky, sexy way of his that made her catch her breath. "Just you."

Chapter 13

"What's all the noise?" Zane asked over the phone the next afternoon.

"I'm chaperoning a field trip to the fabric and craft stores," Nora explained.

"Ah. The Ugly Sweater contest."

She could hear voices on his end, too. Low and businesslike, unlike the ones on her end, which were high-pitched and peppered with eager laughter. "Everyone is getting pretty excited."

"Sounds like it."

Nora sifted through the stacks on the table, picking out a sweater her size, then Liam's. Putting both into a basket. "Anyway, I called to see if you want me to pick up one of the green or red cotton sweaters the craft store just got in."

"No." The smile remained in his voice. "I'm good."

He was in Dallas, where shopping options abounded. Figuring she might as well ask, as long as she was there, she said, "Did you need anything else? Fabric glue? Felt? Glitter? Jingle bells? Extra mistletoe?"

He chuckled. "Maybe the latter..."

Nora flushed at the veiled suggestiveness in his low tone.

The noises in the background faded. "So how are things with you?" Zane asked.

I miss you, Nora thought. Even though it had only been thirty-eight hours, five minutes and a few seconds since they had last seen each other. And less than twelve since they had last spoken on the phone. She rummaged through several spools of satin ribbon. "I'm good," she said. Or as good as she could get without Zane.

"Liam?"

He misses you, too. "Also good." She pretended a chipper attitude she couldn't quite feel.

"How is Mr. Pierce doing?"

"Another rough evening." Russell had wanted to see his late wife and had gotten agitated when she told him why that was not possible. Later, when he had finally understood, he'd become unbearably sad again.

As sad as Nora knew she would be if something happened to Zane, and their earthly connection ended.

"But he's better this morning," she forced herself to continue. And had been up and surfing the web on his computer tablet before breakfast, one of his beloved leather-bound classics sitting on the desk beside him.

The background noise on Zane's end faded even more. She could imagine him slipping away from whatever was going on to get a little more privacy. "Did you

hear back yet on the antihistamine you were research-
ing?" he asked.

"No," she admitted regretfully, doing the same thing
and heading for a more deserted part of the store. She
sighed. "But I've made queries at a dozen different
places, so hopefully, something soon."

"Hopefully before Christmas."

"I know. Speaking of the holiday, is there anything
on your gift list that this 'Santa' should know about?"
She still had no idea what she was going to get him.
Although she'd been thinking about some sort of Good
Luck charm. Something to carry with him.

"Just one thing." His voice was a low, sexy rumble.

Her whole body tingling in response, Nora murmured back, "I'm listening."

"Wait up for me when I get back tomorrow night?"

The following evening at ten o'clock, a rap sounded
on Nora's front door. Pretending like she hadn't been
waiting impatiently all evening for her gentleman caller,
she sashayed to the door.

Zane stood on the other side of the door, a Santa hat
on his head, a small gift-wrapped present in his hand.
She couldn't help but laugh as she rose on tiptoe, kissed
him hello, then ushered him inside.

He shrugged out of his coat, kissed her again, in-
fusing her with the taste of peppermint this time, then
lifted his head. Taking her hand, he led her over to the
sofa, where she had a bottle of wine waiting. "Sorry it
took me so long to get here."

He looked tired beneath the exuberant exterior. Like
whatever it was he'd been doing had sapped the energy

from him. Not an easy feat, with someone as unstoppable as Zane. "Traffic?"

She poured him a glass, then one for herself.

"No." He toasted her silently. "Just some things to wrap up in Dallas."

"Ah."

He picked up the present he'd brought in with him and handed it to her. It just covered the palm of her hand. "And of course I had to stop and get this."

Nora recognized the name of an exclusive store on the gift wrap. "What is it?"

Zane leaned back and folded his hands behind his head. "Open it and see."

Nora's heart skittered in her chest. "You don't want me to wait until Christmas morning?"

He tilted his head, considering. Eyes twinkling mysteriously, predicted, "You might like to have it now."

Now she really was curious. Nora took off the paper. Inside was a velvet jewelry box. Too big to be a ring, too square to be a bracelet or necklace.

Telling herself she was glad it wasn't an engagement ring, she lifted the lid.

Inside was an incredibly beautiful Christmas tree broach, with a pile of colorful, gaily wrapped presents underneath. In the center of each ribbon-tie was a gem.

Confidently, Zane explained, "Sapphire for Liam. Amethyst for you. Emerald for me. And see, there's even a couple extra presents in case you want to add a few more birthstones…"

For more children? *Their children*? Or was she really going off the rails now?

Nora blinked back tears. "It's beautiful, Zane."

"I'm glad you like it."

Silence fell.

"But…?" he asked, sensing there was more.

Nora dragged in another quavering breath. Almost afraid to ask, but needing to anyway. "Is there a special meaning in this?"

His gaze gentled. He pinned the broach on her, then cupped her face in both hands. "What do you think?"

"I think…" *I'm in love with you*, Nora thought.

But wary of inundating him with too much too soon, or putting a boundary on him he didn't want, she rose and went to the center drawer of her desk. Pulled out another jewelry box. "I think I need to give you this now, too." Even though it wasn't wrapped.

He stared down at the solid silver chain and pendant. "St. Michael the Archangel. The patron saint of soldiers and battles."

Nora looped it over his neck. "So you'll be protected wherever you go, whatever you're doing." Nora's voice turned rusty. "And know I'm thinking of you."

He took her all the way into his arms. "Without a doubt," he told her raggedly, "this is the best gift I've ever received."

Their lips met. He kissed her deeply, passionately, and in a masterful move, lifted her into his arms and swept her up the stairs to her bedroom. Then he carried her over to her bed and laid her down.

Parting her knees with his, he draped himself over her and situated himself between her thighs.

"Wow," she teased, "you must have really missed me."

"Darlin', you have no idea…" he growled, taking a wrist in each hand and anchoring them over her head. "But you will," he promised, kissing her mouth, slowly, sensually, and with breathtaking intensity.

He kissed her until they were both shuddering. Until she arched up against him and kissed him back with every inch of her being, until she shook with need, until their bodies melded in boneless pleasure.

They came apart long enough to undress each other and sheath him in a condom, then came together once again. He slid a pillow beneath her hips. They locked eyes, and she opened herself up to him as completely, as unconditionally as she knew how. He opened himself up to her in return, still kissing her feverishly, sliding home.

He lifted her against him, and suddenly she was there. Shattering in overwhelming release. And he was there, too. Clasping her to him. Joining her. Holding her close until the aftershocks faded. And when it was over she did not let him go, but instead, enticed him into making love with her again. Even more tenderly this time.

Afterward, they cuddled together, falling asleep. But at two in the morning, she woke to see him sitting up on the side of the bed. Reaching for his jeans.

Her hair tumbling over her bare shoulders, she rose up on her elbow. "You have to leave?"

Expression maddeningly inscrutable, he shrugged on his shirt. "I've got some stuff at the No Name to take care of first thing tomorrow morning."

Like what? she wondered. She grabbed her robe and followed him down the stairs. "Did you finally decide what you want to do with the land?"

He sat down on the bottom of the stairs to put on his socks, boots. "Keep it, I hope."

"Make it your home."

He rose to his full height, wrapped his arms around

her waist and leaned over to kiss her. One corner of his mouth crooked mysteriously. "Let's just say, like a lot of things, it's a work in progress."

Or in other words, don't ask, Nora thought on a be-leaguered sigh, feeling shut out all over again. "Afraid of jinxing it?"

"Maybe. Then again, maybe not."

She groaned and put her hands over her ears.

He pulled them off. Leaned down and waited until she'd dare look into his eyes, then bent down and kissed her again. Even more seductively this time. He tucked a strand of hair behind her ear. "Good things come to those who wait. Haven't you ever heard that?"

"Yes," Nora pouted, hating how fast their time together was flying by. How soon he would have to return to his unit, at least until he had finished his tour on January 15. "It doesn't mean I like it."

Zane reached for his coat.

"Do you really have to go?" She pouted even more as he shrugged it over his broad shoulders. He had done this before. Started pulling away emotionally before being deployed. She linked her arm through his as he headed for the door. "You could stay a few hours."

He studied her, clearly torn about something. "Don't you have to work tomorrow?"

Darn him for pointing that out. "Yes, but…"

His gaze drifted over her before returning ever so slowly to her face. "Nora wants what Nora wants?"

If he only knew. She folded her arms in front of her. "Exactly."

Zane exhaled heavily. Pulled her into his arms once again. "Believe me," he said, smoothing a hand over her back, "I'd like nothing better than to sleep right here all night."

She splayed her hands across his chest. "Then why don't you?"

"It's been pointed out to me it is not good for your reputation."

"By…?"

"Does it matter? They're right."

Nora hated it when he was right, too. Which made her take the opposite tack. Especially when their days together were numbered. She curved her hands over his biceps. "I really don't care what people think," she said stubbornly.

Zane paused, thinking. "It won't always be this way," he promised finally.

"But for right now?"

She looked in his eyes and knew it definitely was.

"I don't understand why we haven't seen Zane at all this week," Miss Sadie said, the following day.

I'm with you. I've missed him, too, Nora thought, as she finished updating a half dozen medical records. "He was in Dallas, taking care of Lockhart family business."

"But he's back now, isn't he?" Miss Mim persisted from the doorway of Nora's office.

"Yes." Nora shut down her computer. She walked across the hall and into the community room, where a lot of the residents were gathered. "And he's still busy."

"I think this has something to do with that Raquel person." Betty sniffed, following along.

"I think we should be grateful for everything that young man did when he was here." Miss Isabelle looked up from the drawing she and her little visitor, Braden Lockhart, were coloring.

No one could deny that.

The Adopt a Grandparent program was starting to take off and they had Zane to thank for getting the ball rolling. She would be eternally grateful to him for that.

Kurtis Kelley and Wilbur Barnes were engaged in an impromptu Battleship board game tournament with several middle school students in the community room.

High school choir students were setting up for a rehearsal of their annual holiday concert material in the music area.

Darrell Enlow was speaking with a fifth grader, who was doing a social studies report on what it had been like to serve in the military forty years prior.

"The point is, we'd like to thank him," Miss Sadie said. "So we all got together to give him this." She handed Nora a tabletop Christmas tree, decorated with lights and ornaments.

"We'd like you to deliver it to him," Betty added.

Nora would love to but she might be interrupting whatever he was so busy with. She smiled, suggesting, "Why don't you-all save it and give it to him yourselves during the Ugly Sweater contest?"

The women exchanged concerned looks.

"We want him to have it today," Betty insisted, consulting the wall clock. "And since you're just about finished for the day…"

Nora smiled as her sitter, Shanda, came toward her with Liam in her arms. "You want me to drive all the way out to the No Name ranch?"

Miss Patricia laid a hand over her heart. "Unless you want us all to go in the Activity Bus?"

"Seriously, Nora," Betty said, "you need to keep an

eye on that man of yours if you don't want him to get away again. So if you don't do it, we will."

Nora could see the women meant it. So, even though she knew it wasn't necessary, she accepted the gift for Zane, then officially clocked out of work. With her sitter's help, she situated Liam in her minivan and drove out to the No Name.

She wasn't sure what she expected to see when she arrived at Zane's ranch. But it sure as heck wasn't what she found. A property clogged with vehicles of all sorts. Survey stakes dotted not just along the perimeter of the property, but within it, too. Worse, Zane did not look particularly happy to see her and Liam.

Realizing it had been a mistake to come without calling, she parked close to where he stood with several people in business attire. One of them a strikingly attractive woman about his sister's age.

Raquel, she guessed.

Had Betty and the other women been right?

Did Nora need to do a better job of looking after her man?

If she could even call Zane her man, that was. Since they still had no formally defined relationship. Broach or not.

Her heart accelerating as Zane strode toward her, Nora turned to Liam, said, "This will take just a minute, honey." Then turned off the engine and got out of the car.

"I wasn't expecting you."

He wasn't really glad to see her, either, Nora noted, standing next to the passenger door, in full view of her infant son.

"You're right." She wet her lips. "I should have called."

His gaze softened. "That's not what I meant." He stepped closer. "Is everything okay?"

"Yes." She swallowed around the parched feeling in her throat. "I'm just here because..." She walked around to the cargo area and opened it up. "The residents of Laramie Gardens wanted me to bring you this." She handed over the small prelit and already-decorated two-foot tree.

For a second, Zane was speechless.

As was she.

"Wow," he said finally.

Trying not to look as embarrassed as she felt, Nora continued, "They knew you hadn't put up a tree when you last talked with them, so they wanted to be sure you had something. As you can see, this decoration is designed to be set on a tabletop. And it's artificial, so you can pack it away and use it year after year, if you like."

Zane held it in front of him like a trophy. "I'll have to thank them when I see them."

Nora stepped back on shaking legs, chastising herself all the while. "Okay, then..."

"Nora." He caught her arm and swung her back around. Their glances met and held for several long beats. Frowning, he inclined his head at the activity behind him. "I can't explain any of this just yet."

Of course he was shutting her out. Again. His time here was almost up. "You don't have to."

His eyes said he disagreed.

Regret sharpened the ruggedly handsome lines of his face. "I also can't do anything with you and Liam tonight."

"I wasn't expecting you to." A total lie. She had actually been counting on spending the evening together. Just Zane, her and Liam.

"I will be at the Ugly Sweater contest tomorrow, though."

Feeling her heart break a little more, her Christmas spirit diminish, Nora forced a bracing smile and said, "I'll see you then."

"It's not too late to enter the Ugly Sweater competition," Nora told Mr. Pierce the following afternoon. She had just learned the former bookseller was one of the few residents at Laramie Gardens not participating.

"I've got a hot glue gun in my office, a few extra red and green sweaters and all sorts of decorations. We could do *A Christmas Carol* theme. A likeness of Scrooge…" she teased. "Or something from any other holiday-themed novel you like."

"Thank you, dear, but I'm doing my best not to vary from my new routine. I want to be on track when my daughter, Lynn, visits."

Instead of the one leather-bound classic with clasp he typically carried, today he had two. *Treasure Island* and *Great Expectations*.

"I think I'd rather do a little more research on improving memory on my computer, and then rest. But if I'm feeling up to it, I'll join the festivities in time for the judging," he promised.

Aware that was the best she was going to get, Nora told him, "Okay. But just so you know, if you change your mind, my offer to help you make a last-minute entry is good right up until the time of the contest…"

She went down the hall, checking in on residents. Clandestine activity abounded for the rest of the day, with final costume tweaking being done. And everywhere she went, one question was put to her—would Zane be competing, too?

"He promised he would," Nora said over and over, not really sure now that he would show up. Especially if whatever it was that was so important was still going on at the No Name ranch.

"Have you seen his ugly sweater?" Betty wanted to know.

No, and she had to admit, if he had found time to prepare one, she was a little curious.

"What time is he arriving?" Buck Franklin asked.

She had no idea about that, either, since she hadn't had so much as a text message from him after seeing him at his ranch. Probably because he didn't want her to ask any more questions he couldn't—or maybe just wouldn't—answer.

On the other hand, he always had been a man of his word. A man of honor.

"Hopefully he'll be here by the time it starts, at four o'clock," Nora said.

"I'm sure he'll surprise us," Wilbur Barnes said.

So was Nora. No matter what happened.

But she had no idea just how much, until Zane walked through the door.

Chapter 14

The first thing Nora realized as the handsome warrior strode toward her was that she never should have doubted Zane's willingness to participate once he had declared the three of them "all in."

The second was that he was as much a rule breaker as ever.

The base sweater was a worn-to-the-point-of-ruin camouflage design with olive green leather elbow patches. Strands of multicolored blinking Christmas lights had been duct-taped to the sleeves, back and chest. The battery-pack that fueled them was attached to a wide black vinyl belt—that was also duct-taped to the sweater. Completing the ensemble was a bucket hat in the same camouflage green, with reindeer antlers popping up on either side of his head, double strands of mistletoe dangling from them.

It was, Nora noted with a mixture of exasperation and relief, exactly what they needed to break some of the too-serious tension in the room, as the time for competition neared.

Not that everyone agreed.

Betty leveled an accusing finger at Zane. "You're disqualified!" she said, clearly upset.

Zane didn't care.

Nor did Liam, whose eyes had lit up the moment he saw Zane striding toward them, Christmas lights blinking merrily. As the grinning lieutenant neared, Liam's face lit even more. And then it began. A first, soft chuckle that swiftly evolved into a baby belly laugh, Liam's first.

And once Liam started laughing at Zane—who was by now laughing, too—he couldn't seem to stop. Nor could anyone else. The chuckles running through the room grew and grew until everyone was joining in the hilarity.

Betty frowned at Zane, the rule sheet still in her hand. "You're still disqualified," she fumed.

Zane winked at her playfully. He reached for Liam, who had his arms held out toward him. "As I should be," he murmured, moving quickly to catch the suddenly lurching Liam. "Hey there, little fella," he said, holding Liam against his chest and wrapping his other arm around Nora.

In front of everyone, he kissed her soundly on the lips. "Don't you look fetching, too," he murmured.

And in that instant, with tears of mirth still streaming down her face, Nora felt so much. Gratitude that Zane was there with them. Regret at all the time they had wasted over the years. Plus, a boundless enthusiasm for their future. No matter what happened from here on out, she knew what she wanted, and that was to be a part of Zane's life. And he, theirs.

"Tell me the truth," Zane said, hours later, when the three of them had returned to her home and the exhausted Liam was tucked in bed. His ridiculous sweater and hat off, a navy one in its place, he finished lighting the fire in the hearth. He pivoted and sent Nora a knowing look. "You threw the competition on purpose."

Pretending to be indignant, Nora walked over to plug in the Christmas tree lights. "What was wrong with Liam's and my sweaters?" She pointed to the back of the chair, where they were now displayed in all their eclectic glory.

She had sewn an adorable felt elf on the front of Liam's Christmas-green sweater and hot-glued a combination of fabric ornaments, and vinyl green-and-white-striped candy cane decals to the front of her red one.

"Uh-huh." Zane sank down beside her on the sofa.

Nora grinned and snuggled close. There was no use pretending she wasn't completely smitten with the two men in her life. "Okay, I confess that I simply wanted Liam to look cute. Otherwise, he would have had way too unfair an advantage."

Zane chuckled, recalling, "He almost won it with that belly laugh."

The thought of which still brought a sheen of happy tears to Nora's eyes. "His very first, by the way," she pointed out.

And it had all been because of Zane.

So much that was good this holiday season was because of him…

Zane stroked the back of her hand with his fingertips. "I'm glad I got to see that," he said tenderly.

"So am I." She turned her palm up, so it was facing his. "It was a special moment," she confessed softly. Made all the more special because Zane had been there, too. Marveling at how well they had always fit together—as if they were meant to be—she looked down at their entwined hands. "But it was good Miss Isabella walked away with the grand prize."

The handpainted holiday collage attached to the front of the former art teacher's Christmas-red sweater had been outrageously funny and loud, with colors clashing, yet somehow sweetly sentimental at the same time.

He nodded. "It's amazing how much she has perked up since Thanksgiving."

"Amazing how happy a lot of us are. I just wish Mr. Pierce hadn't been so blue tonight."

Zane recollected with concern, "He barely looked up from whatever he was doing on his computer tablet."

Nora sighed. "I think he may have been a little confused, too." She and the other nurses had noticed that happening more and more as the week had progressed, despite the new multitherapy regimen the older gentleman was on.

She forced herself to be optimistic. "Dr. Wheeler is coming in tomorrow morning to see him, so hopefully that will help."

"I'm sure it will." Keeping his dark silver gaze locked with hers, he stroked a comforting hand down her thigh. "So what else is on your mind?"

Nora swallowed around the rising lump in her throat,

wondering if she was going to be able to find the nerve to do what she really wanted, and propose they craft a happily-ever-after. Whatever that looked like to him.

Married.

Engaged.

Or simply committed to each other, in their hearts and souls, from here on out. "I did want to talk to you about something important."

"Okay," he said softly.

She inhaled deeply. "Us."

The width of his smile etched grooves on either side of his mouth. He looked deep into her eyes with all the affection she had ever wanted and hoped to see. "We'll get to that before I leave again," he said soberly, "I promise you that. But right now—" one hand on her spine, he drew her even closer "—what I want more than anything is to make up for the time we lost this week. Because I missed you, Nora, so much..."

His lips fastened over hers and just that quickly all her worries fled. He kissed her in a way that had her senses spinning and her heart soaring.

The next thing she knew he was tossing one of the throws and several pillows on the floor before the fire and guiding her to the bed he made for them. Passion swept through her as he stretched out beside her.

She moaned softly as he clasped her to him and eased a hand beneath her shirt. He kissed her slow and deep, angling his head to get more of her, even as his clever hands moved upward and the fastening of her bra came undone.

She smiled as his palms came around to her breasts, slipping beneath the silk of her bra and stroking her nipples. A slow, warm heat began to fill her as they kissed hungrily, arching into each other, his rock-hardness a seduction in and of itself.

Her hands slipped beneath the hem of his sweater, too, finding the sleek muscles and satin warmth of his skin. He felt so good. So masculine. So right.

They felt so right.

"I want you," she murmured, against his lips.

"I want you, too." The wicked light in his eyes igniting all her erogenous zones, he sat up. Removed his sweater. She sat up and removed hers.

He pulled her onto his lap, so she was facing him, her arms encircling his neck. The clothing still between them was maddening. "Our jeans..."

"We'll get there. Promise..." And then his lips were on hers in a frenzy of wanting. Making her reckless, making her need, the powerful muscles of his chest abrading the softness of her breasts.

And still they kissed. Caresses pouring out of them. Feeling building. Desire exploding in liquid heat. Until unable to stand it any longer, they undressed the rest of the way, found protection and joined each other on the blanket before the fire.

She lifted her hips, her yearning every bit as fierce and all-encompassing as his. The hard length of him pressed into her, slowly, sensually. Hands sliding beneath her hips, lifting her, holding her still. Forcing her to submit to the hopelessly erotic, endless strokes. Deep, then shallow, then deep again.

All the while, their lips clung together, seducing, surrendering. Driving each other to the brink. Until all was lost in a perfect storm of wanting. Needing. Giving. Taking. And there was nothing but the heart and soul of that moment in time, nothing but the two of them. The earthshaking pleasure and the never-ending bliss, the perfection of the present, the sweet hope of the future.

He felt it, too.

It was clear in the way he gathered her close afterward, pressing kisses in her hair, along her temple, her jawline. The way they sagged against each other, spent and breathless. So safe and protected, their connection so strong and so right it felt unbreakable.

Until finally, he captured her lips in another hot, euphoric kiss, then lifted his head and gazed into her eyes, murmured softly, "I want you to know, Nora. There is only one woman on this earth for me. And it's you." His voice roughened even as his gaze grew unbearably fervent. "It's always been you…"

It wasn't the same thing as saying he was in love with her, but it was the closest he had ever come.

She celebrated that.

Heart swelling with all that she felt in return, Nora admitted just as fervently, "You're the only man for me, too." And for the moment, maybe even forever, that would have to be enough.

"So you're going to be at the West Texas Warriors Assistance this morning," Nora said, as she and Zane bundled Liam up and headed out the door to her minivan.

He nodded. "They have a Job Finder session I want to sit in on."

Which meant what? Nora wondered. He was looking for a job? Thinking about looking for a job? Or searching for a reason not to try and find a job outside active duty military? There was no clue on his handsome face.

He flashed a grin. "Try not to miss me too much, okay?" he teased.

She wrinkled her nose right back at him, glad they already had plans to see each other for dinner. She saluted him sharply. "And you do the same, Lieutenant!"

Fortunately for Nora, it was slated to be a very busy day at Laramie Gardens. Which meant their time apart would pass quickly.

A good thing, given how much matchmaking she encountered when she reported for duty.

"Where is that handsome fella of yours?" Miss Mim teased while setting out boxes of undecorated sugar cookies.

Betty added colored frostings and sparkling sugar to the workstations set up in the dining room. "Not with Raquel, I hope."

Miss Sadie put in her two cents. "You have to keep an eye on your man, Nora!"

"As it happens he is with other ex-military personnel this morning," Nora said, as she passed out morning medications to those who required them.

"If I were you I'd get a ring on his finger, pronto," Miss Patricia said.

"Let him know you're serious," Miss Isabelle chimed in helpfully.

I tried last night, Nora thought, in silent frustration, *but Zane didn't let me get very far...*

Aware she'd have to be a lot more proactive if she wanted to get what she wanted out of their renewed relationship, Nora said wryly, "Thanks for the advice, ladies." She propped her hands on her hips, and assumed a total taskmaster stance. "Now, can we get cracking on decorating those sugar cookies we were going to send to the community caroling event at the town square?"

Chuckles abounded.

And there were some sympathetic looks, too.

The women at Laramie Gardens knew Nora well enough to know they had struck a nerve with their teasing. Albeit, unintentionally.

Fortunately, she still had more medication to pass out and a patient to get ready for an on-site medical appointment.

"You want me to wait in your office?" Mr. Pierce asked.

Nora paused while the older gentleman got comfortable, then handed him the insulated mug of green tea she'd been carrying for him. "Just for a few minutes. Dr. Wheeler is reviewing your records as we speak. As soon as he's done, he and I will confer, and then we'll bring you in."

Mr. Pierce set his leather-bound copy of *A Christmas Carol* and computer tablet on his lap. "Doc's got to be very busy with Christmas so close at hand."

Was it her imagination or was Mr. Pierce looking a little manic this morning? "I think everyone is this time of year."

Mr. Pierce rubbed the elaborate buckle clasp on his book. "The weatherman said a cold front is coming in!"

Nora smiled. Moving to tidy up her office, she hung her coat on the hook behind the door, her purse on the one next to it, Liam's fleece hoodie on a third. "I heard."

He crossed his legs, then uncrossed them. "I also read that it'll be below freezing tonight, with a possibility of snow on Christmas Eve!"

Nora had heard less than a 10 percent chance. Still…

"Wouldn't that be wonderful," she said, opening the blinds, so Mr. Pierce could see the people coming and going from the parking lot outside. Her red minivan that he had so admired gleamed in the winter sunshine.

He nodded vigorously. "Your son would love it. So will Lynn."

"They would." Spying her keys on the desk, Nora slipped them into the outside pocket on her purse.

"But it could hurt last-minute business for the retailers," Mr. Pierce predicted.

True. "Or encourage them to buy early!"

He grinned. "The holidays have always been a particularly busy time for booksellers. Including Esther and me."

Aware Mr. Pierce hadn't been this chatty in a long time—if ever—Nora straightened a stack of Welcome folders on her desk. "I remember," she said fondly. The Book Nook had been a treasure trove of gifts during the holidays. The married owners were a delight.

Mr. Pierce settled back in his chair and sipped his tea. "I want Lynn to have a very nice Christmas, too."

It was good he was focused on his daughter and her upcoming visit. Those plans would help keep him grounded. "I know she's excited," Nora said. The actress had already phoned to request that she and her father be allowed to eat at least one meal in the private dining room.

Mr. Pierce opened up his tablet. "I probably should make up a list," he said, as if anxious to get going. "I still have a lot to do to get ready for Christmas."

Didn't they all?

"Then I'll leave you to it." Nora shut the door quietly behind her and went down the hall to the conference room, where Dr. Wheeler was just finishing reviewing the files Nora had set in front of him.

"You're right." The physician looked up from the notes he had been making. "The time frame fits. But you and I have both done extensive research on possible drug interactions in this case. There's no documented evidence that the new antihistamine Mr. Pierce started taking after his move to New York City last summer could be causing his intermittent disorientation and memory issues."

But there was no documented evidence that it wasn't, Nora thought. Quietly, she persuaded, "It's only been on the market a year. Maybe there just isn't enough data yet for it to show up. Or maybe the new drug is fine on its own, but when it's combined with the particular blood pressure and cholesterol medications Mr. Pierce takes, there's an interaction. Or maybe for most people there is no negative side effect, even with that particular combination, but for him there is."

Dr. Wheeler steepled his hands in front of him. "You want to take him off the new potentially troublesome medication and put him back on his previous allergy medicine?"

Eager to get her fellow clinician on board, Nora nodded. "It's the only way to eliminate the new medication as being the culprit."

Dr. Wheeler closed the file. "Okay. Let's go see him."

Together, they walked down the hall.

Nora's office door was open.

Unfortunately, Mr. Pierce was not where she had left him. His travel mug of green tea, tablet and leather-bound copy of *A Christmas Carol* were also gone. "Maybe he went back to his suite," she said.

But Mr. Pierce wasn't there, either. Nor was he in the community room. The music room. The dining hall, or anywhere else they could fathom. In fact, they realized quickly, he wasn't anywhere on the premises, inside or out.

Beginning to panic, Nora called the Laramie County sheriff's department, and then Zane.

Both arrived within minutes.

Deputy Kyle McCabe strode in with several fellow officers. Zane and a whole cadre of ex-military followed.

Zane went straight to Nora and wrapped his arm around her shoulders. "We'll find Mr. Pierce," he promised.

But would it be in time? Nora wondered, distraught. "His brown leather jacket and fedora are still in the closet in his room. Which means all he has on is his flannel shirt and corduroy trousers."

And with it being around thirty-four degrees outside, hypothermia was a real concern for the eighty-five-year-old.

"How long do you think he's been gone?" Deputy McCabe asked.

Nora consulted her watch. "Thirty minutes, at most."

Zane speculated, "If he's on foot, he can't have gone far."

What if he wasn't in his right mind? "He could be confused."

"Is there anything else missing?" Deputy Kyle McCabe asked.

"Like what?" Nora asked.

"Your minivan," Zane said.

Nora rushed to the front of the building.

Sure enough, the space where she had parked was empty.

She dashed back to her office. Her purse was still there where she had left it, with her coat on the hook by the door. The exterior pocket was unzipped. She groaned. "My keys are gone, too."

Zane sobered all the more. "If he was confused, he might have thought he was driving his own vehicle."

Betty joined them. "He was talking about Esther at breakfast, and...well, it almost sounded as if he thought she were still here with us..."

Darrell Enlow joined them. "He asked me where I thought the best place in the county was to find a live tree if you wanted to cut it down yourself. I said I didn't know. I hadn't done it in years."

Miss Patricia said, "He also said something about getting his favorite Christmas ornaments out of storage."

"When I left him, he was making a list of things he still had left to do to get ready for Christmas," Nora added.

"So he's probably out running errands," Zane said.

Kyle took down the license plate of Nora's minivan, then issued a Silver Alert. "Two patrol cars are canvassing the town limits as we speak. No one has caught sight of him yet."

"We can't just stay here and do nothing." Nora wrung her hands.

"And we're not going to," Zane reassured her.

Ten minutes later, Zane and Kyle had worked together to come up with a plan. The sheriff's department would canvass the far-flung roads and outlying areas, looking for Nora's minivan. The ex-military volunteers would cover all the businesses in town, going door to door to see if anyone had come in contact with Russell Pierce since he'd left Laramie Gardens.

Meanwhile, Miss Mim would work with all the residents to come up with any additional clues about what Mr. Pierce might be attempting to do to get ready for the holiday. And Zane and Nora would visit some of the more obvious places. His former bookstore, as well as the home where he used to live with Esther and Lynn.

"I should have seen this coming," Nora lamented, as they rushed outside to Zane's pickup truck.

He slanted her a glance, not about to baby her. "We can go through a debriefing of all the mistakes that were made later. Right now, let's just concentrate on finding Mr. Pierce."

Unfortunately, he wasn't at the bookstore he had once owned. The local storage facility hadn't seen him on the premises, either. And no one seemed to even be at the home Esther and Russell Pierce had once owned.

Undeterred, Zane peered around the side of the house into the backyard. Pointed. The door to the shed was wide open.

He and Nora hurried across the yard.

Inside, everything was neatly arranged except the garden tools area. Several of those looked like they had been picked up and thrown down. Zane said, "What do you want to bet he's after a Christmas tree he plans to cut himself?"

"Maybe Miss Mim or the other ladies might know where," Nora said. While she called Laramie Gardens and got the location of the most popular cut-it-yourself Christmas tree farm years ago, as well as several others, Zane contacted all the military men and Kyle McCabe.

Frowning, he got off the phone, "My brother Garrett has enlisted everyone over at West Texas Warrior Assistance to continue canvassing the town, so I'm moving all my guys out into the countryside. Because it's possible Mr. Pierce got turned around if he's out there, we're going to cover every road. It'd be easier if we had air power, but the sheriff's department's one chopper still isn't available— it's on loan to another county sheriff's department for an ongoing search and rescue. Meantime, Kyle's trying to get a hold of Wade McCabe to see if they can borrow his."

"Of all the times to be shorthanded!" Nora fumed.

Zane looked like he wanted to say something, then closed his mouth. He guided her quickly back to his pickup truck. "Do you have directions for where you want to check first?"

"I do."

His jaw set. "Then let's move it."

It took them eighteen minutes to reach the location of what had once been the most popular Christmas tree farm, fifty years before. A rough-hewn property just east of Lake Laramie that had long ago gone to seed. "Now what?" Nora asked in frustration. "There's no way my minivan could cut through that much underbrush."

Zane drove a little farther down the country road. "Which is maybe why it's parked there." He pulled up beside Nora's vehicle.

The minivan's motor was turned off but the driver door had been left oddly ajar, the keys inside. While Zane quickly made the call to let the others know the vehicle had been found, the general area of Mr. Pierce's whereabouts pinpointed, Nora leaped out of the cab to peer inside the minivan.

Mr. Pierce's tablet was on the passenger seat along with his travel mug of tea and the leather-bound *A Christmas Carol*. Only this time, the buckle was undone.

"Help is on the way," Zane reported. He grabbed a pair of binoculars from his glove compartment and climbed on the bed of his pickup truck.

"Do you see him?" she asked Zane.

He scanned the wooded terrain. "Not yet. What color shirt was he wearing? Do you remember?"

"Green and brown plaid shirt, brown pants."

Zane groaned.

Nora knew how he felt. Mr. Pierce might as well have been wearing camouflage gear.

She grabbed the fleece blanket she always kept in her car, in winter, just in case of emergencies. The tea thermos—which still had a little bit of liquid in it. Then, on impulse, the book.

As she picked it up, it fell open. From the compartment formed by cutaway pages, a small white plastic bottle tumbled out and rolled across the seat. She bent to pick it up, and gasped at what it was.

"Problem?" Zane said.

Nora nodded and swiftly took off the cap, realizing it was empty. "A big one," she confirmed gravely, her panic turning to dread.

"Hey," Zane said, before she had time to explain, "I think I've got him in my sights! Yep! That's him, all right." He jumped down from the bed of the pickup.

Nora followed him through the heavy brush, into the woods. One hundred yards later, they encountered Mr. Pierce. The older gentleman was seated next to a gorgeous pine tree, an ax and a small tree saw, on the ground next to him. Seeing them, he pointed to the faint cut marks on the base of the tree trunk. "Had to stop and rest a minute," he explained, shivering.

"Understandable," Zane said.

Nora nodded. "I'm so glad we found you." Nora knelt and felt his skin. It was pale and cool to the touch. Hypothermia was definitely setting in. She wrapped the blanket about his shoulders.

"But I'm going to have to g-g-get going again soon." Mr. Pierce tried to rise on his own, failed. "Esther and Lynn will be expecting me to b-bring home a Christmas tree for them to decorate."

Zane knelt next to Mr. Pierce. He caught Nora's glance and understood well her concern. "Not to worry, sir. I'll take care of that. In the meantime, we have to warm you up a bit."

"Sounds g-good," Mr. Pierce said feebly, shivering all the harder. "It appears I forgot my coat…"

"And to speed things up," Zane continued, catching Nora's panicked look, seeming to realize that there was no time to wait for an ambulance to get all the way out there, "I'm going to carry you." He lifted Mr. Pierce in his strong arms, stood, and made his way deliberately through the brush.

Mr. Pierce chuckled feebly. "This is a first."

"Not for me," Zane joked right back, all macho alpha male. "It's how us military guys work out."

This time they all laughed.

Tears of worry and relief blurring her eyes, Nora grabbed the tools and led the way to safety.

Chapter 15

"Are you angry with me?" Mr. Pierce asked Nora several hours later, when he had been moved out of the emergency room and into a regular hospital room. "You have every right to be."

Zane walked in with the belongings she had requested him to get from Laramie Gardens. He stood next to her, reminding her they were a team—and a very good one. "Concerned is more like it," Nora clarified.

She removed the stack of leather-bound books from the bag Zane carried. Opened the buckle on each one and removed a plastic over-the-counter pill bottle from each.

"Clever place to hide things," Zane observed.

"And safe, since no one reads the classics anymore," Mr. Pierce returned facetiously.

Aiding Zane in the attempt to get Mr. Zane to confide in them, she asked gently, "Do you want to tell us what this is all about?"

Mr. Pierce sighed. "I've been working on improving my memory. So in addition to eating almonds and drinking green tea, I've also taken a lot of all-natural supplements like herbs and vitamins."

"Every day?"

"Pretty much, when I can remember. I've tried them all, alone or in combination. And before you ask, I kept it quiet because I knew not everyone would approve."

Especially the medical staff. "Did you keep any record of these trials?" Nora asked as Zane arched a brow in her direction.

Mr. Pierce pointed to his forehead. "Just up here."

"But it's been pretty regular since—?" she prodded.

"I moved to New York City to be with Lynn and had troubled getting acclimated. They had a health food store down the block from her apartment, and I went there."

Zane inched closer to Nora. "Did your daughter know this?"

"Lynn would have worried if she knew I needed assistance recalling things. So I didn't tell her I'd started taking supplements to boost my memory and sharpen my concentration skills."

"Or your doctors, either," Nora guessed.

He shrugged.

Nora pushed on. "Was this before or after you switched antihistamines?"

Mr. Pierce thought a moment. "A couple of weeks after, I guess."

His elbow bumping up against hers, Zane asked,

"Were you having trouble staying focused before the switch in allergy medication?"

Mr. Pierce shook his head. "No. It was after that, I started forgetting things. And then, after that I added the natural remedies to counter the effects of aging." He began to look almost as upset as Nora and Zane felt. Glancing from one to another, he said, "Was that a mistake?"

And then some, Nora thought. Basking in the support Zane offered, she went on kindly, "Here's the thing, Mr. Pierce. These herbal supplements are all anticholinergic. Which means they inhibit activity of the neurotransmitter acetylcholine, which plays an essential role in memory and cognitive function. When you combine them with the medications you already take to control your blood pressure and lower cholesterol, they can produce mild cognitive impairment. Or dementia and Alzheimer-like symptoms."

Mr. Pierce turned pale. "So you think this may have been the problem all along?" he asked, aghast. "The combination of my new antihistamine and the natural supplements I added?"

Nora, who had already talked to his geriatric specialist on the phone, nodded. "Dr. Wheeler and I are betting on it."

Mr. Pierce smiled. "So to get better, all I have to do is...?"

"Switch back to your old allergy medication and stop taking any and all unauthorized supplements. Herbal or otherwise."

Nora and Zane talked to Mr. Pierce a few more minutes. Reassured him he would be getting out of the hospital the following day in plenty of time to enjoy Christmas Eve with his daughter, Lynn.

Together, they headed out into the hall. Taking advantage of the momentary quiet, Nora took Zane's hand in hers. "Have I told you how much I appreciate everything you did for us today?" she murmured. She rose up on tiptoe and brushed her lips across his. "You were quite the hero."

He laced an arm about her waist and pulled her closer. "Haven't you heard?" he quipped, kissing her back. "Being a hero is my full-time job."

"How well I know that," she replied, dancing him back into the hidden alcove opposite the elevators and kissing him again.

In fact, she was beginning to see the two were intrinsically interlinked.

The doors slid open.

One of the nurses who'd taken care of Mr. Pierce in the ER stepped out.

"And here I thought there wasn't enough mistletoe to go around," she teased.

Zane and Nora exchanged baffled glances. "Ah, we don't have any mistletoe," he said.

Although that, too, could be remedied, Nora thought happily.

The nurse winked. "And you don't appear to need it, either!"

That evening, the residents of Laramie Gardens threw a party to thank everyone who had aided in the search for Mr. Pierce. While Zane made the rounds, with Liam in a BabyBjörn strapped to his wide chest,

Nora helped the women put out the holiday spread for the guests.

But even as they worked, no one could keep from looking at the soldier in the center of the room. Zane was just so handsome and charismatic, Nora thought on a wistful sigh. So big and manly he made her feel like a woman every time she saw him.

Miss Sadie followed Nora's surreptitious glance. "You have to nail that hunk of burnin' love down and get a ring on your finger before he leaves again!" she murmured, as she put out the cranberry molds.

"I second that!" Betty chimed in, adding a fresh tray of brisket sliders to the buffet.

Miss Patricia handed Nora a sprig of mistletoe and a CD of an old but cherished copy of *Andy Williams Christmas Favorites*. "Just in case you need something to set the mood." She winked.

Nora didn't think she and Zane needed any help setting their mood. They couldn't keep their hands off each other.

Miss Isabelle patted her arm. "Times like this, dear, a woman needs to use every tool in her arsenal."

Nora put the last of the side dishes and salads out. "I'll remember that," she opined drily, already thinking how much fun it would be to recount this conversation to Zane later.

"In fact…" She picked up a tray of cookies and headed for Zane, who was now surrounded by a group of ex-military and sheriff's deputies. She turned and winked at her group of cheerleaders. "I'll get started right now."

As she neared him, she heard Deputy Kyle McCabe say, "…appreciate how quickly you were able to jump into the action today…organize others…a real asset… The sheriff's department could really use you."

That's what Nora had been hearing, too.

Although sadly Zane had told her in no uncertain terms he wasn't interested in doing a job that included handing out traffic tickets…

She stopped to offer refreshment to Buck Franklin and Kurtis Kelley. As the residents helped themselves to cookies, another military guy said, "I heard via the grapevine they've been doing everything possible to get you to reenlist."

Zane shrugged, his back still to her, so she could not read the expression on his face. "That's always the case," he said mildly.

Darrell Enlow walked up to join the group, adding, "Despite what Nora said, she will support you."

Nora's heart stuttered in her chest, listening raptly to every word. Kyle McCabe, who had known her since childhood, agreed. "She'll wait for you," he promised.

Except in the past, she thought guiltily, she hadn't really done that. She and Zane had always eventually gotten back together, but there had been an awful lot of heartache and loneliness in between their hookups.

And that remained one of her biggest life regrets.

They had wasted so much time.

So many opportunities to be together emotionally, if not physically.

As she ventured even closer, Zane's older brother, Garrett, elbowed Zane lightly in the ribs. "And speaking of the gal who's got your heart…"

But did she? Nora wondered, thinking of all Zane had been up to recently that he hadn't actually confided in her.

On the other hand, there were things she hadn't gotten around to telling him, either. Things she still needed to say.

As if sensing her presence behind him, Zane swung around to face Nora. He gave her a slow, affectionate once-over, seeming to see how completely exhausted she was, while as usual he still had tons of energy left. He looked down at the yawning baby strapped to his chest. "I think this little guy's about had it." He reached over to take her hand, his expression radiating the tender devotion she so adored. "Ready to go home?"

She knew it was selfish, but she wanted her alone time with him. Especially now that their days together were dwindling. "Yes," she said, smiling back and gearing up for all that yet had to be said. "I am."

Half an hour later, Liam was in bed, fast asleep, and Zane and Nora were finally settled before the fire.

She had been waiting for this moment for weeks now, even thinking she might dare to propose to him. Yet suddenly she was a bundle of nerves. Worried it all might go awry.

He clasped her shoulders lightly and drew her into the curve of his big strong body. "You okay?" he asked, pressing a kiss on the top of her head.

Nora inhaled deeply and tried to calm down.

Why was he looking at her like that? As if he half expected her to do what she always did when their time together approached an end, and break up with him tonight?

"Why wouldn't I be?" she countered.

He chuckled and stroked a thumb down her cheek. "Maybe because you looked like you were getting some vigorous advice on how to handle your man from the Laramie Gardens ladies tonight."

Perceptive, as always. "You were getting the same kind of life coaching, from what I heard."

Zane inclined his head to the side, unperturbed. "Everyone means well."

Even as they push us together. "They do." Nora nodded.

"But...?" he prodded.

Knowing it was now or never, Nora sighed. Moving out of the cozy curve of his body, she perched on the edge of the sofa and pivoted to face him. Hands clasped together on her lap, she announced firmly, "We also need to talk. And we need to do it tonight."

Zane wanted to tell Nora everything. She had no idea how badly. But only once it was all set. He lifted a staying hand. "I need a few more days, Nora." That was all he was asking.

They stared at each other.

She sighed and ran her hands through her hair. "Until after Christmas," she deduced unhappily.

Or sooner.

He wasn't quite sure.

So erring on the side of caution, he just said, "Yes."

Nora squared her slender shoulders deliberately and huffed out a breath. "No, Zane. You don't need more time before we talk about what's next for us."

"I don't?" he echoed in confusion.

Her slender body quivering with emotion, Nora drew a deep breath. "It's okay if you want to go back to your unit. I understand."

This was new, Zane thought. And not in a good way.

The tip of Nora's tongue snaked out to wet her lower

lip. "You don't belong here in Laramie, Zane. And the truth is, you never have," she said, holding all the tighter to his hands. "You know it. I know it…"

He'd never seen her so overwrought or so incredibly, passionately, beautiful. He shifted her over onto his lap. Adjusted his posture to ease the pressure building at the front of his slacks and felt her begin to blissfully relax.

He rubbed his thumb across the soft dampness of her lower lip. Looked deep into her eyes. "Where do you see me?"

Nora wreathed one arm about his shoulders, splayed the other hand across the center of his chest. Her expressive brows lowering over her long-lashed eyes, she replied, "Where you have always belonged. With your unit in the Special Forces."

He stared at her, hardly able to believe she was pushing him away. The way she always did before any expected deployment.

Again.

He'd thought—hoped—with the connection they had forged, with Liam's help, that they had gotten past all that.

Still, he tried to give her the benefit of the doubt. "And here I thought I'd been making myself useful around here," he deadpanned.

For a second, Nora turned her glance away and the pink in her cheeks deepened. Her lips tightened. Slowly but surely, the walls around her heart began to go back up. With a contrite smile, she turned to look him in the eye. "That's the hell of it. You have. With the Laramie Gardens residents. The ex-military guys over at the WTWA. Liam. Me. Your family."

Her pretty sky blue eyes began to fill with tears.

"We're all going to miss you terribly," she admitted, her lush lower lip quivering. "But we can't let our feelings dictate what you do or where you go." She withdrew herself from his embrace, stood. And walked over to the fireplace. She fingered the less-than-pleasing photo of Liam, with Santa displayed there.

As a reminder that life wasn't always perfect? he wondered.

Swallowing she turned back to face him. "And I know you realize it, too. Even if you're not ready to admit it to me just yet."

His emotions in turmoil, too, he stood. "How do you figure that?"

She waved an airy hand. "It's why you've been putting off having any kind of serious talk until after Christmas Day. The same goes for your family. It's why you are preparing to sell the ranch your father left you."

He joined her at the mantel. The heat emanating from the hearth was nothing compared to the fire roiling deep inside his gut.

He lounged beside her. "How long since you deduced all this?"

To his increasing frustration, his sarcasm seemed lost on her.

Turning to face him, she angled her chin at him and continued blithely, "I realized what was going on the day I delivered the tabletop tree to the No Name."

He lifted his brow, wordlessly urging her to go on.

"You had the most knowledgeable real estate broker in Laramie County out there. A group of surveyors. Sage's friend Raquel, from Dallas."

He shook his head, hoping that would clear it. "So?"

"You didn't want to talk about any of it to me, Zanc. You still don't."

He rubbed at the tension gathering in the back of his neck, said wearily, "I had my reasons, Nora." *And I still do.*

"Yes," she said, determined to keep her blinders on. Her lower lip slid out in a delicious pout. "Because you didn't want our latest hookup to end the way it always does just yet."

"Hookup," he echoed in shock, wondering how this conversation could get any more disappointing.

"Or fling or reconnection. Whatever you want to call it."

Semantics weren't what was bothering him here.

"How about Part Two in Our Never Really Ending Relationship?"

His sardonic humor was completely lost on her.

She propped her hands on her hips. Clearly exasperated, said, "That's exactly what I'm trying to tell you, Zane. Our relationship with each other doesn't have to end."

She came close enough to take him in her arms again.

Said with fierce finality, "I want to be on-again with you from here on out. I want you to know that Liam and I will be here, waiting for you and supporting you, no matter how long or how often you're gone."

Nora wasn't sure why her matter-of-fact declaration was being met with such stunned silence. She'd expected the knowledge that they would be here for him from this day forward would make him incredibly happy.

Instead, he looked stunned. And wary. Too wary for comfort.

"And you'll be content with that?" he asked quietly, keeping his physical distance in a way she hadn't expected. He rested an arm on the mantel. "Seeing each other only occasionally? Making do with what time the military gives us?"

Of course not! But she'd finally found a way to be there for him. To be as honorable and duty driven as he was, deep down. And most especially, to be able to nobly sacrifice the way he did. "I promise, from here on out, I'm going to be a good military…"

He frowned when she stumbled, trying to come up with the right word to categorize what they had yet to precisely define. "Girlfriend?" he asked mildly.

Was he angry? Hard to tell, but it certainly seemed so.

Aware this was all starting to go mysteriously awry, Nora swallowed. "I think—if you're asking—that I prefer the term *your woman*. Or *your significant other*. But—" she drew another deep breath, still floundering under his steady regard "—if you'd like to say something more contemporary, we could always call me your…um…*person*…?"

His expression maddeningly impassive, Zane folded his arms. His gaze sifted over her face before returning with slow deliberation to her eyes. "How about *love interest*? Would that work?"

Like she cared how others viewed them, she thought grumpily. Their relationship was theirs and theirs alone. She thought she had made that clear! Apparently not.

She moved toward him, hands outspread. Suddenly feeling as piqued and out of sorts as he looked. "Why are you so ticked off, anyway? I'm finally giving you what you always wanted from me, Zane! My unwavering, unconditional support."

His dark silver eyes narrowed. He turned and walked away from her. "With one foot out the door, of course."

Tensing anxiously, she followed. "I'm giving you your freedom instead of boxing you in, the way you always hated."

He swung around to square off with her once again. His jaw set. He stared at her long and hard, then shook his head. "I really thought things had changed between us."

Nora took him by the arms. "They have!"

His biceps were rock hard, resistant, beneath her compelling grip. "No," he countered sternly, "they haven't, Nora. My family. The guys in the unit. The fellows at Laramie Gardens and now, *even you*. You all have an opinion as to what I should do."

He stepped back and angled a thumb at the center of his chest.

Anger vibrated in the air between them. "And yet… as much as you proclaim to care for me…you've never once asked me what I want! Or what I think would be good for us."

He was twisting things, deliberately misinterpreting her actions, the way he always did whenever they got too close. Or he risked having *her* ask too much of *him*.

The heat of rejection pushed from her chest into her face. She'd thought things were different, too. But were they, after all?

"I just did that," she retorted evenly.

He shook his head, regret etching the hard, uncompromising lines of his handsome face. "No, Nora, you made a huge *assumption* predicated on what you *thought* I was going to do between now and January 15, when my current enlistment ends. And you let me know you were okay with your expectation." He grimaced unhappily. "Especially now that you have your guard back up."

Nora dropped her hands as if she'd been stung. And to think, she'd been about to propose to this man! She stepped back, feeling as if the entire world were quaking beneath her feet.

Hurt filled her low tone. "That wasn't what I was doing!" Tears filled her eyes. She did her best to contain them.

He quirked a dissenting brow.

"I was finally being supportive in the best, the only way I know how," she continued, feeling utterly humiliated.

Even if he still had yet to be completely forthcoming with her. And maybe, she realized sadly, acutely aware of how he was still shutting her out, he never would be.

But once again, Zane didn't see it her way.

"No, Nora," he corrected bitterly, a muscle working in his jaw. "You were protecting your heart, once again. Valiantly pushing me out the door and out of your life—just in time for the first and only Christmas we've been blessed to actually spend together!" He turned on his heel and grabbed his coat. "And guess what? I'm going!"

Chapter 16

"What's wrong, dear?" Miss Mim asked Nora on the morning of Christmas Eve.

Everything, Nora thought miserably. But wary of spoiling anyone else's holiday, Nora continued setting out small gift baskets at every seat in the dining hall. "What could be wrong? Mr. Pierce is safe and sound and celebrating the holiday with his daughter, Lynn." Plus, his medical mystery had been solved.

She nodded at the community room, which was filled with laughter and music.

"We've had children in and out all day, bringing gifts and spending time with residents as part of our new Adopt a Grandparent program."

A fact which had made Miss Isabella and others very happy.

"And we're set to have a wonderful holiday meal

this evening, and another in the dining hall tomorrow afternoon."

Miss Mim moved behind Nora, adding poinsettia centerpieces. "Have you heard from your family?"

Nora and Miss Mim went back to the storage area to replenish their pushcarts.

"My mother and my sister, Davina, both called this morning to wish us a merry Christmas, and FaceTime with us a bit." Which had been the one-and-only really bright spot of her day thus far.

Miss Mim cast a fond look at Liam, who currently was nestled in Miss Patricia's arms while Miss Sadie entertained him with an impromptu puppet show. "What about Zane?"

Liam let out a belly laugh at the antics of the stuffed lamb and pig, which made everyone within earshot grin.

Aware the retired librarian was awaiting an answer, Nora helped her finish loading her cart with more centerpieces. "He has a family thing this evening."

Together, they pushed their carts back out into the dining hall. Miss Mim slanted her a glance. "Are you going?"

She had been. Until they'd quarreled. Now, given the way he'd stormed out on her, it didn't seem like a good idea at all. Nora worked hard to suppress a self-conscious blush. "I was invited," she informed truthfully.

"But are you attending?" the older woman pressed.

Nora only wished that were still possible. But not wanting to get into it, shrugged and murmured, "It depends on Liam." She smiled as her son yawned. "He's had a busy few days."

We all have.

And though Nora wished she could blame her fight

with Zane on the fact they were both worn-out and dreading the end of their time together, she knew it was more than that.

She had given him every opportunity and he still didn't trust her enough to tell her the truth about his plans.

Mistaking the reason behind Nora's contemplative silence, Miss Mim patted her hand. "I'm sorry if the other ladies and I have given you too much advice," she said kindly, pausing to take a seat.

Nora did the same.

"It's just we don't want you to make our mistakes." Miss Mim shook her head. "Time passes so quickly. When you get to be our age, you realize how fleeting it is. How some opportunities only come once and even if we're wise enough *not* to squander them, the moments are fleeting anyway."

Sadly, Nora knew how true that was.

Zane had been in Texas for almost a month now, and it seemed like their time together had passed in an instant.

Quietly, the older woman insisted, "Whatever is keeping you and Zane apart can be fixed, Nora."

Could it?

She wondered.

"If only you're brave enough to open up your heart and try…"

Zane was chopping wood when Sage arrived at the No Name ranch, already dressed for the Lockharts' Christmas Eve celebration.

He wasn't surprised to see his meddlesome only sister arrive. Nor was he shocked at what she had to say, as she made her way carefully over the rough terrain. "I can't believe you blew it with Nora. Again."

"She's the one who pushed me out the door with both hands."

"Only because she had no clue what you've been up to for the past month. Face it. You made a mistake, not telling Nora what you were doing out here."

He had wanted to. Numerous times. But… "She set the rules, Sage." No more broken promises.

And since there had been no way he could guarantee how it would all work out, he'd had to ignore every romantic impulse he had and remain silent about that part of his future.

"It's not as if I didn't let her know how I felt about her and Liam a dozen other ways."

"Such as…?"

"I set up a little nursery out here for Liam."

"So she could spend the night with you."

He clenched his jaw. "So they both could spend the night out here." What he had hoped would be the start of many.

Sage shivered in the cold December air.

"I took steps to provide for them financially."

His sister persisted doggedly. "But did you tell her you love her?"

"She knows she's the only woman in the world for me."

"So you didn't mention love."

"Listen, Dear Abby…"

She propped her hands on her hips. "I know you think they are just words, Zane. But women need to hear them."

Zane found it hard to believe that Nora would have shoved him out the door over a few unsaid words. "We were more than that, Sage." At least he'd thought they were.

She lifted a brow. "More than love?"

Zane picked up a load of split logs and carried them toward the ranch house. He stacked them neatly on the porch, then went back for another half dozen. "I wanted things to work out."

"Really?" As determined as ever to make him see the wisdom of her words, Sage dogged his every step. "Because it looked to me like it wasn't just Nora who has had her doubts. You haven't been sure you could be happy with her, either."

Zane exhaled. Had he ever seen a gloomier Christmas Eve? He didn't think so.

"It's true." He carried the last of the split logs to the porch. "I've never been the kind of guy who could sit still for even a day."

Sage followed him inside. Watched as he washed up. "And now, thanks to all your very hard work putting together a very big endeavor in a very short time, you won't have to worry you'll get bored in Laramie County. Because every day is likely to be as different and challenging and important to everyone involved as the next."

Zane dried his hands. "Yeah—" he shrugged, discouragement flooding his soul "—but will any of it matter to Nora?"

Would it make her want what he wanted most of all?

Sage took him by the arms and forced him to look at her. "Listen to me, Zane," she said softly. "You're not the first couple to find yourself in a potentially heartbreaking situation. Nick and I went through the same thing."

Hard to imagine, they were so happy now. But what

did he know about what had gone down between them? He'd been with his unit, overseas during most of the courtships of all four of his siblings.

Calmly, he pointed out what he did know. "You never disapproved of Nick's life work."

"But I worried I wouldn't fit into his life. And as it turns out—" Sage paused to let her words sink in "—he was just as worried about making me happy. We didn't know that, though, because we were so busy trying to keep it casual and hide what we were really thinking and feeling that we almost lost each other." Tears sparkled in her eyes. "We would have if we hadn't found the courage to tell each other what was in our hearts."

Zane inhaled deeply. "You're saying I should go to Nora?"

"And make it the merriest Christmas of all, by telling her all you've been doing behind the scenes to see that you will have the kind of future together that will make you-all blissfully happy."

As Zane showered and got ready for the family party, he realized his sister was right. Mistakes had been made. Lots of them. But there was still time to fix everything.

And it had to be done in person.

As he was walking out the door, he saw a familiar red minivan coming up the drive. *Nora.* She was the last person he expected to see and the person he most wanted to connect with, too.

He stood, hands in his pockets, waiting, until the van stopped and Nora got out. She came toward him, her chin held high, her expression so resolute it set his heart to pounding.

He glanced inquiringly at the rear passenger seat.

"Liam is with your mother at the Circle H."

Which meant what? His mother had been involved in the last-minute matchmaking efforts, too? Or Nora and Liam intended to attend the party with him, after all?

Looking gorgeous as ever in a red wool coat, a white scarf wound around her neck, Nora met him at the top of the steps. "I wanted us to be able to talk without interruption."

Talking sounded good. But first…

Zane ushered her inside, out of the cold, and said, "Before we do that, I owe you an apology."

"For what?"

He exhaled roughly. "For overreacting…and for storming out."

He watched her unwind her scarf, then helped her off with her coat. Took off his own. Taking her by the hand, he led her over to the sofa.

"I thought about it," he told her as they sat down, knee to knee. Clasping her soft hands in his, he confided gruffly, "And I realize what you were trying to do, letting me know it was okay with you if I wanted to reenlist again. It was a big sacrifice."

Nora's lips curved ruefully. "Not enough of one." She clasped his hands tighter and looked intently into his eyes. "Because you were right, Zane. I decided your future for you because it was easier than facing my own issues."

This was a big admission.

And a startling one.

"Which are?" he asked, really wanting to understand.

"All my life I've equated love with loss, need with abandonment. And that mindset was even worse after my grandparents died." She choked up. "So I've tried really hard not to let or allow myself to be vulnerable with anyone."

He used his thumbs to wipe away the tears trembling on her lower lashes. "It wasn't just you putting up walls, Nora," he told her, wrapping his arms around her. "I've done the same thing."

She rested her forehead in the curve of his neck. Inhaled a shaky breath. "At least your reason was noble. Made out of honor and duty to your country."

Tucking a hand beneath her chin, he lifted her gaze to his. "In some respects, yes. But in others, it was done out of a fear of being boxed in, bored, restless." All the bane of his youth.

Nora looked at him long and hard. "And now?"

"I found a solution."

He released her and rose. Taking her by the hand, he led her over to his desk. "I didn't want to tell you until the dream became a reality. But now that it has..." He opened up a folder, handed her a blueprint and a business plan.

Nora studied both. Cheeks pinkening, she read in surprise. "Lockhart Search And Rescue?"

"Laramie County does not have a dedicated search and rescue team. Nor do any of the surrounding counties."

She nodded. "None of them have the budget for a service that is only needed part of the time. Which, as we found out with Mr. Pierce's situation this week, is a real problem."

"Right, because in an emergency, they're left to cobble together resources as best they can, sometimes from as far away as San Antonio or Dallas. And they pay exorbitant rates for them, too."

Nora's eyes lit up. "So there is a definite need," she said, beginning to understand.

Zane nodded, relieved to have this all out in the open. "One I plan to fill with ex-military, like me, who are skilled in search and rescue. I'll run it out of the No Name—which by the way will be rechristened with the name of the new business—and have help on-site available to be dispatched twenty-four hours a day, seven days a week for a seven-county radius."

Nora blinked in surprise. "So that's what's been going on out here?"

"Choppers don't come cheap. To get a small business loan, I had to come up with a comprehensive business plan and put my ranch up as collateral. To do that, I had to have the property appraised. Thanks to Sage's banker friend, Raquel, in Dallas, I got what we needed," he announced happily. "The loan was approved yesterday. The funds will be in place by the time I come back to Texas on January 15."

Hurt shimmered in her eyes. "Why didn't you tell me?" she asked, confused.

"I should have. I know that now."

"But while all this was going on...?"

Brusquely, he admitted, "I had promised you stuff before, then was unable to deliver on those vows. I didn't want to do that again."

Her pretty eyes lit with understanding, giving him the courage to go on.

He drew her all the way into his arms. "And to be honest, when I first came back to Laramie, I didn't know what I was going to be able to do here professionally."

To his relief, she understood that, too.

"*Until* I started talking to the people at the sheriff's, fire and EMS departments," he confessed, breathing in the sweet, womanly scent of her. "And realized just how little they had to offer me in the way of full-time work that matched my skills, and yet how deep their need went, too."

Nora nodded, smiling. "So the next time someone gets lost...or wanders off from a campsite..."

"It'll be Lockhart Search and Rescue that gets called."

She studied him a long moment. "You really want to do this?"

Contentment flowed through him. He brought her even closer. "I really do."

Nora lifted her lips to his. "Oh, Zane, I love you so much."

His heart swelled. "I love you, too." He kissed her softly, deeply. Then lifted his head, eager to spill the rest. Smiling, he said, "And that brings me to the second part of my plan to make this the best Christmas ever."

With her watching raptly, Zane produced a velvet box. She flipped open the lid and gasped at the gleaming platinum solitaire diamond inside.

"Marry me, Nora," he urged in a voice filled with all the affection he felt. "And let me be the husband and father you and Liam deserve. Let me make all your dreams come true."

Nora's pulse pounded with excitement and joy. This was the best Christmas present he could ever have given her! Better yet, a start to a new and wonderful life for them all. Happy tears spilling down her cheeks, she threw her arms around his neck, stood on tiptoe and gave him a resounding kiss, amplified by all the love and tenderness she felt in her heart. He really was all she had ever wanted and needed, and at long last she knew she was that for him, too.

"Yes, Zane," she murmured emotionally, basking in the love flowing freely between them, "yes!"

Epilogue

One year later

Looking gorgeous as ever, Nora stood ten feet back from the entrance to Lockhart Search and Rescue, sixteen-month-old Liam in her arms. A Christmas wreath looped over one shoulder, Zane moved the ladder beneath the iron archway. "You're going to have to tell me where you want it," he said.

Nora squinted, considering. "The center would be good."

"Cen', Daddy!" Liam shouted, pumping both his little arms.

Grinning at his son's helpfulness, Zane positioned the evergreen wreath with the red velvet bow. "Here?" he asked his two "helpers."

Nora tilted her head to one side, a cascade of chestnut hair spilled across her slender shoulder. "A little to the right," she said finally.

Trying not to be distracted by the new lushness of her curves—not an easy task—he obliged. "Here?"

She paused, then pursed her soft lips together in a very kissable pout.

But then, her lips were always kissable...

"Maybe slightly to the left," she said finally.

Zane moved it again.

"Another inch."

Not sure what she was going for—weren't they about to get off center now?—he again moved the wreath ever so slightly.

"Again. In the other direction."

Frowning, he did as asked.

"No," she corrected, sighing loudly, "back the other way!"

He turned and saw her peering at him mischievously. She laughed at the baleful expression he gave her.

"Actually," she said drily, "that's good right there."

He regarded her with comically exaggerated admonition. "It's good that's good." He waggled his brows teasingly. "Or we'd be switching places."

"Which would be a real problem since I'm not tall enough to reach that, even with the ladder."

He chuckled. "True."

"True, Daddy!" Liam echoed. Then at their looks of surprise, he pumped his little arms and let out a belly laugh that quickly had them laughing even more.

Finished fastening the decoration, Zane climbed back down and returned the ladder to the bed of his pickup truck.

Aware he had never been more content in his life,

he moved to stand next to his family. Gazing down at Nora's lovely face, he asked, "How long before the activity buses from Laramie Gardens arrive?"

Nora consulted her watch. "Thirty minutes."

"How many times have they been out here?"

She wrinkled her nose. "I think this makes their tenth tour. But the residents never tire of seeing the equipment you use and talking with the guys and gals who work here, so…it's all good."

"It is all good." With a smile, he leaned down to kiss her. "Starting with the fact we're married."

"Agreed."

"Proud parents of one amazing child." He cast an adoring look at Liam, then reached down to pat her tummy. "With another on the way…"

Nora grinned, shifting the son they had both adopted over to his arms for holding. "I really agree there."

Wrapping an arm around her shoulders, while cuddling Liam on the right, he brought her in close to his left side. Brushed his lips across her temple. "I never imagined I could be as happy as I am now."

"Neither did I," Nora whispered back.

But they were.

Smiling, she predicted, "And the best is yet to come…"

* * * * *

IF YOU ENJOYED THIS BOOK
WE THINK YOU WILL ALSO LOVE

LOVE INSPIRED

INSPIRATIONAL ROMANCE

Uplifting stories of faith, forgiveness and hope.

Fall in love with stories where faith helps
guide you through life's challenges, and discover
the promise of a new beginning.

6 NEW BOOKS AVAILABLE EVERY MONTH!

SPECIAL EXCERPT FROM

LOVE INSPIRED
INSPIRATIONAL ROMANCE

What happens when a beautiful foster mom claims an Oklahoma rancher as her fake fiancé?

Read on for a sneak preview of
The Rancher's Holiday Arrangement
by Brenda Minton.

"I am so sorry," Daisy told Joe as they walked down the sidewalk together.

The sun had come out and it was warm. The kind of day that made her long for spring.

"I don't know that I need an apology," Joe told her. "But an explanation would be a good start."

She shook her head. "I saw you sitting with your family, and I knew how I'd feel. Ambushed."

"I could have handled it. Now I'm engaged." He tossed her a dimpled grin. "What am I supposed to tell them when I don't have a wedding?"

"I got tired of your smug attitude and left you at the altar?" she asked, half teasing. "Where are we walking to?"

"I'm not sure. I guess the park."

"The park it is," she told him.

Daisy smiled down at the stroller. Myra and Miriam belonged with their mother, Lindsey. Daisy got to love them for a short time and hoped that she'd made a difference.

"It'll be hard to let them go," Joe said.

"It will be," Daisy admitted. "I think they'll go home after New Year's."

"That's pretty soon."

"It is. We have a court date next week."

"I'm sorry," Joe said, reaching for her hand and giving it a light squeeze.

"None of that has anything to do with what I've done to your life. I've complicated things. I'm sorry. You can tell your parents I lost my mind for a few minutes. Tell them I have a horrible sense of humor and that we aren't even friends. Tell them I wanted to make your life difficult."

"Which one is true?" he asked.

"Maybe a combination," she answered. "I *do* have a horrible sense of humor. I *did* want to mess with you."

"And the part about us not being friends?"

"Honestly, I don't know what we are."

"I'll take friendship," he told her. "Don't worry, Daisy, I'm not holding you to this proposal."

She laughed and so did he.

"Good thing. The last thing I want is a real fiancé."

"I know I'm not the most handsome guy, but I'm a decent catch," he said.

She ignored the comment about his looks. The last thing she wanted to admit was that when he smiled, she forgot herself just a little.

Don't miss
The Rancher's Holiday Arrangement *by Brenda Minton,*
available November 2020 wherever
Love Inspired books and ebooks are sold.

LoveInspired.com

Love Harlequin romance?

DISCOVER.

Be the first to find out about promotions,
news and exclusive content!

f Facebook.com/HarlequinBooks

🐦 Twitter.com/HarlequinBooks

📷 Instagram.com/HarlequinBooks

📌 Pinterest.com/HarlequinBooks

ReaderService.com

EXPLORE.

Sign up for the Harlequin e-newsletter and
download a free book from any series at
TryHarlequin.com

CONNECT.

Join our Harlequin community to
share your thoughts and connect
with other romance readers!
Facebook.com/groups/HarlequinConnection

HSOCIAL2020